The Newsboys' Lodging-house

The Newsboys' Lodging-House

OR

THE CONFESSIONS OF WILLIAM JAMES

William James. Pencil sketch by himself, about 1866.

THE NEWSBOYS' LODGING-HOUSE

OR

THE CONFESSIONS OF WILLIAM JAMES

A NOVEL

JON BOORSTIN

VIKING

VIKING
Published by the Penguin Group
Penguin Putnam Inc., 375 Hudson Street, New York, New York 10014, U.S.A.
Penguin Books Ltd, 80 Strand, London WC2R 0RL, England
Penguin Books Australia Ltd, 250 Camberwell Road, Camberwell,
   Victoria 3124, Australia
Penguin Books Canada Ltd, 10 Alcorn Avenue,
   Toronto, Ontario, Canada M4V 3B2
Penguin Books India (P) Ltd, 11 Community Centre, Panchsheel Park,
   New Delhi - 110 017, India
Penguin Books (N.Z.) Ltd, Cnr Rosedale and Airborne Roads, Albany,
   Auckland, New Zealand
Penguin Books (South Africa) (Pty) Ltd, 24 Sturdee Avenue,
   Rosebank, Johannesburg 2196, South Africa

Penguin Books Ltd, Registered Offices:
Harmondsworth, Middlesex, England

First published in 2003 by Viking Penguin,
a member of Penguin Putnam Inc.

10   9   8   7   6   5   4   3   2   1

Publisher's Note
This is a work of fiction. Names, characters, places, and incidents either are the product of the author's imagination or are used fictitiously, and any resemblance to actual persons, living or dead, business establishments, events, or locales is entirely coincidental.

LIBRARY OF CONGRESS CATALOGING-IN-PUBLICATION DATA
Boorstin, Jon, 1946–
     The newsboys' lodging-house, or, The confessions of William James : a novel/by
   Jon Boorstin.
        p.   cm.
     ISBN 0-670-03115-1
     1. James, William, 1842–1910—Fiction.   2. Philosophers—Fiction.
   I. Title: Confessions of William James.   II. Title: Newsboys' lodging-house, or,
   The confessions of William James.   III. Title.
   PS3552.O64396 N49 2001
   813'.54—dc21   2001046906

This book is printed on acid-free paper. ∞

Printed in the United States of America
Set in Esprit Book with Greco display
Designed by Carla Bolte

For my father

We stand on a mountain pass in the midst of whirling snow and blinding mist, through which we get glimpses now and then of paths which may be deceptive. If we stand still we shall be frozen to death. If we take the wrong road we shall be dashed to pieces. We do not certainly know whether there is any right one. What must we do?

—William James, *The Will to Believe*

Only fools laugh at Horatio Alger, and his poor boys who make good. The wiser man who thinks twice about that sterling author will realize that Alger is to America what Homer was to the Greeks.

—Nathanael West and Boris Ingster

The Newsboys' Lodging-House

---- OR ----

THE CONFESSIONS OF
WILLIAM JAMES

CAMBRIDGE, 1908

Dearest H,

I write this at 6.30, in the library, which the blessed hard-coal fire has kept warm all night. It has been a still, crisp night, and I have watched the constellations gyrate and fade until nothing remains but the big morning star and the porous crescent of the moon. I am kept from my bed not by the decrepitude of age, nor the accursed 'thoracic symptom,' but by the intrusion of ancient events, events which I have suppressed but which, like stars blanked by the dawn, float omnipresent nonetheless.

At my age, false modesty is as unbecoming as false pride. We each see the world in our own way, and regardless of the value of our perceptions most of us are destined to nurture them in secret or to shout them into the echoless void; I have been privileged to have my words resonate about me as have few in my generation. Whatever their transcendent truth, my thoughts have been clasped to the bosom of a nation busy with the conquest of a continent and devoted to the applications of science to life. It has been said that I have revealed to the American people the meaning of their doings, and so enabled them to go on doing them more intelligently and harmoniously.

I flatter myself that my ideas have brought some measure of sanity and solace to this epoch of exuberant exploitation. I know that I have trumpeted a democratic respect for the sacredness of individuality and the outward tolerance of whatever is not itself intolerant, empty phrases in the mouths of politicians but ideals I have endeavoured to invest with passionate meaning. I have fought with some success against the aridity of a world deprived of faith. I have been honoured for these accomplishments.

My notoriety, however, has not deluded me that my particular psyche has any special value in understanding the human mind. I cite it upon occasion for the simple reason that I have unique access to its inner processes. In spite of a possessory fondness for my personal patterns of thought I have laboured to resist wallowing in the minutiae of my own existence and my reticence has spared my readers much trivializing distraction, while promoting the impression that my conclusions, like any scientific propositions, stand independent of the investigating mind.

Yesterday an intruder dragged the past into the present, and in so doing forcefully impressed upon me the hollowness of my position. I have created the illusion that I sit high upon my philosopher's throne in my sepulchral study, gazing down at monks and mystics and men of action and through sheer force of intellect divining in their behaviour fundamental patterns of the human mind. My pose of pure thinker denies the obvious fact that my truths as well as theirs are distilled in the crucible of experience.

Honesty and equity require me to turn my analytic techniques upon myself. However, any such attempt would be inherently contradictory, dependent as it is upon an objective perspective toward one's own psyche beyond my reach, or, I daresay, the reach of any man. I can, however, lay aside my natural inclination for privacy and detail those events that are crucial to the conclusions in my work, no matter how damaging to my good name or amour-propre, *so that others may perform the task. Those who would weigh the worth of my ideas deserve to know the facts of the experiment, as it were, which shaped my hypotheses, though I daresay it is not an experiment any reader will wish to replicate.*

I am willing to suffer the consequences implicit in the telling of this tale. I am unwilling to inflict such humiliations upon the innocent. Let Alice's ashes be spread like mine through the woods of Chocorua, and those of my sons sprinkled wherever they will, before these words are aired. If my writings are by then forgotten, this manuscript will be an irrelevant curiosity, but if my work has endured, these words will provide a necessary corrective.

In point of fact, the stream of experience which constitutes William James was deflected into its present path by a chance encounter with an illiterate child. If our paths had not converged, at that precise moment, for that precise duration, I would not now be the William James whom the world has gilded with praise.

Here then are the relevant adventures told with all the merciless accuracy I can muster, as to both external events and my own mental processes. My actions may appear irrational and self-destructive. My descriptions of my mental and physical states may be mistaken for exculpatory self-pity. I do not see any alternative but to tell the truth.

———

I was seated here yesterday in the glare of the afternoon sun (now that I am old, I am like a reptile or other cold-blooded beast, stirred to activity by the heat of the sun until excessive warmth reduces me to torpor) attempting to fathom the depths of the military mind, and the mystery of how that violent and destructive mentality creates a barracks-yard atmosphere more conducive to honorable service and cooperation than does everyday life on the street, when Mrs. Nutly announced an uninvited guest. Alice usually protects me from such importunate intruders but she was visiting her sister in Montreal, and the kindhearted Mrs. Nutly was incapable of sending the fellow away. He was, apparently, a conductor on the Ohio and Pennsylvania Railroad, and he had come from Cleveland to have words with me.

A conductor who will leave his train five hundred miles behind for the sake of an exchange of views is not a man to be denied. Mrs. Nutly produced a square, solid individual about forty years of age with a face severely framed by dense black mutton-chop whiskers. He rocked stiffly in his heavy boots, and he would neither accept the offer of a chair nor volunteer his name.

He had, he said, in the bluff, four-square voice of a man accustomed to calling station stops, heard me lecture once in St. Louis, on the subject of the 'Will to Believe.' He claimed I had told him that he should believe in God as it was good for him. The problem was, he said, he didn't care how good something was for him, if he had to make himself believe it then it wasn't something he really believed, if I got his point. He was just fooling himself.

I replied that while many eminent philosophers held to his view, I was of the opinion that all beliefs are formed in precisely that fashion, although via a more roundabout process. Ultimately we believe only what we choose to believe.

4

He said that sounded like an excuse for "not believing noth-
ing." Then, scrutinizing me closely, he pronounced himself Mr.
William James MacReady. I did not know what to make of the
coincidence of our names until he informed me that his mother's
maiden name was Emma Larkin. My start of recognition pro-
vided him grim satisfaction.

When I asked after the woman, my namesake informed me
that she had died a month before but would tell me nothing more.
She had, he said, made him swear never to approach me, so he
didn't reckon it right to talk about her.

When I asked him why he had come if his mother had forbid-
den it, he forgot his resolve to refuse my hospitality and lowered
himself heavily into a chair, announcing that his mother had
once told him I had saved her life. Was that the truth?

"Yes," I said. "And she saved mine."

"She never told me that."

"She didn't know she'd done it."

"I don't see how you can save someone's life and not know you
done it."

"Perhaps she knew. I doubt it."

"She never said nothing about it." Mr. MacReady looked at me
suspiciously, as if I had lied about his mother, yet he seemed in no
hurry to leave.

I could think of nothing to do with him but to offer him tea. He
declined. He then leaned close to me and rapped my desk with his
knuckle. It gave me a start.

"What I come for, sir, is this: Is you my father?"

To this I could not reply. He leaned closer still. He smelled of
stale beer and cheap cigars. I turned away.

"I ain't looking for no handout. What you say to me is man to man. I got a right to know."

"You believe I am your father?"

"If I know'd for sure one way or t'other I wouldn't be here."

"Did Emma ever say I was your father?"

"She never said not."

"Then I do not think it proper to speak in her place."

"The way I see it, you got to be my father. Not a lot of other candidates running for the job."

"You'll believe what you wish."

"I want to know!"

"I am honour bound to respect your mother's wishes."

"Her wishes!"

The man's body went rigid. He compressed my desk with flattened hands. I rang for Mrs. Nutly.

He relaxed. A decision had been made. "You're my father. I seen it in your eyes." And before Mrs. Nutly was fully in the room he had brushed past her and banged out the door.

CHAPTER ONE

It is all too easy to make a successful life appear as an inescapable march toward achievement, in which ill chance may briefly deflect one's progress but the momentum of superior character and intellect unerringly rights the course. That is so much warm porridge, served up to console the less accomplished and inspire children. Only the very young or the very arrogant take such a view of their own existence. The rest of us, when the melancholy mood forces us to assess our lives (and when else do we ever ask ourselves such questions), are haunted by botched opportunities and failed aspirations. Absurdly, a lifetime of solid contributions pales beside what might have been.

At my most vulnerable time of life I was poisoned with a dispiriting concoction of these two simplistic attitudes, convinced as I was that the successful followed an unblemished path while I was mired in failure. I was thirty years old, and at a time when others were well along their life's road I was living with my parents, having proved myself ill equipped for a variety of other occupations before completing my medical education, a course of study which had succeeded primarily in teaching me that I lacked both the temperament and the constitution to practice medicine. I was acutely aware that I was living off my father's beneficence without a social or professional presence of my own, a fragile and temporary condition at best. Yet I was incapable of pursuing any constructive avenue. I was paralyzed by the question of evil.

The philosophic disease, blessing and curse of my existence, was then at its most virulent. *On the Origin of Species* was a few scant years among us, and my position had evolved, an all too appropriate word, into deterministic materialism, a polysyllabic term for the very hard fact that after Darwin had done his work there was no place for even a wiggle of our will to take part. The mechanism of evolution was simply too pervasive and overpowering. It removed even the necessity of a Divine Presence. The unfathomably complex organization of even the simplest living creature which had until recently been the best argument for the existence of God now became an irrefutable argument for a world free of Him. The strongest, the swiftest, the hardiest, not the most virtuous, pleased the implacable forces of nature, and those forces, not any higher being, were the final arbiter of existence.

Others have debated these issues and continued to pursue their lives unencumbered by their conclusions. David Hume could prove his armchair to be an insubstantial illusion yet he sat in it nonetheless. I have never been of that constitution. I was haunted, obsessed is not too strong a word, by the proposition that if the human will is an epiphenomenal illusion and the Divine Presence an outmoded concept, then evil and good are beyond human control and irrelevant to the natural plan. I could not with full knowledge sincerely sympathize with the total process of the universe so as to assent to the evil that is inherent in its details.

I was weakened too by my dorsal affliction, and the pain in my eyes, and the tedious egotism of sickness and solitude. Suffice it to say that one twilight evening as I struggled with this conundrum I went to my mother's dressing room to retrieve for her a hairbrush, and suddenly there fell upon me without warning, just as if it came out of the darkness, a horrible fear of my own existence. Simultaneously there arose in my mind the image of an epileptic patient whom I had seen in the asylum, a black-haired youth with greenish skin, entirely idiotic, who used to sit all day with his knees drawn up against his chin, and the coarse gray undershirt, which was his only garment, drawn over them enclosing his entire figure. That image and my fear entered into a species of combination with each other. *That shape am I,* I felt. Nothing that I possess can defend me against that fate, if the hour for it should strike for me as it struck for him. There was such a horror of him, and such a certainty that I could become him any instant, that it was as if something hitherto solid within my breast gave way entirely, and I became a mass of quivering fear.

After this the universe was changed for me altogether. I awoke morning after morning with a horrible dread in the pit of my stomach, and with a sense of the insecurity of life that I never knew before, and I have never felt since. When I considered how to break these bonds, how to assert the will paralyzed by my certainty of its non-existence, suicide seemed the manly form to put my daring into, but it took more will than I could muster to remove myself from bed. I never wrote my intimates about my collapse, nor did I reveal my condition to Mother. It seemed unfair that others should suffer for my weakness.

Father came to my rescue. Full of loving concern, he bundled me in robes and spirited me from the house on the excuse that I was visiting Charles Peirce, newly returned from Europe, and transported me to McLean Asylum for the Insane, which already at that time had earned an estimable reputation for the humane and discreet care of the deranged. As I would not travel at night, the darkness holding too much terror for me, Father transported me in an enclosed carriage so as not to attract comment from the neighbors and, dispensing with the gossip of coachmen, drove me himself. At the hospital he put me in the care of its director, Dr. Tyler, expressing his confidence in the competence and discretion of the institution and his desire to visit with me often.

Dr. Tyler, a jovial man with the open manner of a good barkeep, remembered me as a student who had attended his lectures on mental diseases at Harvard. Talking was difficult for me, because of the dark futility which overwhelmed my words, but his sincere and profound concern for my welfare led me to describe my condition and my pattern of life. It consisted principally in reading, or attempting to read. Before my crisis, weakness in my eyes had already resolved me to restrict my serious reading for the year to the thirteen volumes of Father's works, Schopenhauer, Fechner, Fichte, and Spencer's biology.

The doctor explained to me that crises such as mine are induced by an imbalance of the moral, physical, and intellectual faculties. He prescribed daily doses of phosphorus and a pancreatic emulsion, and as one physician to another he emphasized how the nervous excitement and the drain of vital fluids caused by masturbation would defeat all attempts at recovery. I

did not wish to discuss masturbation with Dr. Tyler, as indeed
I do not wish to speak of it now, except to observe that while
modern medicine makes mock of Tyler's etiology, there being
scant evidence of physiological damage caused by the practice,
the moral toll is incontrovertible in an individual to whom the
urge signifies despair and the act itself a humiliating capitula-
tion of the will.

Dr. Tyler counseled rest and efforts to right the imbalance in
my faculties. If I felt capable, he said, I might avail myself of
McLean's gymnasium, its lawn sports, and therapeutic labor
such as sawing wood and gardening. Under no circumstances
should I read. Reading was scarcely preferable to masturbation.

McLean was then housed in the mansion known as Pleasant
Hill in Somerville, an aptly named estate overlooking Miller's
River erected in the previous century from the plans of Charles
Bulfinch, whose buildings house the nation's political process
as well as its insane, and whose work is justly renowned for its
elegance, repose, and refinement of detail. We were not patients
but boarders, sharing in the restorative rural amenities of forest and river and pond. Unfortunately in recent years railroads
had claimed the land on three sides of the property, compro-
mising the bucolic serenity with their noise and grit, and the
river now stank of slaughterhouse offal debouching into its
waters upstream.

As I was closer in spirit to the slaughterhouse than the sani-
tarium, I was in no condition to appreciate McLean's amenities. I kept to my room and tried not to think. This is perhaps
the most difficult of all human occupations. I certainly found it
so. My blank mind was soon sullied with *graffiti* of the darkest

11

and the most impure sort. I sought succor in dragging myself to the porch and there, swathed in blankets beneath the slender Grecian pillars, watching the crimson and orange play of the sun's brilliance against my closed eyelids, chasing thoughts away by striving to compose a sound picture in that pulsing veinal world from the papery rustles and whispers of the wind in the leaves, the rough clump of boots, the smack of mallet on croquet ball, human voices like the distant rumbling of a train and the rumble of trains like distant voices. I cast my mind upon each sound, analyzing each packet of noise into its component parts, parsing them like sentences, hoping to corral my mental processes within the bounds of concrete perception. Mercifully, the task of listening and that of herding my intellect required all my faculties, and with considerable effort I could spend hours this way, thinking next to nothing, before my resources flagged and morbid thoughts pushed through.

I was thus engaged one day when the sounds of a nearby conversation intruded upon my silent struggle, the connected threads of speech weaving a curtain that obscured my mental landscape. A patient had strolled into my aural arena, reciting in excessive detail the multiplicity of his symptoms. Listening unbidden, I could not escape the conclusion that his principal symptom was the need to itemize his insanity in such detail.

I strove to block out the distraction by creating my own list, calling upon my memory of anatomy class to name the muscles and bones of the human hand. For a brief moment I appreciated the wonderful complexity of the human machine before a nausea of disgust overcame me and that marvelous instrument became so many levers and pulleys, so much slime and pus. My tongue touched a shred of beef caught in my teeth and I thought of my jaws masticating, my digestive juices reducing the pulp to a dry lump of excrement. Still the voice droned on. I tried to rise, to find a quiet spot, but when I gripped the arm of my chair I sensed each bone in my hand as it wriggled and slid, sensed the scaphoid straining against the radius clamped in the mass of muscles in my forearm, tugged by fibrous tendons, and my hand and arm froze in place, and from thence my body solidified into a single rigid mass.

I remained frozen for I know not how long, seconds or minutes, until a lighter more melodic voice cut short the dismal drone. My paralysis eased sufficiently that I might force my *orbicularis palpebrarum* to lift my eyelids and my *sternocleidomastoid* to torque my cranium in the direction of the conversation. The new voice belonged to a short man whose thin bones, rotund belly, and rapid gestures gave the air of a nervous songbird, a finch or tomtit, an impression accentuated by the flowing cape and floppy ascot of the bohemian. His hair and moustache were long in the fashion of poets and Wild West heroes, but his manner was neither world-weary nor full of braggadocio. Though no younger than I he moved like a small boy, speaking with the spirited self-assurance of the precocious child and peppering his remarks with emphatic gestures.

Poking the air with his finger, he talked of the success of his recent book and the inspiration he found among the homeless boys of New York City, whom he described as his close friends, having claimed as his office a desk in the lodging-house established for their benefit in the attic of the New York *Sun*. "Orphaned and penniless," he said, with characteristic hyperbole,

13

"without even shoes for their feet, they are models of American enterprise and pluck."

"Nonsense," said the patient. "They're foul-mouthed, godless guttersnipes." The author's zeal and lack of concern for the patient's symptoms had provoked him to contradiction, and his words stung the author as a child might be nettled by an undeserved rebuke.

"Come to New York," said the author, "if you don't believe me."

"You deny that they're immoral and dissolute? That they dissipate their earnings on cigars and alcohol and lewd entertainments?"

"They're susceptible to the sinister seductions of street life, but in their natural state they exude such generosity and playfulness of spirit that they afford me constant proof of the essential goodness of man."

"Spare me, please. Save the false piety for your juvenile readers."

The author responded tartly. "Before you dismiss my readers, Cousin, you should judge the work yourself. I've brought you a copy." He presented his cousin a brightly bound book, which the man accepted without examination.

"You could be earning a decent living guiding the spiritual life of adult citizens of substance, Reverend."

"My book is selling well."

"What of the next and the next after that?"

The author, remarkably vulnerable to his cousin's aspersions, grew agitated and responded with petulance. "These young men are a constant source of literary inspiration, and I

14

consider it my pleasure and my duty to guide them toward a better life."

"Return to your ministry."

"I'm a purely literary man. Please don't address me as Reverend in future."

They parted frostily. As his cousin left his sight, my fellow patient tossed aside the book.

On Dr. Tyler's instructions I had not held a book since I arrived at McLean. Though I thirsted for the written word I had scrupulously abided by his proscription, not from exaggerated faith in his medical wisdom but because I too feared its seductive appeal. As with the opium eater, that which fueled my pleasure also propelled me into self-destructive realms. This book, however, seemed harmless enough. Red cloth beckoned the young reader with a youth embossed in gold upon the spine. His clothes were comically oversized and ended in picturesquely jagged hems. Lean, almost ascetic, he gazed at me with an indecipherable expression, clutching a blacking brush in each hand like a character representing the boot-black's guild upon a column capital at Chartres. I could not imagine how this lad could pose much threat to my damaged psyche.

With difficulty I formed words to ask my neighbor if I might inspect the volume. He replied that I might keep it for all he cared. I picked it up. Ornate scarlet letters proclaimed *Ragged Dick; or, Street Life in New York with the Boot-Blacks* by Horatio Alger. What pleasure to heft it in the hand. The pasteboard covers felt smooth as vellum. I prised them open. The coarse paper might have been the finest rag. Tentatively I began to read. Alger's words poured through me like a cool and refresh- **15** ing elixir. How I wished for the clear sense of purpose with which these boys pursued pleasure, righted wrongs, or bettered their own condition.

Father came upon me as I was reading *Ragged Dick* for perhaps the fourth time. He had been speaking with Dr. Tyler and was not pleased to see me reading so intently. Seeing his look I held up the book and announced I had discovered a new author. He laughed, pleased that I was perusing something of no consequence. He said I appeared stronger. I did not disabuse him of the notion. He took my hand in his and told me to be of good cheer, I need not accuse myself of morbidity of mind. He had consulted his Swedenborg and he was convinced that my collapse had been similar to the crisis which had overtaken him twenty years before. With a smile he told me that happily my crisis, like his own, had been a Swedenborgian vastation, a positive catharsis which though painful would lead me to renewed vigour and sense of purpose. He produced a volume from his coat pocket and read to me that my morbidity of conscience was caused by "certain ghostly busy-bodies intent upon reducing the human mind to subjection, and availing themselves for this purpose of every sensuous and fallacious idea we entertain of God, and of every disagreeable memory of our own conduct." If I could but cling to the proper idea of God, the ghosts must leave me.

I replied that I entertained no fallacious ideas about God, because I did not believe He existed.

"There," he said. "There you are. *Quod erat demonstrandum.*"

16   "Why do you believe?" I asked.

"I don't believe, I know, just as I know you're lying in that chaise. I've felt His presence as surely as I feel yours."

"When I feel His presence I'll believe."

"If you don't open yourself to God you will never feel His presence."

"You don't have to open yourself to me to see me in this chaise."

"If I close my eyes you disappear." He handed me the book. "Read. We'll discuss it further at my next visit."

I took the book, thinking of Dr. Tyler's prohibition. Father saw my thought. A wisp of cloud darkened his good cheer for an instant, but it soon blazed anew. "Let Swedenborg strengthen you. Open your eyes to God and banish these ghosts."

"If wishing for God or hoping for God could make me believe, I'd already be a believer."

He reached into his waistcoat pocket and produced his treasured watch, his father's watch, a superb Breguet minute repeater. The smooth gold case and simple porcelain face concealed a mechanical masterwork. He touched a button and listened gravely as pure chimes rang the hour, the quarter hour, and the minute. I assumed he was concerned about the lateness of the day. I was mistaken. He detached it from his vest and presented it to me.

"You're my eldest. This will be yours. Take it now." I made no move to accept it. "Please. As a favor to me. It will give me comfort to know that when you feel most alone, when your skepticism prevents you from calling on God and He makes your eyes refuse to function, you can play these chimes and

17

hear that you've a family that loves you and is confident of your brilliant future." He affixed the fob to my buttonhole, slipped the watch in my pocket, and kissed me tenderly upon the cheek. Though the kiss was delivered with love and concern, it burned my flesh, branding me the apostate.

When Father had departed I tried to read the Swedenborg. I opened to a passage on coincidence as proof of the concrete presence of the higher spiritual realm. The harder I pried at the words, the more tightly they clung to the page. Yearning for Father's direct experience of the presence of God, I opened myself to the Spirit. The black waters of evil rushed in. Wishing desperately to believe, I summoned Scripture texts: "The eternal God is my refuge. . . . Come unto me, all ye that labour and are heavy laden. . . . I am the resurrection and the life." All I saw was the morbid squalour of a world without God.

I picked up the Alger book. Ragged Dick buys his friend Fosdick a new set of clothes. The well-dressed Fosdick secures a job in a hat store for three dollars a week. I imagined myself working in a hat store. What would Father have made of that! I thought of my younger brothers striving to earn an honest wage out west. Were they fulfilling their destinies? Father taught us all that the only true calling is the Artist. Not the poet or the painter or the musician, who in his view was a mere fabricator of products, no nobler than the artisan who fabricated chairs or wallpaper; the true Artist, said Father, works only to show forth the immortal beauty whose presence constitutes his inmost soul. He has neither obligations nor connections to society, submitting to no one's demands or judgement. The perfect man, the man of destiny, has but one

18

purpose: to live so that his soul shines forth. "To live or to act is more than to produce," Father said.

I had never understood what Father meant by this. When I had considered becoming a painter I had probed him diligently without success. Now, in my weakened state, I felt the flush of insight. Fosdick in his hat store was the polar opposite of the Artist, yet reading his chronicle hardened Father's dictum into an imperative. If Fosdick could act, so could I. In seeking my Artistic essence through contemplation I had strangulated what I was endeavouring to lay bare. Only through action would I discover if I even had an essence. To find my Artist I must first become pure uncluttered Fosdick.

But I was still William James, with all his paralyzing impulses crowding in upon me. I fought the old thoughts by imagining Horatio Alger at his desk among the boys in their lodging-house, finding in their particular admixture of innocence and experience ample cause for faith in the human spirit, chronicling them with a meagerness of talent manifest on every page yet nonetheless enriching to the lives of tens of thousands of young men.

I asked myself a startling question. What if I were not William James? As I posed this hypothetical, my black fog evaporated. I imagined myself among those boys with Alger, searching for the Divine Presence by actively engaging with these enterprising free spirits. If only I were not William James, son of Henry James of Cambridge, Massachusetts, would-be Artist and professional man. Then I realized that for the moment I was not William James. Thanks to Father, William James had vanished from the world.

This thought created in me a peculiar buoyancy of spirit. I felt as if I were one of Swedenborg's ghostly busy-bodies flitting with the wrens about the staid portico, regarding with pity the stiff blanket-wrapped figure below, free to explore where I would, learn what I would, unencumbered by the granite cares which crushed poor William James.

I arose easily from my chaise. Burning with feverish energy, I searched out Dr. Tyler in his laboratory, interrupting his experiments with a new faradic stimulator. He was surprised and pleased to see me on the move. I said that I wished to discuss my treatment. He asked for my thoughts, noting that perhaps electrical stimulation would help me. I replied that I had little respect for such treatment, or for that matter the phosphorus-gold regimen he had prescribed for me. He said he had found success in similar cases with a broad pharmacopoeia, including Peruvian bark, rubidium, quinine, strychnic, coca, sanguinaria, and Indian hemp, but my presence in his lab suggested the phosphorus was having some effect.

I replied that to me the multiplicity of treatments proved their inefficacy. If all cure, none cures. Save for surgery, I told him, I had seen no medical procedure of any value. Most caused harm. (This negative view, while combative, was not a product of my melancholic condition. At that time, before the discovery of infectious agents, it was a woefully accurate description of the profession.)

Dr. Tyler was not insulted by my candor. He stated simply that he had seen many gratifying cures in his career and that I must maintain a positive attitude toward my treatment if it was
to prove effective. I replied that if my treatment depended upon

my moral condition then doctors were no better than priests, and as I had no faith in his treatment then we were agreed I would derive no benefit from it. I wished to leave immediately.

The doctor examined my reddened eyes and felt my flushed brow. He said my desire to leave was another symptom. My father had visited with me, and such visits were known to cause agitation and feelings of shame. It might be best to request that my family stay away. He could assure me complete quiet and privacy. If I did not believe in medicaments, time would effect my cure.

No, I said, rest was my enemy. I wished to leave immediately. Reluctantly he agreed to summon my father if I felt the same tomorrow. I told him I was leaving this afternoon. He said that was impossible. My father had brought me, and my father must take me home.

I said I had come of my own free will. I was not going home, and I must leave immediately. I would walk to the railroad tracks and flag down a train at the crossing if that were necessary. He said this was more proof of my desperate state and begged me to reconsider. I was adamant.

"But you have no money."

"I have enough." I had calculated that I had sufficient resources to pay for train fare to New York City. I would worry about the rest when I arrived. I thought of the Hindoo mystic who traveled with nothing but his loincloth and wooden bowl, refusing even to beg, so certain was he that his gods would provide. Let me see if my God would provide.

"I cannot allow it."

"Then you must chain me to my bed like a lunatic at the   **21** pauper's asylum." Dr. Tyler, I knew, prided himself on his enlightened methods. I rose to leave.

He put a hand upon me. "You're risking a permanent collapse."

"If you genuinely desire my cure, Doctor, you won't restrain me."

I returned to my room to pack my valise. I heard steps upon the stairs. I fully expected a pair of brawny custodians with manacles. Dr. Tyler entered. He told me that my father had paid for a month in advance. He held out forty-five dollars.

"If I take your money, Father will see your hand in this, and he'll cause you difficulties."

"Take a room in a quiet inn in the country. Tell me where you situate yourself. If you wish, I shall keep it confidential from your family."

I wrote him a receipt and assured him that the money would be ultimately returned to my father. This forty-five dollars was a good omen. Like the Hindoo, I had been provided for. I shook Dr. Tyler's hand. "Sir, you're a genuine healer."

He did not relinquish my hand but looked me hard in the eye. "Please God may you prove me such."

———

⌒CHAPTER TWO⌒

THE NINE-YEAR-OLD SQUINTED INTO THE SOFT SUN. THOUGH early yet, the day promised to be unseasonably warm which pleased the boy, for he was clad for summer still, shoeless and shirtless, and what clothing he had was ill designed for retaining warmth. His trousers, bound by a cord at the waist and slashed off at his ankles, had once belonged to a Union soldier whose thighs were the size of the boy's waist, and while sewn of heavy serge, they flapped about his legs, well ventilated by gaping tears. His coat, once a glove clerk's pride, was equally distressed, and lacked buttons and half a sleeve. As long as the weather held, the boy was not concerned by his odd manner of dress. He preferred his bare horny soles to confining leather, and he was in matter of fact rather proud of his military pants, in particular of a hole near the knee which appeared to be caused by a rebel minié ball.

Nor did his odd attire draw attention from those around him. Indeed, it rendered him invisible to the multitudes who passed as he made his way up Broadway, pushing against the current of humanity rushing itself downtown to work. The boy always walked up Broadway, instead of Seventh Avenue, because he liked the crush and excitement of the grand thoroughfare. Street-cars and coaches overflowing with impatient

23

men and women vied inharmoniously with pushcarts, barrows, and wagons moving thither and yon. Uptown traffic like boulders cleaved the downtown stream, larger wagons like mighty logs hanging up as they navigated the tight bends from the tributary streets amid a cacophony of imprecations.

To the boy's amusement a scene of frenzied futility dammed the flow entirely at Twentieth Street. A street-car crammed with clerks and shop assistants had halted irrevocably, its overmatched horses incapable of pulling it further and its human inhabitants equally incapable of voluntarily relinquishing their conveyance. The driver flogged the horses to no effect and yelled at the conductor to reimburse the passengers and lighten his load; the conductor argued with his passengers who clung stubbornly to their places and shouted insults at the driver.

The boy picked his way through the confusion and at Twenty-ninth Street turned toward Seventh Avenue. He soon descended beneath the dusty smell of manure into a basement emporium redolent of pine and sulphur. There he waited with dozens of other equally ill-clad boys and girls, until Jake the German shopkeeper could exchange the boy's twenty-five-cent piece for two packets of thirty-six match boxes and a penny change. Jake's shop, one of six dozen similar establishments, devoted itself exclusively to wholesaling the product of the match factory on Thirtieth Street.

The boy gave his penny to a girl for a skein of twine and repaired with his purchases to a bench along the wall. There he carefully removed enough matches from the seventy-two boxes to create another twenty-five bundles, which he bound with the twine, and placed his ninety-seven bundles of matches in his basket. Though he had never studied mathematics, he worked quickly and precisely, cognizant that selling all his matches for a penny a bunch would clear him a profit of seventy-two cents. Then he took himself to the brown-stones on Eighteenth Street near Fourth Avenue where he had left off the day before.

The morning did not go well. The day was as hot as the boy had predicted and on hot days, the boy remarked, people often deferred the purchase of matches. Then, too, the boy had a large swollen bruise around the socket of his right eye, which had turned ugly hues of green and purple. This blemish was the more shocking because beneath his comical attire the boy himself exhibited an extraordinary beauty. His symmetrical features wore the solemn grace of a prepubescent David sculpted by Donatello, and the swelling and contusions were almost blasphemous in their desecration of his purity of form. When he knocked at a door he tried to hide his disfigurement from his customers by presenting his left profile and looking at them askance, but this attitude gave him a furtive aspect, as if not only the appearance but the cause of his injury were shameful, and the servant girls quickly moved him along.

By noon he had but six cents. He spent two upon a belated breakfast of corn cakes. He ate them slowly, to perpetuate the creamy sensation of the warm meal against his tongue, and fed a scrap to an organ grinder's monkey whose antics he enjoyed. He decided to gamble his four remaining cents upon ferriage to Brooklyn in hope of improving his luck.

Jemmie did not often work the Brooklyn side of the river. When asked, he could not articulate what drove him on this particular day to wager his precious pennies on the attempt; yet this decision, born of whim, or pluck, or the covert pressure of some higher force, would alter the course of his existence, and the author's.*

When the sun set, Jemmie was still in Brooklyn and still had seventy-three bunches of matches in his basket. He thrust his hand into his ragged pants to count his remaining pennies. The threadbare material was torn in many places but this pocket was tightly sewn. Eighteen cents remained to him.

He spent four cents for his return to Manhattan. As the ferry lurched from the dock he fingered the fourteen pennies in his pocket. If he allotted four cents for supper he would have only ten to bring home. He looked apprehensively at the dark forms of the fast-approaching city lurking behind the colored lights of the ferry houses and the forest of masts clinging to the coast. In desperation he accosted the passengers standing at the rail. They ignored him, preferring to savour the ocean air which escorted the swift waters that smashed against the hull.

He retreated to a coil of rope. The city was close enough now that he could make out street lamps etched into its mass, and rising over all the full moon of the illuminated clock that

*What I write of Jemmie is his version of the truth, as told to me in our many hours together when he finally chose to speak; where I have embellished with my knowledge of his life in the streets, in order more completely to render his adventures, I have done so with a scrupulous adherence to both the essence and the texture of his tale—W. J.

topped City Hall. Soon he would be close enough to read its face.

A solidly built man approached. He wore the fine cloth of a gentleman, but he spoke with the soft, harsh tones of a pugilist who had taken too many punches to the throat. He nudged the boy's basket with his foot.

"Them matches gettin' heavy I bet."

"No sir."

"Too hot for matches." He clasped the boy's cheeks in a large scarred hand. The boy tried to twist away, but with the gentleness of great strength the man turned him effortlessly to expose his contusion. "How'd you come by that little flower?"

"Kicked by a horse."

"A horse with knuckles." He let the boy squirm from his grasp. "What's he like when he's not beatin' on you?"

"Right enough."

"He ain't gonna like all them unsold merchandise though."

"No."

"You'd kip on them ropes, but even if you sell the goods to-morry, when you goes home he'll give you what fer twice over."

The boy shrugged his shoulders.

"Yer in a right box."

The boy nodded. The man looked at him with the steady eyes of a boxer gauging his opponent. "What you callin' yourself?"

"Jemmie."

"Here, then, Jemmie." The man held out a small shiny   27 coin. In the darkness it glinted like a dime. The boy didn't take it at once. He was gauging the man's intentions. "Fer a box of them matches."

"I don't got no change."

"Keep the difference."

"Thank you sir." The boy gave him a match box and pocketed the coin.

The man looked at him queerly. "Yer a sacred vessel." He cuffed the boy upon the back of the head. "You got a choice now. You take it."

The boy's exertions had taken their toll, and the thought of the uncertain welcome awaiting him made him listless and drowsy. When he reached the New York side Jemmie decided to indulge in a ride on the Broadway car. He handed over his ten-cent piece but the conductor looked at him askance and demanded other money. It would seem the strange man had suckered him with a brass farthing.

He alit at City Hall and dragged himself past that marble monument to a brightly lit saloon at Broadway and Park. There he examined his farthing beneath the hissing gas. It bore a crown. English money. It shone a burnished yellow. Perhaps gold. Jemmie made out a one and a two with a slash between, and never having seen such a mark before deciphered it to mean one two-shilling piece. Two dollars and twenty-five cents in gold. The small heavy coin was worth almost a full week's labor. His exhaustion transmuted into a giddy exhilaration. He was suddenly aware of being extremely hungry.

28   He entered the saloon and asked the bartender to change

his two-shilling piece. The bartender took the coin and in-spected it carefully. He stroked his waxy moustache. "Where'd you come by this?"

"Sold a man some matches."

The bartender gave Jemmie a shrewd look. "What makes you think it's worth two shillings?" The boy pointed to the mark on the coin. The bartender nodded and emptied out the cash box. It only contained a dollar and a quarter. "Give me a minute here." The bartender emptied out his own pockets. Still one quarter was lacking.

Jemmie held out his hand. "Give it me back then."

The man dropped the coin in his little palm with a smile. "Get yourself to school, laddy." He drew upon the counter. "This here mark don't mean two shillings. It's a half. You're holding a whole half pound. You got yourself ten gold shillings."

The little coin winked at him. Jemmie closed his hand tight about it and felt it burn inside his fist. Two shillings was a stroke of luck. Ten shillings was more than he could fathom. He had never seen so much money before and he doubted he would again. Such a sum was more than a gift, it was a burden. Now he understood what the man had meant by choice. This was his chance to change his life. He thought of all he had ever seen that he had not dared to desire. A red wagon to pull behind. A soldier's hat. A prancing white horse.

Jemmie didn't know any person who could change ten shillings. He stuck the coin deep in his good pocket and strolled among the crowds of pleasure-seekers to a nearby   29 oyster saloon, where he placed his remaining pennies upon the table and ate corn bread and oyster stew until the money was exhausted. Then he headed downtown to Baxter Street and turned east.

In minutes he had left the marble glow of Broadway behind. The street narrowed and blackened into an opaque odoriferous alley. Heat had driven the populace to the windows and deposited dark clumps of humanity upon the rickety stairs. Curses drifted from one flickering window, mocking laughter from the rooftops. Jemmie picked his way through the piles of manure, trying to stay in the darkest shadows while sparing his naked feet the worst of the filth that clogged the way. His treasure weighed heavily in his pocket.

He stopped outside his own dwelling, before a basement entrance proclaiming itself a distillery. There he squatted and waited, lagging stones against the wall for practice, until his sister appeared carrying the baby in one arm and a pail in the other. He stepped suddenly into her path, which frightened her, and she punished him with an angry look.

"Where you been? Daddy got tired a waitin'. Here." She thrust him the pail. "He's hellish mad."

"Lookit this." The boy ignored the pail and produced the tiny coin. The girl couldn't see much in the darkness. " 'Tis gold, it is. Ten shillings' worth."

"Naw!"

" 'Tis. I's not comin' home no more."

"You runnin' off West and be a cowboy now?" She tried to hand it back. He wouldn't take it.

30

" 'Twon't stick to me. 'Tis for you and the little one. Take it to Dad and tell him I ain't comin' home."

She dropped the pail to receive the coin. She'd never felt gold before. "He's gonna track you down. You don't wanta be you when he finds ya."

"Tell him I's West. Maybe he'll give up on me."

"What's he usin' fer money then?"

"Tell him he's got all I got. This makes us quits."

"If he knows you got nothin' he knows you ain't gone West."

"Ten shillings should keep him drunk long enough fer me to get outa his way."

"Where you goin' to?"

"Around."

"So yer gone then." She gazed upon him with tired eyes.

He gave her an awkward hug. "Nothin's forever."

———

Jemmie slipped away through the black alley and wound through the crooked thoroughfares until he reached the East River. He walked along the wharves, swinging his basket of merchandise in practiced arcs, until he came upon the clustered hay barges, on such a hot night densely sown with bodies of the vagrant population. Clambering among them to a barge moored outside its brothers, he planted himself in an empty spot. The gentle swaying of the craft and the light breeze from the river soon sent him into a deserved sleep.

Shouts and heavy thumping woke him. Thick-armed men pounded upon the barge hulls with barrel staves and pitchforks to roust the human cargo. Jemmie sat up in luminous

31

darkness, ripples in the river reflecting a lightening sky. He reached for his basket but found only hay. As the pounding grew nearer he threw aside the stiff stalks in frantic haste. A big pock-faced Irish boy pulled at his arm. "The pitchforks are comin'."

"Me goods is gone."

"Kiss 'em good-bye then."

Men climbed over the nearest barges, clearing laggards with well-placed blows. Jemmie kept digging. The older lad knelt beside him and used his greater size to lift armloads of the straw. "What're we looking fer?"

"Basket of matches."

"Lifted most like."

A man with bare freckled biceps leaped upon the barge. "Pissin' in my straw, are we?" He tramped toward them, waving an axe handle to coax them within range.

The older boy yanked Jemmie's arm. "Can ye swim?"

"Don't know."

"Ye know now." He dived into the river with his fist still encircling Jemmie's slim arm.

When the water engulfed them the older boy relinquished Jemmie to the river. Frigid tendrils crept through Jemmie's torn clothes and caressed his body, drawing him down to the river's clammy bosom. Above him the dark legs of the older boy kicked toward the light. Jemmie heard his benefactor's words resounding in his head. He had a choice. What choice? He could fight the river or he could join the river. He flailed his body, but his exertions only drove him deeper. The river used his own strength against him.

To fight the river, he fought himself. Quenching his urge to lash out, Jemmie spread his arms wide and turned his face to the light. He stopped sinking. He hung suspended in the cool fluid, up or down in the balance. Placing his hands above his head in prayerful mode, he propelled them toward his sides. He rose.

He crested, sating himself on sweet air with high sputtery gasps. Ahead the older boy dog-paddled in the watery canyon between the barges. Jemmie followed suit. He could swim.

The older boy hauled him onto the dock. They were pimpled with cold but the air was hot and they stripped off their clothes and wrung them out, laughing. "So you lost yer capital?"

"Me what?"

"Yer wherewithal."

"Them matches?"

"What else you got?"

"Nothin'."

"C'mon with me then."

"Where to?"

"Printin' House Square."

"You a newsie?"

"C'mon. We're late. We got to put the *Star* on the street afore the factory hands come off the ferry."

CHAPTER THREE

I arrived in New York aboard the *Bristol*, a palace afloat which transported Boston passengers from the Connecticut shore to Manhattan. Why this brief passage should require such an abundance of velvet and gilt and crystal I could not discern, but my damaged back was exceedingly grateful for the finely upholstered respite from the jagged gait of the railroad train, a sooty coughing beast leaping from rail to ill-laid rail with rattles and lurches which shot arrows into my lower vertebrae. Once my voyage eased I pored over my Alger volume as long as my eyes allowed me.

Today the Alger books are an institution. The many titles are in fact a single book. Parents look on with approval while their sons ingest the elevating adventures of a stalwart street arab. Cunning but honest, he outwits crafty swindlers and bests wealthier but less virtuous rivals. Through luck and pluck he impresses a generous mentor who teaches him to spurn gambling dens and gin mills, stogies and nights at the Bowery Theatre so as to study French and mathematics and make of himself a solidly respected clerk or accountant. Communists denounce the books and with reason as insidious capitalist mythologizing. Mark Twain parodies their breathless positivism and childish puns. Yet boys read them still.

Ragged Dick was the first of Alger's street arab books. The others were formed upon this template and bore therefore a stale and repetitive stamp, but *Ragged Dick* was modeled on life. It had a spirited verisimilitude. Alger did not pretend success was easy or inevitable. He valued hard work, yet he also bore a healthy respect for the role of chance. The dialogue lacked the substrate of meaning which words carry in life or serious literature, but the diction was that of the street, and phrases stood out as taken from the mouths of the boys themselves. I remember a match boy who described himself as in the lumber trade. I suspected that the chief appeal of *Ragged Dick* to its young readers lay in its seductive portrait of the decadent liberties of street life, yet I did not doubt that they also took comfort in the strength of the young man who turned away from easy pleasures to make a place for himself in the world. I know I did.

In my febrile state I was acutely aware of the principal flaw in Alger's vision. The world he limned was impossibly benign. Evil existed only as a series of annealing temptations that when denied forged a stronger spirit. I had led a sheltered life, but even I had seen enough to know that evil had a more sinister aspect. Innocents suffer and good goes unrewarded.

Yet I flattered myself that I could see beyond Alger's childish optimism. Perhaps Alger was more profoundly correct than he might himself have understood. Evil is a slippery snake. On balance would the human race be a nobler species had we remained in a state of grace? If, so to speak, we had never left the Garden of Eden? I thought not. Since man bit into the serpent's apple and became conscious of his own will, became a creature capable of at least the illusion of choice, there is greater evil in the world but also greater virtue. Perhaps some higher calculus yet to be derived would show us how the mathematics of human morality balanced to the good. Or so I fervently hoped, steaming in red velvet luxury toward the city of New York. I had not one shred of proof that in our universe good would outweigh evil, yet I told myself it must or we faced an inevitable descent into squalour and moral destitution, a future too terrible to contemplate. Even as I demonstrated this proposition, my mind could not abandon the awful alternative.

Stretched on the rack of conflicting belief, sundered between my irrational hope and my all too rational fear, I determined that Alger's street arabs would become my agents of liberation. They would constitute my laboratory of the human soul. Without a past, owning nothing, alone in the world, they were as close an approximation of the naked human spirit as could reasonably be discovered. If some ineffable force propelled our species toward a better world, then I should find it working its mysterious ways among these boys. I allowed myself a prayer that I might find it. I refused to contemplate what should become of me if I did not.

———

When the *Bristol* docked I had more immediate concerns. I arrived well into the evening, having made no provisions for lodgings and wishing to conserve my small amount of capital, but resolved to find suitable accommodation in the vicinity of the Newsboys' Lodging-house. With difficulty I commandeered a hack whose driver assured me he knew of reputable quarters near Printing House Square. Citing the length of the journey and the size of my portmanteau, the man demanded a dollar and a half for the trip, and I had no alternative but to accede.

The streets at that time were paved with Belgian blocks, granite slabs which tipped in their beds so the wheels of the cab rode up and down an endless succession of jarring hillocks. I was still contorting myself to find a suitable angle of repose when the driver abruptly pulled to a halt. He now announced that he was forbidden by charter to proceed beyond the bounds of the immediate ward, and with regrets entrusted me to the stage driver for the rest of my trip, explaining that the stage was the favourite means of conveyance for the better class of New Yorkers, as the fare was sufficiently high to exclude the rougher and dirtier portion of humanity that frequented the street-cars. Of course he would defray any further expenses. When I inquired as to the lodgings he had promised me, he said that he had been mistaken, and on second thought the place was fully occupied, and probably not to my liking in any case. He transferred my baggage as he talked, with great ceremony presenting the driver a dime for my transport, and rapidly clattered back to the docks.

I clambered into the coach beneath the Olympian stare of the driver. The passengers consisted of well-dressed men and women on their way to an evening's amusement. Apparently I was their first diversion. Having overheard my dispute with the hack driver they informed me I had been cozened, and proceeded to debate among themselves the optimal lodgings near Printing House Square. With much vociferous dispute it was ultimately agreed that the best value was the St. Nicholas, but that it was certain to be completely booked, as would the

37

Metropolitan or any other hotel of decent quality, save perhaps the Grand Central, newly completed and the largest in America, fully eight stories tall. Exhausted, I welcomed their solicitude. Of the dozen hotels bandied about only the Metropolitan and the St. Nicholas remained from my childhood days at Fifty-eight West Fourteenth Street.

The lively discussion among strangers awakened in me the peculiar thrill which I felt upon my infrequent visits to this city, where public encounters share an informality usually reserved for the playing field. With a rush of elation I gazed across the dancing shadows of the evening traffic at the might and vigour, the imperial scale of this thoroughfare, spine of the city, clearinghouse of the nation. Moving uptown we passed first the ramshackle express companies crammed with goods from across the continent, then the ponderous edifices of those who moved not goods but gold, culminating in the massed muses and cascading columns of that proudest monument to capital accumulation, Park Bank. Paris or London was more magnificent, but here I felt an odd kinship, an irrational thrill of achievement, as if simply by being American I had helped create this potent engine of commerce. I had chosen the ultimate laboratory.

We approached Printing House Square. City Hall blocked its view, the shining clock face of the tower peering down impartially upon Boss Tweed's subjects. In the shadows above, capping the tower, the figure of Justice hid her eyes. They said she was blindfolded so that she might be spared the sight of the newly completed Courthouse, a modest building for the construction of which Tweed's cohorts extracted millions more than the British Empire expended upon its Houses of Parliament. As the skeletal columns of the Courthouse marched by my pride evaporated. Tweed, subject of superior amusement in the Boston journals, here took on threatening force.

I caught a brief glimpse of the *Sun* building behind Tweed's pair of monuments, but continued uptown. We passed block after block of iron warehouses filled to the trusses with the goods of the world, until the impersonal repositories gave way to purveyors of individualized treasures, Ball & Black's jewelry store and A. T. Stewart's Venetian palazzo of dry goods, to theatres, restaurants, and hotels, among them the Grand Central.

By the time I reached my destination I had long ceased congratulating myself upon my clever choice of laboratory; rather I was appalled that in my *hubris* I would view such an agglomeration of wealth and power as my experimental subject, as if I could stand apart in a clean mental smock and observe with objectivity the desperate travails of my fellow humans in their daily battles for survival, here where the stakes were the highest, when all that separated me from my laboratory subjects was the thirty-two dollars and fifty cents in my coat pocket.

I bore no illusions about the darkness lurking beyond the gaslit glow. Like any man who read a newspaper I knew that the great edifices of Broadway barely concealed the great pit a few blocks beyond. To associate with the have-nothings of New York was to immerse myself in the most squalid urban aggregation in the civilized world, abandoned by its politicians, victimized by its police, in fact a place I had selected by very reason of the ruthless Darwinian struggle that filled its streets. I had proclaimed myself a new man, freed from the baggage trailed by William James, yet I took comfort in the thought that should I prove inadequate to my task a single telegram would transport me back to the safety of Cambridge.

My experiment was fundamentally flawed. I was relying upon William James to insulate me from the horrors I was about to witness. If I did not wish to shoulder the burdens of William James then I could not summon his resources. I resolved to exist as if William James were an utter stranger to me. I told myself that even while I watched these boys earn their way, I must earn mine. I must be as much subject as observer, and I must maintain my new identity until the conclusion of my adventure, despite cold or hunger or disease. Unless I was willing to follow my experiment to its ultimate resolution, whatever that might be, the undertaking had no meaning whatsoever. Better to return post-haste to Boston. I did not doubt that I had the necessary strength of will should the worst occur. I had contemplated suicide often enough to believe I could embrace the idea of my own death.

The irony of my position did not escape me. I who did not believe in the reality of free will believed that I could by choice reject the saving offices of William James, even at the cost of my life. Whatever my theoretical quibbles, I had no doubt that when the moment arose I might assert my freedom of will by accepting my own death.

The proximate result of my morbidity of thought was a heightened resolve to husband my capital. Even as I signed the register at the Grand Central Hotel, committing myself to

the expenditure of five dollars for a single day's food and lodging, I resolved that this night would be my last in such an
establishment.

————

I requested the least expensive accommodations, and to my
surprise was assigned a chamber upon the second floor, the ad-
vent of the 'elevator' rendering the upper floors the more desir-
able. The topsy-turvy effect unsettled me, calling to mind my
own inverted situation. I spent a troubled night. By morning
my lower spine was punishing me for the rigours inflicted
upon it the day before. My eyes too were uncooperative, forcing
me awake at the merest sliver of sunlight which slipped
through the juncture of the curtains. I could not rise to close
them. As I lay supine, through my tightly compressed eyelids
the line of sunlight worked its way across the interior of my
skull with the keen precision of a boning knife scraping brains
from a boiled sheep's head.

I refused to remain hostage to my frailties. When the sunlight had passed I forced open my eyes. I pulled myself erect in
bed and swung my legs to the floor in the gray light. With a
feminine delicacy of movement I prepared myself to be seen by
the world.

I vacated my room and settled my accounts, entrusting my
valise with the bellman, then supped in a vast domed hall
which my waiter told me with pride accommodated six hundred. I could not imagine what kitchen could provide decent
provisions for half that number. My meal lived up to my imag-
inings. I ate a full but rapid repast, mindful of my five dollars'
investment, and hastened or more accurately hobbled out

to Broadway. Newsboys hawked the *Evening Express*, boldly shouting the latest murder-suicide in their reedy voices. Soon they would be making for their Lodging-house, and I would be there to greet them.

Lamps were being lit. I was startled by the newness of it all. The freshly minted buildings, creamy in the gaseous glow, brought to mind my Broadway excursions twenty years ago, when Harry and I wandered the avenue in joyous release from our daily incarceration at the Institution Vergnès. Broadway then promised a mysterious world pregnant with potential. I passed a vacant lot and remembered that same untenanted lot twenty years before, when we used to feed a friendly goat scraps of paper through the relaxed wooden palings. It seemed miraculous that this precious space had never been exploited, almost as if it had awaited my return. Perhaps my pilgrimage was nothing more than a childish attempt to recapture that sensation of the freshness of the world. I flagged a downtown stage.

Upon my entering the coach a well-dressed man requested ten cents, then rang a small gong affixed near a slot in the roof and handed a paper ticket up to the driver. The driver accepted it with a cheerful "Go it boots." I inquired of the gentleman if he worked for the stage company. He replied in the negative. He was the third in a well-to-do brokerage firm. He simply made it his habit to purchase a booklet of twelve tickets for a dollar, so that he might dispense them for a dime apiece and increase his capital.

⌒CHAPTER FOUR⌒

BAREFOOT JEMMIE HURRIED TO KEEP PACE WITH HIS WELL-SHOD longer-limbed companion. Damp clothing pulled heat from his body, and while movement restored it cold and activity drew down his stores of energy, causing hunger to gnaw at his stomach. Though penniless, cold, and hungry he skipped along at a cheerful trot, for he was not alone.

"Here's the deal," said his companion, Tom. "You buys the papers for a penny and a half and you sells them for two and you keeps the difference."

"I'm bust."

"I'll cover you fer fifty papers. That's seventy-five cents."

"I'll pay you back."

"You will that. Plus ten cents."

Jemmie calculated that selling all his papers would leave him with fifteen cents for the morning's work. That would afford him a passable breakfast with a nickel to spare.

They were late at the *Star* office. Tom chafed behind a line of boys until the dispatcher handed them their papers, then led Jemmie double-quick to the Fulton Street Ferry, as it would take them too long to assume his usual post farther uptown at the Greenpoint line on Tenth Street. The *Star* was a breezy journal, four full pages, which presumed to be the organ of the working classes and must therefore be disposed of before that class was attendant upon its labours. Jemmie and Tom joined a host of other boys running among the debarking men and women while shouting the discovery of a dismembered body in a spinster's steamer trunk. Newsies who claimed the ferry as home ground contested their presence but Tom was strong and resolute, and quick to succour Jemmie when an angry regular threatened to push him and his goods into the East River. A misfortune midstream where a young woman fell or jumped into the swiftest current delayed traffic sufficiently to compensate for the boys' late arrival, and by nine o'clock, when Tom declared the last stragglers to be upon the Manhattan side, Jemmie had sold all but three of his papers. He paid Tom eighty-five cents and together they repaired to a coffee and cake saloon, where he spent his remaining nine cents upon coffee and six griddle cakes, filling his belly as he emptied his pocket. Jemmie from long habit bolted his food, the better to have it in his stomach than on the plate in his uncertain world. Tom noticed with disapproval.

"What's yer hurry? Them cakes ain't going nowheres."

"Not oncet they's in me stomach."

Tom carved his cakes with precision and chewed his food with care. "Eat too fast it shoots right through you. Might as well not eat at all."

"Naw."

"The truth. Me daddy told me."

"Yer daddy said that?"

"Yeah."

"You got a daddy?"

"Naw. Not no more."

"You 'members him though."

"Course I 'members him. He was a doctor. With a gold watch chain."

"Show me."

"You thinks I'm sellin' papers, I got me a gold chain? A gold chain's capital. I got me a gold chain I'm buying me a pushcart, sellin' house goods."

"How'd he die?"

"The pox. Him and Ma." Tom stroked his pitted cheek. Jemmie could tell it was all he had left from his parents. Jemmie placed a finger on his own purpled bruise.

After breakfasting they made for the ferries on Courtlandt Street, where they accosted the travelers who debarked, offering to carry their bags. Tom's size and strength made him the more attractive candidate, but Jemmie's persistence was rewarded when a lady appeared with a moderately proportioned bundle which she was reluctant to entrust to the larger boys but willing to commit to his smaller and weaker person. He toted it to the Sixth Avenue cars, where he was rewarded with a dime. Hastening back to the ferry he convinced a tall, gaunt individual to allow him to haul an overstuffed traveling bag a mile across town, for which he was rewarded with a three-cent piece. When Jemmie argued for more the man told him such a weak thing as he was lucky to be paid at all.

He *rendezvous*ed with Tom for his main meal, a six-cent steak, then proceeded with Tom to the *Evening News,* a penny paper chronicling tales of vice and chicanery in lurid detail. They were burdened with the one o'clock edition, a harder sell after the two o'clock was distributed, and when they returned were given the four o'clock edition, which was superseded by the five o'clock, but after settling accounts with Tom, Jemmie was pleased to find twenty-seven cents jingling in his pocket, his own ready capital, to be dispensed as he saw fit. Tom, though profiting thirty cents from Jemmie's toils, thought their labors only moderately remunerative.

The *Evening Star* was not located with the other papers but further east off the Bowery. Jemmie looked uptown where the broad steps and fluted pillars of the Bowery Theatre beckoned. "How much to see a show?" he asked.

"Twelve cents."

"Let's go then!"

Tom viewed him with the eye of the experienced capitalist. "Maybe you got money to throw away. Not me." He waved and headed off. "Meet me right early at the *Star* tomorry and I'll front you again."

"Where you goin' then?"

"To a soft bed and a hot meal."

"How much?"

"Six cents."

"They slathers you with sermons and you prays all night?"

"No preachin'. They makes you wash up. Can't smoke. Can't cuss."

Jemmie watched his friend depart. The glories of the Bowery Theatre faded at the thought of sharing them with a raucous crowd of strangers. He trotted after Tom.

"Can I come too then?"

"You a orphan?"

"How come?"

"Gotta be a orphan."

Jemmie followed Tom down the Bowery. Under the darkened sky the street was assuming its nocturnal character. Early pleasure-seekers drawn by its theatres and restaurants strolled between iron piers that supported the newly erected elevated railway. Tom pushed forward resolutely, but Jemmie lingered, gazing at the enticements with the eye of a man flush with disposable surplus. He pulled Tom to a halt before a small self-styled museum. A man with an impressive beard was gathering passers-by, waving his cane before a crude image of a half-naked spear-wielding savage dwarfed by a fiery-eyed, smoke-snorting, massively horned monster.

"See Proud Axe, haughty foe of the renowned Wild Bill Hickok and brave conqueror of Giganta, most fearsome bison ever to haunt the Great Plains. See the actual body of Giganta himself, and hear in Proud Axe's own words how he brought low the creature that destroyed his village, trampled his mother, and gutted his father with one swift shake of his massive head. One nickel is all for this harrowing tale of bravery and destruction!"

Tom made to move on but Jemmie restrained him. "Gimme a minute."

"You're wastin' a nickel."

"I's goin' West. I is. Maybe I's fightin' me a bison. Time comes I gotta know about this."

Tom considered. The wait would cost him nothing. "Be quick then."

Jemmie paid his nickel and passed through a curtain to join a sparse group of curiosity-seekers on benches in the dark narrow room beyond. A hatchet-nosed fellow bare to the waist, face and chest smeared with warlike daubs, sat stoically upon a stool. A short moon-faced man stood beside him emoting with the skill of a practiced thespian. He gesticulated at a shroud which concealed a large, mysteriously lumped mound.

"Proud Axe knelt beside the crushed form of his dear, sweet mother and cried hot tears of agony. He swore he would avenge himself upon the fiendish creature. And he did not have long to wait. As he cradled his darling baby sister in his arms the ground shook beneath his feet! The sky was torn with a thunderous roar! He had barely time to clutch his spear when the beast appeared, charging through the campfire like a monster from hell!"

A lantern sputtered in imitation of the aboriginal campfire. Mallets pounded with deafening intensity. The orator's spherical head turned majestically toward the shrouded mound. With a flourish he yanked the cloth, revealing a stuffed bison, mangy about the shoulders, bearing upon its forehead an impressive set of steer horns. The thespian mimed heroic thrusts with an imagined spear.

48

"The creature snorted blood and bared his fangs at our

doughty warrior as he bore down for the kill. Quick as a thought Proud Axe thrust his spear like a lightning bolt into the heart. One inch off target and Giganta would have crushed our warrior, but so precisely did the great hunter gauge his huge attacker that the missile stopped the creature in its tracks. It sank to its knees, bowing its great head in homage to its mighty vanquisher, and expired on the spot."

The lantern died. Jemmie gasped and clapped his hands louder than the others. When light was restored the shroud was again in place. Jemmie looked back toward the curtained entrance, wishing to hear the saga from the beginning but fearing that Tom would lose patience with him.

————

Why did Jemmie wish to become an Indian fighter? That I cannot say. Nothing in his experience would make him believe that he had either the aptitude or the inclination to ride the plains and kill. He had never bestrode a horse, and he was a gentle boy who shrank from violence. Surely he was drawn by the majesty of the steppes, the romance of buckskin and fringe, the adventure of the hunt, the challenge of battle, but why this particular adventure, this particular challenge, this romance and majesty should so forcefully resonate in his tiny soul are questions which do not lend themselves to rational response. Thus was he constructed, by God or the struggle of his species for survival, and while he may appear mysterious to us, any nine-year-old would accept him without explanation.

CHAPTER FIVE

I alighted from the coach at City Hall Park amid a throng of importunate entrepreneurs. Ignoring the opportunity to test my lung capacity, discover my weight, or peer through a telescope at the heavens, I crossed Printing House Square, past the more imposing *Times*, *Tribune*, and *Staats Zeitung*, toward the sturdy, four-square building which housed the *Sun*. The ground beneath the paving blocks of Fulton Street shook under my feet to the rhythm of a distant rumble, vibrations of the powerful engine in the bowels of the square and the subterranean shafts and leather belts which connected it to the presses it drove at the various papers. I was directed to the loft, *via* a flight of narrow stairs.

Trudging upward, Alger's book in one hand, the other upon the wall for support of my tender spine, amid the distant roar of presses and the odor of linseed oil and printer's ink, I could for the first time see my plan from an outside perspective, as a journalist might report it: the obsessive musings of a fevered brain, the ill-conceived product of an overly bookish man deprived too long of literary sustenance. At the third floor I halted, strongly tempted to retrace my steps and embark on the luxurious *Bristol* for Connecticut and the Boston train. I could yet reclaim my place at McLean, to the relief of Dr. Tyler, and with luck Father would be none the wiser. Once I had seen the Lodging-house, for good or ill, I knew I could never abandon my adventure, for then abandonment on whatever excuse would be a simple failure of the will, cowardice and weakness by a loftier name. Here in the stairwell my adventure had yet to fairly begin. To turn about now could be an act of sanity and proportion. What did I intend to learn from these boys? How could I justify my presence among them? How could I even maintain my anonymity?

As I lingered wavering in indecision two young men leapt up the stairs past me, laughing in their eagerness to reach the top. The elder's visage was pitted with pox scars; the younger was barefoot, his face disfigured by a frightful bruise. Their happy voices and their acrid odor of dirt and sweat cut short my vacillation. I had already passed the point of no return. I followed the echoing slaps of boyish feet upon the worn wood.

At the top of the stair I joined a brief line of boys at the door of a large, beamed room encircled with windows which admitted a refreshing breeze. It easily accommodated the few dozen young men who disported in small groups, laughing, arguing, gossiping, or wrestling. I awaited my turn to be interviewed by a man who sat just inside the door upon a raised platform, entering names of newcomers in a large registry. He was a calm, pale man whom the boys called Mr. O'Connor, a man of sandy hair, sandy complexion, and watery blue eyes, so bland a presence as to be virtually invisible. He spoke in a neutral tone, with an Irish lilt, and wrote at a steady pace. He did not challenge and he did not berate, but his quiet direct manner provoked a like response. He greeted the elder of the boys who had passed me in the hall as Thomas, and let him sign in with his own hand.   **51**

Thomas told O'Connor he wished to make a deposit to his account of forty-three cents, which Mr. O'Connor noted while the boy inserted the coins into one of a hundred numbered slots in Mr. O'Connor's table. Thomas introduced the lad with the bruised face as Jemmie, which the lad elaborated to James Hickok. While Thomas seemed confident of his place, almost the man of fashion visiting his club, slender young Hickok had a tentative air.

"Tom says I can bum here if I's a orphan."

"Are you an orphan?"

"Yessir. Me mother bled away givin' birth to me little brother an' me father drank hisself to death."

"Where is your brother now?"

"He's gone, sir."

"Where have you been sleeping?"

"Anywheres I can. Slept in a hay barge last night."

"Is that where you got that shiner?"

"No sir. Kicked by a horse."

O'Connor entered the boy's name into his registry. "Thomas no doubt recounted our rules. The cost is six cents for lodging and four cents for supper, cash in advance. No alcohol. No cigars. No gambling. You don't eat if you don't wash. If you have no shoes you must wash your feet before sleeping on our linen. Rowdiness will put you on the street. Theft or vandalism will put you on Blackwell's Island."

Jemmie Hickok paid his fee.

"Do you wish to deposit any savings in our bank? We pay no interest, but you're protected from temptation until we open the coffers at the end of the month."

"No sir. I don't have no capital."

"How long has it been since you washed?"

"I swimmed this mornin'."

"Take the soap to him, Thomas." He turned to me as Thomas led the younger boy away. "I take it you are not in search of lodging."

"No, sir." I extended my hand. I had resolved that my best chance at avoiding exposure was to tell as much of the truth as possible. "My name is William Henry. I've heard Mr. Alger speak of your work here and I'm interested in being of some assistance."

He shook my hand, though without rising from his chair. "Money is always welcome. As you can imagine ten cents per boy hardly covers expenses."

"Unfortunately I'm not a wealthy man. I was hoping I might offer my services."

"Frankly, sir, we've become something of a darling among the socially committed. I've found such people as a rule to be more concerned with their own salvation than with the needs of my charges."

Mr. O'Connor's pale gaze settled upon me, seeing rather too much. Before I could frame a reply he passed on to the boy behind me, a large muscular dark-haired lad with a strong jaw and a self-assured demeanor. A red comforter was rakishly wound about his neck. Had it been brocaded silk he might have been a Venetian princeling in a portrait by Bellini.

"And your name?"

"Dannie O'Connor. Though no kin of your'n."

"How old are you, Dannie?"

53

"Fifteen."

O'Connor eyed him skeptically.

"I look older than I be. It's me chin. A man's chin I grant you, but I be fifteen, I swear it on me poor parents' heads, and me orphaned when the Westfield ferry blew its boiler."

"You're recently alone."

"How long you gotta be a orphan to bum here? Me mummy was boiled like a chicken and me daddy was crushed by the pilot house when it came to earth. Lucky fer me I was off blackin' boots or I'd a got it too. Course the pilot walked away a whole man."

A boy behind snickered. O'Connor merely entered Dannie's name in the register. "Nights are warm still. We have space. First cold night you're on your own." While O'Connor took Dannie's ten cents I pressed my case.

"I have recently completed a course of medical training—"

O'Connor cut me off. "The boys are as a rule hale and sturdy. Dr. Brugge, an expert on the diseases of poverty, is a frequent visitor."

"I could perhaps provide useful discourse upon natural history—"

"These are self-made young men. They share a profound aversion to instructive talk. If you speak well and can tell an inspiring tale I suggest you try the paupers and the beggars of the Children's Aid Society."

Stymied, I raised my copy of *Ragged Dick*. "I'm an admirer of Mr. Alger. I was told he writes here. Might I be allowed to pay him my respects?"

"That's his desk." O'Connor pointed to a large unattended *escritoire* near the far wall. "It appears he's gone for the day."

"Might I leave him a few words?"

O'Connor gestured toward the desk. "In the future I suggest you arrange to *rendezvous* at his publisher."

I strode toward the desk dismayed. Moments before I had been ready to abandon my project as a fool's errand, but now the prospect of failing before I had truly begun made me burn with shame. I had no desire to lecture at the Children's Aid Society to beggars and paupers. Yet I could not fault O'Connor's logic or his distrust of my motives.

I looked about at the boys I passed. This would be my last opportunity to study them *en masse*. They had been forced, many from infancy, to rely upon their own energy and application for survival. Only the strongest and the most resourceful had reached this attic room rather than a Blackwell's Island workhouse or a potter's field grave. I detected a heightened alertness, an air of defensive calculation, a constant apprehension not unlike the look in a sparrow's eye when it sips at a fountain. Equally, however, the boys projected an impressive aura of self-reliance. They were certainly a class of humanity worthy of study.

As I leaned over Alger's blotting paper, framing in my mind a suitable letter of introduction, a skittering and clattering directed my attention behind the desk. There I saw Alger's diminutive form huddled out of view of O'Connor, his long locks swirling as he hurled a pair of dice against the dark wood while three boys looked on. He was completely absorbed in his game, urging the cubes to fall as he willed them, bitterly disappointed when to the glee of his spectators they did not.

A chortling boy saw my startled face. His sudden silence quietened the others. Alger looked up in alarm, then straightened, embarrassed. "No gambling, you understand, no money whatsoever, not a farthing, research, these lads are teaching me some fine points—"

"I quite understand." Had I not cut him off, he would have continued to explain himself into ever deeper discomfiture. "Please. Don't let me interrupt."

"No, no . . ." He gestured at the vanishing boys. "To O'Connor they'd just be playing at craps." He saw the book in my hand. "You have *Ragged Dick*."

"I'm here because of it."

"Really!" Pleased, Alger dropped into his chair and gestured to the corner of the desk. "Seat yourself. We aren't very formal here." I perched upon his desk. My back gave a momentary twinge of objection but Alger took no notice of my fleeting grimace, absorbed as he was in the pleasure of greeting an admirer. "The book had an impact then."

"It depicted the spirit of these young men with such force that I felt compelled to meet them for myself."

My words provoked a grin. He took my compliment without irony or false modesty. "You're a literary man."

"I like to read."

He snapped his fingers. "I know you."

"I don't believe we've ever been introduced."

"I've an excellent head for faces." Alger's brow furrowed. I
feared he was summoning to mind a rigid blanket-wrapped

form upon the porch of McLean Asylum and I started to speak, but he stopped me with a crisp gesture, as if forestalling me from telling him the answer to a riddle. His brow cleared. He aimed his fingers like a pistol. "You're a Harvard man."

"Not precisely. I attended the medical school."

The thumb hammer fell. "Close enough." His hand thrust forward for mine. "I'm a toodle. B.A. Class of Fifty-two. Divinity School class of Sixty. I attended some Agassiz lectures. We must have met there."

"I voyaged in Brazil with Professor Agassiz cataloguing the fish of the Amazon."

Alger was impressed. "So you're a naturalist."

"I fear not. The expedition convinced me I belonged somewhat closer to home." I did not wish to mention that I had been functionally blind much of the time. "But I had hoped to share my knowledge of the natural world with these young men."

"An excellent thought."

"Mr. O'Connor doubts I'd find an audience."

"Nonsense! Tell them about the Amazon. They love adventure tales. Stress the danger and derring-do. You provide an excellent example, a man of substance leading a life any boy would covet. Did you encounter the man-eating piranho? The head hunter?"

"My travels were remarkable only in their lack of drama."

"No matter. You'll teach them valuable facts about the natural world."

"O'Connor's refusal was definitive."

"He's a tight old bear. Leave him to me."

I waited at his desk while he propelled himself briskly at   **57**

O'Connor. Alger's words were lost to me, but his sincere enthusiasm was manifest even at this distance. Though he knew nothing of me save my appreciation of *Ragged Dick* and our purported acquaintance at Harvard, his faith in me was absolute. Was he an innocent, or a fool?

O'Connor, apparently, had no such reservations. He accepted Alger's effervescence as proof of his strength of purpose and purity of motive. Finally Alger summoned me with an energetic wave, and nodded encouragement while O'Connor told me that I might deliver a trial lecture after supper.

Mrs. O'Connor, a cheerful, fat-armed woman, supervised the feeding of the boys in the refectory on the floor below. I prevailed upon Alger to look in on them. Mistaking our intent, she brought us each a plate of simple, filling fare. I declined the invitation, but Alger dispatched the food with an efficiency which implied that this was a not uncommon occurrence.

The boys dined with loose good cheer. Mrs. O'Connor, whom Alger called Minnie, ran the meal with a tolerant hand, and the boys, conscious no doubt of Mr. O'Connor overhead, did not exploit her easy ways. Between bites Alger remarked that she had lost her five children, all under ten years of age, in a cholera epidemic, and in her husband's view treated their lodgers with too much motherly indulgence.

After dining, all gathered about Mr. O'Connor's platform in the main hall. While O'Connor looked on from his slotted table, Alger introduced me as a gentleman who was expert on the natural world having traveled among the Indians of the Amazon. He took pleasure in a lengthy and impassioned description of the perils of that river, in particular the anthropophagous

58

fish, which he said could strip a man to his naked skeleton in seconds, and the savages he claimed thronged its shores in canoes decorated with the smoked and shrunken heads of their foes. Then with the fanfare of a Barnum he led me forward to the delighted cheers and applause of the boys. He had succeeded in focusing the attention of my audience, but he had made a difficult task impossible.

Discounting classroom exercises and drawing-room dramas for the diversion of the family, this was my first public address. I have since spoken on two continents, before princes of the blood and princes of the intellect, in more universities and academies and draughty public halls than I can count. I have dreaded each and every appearance, but I have never approached any public address with more trepidation than this little lecture to the newsboys. Later I developed the defensive strategy of excessive preparation, polishing and rehearsing my speeches until I overcame my apprehension by brute familiarity with my material. This night found me nakedly exposed.

I perceived that this was more than an exercise imposed by chance to charm my hosts. This was an essential part of my adventure. Before I presumed to use these boys as subjects of my observation, I must serve as theirs. With honesty and candor I must prove myself worthy of their moral contemplation.

I surveyed my audience. Never after did I speak to a more demanding public. These boys would stand no fooling. They were accustomed to gammon; they lived by it. Hands in pockets, legs stretched out, heads generally up, eyes full upon me, mouths closed tightly or gaping wide, they were keenly alive and completely attentive. I stood in silence, searching for an opening

59

thought, until my audience lost patience and spoke out. A boy with a harelip asked how many of my friends had been scalped by Indians. He had seen a scalped man in a storefront museum. The boy named Hickok with the bruised face wished to know how many Indians I had killed "with me own hand."

"My adventures with wild Indians consisted in seeing two of them naked at the edge of the forest. It gave me a very peculiar and unexpected thrilling sensation to come suddenly upon these children of Nature."

"They carry spears?"

"They paint thesselves?"

"They jump you?"

"I shouted to them in *Lingua Geral,* and they ran away."

"What about the shrunken heads?"

"We discovered a few hours later that these wild men were in fact a couple of mulattoes from our own expedition who happened to be bathing."

There was a general restless stirring. "Who got et by the fishes?"

"We were very careful where we bathed. I saw a jaguar, however."

"What's a jaguar? Is that like a bison?" asked the Hickok boy.

"A large spotted cat, like a small tiger."

"What's a tiger?"

"A lion with stripes," a boy shouted out. "I seen 'em at Barnum's."

"So this was like a lion with spots?"

"Yes. Smaller, but equally fearsome."

"Did it eat anyone?"

"Did you kill it?"

"Its roaring kept us awake all night."

The boys were noisily disappointed. "Go off!"

"Broadway's scarier."

"So what was huntin' you then?"

"You wasn't in no Amazon."

"Insects abounded. Mosquitoes attacked us in clouds. Worms burrowed under our skin and caused large ulcerating sores."

"Skeeters and worms! Go on home! Won't find me in no Amazon!"

"I was there for good purpose. I was looking to discover animals no one had seen before."

"What'd you find?"

"Over seventy new species of fish."

"What's species?"

"An excellent question. By species, I suppose I mean a particular kind of fish that resembles itself but no other kind of fish. There are hundreds of species of fish."

"But they's all fishes."

"He says different kinds. Like bulldog or fox terrier is dogs."

"Yes, something like that, except that different species can't mate with one another."

"Terriers and bulldogs sure can!" Raucous gaiety ensued, and whispered arguments about the interbreeding of dogs.

"Ain't no hundred fishes. That's bull."

"There's cod! There's mackerel! There's halibut!"

"Ain't no hundred fishes!"

Chaos threatened. Beside me O'Connor pushed back from his desk, preparing to restore order and no doubt abort my   **61** address. I signaled him to refrain. To regain the boys' attention I took up O'Connor's pen and boldly sketched the piranho fish, emphasizing its fearsome jaws.

"This is the man-eating piranho fish. He's no bigger than my fist, but he travels packed together in schools, feasting upon large game such as monkeys and wild pigs. He's nothing but a gigantic pair of jaws designed for ripping flesh." I handed my sketch into the audience and limned a few more toothy jaws. They quietened somewhat. "The blue whale is the largest animal upon the planet, and he eats plants so small they're almost invisible to the eye. He catches his food with a sieve in his throat. Nature is a wonder of diversity."

The boy who called himself O'Connor spoke out. "How come?"

"Excuse me?"

"How come they's so many?"

"Who sells papers here?" Hands shot up. "Who blacks boots?" Other hands. "And the rest?"

"I sells matches."

"Oranges."

"Candles."

"Books."

"Cards."

"Neckties."

"I hawk firewood."

"You *swipes* firewood."

"Just as you find every way to make a living in the city, species develop to find every way to make a living in the jungle. They're all competing for a place at the table."

62

"Maybe I sell papers today, maybe I sell books tomorrow or oranges come Christmas." The O'Connor boy persisted. "Ain't no species about it."

"You're blessed with a brain that can learn. These creatures are driven by instinct."

"Goats eat pretty near anything."

"That's their niche. They possess a particularly strong set of stomachs which allow them to digest almost anything, but they're not fast runners or good at stalking prey. Other animals developed those skills in competition with each other, until each species grew so adept at its specialty that it kept others out. Their struggle created the natural order."

Mr. O'Connor looked at me sharply. "Surely, sir, you mean to say that God created the natural order to strengthen His creatures through struggle?"

"Shall we spare these boys from theological debate?" I had no wish to go down that road.

"I'd like to know where you stand, sir. There's no place here for godless men."

"Should God exist He doesn't require my good opinion."

"But you require His."

Alger interjected soothing words in an anxious voice. "We're all God-fearing men. Certainly."

I ignored him, speaking to O'Connor. "I can assure you that no man is searching harder for evidence of the Divine Presence than I, and none would be more delighted to find it."

O'Connor was hardly mollified by this reply, but I was spared further discourse by young Hickok, enamored of my pi- ranho jaw, urging me to "Draw a jaguar!" I busied myself and

63

sketched a fair image of the beast. I drew a few of the peculiar trapezoidal rings which we call spots, and handed the paper and pen to the boy. "The markings break up the lines of his body. Imagine them as leaf shadows."

Hickok went at it while others crowded around. One boy asked if I could draw a horse. I sketched a horse's head. Hickok looked up from drawing his spots, entranced. "Can you learn me that?"

"Who would like to learn to draw horses?" Half a dozen hands went up.

"And injuns!"

"Locomotives!"

"We'll begin with the horse's head." I addressed Mr. Alger. "If you'll allow me the use of your paper and pens, I'll replace them tomorrow."

"With Mr. O'Connor's permission."

O'Connor took my measure, noncommittal.

"I'm well trained as a draughtsman. I apprenticed with a prominent New England artist. I might detect talent which can elevate these boys from their present situation."

"Not one word about your so-called natural order."

"I assure you I'll avoid any discourse even remotely philosophical."

O'Connor gestured faintly toward Alger's desk. Alger and half a dozen boys followed me over and we were soon at work. Realizing that my future welcome depended upon these boys' good opinion, I strove less to inculcate general principles than to gratify with immediate effect. I stripped off my coat, and with the young men gathered about me I demonstrated how to construct a horse head from cylinders, cones, and spheres. Soon to their amazement they were producing passable representations.

My two most enthusiastic artists were Hickok and the big O'Connor boy. Hickok showed remarkable aptitude for one who had never held a pen before and impressive concentration on the work at hand. He possessed that rarest of qualities in an artist, or for that matter in any creator, an instinctive feel for the whole. Dannie O'Connor laid down a facile line and found excitement in the process as a sort of magic trick.

Alger joined in, eager as any boy to master the draughtsman's secrets, but he was uncomfortable with the process and was disappointed when his cones and spheres refused to coalesce into an animal, stubbornly remaining mere geometric forms. When Dannie commented that with his new skill he could win a nickel bet at any bar, Alger in frustration lashed out at him for talk of betting. Dannie serenely replied that Alger needn't worry because he'd never bet on Alger, and the boys laughed hard at this in spite of Alger's discomfiture. They treated Alger as one of their confraternity, and although Alger felt slighted by young O'Connor he took pleasure in being so well accepted that the boys felt comfortable ragging on him.

I too was pleased with the progress of events. I was most impressed by these boys' ability to bring their intellects to bear upon unfamiliar issues. They were high-spirited, quick to accept a challenge, and they reveled in the forms of humor which signal a quick intelligence. Diffidence and inhibition were not in their constitutions. No doubt their mode of living had selected those who were the brightest and most confident, and success upon the streets had increased their self-reliance.

65

They had the child's straightforwardness and the adult's self-possession. When I compared my own condition to theirs I was humbled and inspired. I enjoyed the prospect of earning these boys' trust and learning more about their processes of mind.

Collecting the best examples of the boys' work I presented them to the senior O'Connor as a peace offering, suggesting that he might wish to display one or two as encouragement. O'Connor accepted them with no particular pleasure. "So you're artist as well as naturalist."

"I'm trained as both, but alas I'm neither."

"I warrant you've been trained in all manner of rarefied activities," he said in quiet and meticulous tones. "Speak a fistful of languages, ride and shoot and dance and recite poetry too, I warrant."

"I'm no outdoorsman, but I've had the privilege of a broad education."

"Then you might tell me why the thought of natural struggle is so attractive to folks like yourself who never tasted the fact of the thing."

"The laws of natural selection function independently of my personality."

O'Connor grunted dismissively.

My success with the children emboldened me. "What have I done to have so offended you?"

"You're a gentleman. You dabble. You try on accomplishments like so many new silk suits. Work to you is an amusing diversion. You didn't earn what you possess, so you don't value your possessions. You're a bad example to the boys. They see all too many of your kind in the gambling saloons."

I was taken aback by the intensity of his reply. "If you knew me better you'd acknowledge that I'm capable of serious application."

"I'm sure you are, when the mood strikes you, but you've had the rare blessing of inherited wealth and privilege. Those jungle animals you admire didn't share your advantages, and neither do these boys. You cannot imagine what it costs these boys to be honest, to be clean, to help others. Do you think if you were born without privilege, alone as they are, you could have survived to be their age?"

"I doubt it."

"Then how can you presume to advise them?"

"I only wish to teach them drawing."

"That I do not believe. But I thank you for your time. Good evening."

I had no reply. O'Connor was rude but he was not stupid. Upon the barest of acquaintance he had summarized my position more astutely than my friends, family, or doctors. His words resurrected the crushing doubts which had propelled me to McLean. My dark mood descended like a curtain between myself and my surroundings. The yellow gaslight, so warm and nurturing moments before, bathed the room in a sickly jaundiced pall, as if I were drowning in my own urine, and those rambunctious boys were leeches wriggling in the fetid pool. Their gay sounds assumed a dull subaqueous tone. My sight dimmed. The musculature of my lower back seized my spine like a hawk's claw upon a helpless rabbit. I staggered for a seat.

Alger's voice intruded, grating in its concern. Not wanting his pity and having no intention of explaining my condition, **67**

I waved him roughly away. He ignored my rude gesture and cheerfully insisted upon returning me to my bed. When I curtly replied that I planned to devote the evening to finding one, he urged me to join him at his lodgings. It was, he said, a fair bargain at five dollars a week. The food was plentiful, the landlady tolerable, and he would welcome my companionship at table. Making light of my affliction in a comradely fashion, he played the host and insisted upon hiring a hack and escorting me to retrieve my valise at the Grand Central Hotel.

I was in no position to spurn his offer. In my decrepit state I longed only for a dark bed in a silent room. In truth, Alger's combination of genuine concern and blithe disregard for the severity of my condition was exactly what my sinking spirits required. In the hack he flattered my performance with the boys. My own dark mood detected desperation in his good offices. Away from the boys he was, I sensed, a lonely man.

Alger's landlady, Mrs. Frye, presided over a brown-stone in St. Mark's Place that had been a mansion when last I lived in New York. As the wealthy were pulled uptown by the currents of fashion they left their dwellings behind like empty sea shells upon the shore, and landladies like fiddler crabs took up residence therein, apportioning each chamber to some forlorn creature that floated in with the fall tide and out with the spring. Alger himself was newly ensconced. Mrs. Frye, I was relieved to discover, was neither inquisitive nor loquacious, though dauntingly stern. Widowed since Gettysburg, she still wore mourning.

Mrs. Frye was not the trusting sort. She showed me a clean room and informed me that guests or noise after nine were evictable offenses. I assured her that I was a quiet soul who valued his rest, a self-evident proposition, given my decrepit posture and hesitant movements, but one to which she gave credence only when assured by Alger that my affliction was authentic. She required two weeks' payment in advance. If I did not pay on time I would find my belongings in the street.

I was in no condition to search further. In truth, Alger's presence and the imposed serenity seemed worth the aura of grim gentility which festooned the place like funereal crepe. I reached for my wallet to advance milady a month's rent.

To my chagrin, the wallet was missing. A thorough search of my person did not produce it. I was forced to admit that I had forty cents to my name.

I swore to Alger and Mrs. Frye that I possessed a wallet containing thirty-two dollars, which I had placed in my jacket pocket. I had last remarked upon it when I had draped the coat over Alger's chair at the Lodging-house. I speculated that it had fallen out when I had donned the coat or perhaps in the hack on the way to the boarding house. In my condition I would not have noticed its disappearance.

Alger did not doubt me for an instant. He was if possible more upset than I. He was certain it had fallen out in the Lodging-house and said we must return there immediately. No doubt a boy had discovered it and entrusted it to O'Connor. Mrs. Frye, stony as her St. Mark's Place façade, remarked that she had been running a boarding house for many years and cautioned Alger to stifle any impulse to advance me money.

CHAPTER SIX

Alger and I rode back to Printing House Square in silence, both praying that O'Connor would have my wallet intact in his possession. We neither of us wished to conjure up the likelier scenario. Upon arrival, my dorsal predicament required that I mount the long stair delicately, while Alger rushed ahead. Reaching the upper floor I was met with grim silence. The boys were in their beds, and O'Connor and his wife had been shutting off the gas when Alger intruded. The wallet had not been turned over. I immediately apologized for our imposition, declared that I must have lost it in the hack, and turned to descend. O'Connor would not let me leave. He re-illumined the upper floor and the four of us searched beneath every chair and in every crevice in the floorboards, to no avail. Though I was facing utter destitution I was in fact relieved we had not found an empty wallet. Better to have lost my last penny than to have lost my esteem for these boys.

I was repeating my apologies to O'Connor and his wife when O'Connor, looking out the window, pointed to a small dark object in the side alley. Alger rushed down and returned with a familiar square of green Florentine leather, flaccid and forlorn. I thanked O'Connor. "I must have dropped it when we boarded the carriage."

"That would have been on the Printing House Square side of the building."

"No doubt someone found it where I dropped it and took himself behind the building to inspect its contents."

O'Connor shook his head. "Your 'someone' threw it from this window. Excuse me please." Picking up a broom, he disappeared to the floor below.

We heard the muffled clatter of O'Connor's broom handle rapping bedsteads, the clump of two hundred bare feet upon boards, the rumble of distant talk. I could see that Minnie O'Connor shared our distress. "I've no wish to disturb the boys," I said, "but I have no influence with your husband. Could you prevail upon him to let this pass?"

She looked at me as if I had asked her to reverse the tides. "Mr. O'Connor," she said, "was sergeant major with Her Majesty's Guards in the Crimea."

The door opened and the sergeant major entered trailing a double line of barefoot half-clad boys, whom he arrayed in ragged rows before Mr. Alger's desk, speaking in his usual quiet tones but with a new note of dry precision which provoked from the boys deferential if sullen attention.

"Mr. Henry," he said to me, for the benefit of his young audience, "I've explained to these boys that the theft of your money is a serious offense which stains the personal honour of every one of them. I've urged them to clear their own names and the good repute of this institution by identifying the thief. Unfortunately no one sees fit to report anything." He gazed mildly over the rows of boys. "No one shall sleep until we've discovered the thief among us and seen him duly punished. Mr. Henry, will you kindly show me exactly what occurred from the moment you removed your jacket?"

"Mr. O'Connor," I said, "we've no proof any of these boys took my wallet. Let's assume the best of all concerned and agree that I lost my money in the street. Send the boys back to bed."

"As long as I am in charge of this Lodging-house I shall punish thievery. You're not helping these boys by doing otherwise. Please tell me what occurred from the moment you removed your jacket."

Reluctantly I approached Alger's desk. "I removed my jacket before seating myself." I draped my jacket over the chair and sat in demonstration.

He turned to the boys. "Which of you accompanied Mr. Henry?" Half a dozen came forward. He turned to me. "Is that all the boys who came with you?"

"I believe so."

"Mr. Alger," he said, "were these the boys who accompanied Mr. Henry?"

"Yes."

"There were no others?"

"No."

The boys eyed one another.

"Mr. Henry, can you describe how they were gathered around you?"

"I'm uncomfortable with this whole proceeding."

"If necessary I'll see all six of these boys punished to root out the thief. I'm quite sure they all know who took the money."

He surveyed them with his deceptively gentle gaze. "Better to tell me now than later."

The boys said nothing.

"Show me how you were standing."

The boys arranged themselves approximately as they were when we were drawing.

"Is that accurate, Mr. Henry?"

"If the boys say it was so."

"Mr. Alger?"

"That's about right," said Horatio.

"What's different?"

"Dannie was closer to the desk."

"Where exactly?"

To my surprise, though Alger must have shared my distaste for the proceedings he strove to abet them, taking Dannie by the arm to position him. Dannie pulled himself away. "I knows where I was standin'."

O'Connor looked the six boys in the eye, one by one, in unhurried assessment of their souls. "Mickety, Fat Jack, Cranky Jim, Pickle Nose, you were on the wrong side of the desk, and you I know to be honourable young men. Did you see any suspect behaviour by these other two? Fat Jack?"

"No sir, we was hard at our drawin'."

"The rest of you?"

The boys looked at the ground and mumbled in the negative.

"Jemmie Hickok, you're new here. I don't know you. Are you the sort of boy that steals money?"

"No sir."

"Swear on your mother's head."

"Me mother's dead, sir."

"She's up in heaven looking down. Swear on her sainted head."

"I swear on me mother I didn't take no money."

Satisfied, O'Connor turned his attention to Dannie. "Mr. O'Connor. Another debutant. Usually a boy your age has come through here a few times."

"I told you, I was only orphaned this year."

"And you told me your name was O'Connor. Remarkable coincidence that."

"I know twenty O'Connors live in Mulberry Bend."

"I'm thinking you lied about your name. I'm thinking you were standing next to Mr. Henry's coat. I'm thinking you're the type of boy that comes to no damn good."

"Think what you like."

"Turn your pockets out."

"You turn 'em out."

"Mickety, Fat Jack, go through his pockets."

Dannie was wearing only a long shirt. The boys found nothing.

"If I stole your money you think I'm thick enough to keep it in me pocket?"

"Who knows where Dannie was bunking?"

Pock-faced Thomas spoke. "In the Eagle's Nest."

This information further displeased O'Connor. "What's he doing there?"

"Don't know, sir."

"Search his belongings. Search his mattress. Mrs. O'Connor, help Thomas."

Minnie mutely led Thomas downstairs. O'Connor squared off with Dannie. "Better for you it comes from your own lips."

"Me pocket, me mattress ain't no difference. What you thinkin' to find?"

In the presence of such arbitrary justice I could no longer hold my tongue. I drew Mr. O'Connor aside and spoke in confidential tones. "Aren't you being rather presumptive? There's no evidence against this boy. Anyone might have brushed by my jacket. We don't even know my wallet was stolen."

"You've done quite enough, leaving your money lying about like the rankest greenhorn. Now I must see to the end what you began."

Mrs. O'Connor and Thomas returned. Thomas was rifling Dannie's worn clothing. "No money I can see."

"None you can't see neither."

O'Connor's voice dropped a notch. "Make a clean breast or you'll rue this day."

Dannie smirked. "Nothin' I says changes nothin' no ways."

O'Connor took from Alger's desk a pearl-handled pen knife. He snapped it open and approached the boy. Dannie stood defiant. They stared at each other for long seconds. Then O'Connor reached out and with a deft flick cut a notch from the boy's left ear. The boy gave a bark of pain and surprise.

As for the rest of us, such silence greeted O'Connor's act that we could hear the faint plop as the gobbet of cartilage hit the floor. Dannie crouched, to protect himself or leap at

O'Connor, but O'Connor aborted both intentions by grabbing his good ear in a powerful grip and dragging him toward the door, muttering through gritted teeth loud enough for all to hear, "You've got the mark of Cain now, my lad. The thief's ear."

I flushed with shame at the sight of such cruel and impetuous jungle justice, made doubly horrible as I was its root cause. From the stair as from infernal depths I heard bumping and shrieks, and I forced myself to the window, where I watched O'Connor hurl the half-naked boy onto the pavement and slam the door. Jemmie, owl-eyed, came up beside me and jettisoned Dannie's shoes and pants from the window. The shoes dropped like stones, but the pants spread legs like wings and floated gently through the medium of the air. A dorsal spasm threw me to the wall.

Superficially at least the other boys were more amused than distressed by the events. Whatever their deeper feelings, and I presume they must have been appalled by the tyranny and brutality they had just witnessed from a man who called himself their protector, they loudly proclaimed the younger O'Connor culpable and well deserving of his treatment at the hands of the elder. Alger, however, sat silent, a bloodless ashy color, his lips liver-hued. We exchanged despairing looks as O'Connor's tread resonated upon the stair.

When O'Connor entered, the boys clamoured to be returned to bed. He silenced them. "My count today was eighty-four. Less O'Connor, eighty-three." Some boys laughed at that. "Mr. Henry lost thirty-two dollars. That means we each of us owe him thirty-nine cents. I will charge it against your account, if you have savings here, or you may pay this morning as you leave."

I forced myself to stand. "That I cannot allow, and if you insist I'll return the money to the boys."

We had arrived at a stand-off. O'Connor stared at me with something more than contempt but less than respect. "A gentleman allows another gentleman to repay a debt of honour."

"If you truly believe you owe me a debt, you may repay it by allowing me to teach these boys to draw."

My suggestion displeased the man. "Corruption feeds on weakness."

"Corruption feeds on injustice."

"You've no stomach for justice. Your concern is peace of mind. What's thirty-two dollars to you? A cheap suit. You'd go naked for peace of mind, but you don't have to. You've a rack of silk suits and a butler to dress you."

"I'll be going, then." I made my way with some difficulty for the door. With each step knives stabbed my lower back. I did not know how I would navigate the stairway, but I had no intention of remaining, or requesting O'Connor's assistance.

"A debt's a debt. Come whenever you like."

O'Connor inclined his chin as if to say that I had won this round. Oddly, I found his good opinion gratifying. I straightened myself as best I could, and turned to the boys. "Is that agreeable with the rest of you?" My words were greeted with weary and relieved assent.

I walked tall, stiff-faced from hiding my pain, until I was in the shelter of the stairway. Once free from the children's eyes I clutched the wall, taking the first stair gingerly with one foot,

77

then the other. I took a second stair, and a third. Tears clouded my vision. I paused for breath.

I felt support beneath my arm. Alger was offering his shoulder, which his bantam stature placed at the pit of my arm, a welcome crutch.

"Thank you."

"Take your time."

I let him help me down the flight. We were soon passed by the boys rushing back to their beds and then we were alone again, our only company the rumble from the great press machinery. I leaned heavily upon the little man and he took my weight without complaint. I thought of him before I intruded, playing at dice as happily as the boys. "I've served you poorly, Alger, and I apologize. I came here to learn from these boys, and instead I've brought conflict and pain."

"Nonsense. Could have happened to anybody."

"Only to someone as naïve as myself. I hope I haven't jeopardized your standing here."

"Not at all." He bent briefly under my weight. "O'Connor's a hard man, but he has the boys' interests at heart."

"I forced you into a position where you had to play his game. I hope I didn't hurt you with the boys."

"The boys agree with him."

"Do you?"

"I don't disagree. I've learned better."

"He's a powerful man."

"Yes."

O'Connor's a man with his will intact, I thought. *Ein ganzer Mensch—ein ganzer Wille.* A whole man is a whole will.

"You were saying that you had no money left."

"I don't."

"Do you have family or business associates you can appeal to?"

"No."

"Do you enjoy a monthly income?"

"No."

"You appear in New York City with no means of support."

"Yes."

"How on God's earth did you expect to survive?"

"I thought I'd find a way. I shall find a way."

"But what?"

"I've no idea. I thought I'd have a month to sort that out."

"And for tonight?"

"Aren't the poor allowed to sleep in the basement of the station house? Perhaps you can lead me there."

"That's a foul and perilous place."

"It's what I have."

We descended in silence, intent upon navigating the staircase. At the bottom Alger spoke. "I won't allow it. You must return to my boarding house."

"I doubt the good Mrs. Frye will accept my credit."

"Don't concern yourself. I'll advance you the funds."

"I can't ask you for that."

"You aren't asking. I'm offering."

"I cannot accept your charity."

"It's not charity. I'm investing in your future. I'm sure we shall realize a handsome return."

"You've no reason to think I have a future." **79**

"I watched you up there with O'Connor. You're every bit as powerful as he is."

In my morbid isolation I had seen only that my naïveté had inflicted needless suffering on others. Seeing through Alger's eyes, I realized that I had deported myself honourably enough in the course of the evening so as to allow myself a modicum of satisfaction. Alger was benefactor indeed.

=

⌒CHAPTER SEVEN⌒

JEMMIE STOOD BEHIND TOM WHILE MR. O'CONNOR ENTERED Tom's name in the Lodging-house registry with a steady hand. That careful pen laid down solid fact. It could never scratch down a lie.

Jemmie observed the boys cavorting in the room beyond and heard their gay shouts and laughter. He imagined the smooth bed awaiting him. Tom said it felt like petting a dog to slide between the sheets. Tom conversed with O'Connor as with a business associate, entrusting him with forty-three cents. Then he placed a hand upon Jemmie's shoulder in proprietary fashion. "This here's Jemmie."

O'Connor's granite gray eyes peered into his and sank straight through to his gut. Jemmie figured for sure they saw the hot thumpety-thumping of his heart.

"Jemmie?"

The boy nodded. "Yessir."

"That is James, correct?"

"Yessir."

"What's your surname?"

"Surname?"

"Your parents' name."

His true name could only lead back to his father. Then he wouldn't be an orphan any more. Jemmie thought of Proud Axe fighting the raging bison. O'Connor in his mild fashion was more terrible than Giganta. "Hickok. I's Jemmie Hickok."

O'Connor dipped his pen. Slowly he wrote in his ruled book. Jemmie couldn't read, but he figured the swirls for James Hickok. O'Connor's pen was not infallible. Giganta lay at his feet. "Tom says I can bum here if I's a orphan."

"Are you an orphan?"

"Yessir. Me mother bled away givin' birth to me little brother, an' me father drank hisself to death." It was a small matter now to concoct a tale of orphandom. The part that was made up hardly felt different upon his tongue from the part that was true. Hearing the words spoken aloud half convinced him it was all true anyhow.

Tom, at O'Connor's behest, took Jemmie to the wash room, where he stripped naked and stood beneath a perforated nozzle which sprinkled him with cold water that burned at first like red-hot needles but soon became a pleasant pricking tingle. The soap smelled bitter and felt rough. Tom rubbed some in his hair. The soap itched his eyes and the cuts upon his face and turned his whole body slippery as a fish. He couldn't rub the slippery off. Tom threw him a cloth to dry himself with, as clean and stiff as the papers they'd sold. Another boy used his towel like a whip against Jemmie's body, stinging him with a crisp snap. Jemmie imitated the boy, and the two dueled with the towels until by accident his towel snapped an older boy and was grabbed away. Then they dressed and ate a plentiful meal of mutton and potatoes and beans and carrots under the gentle hand of Mrs. O'Connor. Jemmie felt all polished and filled up like a bright brass kerosene lamp.

After the meal the boys were directed to the large room, where a pale, stiff, neatly dressed gentleman tried to talk about Indians. He used long words, but he didn't know much. He spoke in low hesitant tones, and sometimes would stop speaking entirely and stare at them in a daze, as if expecting his next thought to be sitting in the audience. He didn't say anything at all about bison or scalping. However, he had eyes which changed color with his moods, from placid gray to irascible blue, and he could draw a horse's head. He showed Jemmie and some others how they could as well. Jemmie wanted to keep his picture but the man took it from him and presented it to O'Connor. That was better than keeping it. He wanted O'Connor to think well of him, particularly since he'd lied.

Jemmie drew his picture near a big funny boy named Dannie, who spoke in a loud voice and talked to the adults as if they were just other boys. He didn't care that this made the adults uneasy. When he seemed headed for sure trouble he would make them laugh and be in the clear again.

After they finished drawing horses the boys were ordered downstairs to bed. Jemmie was in the back of the room with Dannie, and in the clamour of movement he noticed the older boy act in a peculiar fashion. At a moment when he thought all eyes were elsewhere, Dannie slipped a small green object from his pocket and chucked it out the window. Jemmie watched it land upon the street below. When he looked up

83

Dannie was studying him. Jemmie smiled. Dannie smiled his devil-may-care grin in return.

The dormitory was nothing but stacks of beds. While regular tenants hurried to claim their usual berths, Jemmie joined Tom in one corner where a platform raised a few beds to a higher level, only to be shooed away. "Not here, Jemmie. This here's the Eagle's Nest." Jemmie obediently retreated to a nearby empty berth. Dannie, close behind, was not as obliging. When he climbed upon the platform Tom hopped off his mattress to meet him. "This here's the Eagle's Nest. It's a right you gotta earn." The other boys on the platform sat up to watch, in their manner clearly supporting Tom, but their numbers had no effect on Dannie.

"Don't see what's so special 'bout these here bunks."

"Then you don't mind sleepin' somewheres else."

Dannie was not deterred. He pointed at the berth behind Tom. "That there one's callin' me name right sweet. 'Dannie,' she says, 'Dannie me lovely lad climb onto me soft warm body.' " Dannie moved toward it and Tom stepped in his way. The two boys were well matched in size and strength. Dannie smiled. "So you're the jealous lover? I gotta whip you to spend a night wrapped in me lovely bed?"

"Fight and O'Connor'll toss you in the street. You don't earn the Eagle's Nest by fightin'."

"How's I earn it?"

"You're a leader."

Mr. O'Connor walked by. "Settle down, lads. Dannie, find a bed."

Dannie backed off the platform and leapt into the bunk above Jemmie. O'Connor turned down the gas. "Say your prayers and shut your eyes."

O'Connor closed the door. Dannie sat up in the darkness. "Hey! You! Eagle! What's a leader?"

"If you gotta ask you ain't one."

"Jesus, he a leader?"

"Jesus Christ?"

"That one."

"You sayin' you is Jesus Christ?"

"What's the hardest thing Jesus ever done?"

"Take on the sins of the world."

" 'sides that. He come back from the dead. Right?"

"You comin' back from the dead?"

"I seed a man hung. You ever seed a man hung? He shits his pants."

"So?"

"Hang me. I'll come back from the dead."

"G'wan!"

"Won't shit my pants neither."

"I ain't gonna hang you."

"Who's leadin' now?" He turned to the others. "Know somewheres I can hang meself?"

"There's the plate room downstairs."

"Show me."

Jemmie watched the boys march off to Dannie's execution. Dannie remarked on his wide unblinking stare. "Come along, baby boots, you're sheriff."

Jemmie followed the others down the black stairs to the floor below, where a lanky hawk-faced boy pushed open a door to reveal an abandoned composing room lit by a faint glow from the street. With exaggerated gestures, Dannie removed the comforter from around his neck. Jemmie knew it was crimson red, but in the darkness it looked black and ominous, like a thick snake. Dannie deftly twisted one end into a slip-noose and placed it around his own neck. "I seed this at the Tombs. Had to wait most of a day to get a good spot. Right up front I was. They was hangin' a man for killin' his wife. He was a big barrel a lard. They used a extra-strong rope. He was so heavy, when that trap door opened he dropped like a sack a cannon balls and thwack!"—Dannie snapped his fingers—"his body comes right off his head. A fire hose fulla blood pumps out his neck, and his head don't have no body holding it, so it pops outa the noose like a India-rubber ball and bounces offa the scaffold into me lap." He climbed atop a table and threw the free end of the comforter above a convenient beam. It swooped over lazily, like a prowling anaconda, and Dannie snared it. In his hand it transformed into a tight V from neck to beam to fist. He proffered his fist to Tom.

"You're hangman."

"I is not."

"Who is then?"

The beak-nosed youth climbed onto the table. "You never saw no head fall offa no body."

Dannie tightened his noose. "You, baby boots," he said to Jemmie, "you're sheriff. Sheriff says a prayer."

"Don't know but the Lord's Prayer."

"Say that then."

" 'Now I lay me down to sleep. I pray the Lord my soul to keep. If I should die before I wake, I pray the Lord my soul to take.' "

"First-rate. Go it, hangman."

Beak Nose pulled. The cloth rope sighed as it stretched under the weight. Instead of breaking, as Jemmie hoped it would, the noose closed around Dannie's throat and lifted his heels, but his toes held him to the table. Beak Nose strained under the load. "He's a right sack a shit. Help me out here." Two other boys took hold and yanked.

Dannie's body swung free, arms atwitch, throwing its shadow upon Jemmie's upturned features. The little boy shut his eyes and prayed to the Lord to save Dannie. He heard the creak of the rope upon the beam and felt the darkness pass back and forth. He kept praying, and the body kept swinging. He heard a gurgle. He opened his eyes. Even in the dark he could see that Dannie's face had turned black. He screamed.

With muffled oaths the boys released the rope, dropping Dannie to the table in a heap. The hawk-faced boy cuffed Jemmie for shouting out, but it was a blow struck in anger at himself for being caught in Dannie's spell. Released by Jemmie's outcry they all crowded around the inert figure, slack-faced with concern. Tom leaned his ear close to Dannie's purple lips. Everyone held his breath in the dark.

Tom straightened. "Breathin'. Let's get outa here."

The beak-nosed boy opened the door stealthily and peered

out. Jemmie lingered by the table until Tom's fingers clasped his bony arm and drew him away.

———

Jemmie was lying face up, staring at how the gas tube was twisted into a hook shape, like a snake to hang things from, when Dannie slipped back into the room. He climbed into a free bunk in the Eagle's Nest while the other nesters pretended to sleep.

"Dannie?" asked Jemmie.

"What?" Dannie sounded raspy rough.

"You okay?"

"Course I's okay. I said I's coming back from the dead, didn't I?"

"You wasn't dead."

"They said that 'bout Jesus too I bet."

Jemmie remembered fighting the dark river, the moment when he could go up or go down. He thought of Dannie not fighting death. Maybe if you let death carry you along you could ride it back to life.

A pounding woke him. O'Connor was hammering a broom handle upon an iron bed post. "Up, boys, up." Jemmie rose with the rest, groping for his coat. "Leave off your clothes." Voices raised in good-natured complaint, and O'Connor rapped the bed post sharply. "A crime has been committed. Stand down."

Sobered, the boys lined up before the bunks. Jemmie followed the others and watched Dannie do the same. Dannie's neck was red and bruised. Hanging yourself was wrong, but Jemmie didn't see how it was a crime.

O'Connor walked between the rows, looking each boy in the eye while he told them all of Mr. Henry's missing wallet, and the precious worth of their good names, the only things of value they owned on this earth, and their duty to tell what they knew of this crime which besmirched them all. Some boys looked back bold, some anxious, most with a blank plea for anonymity. Dannie was a bold one.

Jemmie knew the green square he'd seen tumbling to the pavement was the missing wallet. "Jay Gould can be a liar and a thief," said O'Connor, "and live in his mansion and drive his horses straight to hell. You don't have his mansion and his millions. Your honour is your capital. The respect and trust of men like me is your one true hope for advancement in this world."

Dannie caught Jemmie staring and returned a slim reassuring smile. Jemmie did not fear Dannie, though he respected him. He did not feel any debt to Dannie, or boyish honour in maintaining silence. Jemmie knew, however, that if he spoke he would stir up tumult, and while he could not predict an outcome he knew he would be the center of the maelstrom. Silence, he thought, changed nothing. Choosing silence didn't feel like making any choice at all. Jemmie remained silent with the others, and in that moment, in that choice which was no choice, Jemmie's life changed utterly.

O'Connor led the boys upstairs, where he repeated his performance for the benefit of Mr. Henry, who seemed very aggrieved, ill even, at the loss of his wallet, though his anger was not expressed as Jemmie would have expected, by lashing out at the boys. His fury appeared to consume him from the inside, like a gas fire in a garbage dump. He was no help to O'Connor in ferreting out the culprit.

Jemmie was singled out with the others who drew pictures. Now that he had chosen his course, silence was as simple as doing nothing. Only when O'Connor looked him directly in the eye and asked him point blank if he was the thief did silence require any effort. Had O'Connor asked him then to name the thief, he could not have kept his lips from speaking out. O'Connor, however, was not concerned with Jemmie, but with Dannie.

Dannie cared not about O'Connor. Even when O'Connor slashed his ear and dragged him down the stair Dannie conveyed the impression that the whole occurrence weighed heavier upon O'Connor than himself. When O'Connor deposited Dannie in the street Jemmie ran to the window and threw down his clothes. Pulling on his pants, Dannie waved his thanks. Jemmie waved in reply. Dannie hopped into his shoes, smiled his carefree smile, and shouted up to him, "Harry Hill's! Tonight!" before he strode away.

⌇CHAPTER EIGHT⌇

COME THE MORNING JEMMIE ACCOMPANIED TOM TO THE *STAR* and spent the day with him selling papers under their previous arrangement. Tom was businesslike and fair, but it was lonely work, as Tom didn't see much purpose in talk. When the evening papers had been distributed and Jemmie had divided the day's earnings with his financier he counted a profit of thirty-two cents. Tom showed the same mild displeasure with the day's earnings he had evinced the night before. As before, he turned toward the Newsboys' Lodging-house. Tonight, however, Jemmie hung back.

"You comin' then?"

"I's comin'. Jes' not right now."

"You're working for me?"

"Yeah, course."

"You sleep at the Lodging-house."

"Said I was." Tom turned away, and Jemmie headed up Broadway toward Houston. There, around the corner from the police precinct house, a red and blue globe beckoned the curious and the unwary to a rambling two-story structure, to all other appearances a private dwelling, Harry Hill's Concert Saloon.

Jemmie entered a low dark establishment thick with

tobacco smoke, and passed between two counters lined with large men drinking in a serious manner, on the lookout for Dannie but careful not to intrude upon the drinkers, who appeared to be the sort who would welcome an inquiring boy with curses or worse. Laughter and applause wafted down a staircase, beckoning him, but his way was blocked by a booth inhabited by a wizened crone.

"Twenty-five cents."

Jemmie cranked up on tiptoes to speak at the window. "Is a boy named Dannie O'Connor up there?"

"Lord, I don't know."

"Plain Dannie maybe. Maybe not O'Connor. He's strong and talks stories. His ear is cut."

"Twenty-five cents."

Jemmie exchanged his coins for a ticket and mounted the stair, toward the tickle of applause and then a jaunty tune.

He emerged into a brilliant energetic world. Below, smoke hung like a black fog, but up here the cloud shone golden-haloed from a profligate outpouring of gas. Men and women swirled gaily through the warm light, existing, it seemed, purely for their own amusement, chosen creatures dancing in their heavenly bower. Walls which once partitioned the lives of a comfortable family had been torn out, but further refinements had been eschewed, leaving a large space, all the more a world unto itself because it was composed of subsidiary continents of varying décor and dimension, united by the movement and the music and the thick golden smoke. Jemmie drifted through this numinous vision, invisible to the heavenly revelers, expecting at any moment to discover Dannie cavorting past with some pink young maiden.

He was distracted by a table heavy with delicacies, where he sampled corned beef and boiled ham and minced pie before a serving girl moved him along. With hands full of pig's feet he approached the stage, upon which three young men extracted a spirited quadrille from a piano, a violin, and a bass viol, weaving the gliding bodies into a complicated pattern of black wool suits and shimmery silk pastels.

He heard a crash, and turned to see a table upended and one top-hatted gentleman pounding upon another. A young woman cried in alarm. Dancers backed away. The musicians lost their rhythm.

This was not heaven, then, the gaiety was stoked by drink. Jemmie knew what would ensue. Glasses would fly and explode into shards. Screams and oaths would silence the orchestra. The combatants would careen into their neighbors, inciting further confrontations.

Dancers parted for a square man with the thick neck and massive arms of a professional pugilist. One block-like hand clasped each fighter by the neck. "Order, please, or your necks I'll squeeze." He shook them as if breaking the necks of a pair of Christmas geese, until they removed their hold upon each other to grab at him. "Fight with Harry Hill and he dumps you on the door sill." He dragged them along the dance floor and down the stairs. No sooner was he gone than music recommenced and dancers resumed as if there had been no disturbance.

Here was a man the equal of this place, thought Jemmie as he munched his pickled delicacy. Feeling a heavy hand upon his own shoulder he gave a start but, looking in that direction, saw no one. A tap on the other shoulder turned his head to reveal Dannie, his wounded ear hidden under a cloth cap.

"Harry Hill can hold a barrel a flour at arm's length in each hand. They say in a fight once he tore a man's arm off and clubbed him to death with it. Course that was afore he made hisself respectable with this here drum."

Jemmie smiled. "He talks in poems."

"A regular bard." Dannie pointed to signs posted at strategic points along the walls. "He wrote all them."

To Jemmie, the letters might as well have been hieroglyphics. "They's poems?"

Dannie read the nearby postings. "If a woman stands while a man sits, the man gits." "If you speak profane, you will know pain." "Dance and stay, when you stop go away." "Buy refreshment each dance or you'll no longer prance."

Jemmie was impressed. "You knows him?"

"Course I do. We're best chums. This is me second home."

"Yer raggin' again."

"No sir. I's a val'able segment of the population. I pervides amusement. Not like the ladies, mind you, but I does me part."

"Go on."

"Harry Hill, he figures men in this town is ever' day riskin' everythin' they got to git more, always on to somethin' bigger and crazier, knowing when Gould sneezes, they's covered in snot. Harry, he says the pressure builds up inside 'em like the boiler what blew on the Westfield ferry, and this place, the women and liquor and music and all, it's like the safety valve, letting steam out so's they don't go BOOM." Dannie shouted the explosive sound.

The quadrille had ended. Dannie's sudden exclamation turned disapproving glances in their direction. He approached a table where two young men sat, clad in coarse rural attire, in the company of two young women in sealskin sacques. "Me apologies, sirs and madams. We was discussing matters a high finance." His comment elicited a smile from the women.

The bigger, stiffer fellow spoke out in a country accent. "What kin you know 'bout high finance?'

"I know as much 'bout stocks and bonds as you know 'bout plantin' turnips. An' that's a whole lot."

His smaller, more inebriated companion chortled. "Got ya there, Custis."

Custis was not amused. "Don't matter what I do do or don't do. He don't know jack 'bout stocks and bonds."

"Me granddaddy taught me. He was slicker'n Jim Fisk hisself." Dannie struck an histrionic pose and continued:

Me grandfather was a most wonderful man,
He could do, or invent, a most wondrous plan,
He traveled around through vast regions unknown,
And always found out the philosopher's stone.
And just like a duck or a goose he could swim—

"Speakin' of swimming, oncet he swum from Albany to New York, and beat the steamboat by two hours and a half." **95**

So what a pity that life is a span!
For me grandfather was a most wonderful man!

"Grandpa'd plant tenpenny nails in the ground at night, in the morning they'd spring up crowbars. Oncet he made a steam wheelbarrow and put me grandmother in it, and sent it away up forty miles into the air, and she never been heard of since!"

Dannie performed his oration with such energy and mobility of expression that he induced considerable gaiety among the young women and their escorts. At the conclusion he bowed low and held out his cap. The drunk young man reached into the pocket of his companion and extracted two quarters, which he dropped into the outstretched headgear. The larger fellow protested, but Dannie deftly replaced the cap upon his forehead with quarters intact. The two farmers began to dispute in earnest. As their voices rose in anger Dannie pulled Jemmie away. "Let's find us friendlier surroundin's."

Dannie and Jemmie descended apace into the thick gloom below, followed closely by a call summoning Harry to the dispute. As Harry rolled from a stool and lumbered upstairs the man beside him raked the boys with his look, causing Jemmie to turn away his face. The man powerfully resembled his gruff-voiced benefactor on the Brooklyn ferry, and Jemmie had no desire to explain to his guardian angel the use he had made of the choice he had been given. He thought of his sister and the little one and wondered if the gold was drunk up yet.

When they reached the street Dannie doffed his cap and

retrieved the quarters. "The Bowery beckons, boyo. Turnip's treat."

"The theatre?"

"What else, me man?"

"I's to be at the Lodging-house."

"And so you shall, you have me word upon it. Many a newsie slips in with the fall of the Bowery curtain. You must a seed."

"I was sleepin'."

"You ever seed a play?"

"No."

"You sure you's a orphan?"

"Course I's sure."

"Tonight's your night."

The Bowery Theatre was a massive white structure in the classical mold, a Corinthian Temple to the Dramatic Arts, but its acolytes were a scruffy and ill-attired lot. No toga-clad kouroi with Olympian poise, but tiny homunculi in out-sized garb of all description, as if some prankster deity had shrunken his entire community of believers, soldier, sailor, clerk, and laboring man, even the man of affairs, and left them to caper about in clothing which had once defined their occupations but which now flopped at the arm and gaped at the waist, torn and tattered and filthy but still glinting with the occasional brass button or twist of braid. The miniature men, however, seemed oblivious of their misfortune. They scampered and pranced and climbed the lampposts, and to Jemmie they appeared as daunting and doughty as would the original owners of their attire.

Jemmie was particularly impressed by a soldier's great-coat walking on its hands down the steps to the vocal encouragement of a cluster of tiny military men who stood about fists clenched in breech pockets, nudging one another with sharp elbows. Dannie led Jemmie into this merry crowd and smashed down the hat of a swaggerer whom Jemmie judged to be their leader from his tycoon attire, a cut-down long-napped white beaver coat, the lapels of which were a foot square and shingled his ankles as if he stood between a pair of placards.

The tycoon smashed down Dannie's cap in reply, compressing Dannie's wounded ear and provoking a wince. The tycoon took notice. "Someone's taggin' you fer their sow. Hope you didn't squeal or nothin'."

Dannie's disfigurement was not exceptional. While none had a face as purple and swollen as Jemmie's, all were grimy and gap-toothed and scarred. To Jemmie their scars were as much badges of honour as the dueling scars of Prussian students, and created a similar aura of privileged participation in a secret association, a fellowship akin to the Eagle's Nest but jollier and more mutually supportive, to which, like the Eagle's Nest, he scarcely dared aspire.

Dannie gave Jemmie's thin shoulder a shove. "This one's never seen a show."

"Naw!" The beavered tycoon clutched the boy's coat. "That right?"

"I seed shows. Jus' no theatre shows."

"Then you ain't seen nothin. Right?" His companions cheered assent. The tycoon gave Jemmie a good-natured cuff upon his purpled bruise, causing a moment of scalding pain. "You got one handsome petunia on that cheek a your'n. You get tired a Dannie beatin' on you, come with me, I'll beat on you."

When the theatre opened its doors, admitting the larger and more comprehensively attired customers, the raggedy band made a general dash down through a sort of cellar door, and shoving and uttering oaths pressed in a mass through a narrow passage to emerge in the bowels of a great gilded space. Peanut shells crunched beneath Jemmie's bare feet, and he saw himself as a peanut at the bottom of a very large bowl while he clung to Dannie's coat and clambered over benches toward the sounds of a lively tune. He gazed upward through air heavy with the gas-tinged odors of two thousand bodies, the unwashed and the overperfumed, past 'prentice boys and shop girls, pale German tailors, gaudy young women, and sailors moored to their black-eyed Susans, searching the shadowy heights for families: Jew boys bearing their fathers' ringlets, red-faced Irish fathers urging tots to sit down upon their seats, plump mothers suckling infants while passing apples and sausage slices among their brood, brothers and sisters jostling in a perpetual tug of war. A boy his own age ate a chicken wing in the pillowy ease of his mother's lap. He tossed the bone over the rail and it bounced off a bowler hat near Jemmie.

A bell tinkled and tinkled again. The orchestra subsided, quelling the turmoil. Expectant silence gripped all but puling infants. All eyes fastened upon the great expanse of green baize. Of a sudden it shot upward with surprising speed, and

Jemmie saw before him a sumptuously decorated space domi-
nated by a cut crystal chandelier. He recognized that the people in the scene lived in this room, though no one slept there.
The heavy furniture with its curlicues and tassels, shiny
with silk brocade, was used exclusively for sitting or the
draping of elegant capes and scarves.

The principal inhabitant was a young woman of exceptional grace and presence named Laura Courtland. When the
curtain rose, she was poised on the brink of a life of happiness and ease as the intended wife of a handsome blood
named Ray Trafford. As such she held small interest for Jemmie or his friends, but soon she was revealed as an impostor
of sorts, an erstwhile street urchin like themselves whose
hand had been caught in Mrs. Courtland's pocket, on whom
the good woman had taken pity and whom she had raised as
her own. Jemmie watched saucer-eyed as the azure luxury
of Delmonico's Blue Room materialized, wherein Mrs. Van
Dam labeled Laura a beggar and a thief and expelled her from
Society as the curtain fell.

Jemmie spent the interlude in considerable suspense as to
Laura's future, and was reassured when the curtain rose
upon a lofty room, described as a basement but not like any
basement of Jemmie's acquaintance, not low and dark and
crowded and foul-smelling but clean and spacious, inhabited
exclusively by Laura and paid for in its entirety by her color-
ing of photographs. Though her clothes were plainer, in Jemmie's eyes she had lost nothing of great value, except her
friend Ray and cousin Pearl, and in her stead he would have

chosen her present tranquil solitude over the carping demands of Mrs. Van Dam's Society.

Her peace was short-lived. Mr. Byke, a man of mean and devious temperament, descended into her abode, claiming her as his daughter. Jemmie watched in horror as a black-robed judge awarded this despicable man sovereignty over her, and amid a hail of peanuts and imprecations from Jemmie's companions Byke dragged Laura off for unspecified evil purposes, hinting at her sorry end.

Jemmie's neighbor, dismayed at the absence of swordplay, pronounced the production dull as lead, but Jemmie was captivated by Laura's peril. He could well imagine the terror of her situation, and was mightily relieved when she eluded Byke's scheme to drown her in the Hudson, though he feared for her safety, alone and vulnerable as she was, and Byke still after her.

Curtain rose on a railroad station at night. The station shed, train tracks, and platform looked so real that Jemmie forgot he was indoors. He basked in moonlight, wrinkling his nose at imaginary wind. He remembered sitting in a train station with his mother and his father. His sister held a bundle wrapped in a fringed scarf. They had many bundles then. They had valises and trunks and even a big bed.

Laura appeared, walking feebly, and the kind signalman allowed her to sleep in the station shed. He even locked her inside for good measure. Jemmie was relieved to see her safe.

Her safety was illusory. Snorkey the one-armed veteran appeared hurrying to warn the Courtlands of Byke's latest plot, pursued by Byke, who lashed him tight and placed him upon the railroad tracks. "You dog me and play the eavesdropper, eh? Now do it if you can. When you hear the thunder under your head and see the lights dancing in your eyes and feel the iron wheels a foot from your neck, remember Byke!" In the distance, a train whistle blew. Jemmie and his companions grew still as death.

Laura tried helplessly to break free from the storage shed while the whistle cried again, louder. Lo and behold, a shipment of axes! Whistle shriek conjoined with the menacing rumble of train upon track as Laura shattered her prison door.

The rumble grew to a cacophonous roar. Locomotive lights glared upon the scene. Jemmie and his fellows in the pit stood upon their benches urging her on, their words submerged in a deafening screech. Just as Laura was lifting Snorkey's head from the rail the black behemoth shot into view spouting gobbets of steam, wheels like huge claws grabbing track. As the iron monster clattered by, missing him by inches, Snorkey exulted. "Saved! Hooray! And these are the women who ain't to have a vote!"

Horror sucked the air from Jemmie's lungs. He didn't question how the massive contraption could have coursed through the theatre or where it went when it left the stage. This was the locomotive of his darkest dreams, the smoky, snarling thing that had carried him to the filth and darkness of New York City; in his dreams it sprang upon him with the same terrifying ferocity and vanished as inexplicably, leaving behind only a miasma of dread. Tonight, however, the sticky residue of fear did not adhere to Jemmie. Tonight he felt as proud and strong as Laura. The locomotive couldn't touch him. He suspected that it had rushed from his dreams forever.

The ensuing mêlée though energetic and righteous in outcome paled in the shadow of the locomotive's visitation, but Jemmie was intrigued to learn that Laura was not in fact Byke's daughter. She had been switched at birth with cousin Pearl! "There is tomorrow," Laura proclaimed in vindication. "It cannot remain dark forever!"

Jemmie cheered with the other boys. Never had he felt such a satisfying emptiness. A leaden weight had been lifted from his gut. He hadn't even known of its existence until he felt it gone, but the weight had been there, surely, pressing upon his stomach and his heart, and now that it was absent he felt a comfortable lightness in his body. He decided that this is how it must feel to be rich, like Laura. When Dannie asked him how he liked the show, Jemmie gave a double hop.

"That locomotive is a right marvel," said Dannie. "I like to jump outa my seat when that came through."

"Is Laura a orphan?"

"What?"

"Mrs. Courtland, Pearl says she's dead, and nobody says no word 'bout Mr. Courtland."

"Nah, he's not dead, he's out makin' money. How else they gonna have all them fancy goods? Can't 'spect him to be wastin' his time dancin' and marryin' people off."

"Oh."

"Course."

103

"That switched-at-birth. That happen lots?"

"Sure. Happens all the time. I was switched at birth."

"G'wan."

" 'struth. Me real daddy was the Prince a Pennsylvania."

"How you know?"

"You jes' knows. You feels diff'rent. Like this family what yer living in ain't rightly your'n. You ever feel that way? I mean afore you was orphaned."

"Sometimes."

"Well I bet you was switched at birth."

"That mean me sister ain't me sister?"

"You got a sister?"

"Yeah."

"She feel like your'n?"

"Yeah."

"Mos' likely you two was switched at birth together."

"But she's younger'n me."

Dannie cuffed him. "Why you goin' on 'bout this?"

"I ain't. You says I's switched at birth."

"Well maybe you is and maybe you ain't. You's a orphan now so's you'll never know noways."

"I gotta get me to the Lodgin'-house." Jemmie felt very tired.

"C'mere." Dannie approached one of the many hacks which waited outside the theatre. "Climb in." Jemmie hesitated. "Go on. Courtesy a Mr. Turnip."

"Why you so nice to me?"

"I owes you. I always pays me debts."

"I's never gonna rat you out."

"It's God's way. Now we's bound together, you and me. G'wan in."

Jemmie mounted into the hack and Dannie followed behind. It was a clean well-maintained conveyance. "What's this?" asked the driver.

Dannie handed him a quarter dollar. "There's a good man, run us down to Printin' House Square." The cabbie inspected the coin and placed it in his pocket. "We's square," Dannie said to him. "Don't go askin' for no bump when we gets there."

In reply the cab started with a jarring jolt. "Guess he's not so proud a his new employers." Dannie grinned. "Yer still working for Tom Lackey, aintcha?"

"I gotta. 'Til I gets me some capital."

Dannie reached in his pocket and brought out four dollar bills. "Here. Now you don't gotta no more."

"Four dollars!"

"So's you can set up on your own."

Jemmie looked at the money with longing. "Nah."

"Why not?"

"Workin' for Tom's okay."

"No it ain't. It's slavery and you knows it."

"I's near 'nuff to bein' on me own."

"How much capital you got?"

" 'Nuff."

"How much?"

"Seven cents."

"That ain't capital. Here." He proffered the bills again. Jemmie did not reach for them. His eyes wandered to the   105 scabbed-over slit in Dannie's ear. Dannie caught the look. His voice took on an accusatory edge. "What's this? You attends me play, you rides me cab, so what now?"

" 'sdifferent."

"How?"

"Four dollars . . ."

"You're askin' yourself where'd I be gettin' four dollars? You're askin' yourself whose four dollars is I givin' you?"

Jemmie nodded, afraid to speak. Dannie grinned.

"It belongs to the U.S. mint in Philadelphia. Says so on the paper. You're jes' borrowin' it. G'wan."

When Jemmie made no move to take the money Dannie shoved it in his face. Jemmie turned away. "Smell. What's that smell like?"

"It smells like shite."

"Yessir. Me own shite. Knows why?"

Jemmie shook his head.

" 'cause I shoved it up me arse at your precious Lodgin'-house. Take it."

Jemmie did not move. Dannie's features hardened. Jemmie had seen that stone look on a man before. It meant he was in for a beating. Jemmie sat as still as stone himself. He knew the least movement would start the blows.

Dannie laughed. "Have it your way then." He called up to the driver, "Hold a minute!" When the cab slowed he threw the bills upon the floor and jumped out.

The cab resumed its journey. Jemmie stared at the rectangular bits of paper bouncing with the uneven pavements as if they were tiny creatures striving to be free of the coach. He reached down to retrieve them and liberate them over the side. When he had them in hand he smelled them again and put them in his pocket.

Jemmie was not alone in his late arrival at the *Sun* building. He joined a sparse line of sybaritic stragglers who washed their feet and proceeded to the dormitory, talking of that Eighth Wonder of the World, the Bowery Theatre locomotive. Complaints of the bedded boys brought answering oaths, then silence. Jemmie climbed onto an upper bunk. He smelled the boiled starch of freshly laundered sheeting.

———

"Up, boys, up!"

Jemmie forced his eyes to open. He was not aware of having slept. He donned his trousers and thrust his hand in his good pocket in search of the offending bills, hoping they'd been stolen or perhaps had crawled away as they'd attempted to in the hack, but no, they resided in a damp wad at the bottom.

He went with the other late arrivals to register with O'Connor. Jemmie proffered six cents, and O'Connor entered his name in his usual solid meticulous fashion. Jemmie heard disapproval in the scratching of the nib.

"Mr. O'Connor, I'd like to open a bank."

O'Connor pointed the pen at a slot in the table. "You are number ninety-two. Can you remember that?"

"Ninety-two. Yessir."

"And how much are you depositing?"

Jemmie produced three of his four dollars. "These here dollars."

107

O'Connor counted the three carefully and slipped them in the slot. "That's a great deal of money."

He entered the sum and the Hickok name in his log book. "Where did you come by three dollars?"

"It was a kinda present you could say."

O'Connor peered into Jemmie's face. Jemmie could feel the weight of his granite gray eyes. "A present?"

"Yessir. A gentleman give it me. He said I has a choice now."

"You're a very lucky young man."

"Yessir."

"Know what he meant by having a choice?"

"Yessir."

"And what did he mean?"

"He means I can do good and elevate myself or I can throw it away on stuff."

"Where were you last night?"

"Bowery Theatre."

"What would your gentleman say about that?"

"It was only a quarter."

"He gave you that money in trust. You must use it to better yourself. That's your part of the bargain."

"That's why I's startin' the bank."

"A wise move. Now you must give yourself a goal. Do you have a goal?"

"Yessir."

"What is your goal?"

"I mean to go out West and fight injuns."

"Then you must save your money for the trip."

"Yessir."

"Every time you visit the theatre, your trip out West slips farther away."

"Yessir."

O'Connor's hard eyes were delving into Jemmie's again. Jemmie looked away. His gaze fastened upon the sharp point of O'Connor's pen.

"I can see the truth in a boy's eyes, Jemmie. Did you know that?"

"Yessir."

"A true boy's eyes are clear and bright. Yours are muddy and dim. You're lying, Jemmie."

"I gotta pee. Can I go, please?"

"That is your bladder telling your mouth to speak truth. Speak truth, Jemmie Hickok."

Jemmie looked at O'Connor in anguish. O'Connor nodded in his placid fashion.

"Me name ain't Hickok."

O'Connor's eyes did not blink or waver. "What is it, then?"

"Do I gotta say?"

"Why are you afraid of giving your name?"

"It's me daddy. He's lookin' fer me."

"So your father is alive."

"I ain't no orphan. I lied 'bout that too. Me mum, she died jes' like I said, birthin' the little un."

"Your father give you that?" O'Connor touched the iridescent bruise.

"Yessir. He's wild mean when he drinks. He drinks most all the time. He finds me, he's like to beat me to death." Jemmie's eyes had been avoiding his inquisitor's. Now he peered   109 into them so hard he could count the little green flecks. "Please, sir, kin I stay anyways?"

O'Connor nodded.

"Thank you, sir. Thank you. Must I say my name?"

"I've entered you as Hickok. That will do."

"Thank you, sir. Thank you."

"We'll not speak of this again. You save your money, young man."

"Yessir."

"Now be off with you."

Jemmie turned away, but paused for one last question. "Mr. O'Connor?"

"Yes?"

"Is I damned to hell?"

"I'm not the man to ask. Find the answer in your prayers."

Jemmie skipped off for the square. In the shelter of the stairwell he jammed his fingers into his pocket until they touched his solitary bill, velvet with wear. He found its presence more reassuring than admonitory. He had not planned his responses to O'Connor. He had been stuck for words and when they finally came they were all he could think of saying. He had not planned on taking Dannie's money, either. He had refused the money even when it might have meant a beating. Jemmie knew he had choices to make, but he wasn't yet sure what they were, or how to make them.

CHAPTER NINE

Mrs. Frye was loath to accept Alger's money on my behalf, stating that in her experience charity should never begin at home, generosity toward one's fellow tenants invariably resulting in rancor and disputation. Alger however prevailed upon her, and I was allowed to enlist as a provisional, probationary lodger. She situated me in a small chamber at the top of the house, far from the facilities.

The horizontal position was a most welcome change of posture, but sleep was a distant friend. As I lay enveloped in darkness, freed from the necessity of charming Mrs. Frye and bereft of the support of Horatio's good opinion, the black despair that I had fled found me out and wrapped me in its suffocating shroud.

I reached for the smooth comfort of Father's Breguet repeater. I pressed the knurled knob, hoping for melodious consolation. Instead shards of sound mocked the absurdity of my enterprise: I had come to New York seeking the antidote to evil, and had succeeded only in instigating mayhem of the cruelest sort.

Evil, dense and implacable, congealed in my chest and crushed the breath from my lungs. I tried to call for help. My jaw clamped in isometric opposition. I was a prisoner, suffocating in my rigid body. In desperation I summoned to mind what I would call upon were I a believer, clinging to the fragments of Scripture I could invoke in my asphyxiated state: "The Lord is my shepherd. . . ." I focused upon the words. My lungs found space to breathe. I slept.

———

My head throbbed with morning light. I willed my hand to my eyes. What pleasure to see it respond! I pulled myself upright, drained of energy, but the vacant sensation was not entirely unpleasing. It left space for thought.

I had an immediate problem. I had to earn my living, and I did not see how I could exploit my scientific skills without revealing my identity. Medicine was a profession, not a source of ready cash, its practice required capital and references.

The boys had taught me a useful lesson: My most appreciable asset was my skill as a draughtsman. Though I had continued to sketch as a diversion, I had years before abandoned the idea of an artistic career. I had only dim recollections of my urge to paint. I remembered the pleasure it afforded me—indeed I still enjoyed scratching my pen—but I could not muster even the shadow of that intensity of purpose which had driven me to compel Father to uproot us from Europe and bring us to Newport so that I might study with William Morris Hunt.

Father harbored undisguised scientific aspirations on my behalf, but he restrained me with indulgence, hoping that immersion in the work of painting would soon exhaust my dedication to the muse. Instead I found it liberating. To spend one's days striving to see the world clear is to put oneself in a very particular relationship with nature. When one strives to express substance in the play of light upon surface, things hollow out. What is not surface is not. One's being becomes purely a vehicle for capturing the fleeting gleam. Light becomes the binding element in the universe. All things, even oneself, fit as tesserae in the light mosaic.

"Do as you feel," Hunt would say, with his characteristic hyperbole. "Hang duty! Duty never painted a picture nor wrote a poem. Do it *as it seems to you to be.* Don't talk of what you're going to do. Do it!" Why had I abandoned the muse? I was healthy yet, eyes keen and back sound. I suppose I lost the feeling for it. Father's misgivings did not dissuade me. He feared the pursuit of art would corrupt me and I knew him to be mistaken on that count. Perhaps the sensual pleasures simply lacked a philosophical rigour that my soul required. When Father's fainting spells and morbid intimations made departing Newport inevitable I enrolled at the Scientific School without regret. When in the grip of an obsession it appears as an impregnable fortress, and we are willing to sacrifice comfort and approbation and even our lives in its defense, but when the passion vanishes it seems in retrospect to have been a castle built of sand.

"Doing is bad enough," Hunt would say, "but not doing is worse." If my pursuit of art before had been driven by inner compulsion, the sensation that I had no choice in spite of my manifest multiplicity of choices, now my world had constricted to the point where it was indeed my only course of action. Sustenance not vocation was at issue. The incomparable Ingres had lived for many years in Rome by drawing portraits of   **113** tourists. His masterpieces were sold like piece goods, so much for face only, more for full figures, or showing the hands, or filling in the background. I would do the same.

Even such a modest ambition required capital. I was forced to approach Alger in his capacity as my banker and he received me with characteristic generosity and enthusiasm eager, he said, to invest in an artist to be. When I told him I harbored no such aspirations, he chided me for my shortness of vision.

"You have the gift," he said. "You've studied. This is your opportunity to earn your place in the world."

"I'll be happy to earn ten dollars a week."

"I can't believe that a man of your abilities would be satisfied with that."

"For the moment that's all I require."

"Never aim beneath yourself," said Alger, distressed by my sentiment. "If I had thought as you do, I'd still be a miserable minister, living comfortably and unhappily in a sleepy hamlet on eight hundred a year."

"Surely you found a way to write."

"Indeed I did," said Alger. "My father is a minister, from ill luck or principle the sort of genuine Christian for whom poverty is a necessary virtue. I lived on scholarship at Harvard, and my father secured me a congregation. The week of my ordination service, at which my father gave the benediction, was the week *Frank's Campaign,* my tale of a Yankee drummer boy, was published."

"My point exactly. Your vocation searched you out."

"On the contrary. The book made no money to speak of. Only by abandoning the security of the ministry and risking destitution in this daunting metropolis, just as you do now, by committing myself to my art, do I find myself in the enviable position of a man who is spending the brief time allotted to him doing exactly what he wishes to do." He puffed his cheeks with satisfaction at his success.

I could not resist a verbal poke. "Surely you've some goal unfulfilled."

"I'm not yet Harriet Beecher Stowe, but where would we be without aspirations? Don't think of yourself as a street hawker. Your work will attract the attention it deserves."

I found myself succumbing to the sunny charms of Alger's relentless naïveté. Perhaps performing the work would summon up the vanished sense of vocation. For a moment I allowed myself to view my new occupation in a more ambitious light, limned in Ingres's perfect line, before a dorsal twinge terminated the fantasy.

We agreed that I must establish myself in a public thoroughfare heavily traveled by folk in search of diversion. City Hall Park seemed a likely spot. We acquired the necessary artist's supplies, Alger insisting upon a higher quality of paper than I would have thought necessary, purchased a pair of folding chairs, and engaged a street urchin to tote them to the park.

When we arrived at mid-morning the weather was crisply splendid. A balmy sun warmed without overheating, and the shaded walks were refreshingly cool. The crowds of clerks and office workers had thinned. Businessmen of a more substantial sort were dispersing to their places of employment, and a stream of supplicants moved to and from City Hall and the Courts of Justice. Viewed from my new perspective, as a street vendor attempting to attract their custom, I was forcibly impressed by their sense of purpose. Each pedestrian followed his unique trajectory, propelled by his own explosive combination of hope and fear, aimed by his ambitions, as impossible to divert from his course as an artillery shell.

More likely candidates were the mothers who exercised their small children in the park. These women were not in transit. Certainty of purpose was replaced by certainty of place. They watched their charges with the possessory air of a woman in her sitting room, congregating upon a gravel path beneath a row of plane trees which also sheltered an array of would-be entrepreneurs, drawn to them as I was. Apples, oranges, and grapes were proffered; girls sold hot corn; boys picture post cards and ribbons and sheets of paper. A monkey danced to the Italianate tunes of a hand organ, and a gentleman provided electric stimulation with a galvanometer not unlike Dr. Tyler's device at McLean. Alger seated himself among them and bade me draw his likeness. When the portrait took shape, however, and my intentions and abilities became evident, my neighbour, an obese Greek who offered crude tracings via a *camera obscura,* uttered such threats and imprecations that I feared for my safety. Alger was not intimidated, and engaged the man in dispute, but I packed up my effects and moved to the periphery of the vendors, far from the Greek and my potential clients.

I have a talent for capturing a likeness. This is not a photographic act. The work of drawing is a process in which the lines reveal themselves to me, and reveal to me my deepest feelings toward my subject. No matter what I wished to see, my ac-

116

tual view would emerge. My hasty portrait of Alger conveyed his keen eye and his positive, energetic demeanour, and it also revealed my admiration for the man. Had I thought him a charlatan or a self-deluding fool my portrait would have shown him as such, but it exhibited a sincere man of warm and generous spirit.

This noble portrait gave me unexpected pleasure. Alger was no Emerson. He lacked the quickness of wit and the subtlety of intellect which I valued in a companion, and had we dined at my father's table in Cambridge the family would have dismissed him as dull and simplistic. I was gratified to see that in the present context I could appreciate his strengths without condescension. Though he lacked the insight and verbal skill required of a competent author he had fashioned for himself a writer's life, acting upon his convictions, elevating his life above his art. I was his beneficiary, and he deserved my respect. I was pleased that my drawing showed that I could give it without reservation.

My labours attracted a small crowd, primarily of street children, who clucked at my facility and sang my praises. Rather than attract paying customers, however, my ragged admirers formed a barrier to their approach. My attempts to chase away the children were ineffectual, for they sensed my lack of resolution. Alger of course was incapable of scattering them. Ultimately I released my kind Horatio to return to his own labours and he took my leave, counseling patience and perseverance.

One grimy young man in a brimless hat demanded I do his portrait. When I obliged, he pronounced it worth keeping, and offered me three cents for it. That sale provoked more. I spent

117

the morning in drawing a rogue's gallery of street faces, gap-toothed, scarred, and filthy, but exhibiting a spirited self-satisfaction and an admirable pleasure in the present.

I lunched on hot corn and apples. I did not wish to leave my post, for I hoped that the lunchtime crowds would afford me more lucrative employment. The park filled with briefly idle workers from the brokerages and counting rooms and courts, who swelled my ranks of onlookers but would not commission me. Their presence however attracted the attention of a slab-sided constable, who remarked that I was a newcomer, and demanded payment for the privilege of my place in the park. I told him I had garnered a total of thirty-three cents from my morning's labors. He replied that a payment of twenty-five would be sufficient, but that in the future the fee was fifty cents a day for a man of my gifts. I offered to draw his portrait in lieu of payment, but he refused with a laugh, saying he might lose his position if he was discovered sitting for a portrait while on duty.

After paying the constable his quarter dollar I was in essence where I had begun, though I had expended a considerable stock of paper. A morning bent before an easel had inflamed my spine until I could sit no longer. I enlisted one of my young subjects to watch over my materials while I stretched myself unceremoniously upon the grass verge. My donation to the constable had I hoped purchased me this small right. I closed my eyes and felt the sun warm my forehead. I heard the rustle of gowns and the slapping of boots and the murmur of language. I thought myself back upon the porch at McLean, frozen in my auditory mode. I heard leaves turn in the wind, dog's claws scratch paving, perambulator wheels crush gravel. I longed to yield myself to that symphony of sounds, but I had not the luxury of incapacity. I forced myself up on one elbow and back to my easel.

I decided to broaden the appeal of my work by sketching landscape, and devoted myself to depicting the visual equivalent of the sound tapestry, a scene of human bustle amid arboreal tranquillity. I became sufficiently taken up with my task that upon its completion the shadows were lengthening into darkness. I had created a fair urban landscape, but my absorption in my work had rendered me completely ineffectual as an entrepreneur. In sum, my first day earning my bread as an artist of the streets had been a bust.

I paid a young man five cents to carry my belongings back to my lodgings. There I rested briefly until summoned by Mrs. Frye's chimes. Alger was not at supper, and I ate the bland, greasy food in silence, muted as were my table mates by Mrs. Frye's strict regime. She forbad inappropriate discussions at the dinner table, and this she defined as any topic likely to cause disagreement. Politics were explicitly *verboten*. So were business and the discussion of horseflesh. Little remained but pious homilies and fashion talk.

Mrs. Frye was well informed on the goings and comings of the social elite and eager to expand her knowledge. I underwent an awkward interrogation about my possible connections to the blue of blood, my alias Henry being the patronymic of the eloquent patriot Patrick Henry, but ultimately I convinced

the woman that any possibility of our consanguinity was remote in the extreme. Once she lost interest in my family tree
she moved on to the question of pongee silk, of which she dis-
approved, and of which I was mercifully ignorant.

Freed from the table, I hastened to the Newsboys' Lodging-
house with all the speed my tender spine would permit. O'Connor greeted me coolly, mildly surprised that I had returned to
the scene of my humiliation. I had engaged a boy to carry my
easel and supplies, and the sight of the overburdened lad did little to endear me to that stern gentleman.

Alger was not in evidence. His empty desk reminded me
forcefully of the gulf that I had yet to span. What was I hoping
to discover among these boys? Nothing which could be articu-
lated. Had I been searching for words I would be reading more
philosophy. I had come in pursuit of an essential experience,
some direct perception of the divine in the bearing of these
young men, definitive evidence of the existence of the Good
which would blot out my abysmal dread. I saw the absurdity of
my mission and yet I could not abandon it. To do so would be
to acknowledge the unalterable reality of a world indifferent to
Good and Evil.

I had learned little as yet, but I had learned this: Somehow
my own efforts at self-reliance were an essential component in
my ineffable quest. In this area I had fared poorly. In coming to
New York to try myself on purely my own merits, without the
benefits or expectations of family, I had only succeeded in ex-
changing one patron for another. How had I become Alger's
dependent? Negligence on my part and generosity of spirit on

his had conspired to place me in his debt. Had I cultivated my carelessness in order to place myself in a dependent situation?

Teaching the boys provided an opportunity to transpose myself. Here I was to lead. These boys, however, had no good reason to follow me. I must not only teach them to do the work but also inspire them with a passion for it. I could not recollect my own vanished lust for drawing. How could I inflame theirs?

My doubts caused me to exhibit an exaggerated respect for the boys' sensibilities. Some had been among my audience in the adjacent park, and when the beak-nosed boy called Mickety displayed his three-penny portrait they all wished their portraits drawn. Thinking to capitalize upon their enthusiasm I bade them draw each other. This they attempted, but they soon became mired in frustration, the endeavour being beyond their capacities, and their fellows, however bad as artists, being merciless bloodthirsty critics. Fat Jack, a clumsy man-child, attempted to render Mickety, who pronounced his portrait a perfect likeness of a pile of steaming horse manure; Fat Jack responded by calling that a fair description of its subject, precipitating an assault by Mickety and general riotous tumult which was quelled only by caustic words from O'Connor at his desk across the room. I set the boys the less contentious task of using their own hands as models, but the mood was soured.

O'Connor would have thrown me out had my negligence not put him in my debt. When he considered the scales balanced he would surely show me the door, unless I could demonstrate some utility to the boys. Unlike reading or mathematics, drawing was a useless skill *sans* talent. I plodded through the lesson, sorely missing my two best students, Hickok and Dannie O'Connor, not only for their facility with the pen but for Dannie's leavening wit, which would have freed the rest of them to enjoy the foibles in one another's work without coming to blows.

My efforts were further diluted by the appearance among us of a handsome woman a few years younger than I. She was like myself a volunteer, but her good offices were greeted by O'Connor with notably greater enthusiasm than my own. She was indeed a more striking presence, soberly but stylishly dressed, a tall woman with a figure well suited to the high-waisted, full-busted corset then in fashion. Her hair in the current 'careless look' cascaded in waves and curls, extending soft ebony tendrils about her face, serpentine curves contrasting with a sheer brow and noble features as pale and translucent as Carrara marble, and as symmetrical as if carved by Michelangelo. Like the faces of most Michelangelo women, hers was too strong to be ideally feminine, but it bespoke an intelligence and a firmness of purpose which that sculptor would have been proud to capture in stone.

She comported herself like a sculpture come to life, with careful, languid movements, but her manner had nothing of the somnambulistic or ethereal. Rather, she moved with deliberate grace, bidding us to honor her gestures for their careful meaning. Though I later learned O'Connor had institutional reasons to treat her with deference, I believe his admiration was genuine. He respected her tranquillity of manner, so similar to his own, but so much more profound. Where his masked a harshness of spirit, hers seemed as fathomless and refreshing as an Alpine lake.

In short, I was smitten, and in this I was not alone. She held court in one corner of the large room, where she endeavoured to teach the boys to read and write, using as her text the Lord's Prayer. She drew the words upon a slate, her long fingers clasping the chalk as lightly as the stem of a thorny rose. She walked among her students while they struggled to copy her work, pausing to praise in a soft Georgia accent, her hand upon an arm, or wiping out an error with the dab of a cloth. She seemed incapable of an insensitive word or a rough movement. The boys took her corrective comments without complaint. I believe two or three of her students wrote perfectly well, but attended simply to be near her.

All this I observed from across the room while my young artists extended their left hands like claws or pistols and scribbled their crude approximations. They responded to my distraction with an equivalent lack of concentration. Some abandoned their work to disparage the work of others. Fat Jack drew a crude dagger into the sketch of his neighbour's hand, and the puny boy defended his labours by poking Fat Jack with his pencil. Fearing O'Connor, I returned my attention to my charges. Eventually we produced some creditable results. When next I looked at the readers' corner, my Pale Lady was gone.

CHAPTER TEN

The mysterious woman shone forth for precisely two hours each Tuesday and Thursday evening. Though I regarded her with curiosity bordering upon fascination, I could not bring myself to speak with her beyond the inevitable exchange of pleasantries. She radiated such serene self-containment, such singleness of purpose that I did not feel justified in intruding. Without her being in the least remote or condescending, her every movement bespoke a life lived upon a higher plane. She descended among us to do God's work with these boys; then she ascended to her proper sphere.

I myself lived on a decidedly mortal plane. I ceased shaving so that I might conceal myself behind a full beard, a prudent act but one which made me feel permanently dirty. I spent as little time as I could manage in my chambers at Mrs. Frye's, for there my personal demons lay in ambush, in the form of dark despondent thoughts or more lurid distractions. I have no wish to discuss the latter, except to remark that their crude and fantastical content was, I believe, a blind cry for procreation, an animal shriek, a refusal upon my body's part to accept life's bleak realities—occurring, I remarked, at moments of greatest despair or moments of extravagant, nonsensical hope.

The grim ambience of my chamber did not make it easier to

eschew it. Had exigency not required me to earn my keep, many mornings I would not have pulled myself from bed. Once at the park, my labours diverted me from my darker thoughts and the Lodging-house beckoned as refuge and reward, but once among the boys, I all too often yearned for the solitude of my room.

My attempts to emulate Ingres as a street artist met with as much success as my talent bore relative to his, which is to say that with luck and application I could satisfy the constable and retain almost a dollar on a profitable day. I was compelled by competition from the *camera obscura* and from a Spanish woman adept at cutting black paper shadow portraits to charge such a small sum for my drawings that I could not earn the respect of my clients no matter how well I performed. I worked seven days a week, Sundays after church being my most lucrative span of time, when I might earn as much as a third of my week's earnings. One Sunday my constable appeared with his six children and sat for a group portrait, *gratis,* of course, which honour consumed most of this golden period. I might have earned more had I worked the Bowery in the evening and snared the theatre crowd, but my back would not support such a schedule and I would have defeated my reason for remaining in New York, the opportunity to spend time with the newsboys.

Each week, with care and abnegation, I could pay Mrs. Frye her five dollars for the following week, but I could not make restitution to Alger. Horatio behaved splendidly. He barely seemed to remember that he had subsidized me at all. If I attempted to discuss my debt he would flush and stammer and pat my arm and tell me that one day I might do the same for a needy Harvard man. Mrs. Frye, however, was less forgiving, and when she saw us together missed no opportunity to recall my obligations.

I found some satisfaction in my current self-sufficiency, but I realized that if I did not improve my earnings I should soon require an additional infusion from my benefactor. I did not know what would befall when cold weather froze up my pool of clients. I was living day to day and slipping slowly under.

Inevitably my relations with Horatio suffered the price of his generosity. Neither of us wished it to appear that he was purchasing a friend. Our relations were cordial and respectful, and we laboured with the newsboys in comradely fashion; at Mrs. Frye's table we would banter together upon the allowed topics, on which we shared a profound ignorance. Alger would amuse Mrs. Frye and the rest of us with tales of the Seligmans, a prominent banking family whose five adventuresome boys he had been retained to tutor. Otherwise we kept our own counsels. We were both the lonelier for it.

In justice to Alger our lack of communion was more my doing than his. My inner struggles did not allow me to forge a true friendship. I borrowed more than money from Alger; I borrowed his sunny spirits. Working with the boys required a patient optimism completely at odds with my current state of mind. When we bent to the task together, like sled dogs in harness, I would let Alger pull me along in his traces. Apart from the boys, in my dark moods I found his relentless good cheer naïvely deluded and deeply dispiriting.

126　　One evening O'Connor aborted my class so that the boys

might hear a sermon. Knowing his aversion to empty exhortation, Alger and I joined the boys to hear what he counted worthy preaching to his young charges. The occasion explained itself when O'Connor introduced the orator as Charles Loring Brace, founder of the Children's Aid Society and that very Lodging-house. He was a slim, pale gentleman garbed in ministerial black, with unkempt hair and anxious eyes, and he spoke in a halting voice, often compressing his full lips into a firm line as if constraining the liberties of the flesh.

He did not abuse his privilege. After ascertaining by acclamation that his young charges were well satisfied with their treatment, he spoke briefly and concretely of the loneliness of a life on the street, and having touched the boys in that most private of places, the loss of their families, and brought to their consciousness the perpetual isolation of their peripatetic lives, to the point that some were stabbing at their eyes to stanch the tears, he spoke of their one constant companion, the Superior Being, who shared their privations and their temptations, and was pleased at their signs of true manhood. From long experience addressing young men he spoke simply and directly, relying for effect not on hortatory flourish but on the obvious authenticity of his belief. His faith shone through his words, and his belief in the goodness of the boys, and their potential in the world, lit up their faces and lifted their hearts.

His business, however, was not to offer them merely the consolation of faith, but to stir them to action. The lands to the west, he said, were hungry for young men. Farmers and their wives would care for them as for their own children, feeding them well, schooling them, and teaching them the skills of a   **127** farmer's life. They would achieve maturity as strong and capable men, who could forge their own futures.

His words had mixed effect. Some hardy urban souls were driven to justify their own mode of existence, scoffing at a life spent among pigs and cows and mocking Brace's portrait of the doting farmer parent as slavery by another name. Others, primarily the younger and the weaker, crowded forward to register their names for the pilgrimage, carried as much by Brace's luminous sincerity as by any evidence he provided.

I found myself as moved as the weakest child by Mr. Brace's speech. Faith as pure as his was rare indeed, but faith in action rarer still. Brace was not consumed with perfecting his own soul, as my father was. His faith impelled him to help these children as his lungs impelled him to breathe, and his empathy made him a genuinely humble man.

While I could not make his faith my own I could find inspiration in the man. I was a planet, albeit a peripheral one, in the universe Brace had created for his young charges, influencing the others with the pull, however weak, of my presence. I must behave as if the warmth of Brace's sun were reflected from myself onto them. Brace transformed belief into action. I had set into motion events which caused O'Connor's disfigurement of Dannie, and then passively witnessed the outcome, as if I were outside the forces at play.

I had a moral obligation to act. The only appropriate action which I could imagine was to inform Mr. Brace of O'Connor's behaviour, and offer myself as eyewitness to the crime. I was loath to do so, for the ensuing ruckus would bring my own experiment to an acrimonious halt, and most probably lead to exposure of my true identity with the concomitant family scandal. Yet whatever the personal cost I could not in conscience allow Brace to depart without informing him of what had transpired in his name, under his roof.

Accordingly I waited until Brace had taken his leave of O'Connor and moved to confront him in the partial privacy of the stairway. Alger, no doubt divining my intent, restrained me with a hand upon my arm.

"Where are you going?"

"To talk to Mr. Brace. Would you care to join me?"

"To talk of what?"

"You know what."

Alger's grip tightened. "I beg you. Don't. Think of the scandal and the disruption for the boys."

"I only intend to inform Mr. Brace of O'Connor's behaviour. What he does with the information is entirely his decision."

"If you make the accusation he'll be constrained to act."

"I don't see how I can keep silent."

"Don't be an ass!"

Fearful of missing Brace, I pulled away abruptly from Alger's grasp. Our brief confrontation had attracted O'Connor's attention, and he watched me pursue Brace into the stairwell. Alger's words gave me pause, reinforcing as they did my own desire to remain silent, but examining my motives I decided I must speak out. Silence was merely another form of self-absorption. I forced myself to hasten and do the deed before my baser impulses seduced me into inertia.

In my hurry I descended the stairs heavily, and Brace turned at the sound of my boots. He was not surprised to see me.

"Mr. Brace," I began, "I am Mr. Henry."

"Yes, I know. Mr. O'Connor has spoken of you." At my startled look, he favored me with an apologetic smile. "I believe he bears you a certain grudging admiration."

"I'm afraid his good report only makes my present task more difficult." I spoke stiffly, discomfited by O'Connor's reputed praise but determined to press forward.

Brace, however, chose to ignore my obvious intention. "He fears your Darwinist determinism will pollute the minds of our charges," he continued, pleasantly, "but he adds that you've been teaching the boys a useful skill, and they have a liking for you."

"I've avoided philosophical discourse."

"I've read Darwin thirteen times, and I must admit I don't share your doubts. Evolution is proof for the nobility of the Spirit. It's a matter of scale, you see. Your Darwin says that the finch's beak develops over aeons, yet you expect Christ to lead us to moral perfection in a mere two thousand years."

"True faith has the enchanting property of seeing its evidence everywhere."

"Spoken like a man who wishes to believe."

"I'm afraid I've brought cause to question if not your faith, then its execution. I have witnessed—"

"Yes," he said, cutting me off in mid-sentence, obstinately oblivious of my words. "It is all a matter of scale. Mr. O'Connor—and his wife, she is equally important to these boys—the pair of them have saved thousands, and God willing will save thousands more, by appealing to their manly desire to make their own way, and providing them the tools to succeed.

They can't save every child though, can they?" He posed the question as if he hoped they might.

"They must not harm any."

"You might say they're physicians for the children's souls. They must follow the Hippocratic dictum: *Primum non nocere.* 'Above all, do no harm.' "

"Exactly."

"Well, sir, the only blameless doctors are those who've never practiced their profession. Those who've done the most perforce have bloody hands." He looked at me with eyes that bore a strange admixture of anxiety and peace. "The O'Connors are veteran practitioners. They've saved legions. God willing they will save legions more. Now what do you wish to tell me?"

As Brace spoke, my mission crumbled. Alger was correct: I was an ass. Brace already knew more than he wished to. Unburdening myself would lighten my load by weighting him down and he, not I, was the man who bore a mountain upon his back. Hot with shame, I ran out of words. He waited patiently until the pause grew awkward.

"If you will excuse me, Mr. Henry, I must be on my way. We've just been cheated out of thirty thousand dollars by the Tweed ring, and I must find a way of making up the shortfall."

"Godspeed," I stammered.

"Thank you." We shook hands, he with a final, rueful smile, as if to acknowledge the true reason for his gratitude.

I encountered a fretful Alger at the top of the stair. I motioned that my lips were locked. Alger grinned and clapped me upon the shoulder. O'Connor, enrolling boys across the room, took notice.

———

My sobering encounter with Brace had an unexpectedly salutary effect. My aims compared to his appeared egotistical and
petty, and seeing them smaller made them appear closer to
hand. My commitment redoubled. I led a strictly regulated existence. Every moment not working or horizontally summoning
my strength I spent at the Lodging-house with the boys, where
my constant presence had rendered me as invisible to them as a
desk or slate board, a position from which I could observe my
subjects with surprising freedom.

These were not dark and secretive souls. Their open ways
were, I believe, a natural product of their daily struggles. While
money was scarce and difficult to acquire, for most it was ob-
tainable, each and every day, in sufficient amount to defray the
pangs of the moment. Hence while the boys exhibited a sharp-
ness of manner which resulted from their struggle to survive,
they also evidenced a muscular confidence in the morrow.

I could not determine whether their optimistic attitude was
moulded by their style of life, or whether their style of life was
such that only the most optimistic survived. Most were cast
into this undisciplined existence, but not a few had chosen it.
Alger remarked that these boys were not as anxious as children who remained with parents crippled by illness, injury, or
drink, and who felt the insupportable burden of providing for
the entire family, nor as careworn as boys who labored in the
sweatshops from dawn into the gaslit hours, deprived of the
natural rhythms of childhood. Whatever the cause, living as
they did self-sufficient and in the present moment these boys
evinced a freedom of spirit which would have been the envy of

an itinerant Buddhist monk, were a monk sufficiently remote from *satori* to feel envy.

Living in the present is the privilege of the innocent. It was the acknowledged duty of the adult denizens of the Lodging-house, myself and Alger included, to imbue these young survivors with a sense of future. To this end, O'Connor's bank proved an effective device. On the last day of the month when the padlock was removed and the sums totted up the boys were delightful to observe in their pleasure, their pride, and their surprise at their own good fortune. Savings of a few dollars were soon squandered, but sums were often in the tens of dollars, too substantial even to gamble away, as the boys were not as a group prone to wagering more than penny stakes. They used the larger sums to purchase clothing, of which they were all in short supply, in view of the approaching winter, or they reinvested in the slotted table.

The boys with substantial accounts carried themselves differently from the others, and were viewed as a group apart. O'Connor allowed them to bed together in a special section of the dormitory he dubbed the Eagle's Nest, in order to excite admiration—and emulation—in the others, and to cement their own frugal instincts. His plan enjoyed a limited success. These young men, who were also as a rule among the oldest, did indeed act with less abandon and more authority, but for this they were not admired by the others. Some were feared, some ridiculed, but all were excluded from the general camaraderie of the indigent.

I found myself in sympathy with the general opinion. The Eagle's Nesters were O'Connor's proud successes, and I admired his achievement in forging a sense of purpose in these unregulated souls, but these boys were of no interest to me in my own researches, and I found them a dour and self-important lot. Indentured to the future, they had crossed over into the world of men.

As I reflect upon my actions from my current vantage point, I am struck by the extent to which my own situation was mirrored in that of the boys. Although I was cognizant of the need to plan a future and they were not, I resisted that imperative with all my soul. In truth my flight to New York was as much a flight from my own future, whatever that might have been, as it was an inquisition into the Darwinian world of the street boys.

I do not believe I was conscious of this irony at that time. I would not have accepted that I was running from the expectations which my expensive extended education had instilled in my parents. However, I was keenly aware that I was on the cusp of my life, and my personal crisis translated into an exaggerated concern for the futures of these young men, balanced upon a similar fulcrum. I wished them all to find a secure and rewarding place for themselves, yet I did not wish them to transform into the somber, narrow, and plodding men of the O'Connor model. O'Connor's tool was the slotted, padlocked table; mine was the drawing pad.

For these creatures living in the here and now curiosity was mental capital to be invested in their futures, for it was expended in the pursuit of knowledge, an outlay immediately consumed but of lasting value. Those boys not yet Eagle's Nesters displayed as a group a gratifying desire to learn, though they also bored rapidly. Most had never been to school, lacking both the time and the required attire. Though explicitly limited to artistic instruction I endeavored to instill a taste for inquiry and self-discipline, and I searched for pupils whom I could reasonably incite to pursue their artistic abilities into a gratifying and remunerative future. I met with scant success.

The Hickok lad was my principal cause for hope. Alone among the boys he showed evidence of true artistic gifts, though in their nascent form they were clearer to me than to his compatriots. Most neophyte artists concentrate upon small irregularities in their subject, and in capturing some minute foible they lose its general lineament. Their drawings are literal in the specific, but amorphous in the general. When Jemmie drew an apple, he saw its mass. His apple might have a fanciful form but it had a life off the page, a weight in the hand.

After that first absence he was a regular presence at the Lodging-house and in my little group of artists, save when the Pale Lady appeared to teach letters, when he would sit among her pupils near the front. Despite his gifts, however, Jemmie viewed his time with me as a mildly amusing diversion, and invested no more of himself in the work than he invested in a game of craps. His assiduity rose less from love for the work than a desire to be close to a gentle adult.

Many of the boys preferred the company of those their own age, but Jemmie Hickok gravitated toward his elders. Of all the boys he exuded the most dependence, and by that I mean he was the most incomplete by himself, the most in need of an older person to whom he could attach himself as family. When alone and thinking himself unobserved, he betrayed a forlorn air which commandeered the attention of any sensitive adult.

Alger and I, already attracted by his artistic ability, found ourselves spending more time with the boy than was perhaps advisable.

He was an easy companion, an extraordinarily gentle lad with an artist's dreamy temperament, quiet, but lively-eyed. One sensed he was silent not because he was dull or shy, but because he was watching some inward parade of images. Whatever he saw, however, he kept to himself. No amount of subtle coaxing could induce him to share it. Alger and I found ourselves ever more fascinated by the mysteries within those eyes, by his talent without the pride in it, by his clinging and his reticence.

As Jemmie's bruises healed we questioned whether we might be ascribing to him greater complexity of character because he was so astonishingly beautiful. I would see him standing beside my desk, one hip cocked, holding his drawing in the air as the Bargello David dangled the head of Goliath, and I would lose my train of thought in contemplation of his transcendent grace.

Confronted with this child who had so much yet so little, cognizant of Mr. Brace's labours for thousands like him, I made it my goal to help Jemmie find a future through his talents. Upon Alger's advice I showed the best of Jemmie's work to the gentlemen at St. Joseph's Industrial School, the principal institution in the city devoted to training the indigent. They were duly impressed, but regretted that they could not help an orphan, as they were a day school, and their students could not reside in the street nor had they time to earn their own livings. If Jemmie had a home and a patron they would train him.

I had not the resources to adopt young Hickok. Alger professed some interest, and even discussed it with the boy, in a general way, but in spite of his obvious desire to be part of a family and his obvious affection for Alger, Jemmie had no interest in becoming Alger's ward, and refused as well to entertain the possibility of living in an orphanage where he might be instructed properly. A fruitless search of the other charitable schools left us no choice but to abandon hope of placing the boy.

When we could not find a trade for Jemmie I undertook the subtler task of trying to instill a sense of calling. Coaxing and flattery had an antithetical effect. He discouraged my praise for the resentment it created in the others. When I persevered, I could not find words to make him value his ability.

Alger thought the Old Masters might inspire him and volunteered to purchase him a reproduction. I selected the Michelangelo frescoes of the Sistine Chapel for their clarity and drama, hoping a Renaissance work might strike a resonance in Jemmie. As I have noted, I had seen in the faces and bearings of the Lodging-house denizens qualities which brought the subjects of the Renaissance artists forcibly to mind. This was more than coincidence. Life for these young men on the streets of this city rewarded the same boldness of personality, the same strength and resourcefulness as life in Medici Florence.

Whatever the merits in my theory, the reproduction did not have the desired effect upon Jemmie. When Alger and I pored over it, trying to excite him to emulation, Jemmie showed only mild curiosity. He was most smitten, oddly enough, not with the agonies of the damned or the majesty of the Lord Almighty but with downcast Eve being driven from the Garden. I theo-

137

rized that as an orphan exiled from the bosom of family he felt a special affinity for her condition. Alger pointed out that Eve bore a remarkable resemblance to our Pale Lady. His remark inspired my final desperate measure. I would place Jemmie's future in her hands.

I was bemused by the power this woman held over me. At a Cambridge party I doubt I would have looked at her twice. I had always been attracted to women of an entirely different sort, high-spirited, energetic creatures, women with the flash and bite of my beloved sister. This woman lacked such *éclat*. I did not even know if she possessed much wit. To pose such a question seemed indecent. Hers was the strength of the shadowy arbor.

She always arrived on the stroke of seven and set to work immediately, and she left at the stroke of nine. I could not bring myself to delay her coming or going, so I chose to approach her during a lull in her teaching, when she had just inscribed the Twenty-third Psalm upon her slate and was seated at her battered desk, composed and silent, waiting for the boys to copy out the words. Jemmie Hickok sat in the second row.

"Hello," I said, in a low tone from a dry mouth. "My name is Henry. William Henry. I am teaching the boys to draw."

"I know." Her soft Southern vowels caressed the words. Of course she knew. She did not offer me her name in return, but favoured me with a welcoming gaze which acknowledged me as a fondly regarded acquaintance.

"I apologize for intruding upon you, but I have a matter of importance to discuss regarding one of your students. If I may . . ." I proffered her a sheaf of drawings. "These are the work of young Hickok."

She spread them upon her desk. Hickok recognized them but pretended ignorance and bent closer to his slate. I leaned closer to milady. We spoke in undertones. With too much enthusiasm in my voice I pointed to some details. "You see, he has an exceptional sense of balance and proportion for one so young." She ran her hands over the renderings. Beneath her shapely fingers they looked crude and ill formed. I stammered. "I know they're rough and childish. He has a crude line—"

"Remarkable." Her tapered index finger caressed the lumpy visage of a boy in an oversized hat. "He captures Marco's soul in the jut of his chin." She had chosen my favourite and described it perfectly.

"Unfortunately, Marco doesn't agree, and Hickok pays more heed to Marco than to me. I can't convince the boy to commit himself to perfecting his talents."

"Perhaps he'll listen to me." Exactly. "If you'll leave these with me, I'll talk to him after class."

I was still with my students when the Pale Lady concluded. She had finished five minutes early to allow herself time with Hickok. I hurriedly finished and moved within earshot.

She sat at her desk with an arm encircling Hickok's waist. He leaned into her, explaining his drawings. "That there's a bison. It's as big as a coach. When it runs the ground shakes. That's me hand. I don't got no dagger, but I seed it at the Bowery Theatre. Swirly like that. Like the blade is a flame." Jemmie never talked about his work with me.

She traced the sinuous blade with her nail. "I've seen just that dagger. It was covered in jewels."

"That's the one."

139

"It comes from the Orient. King Caspar wore that dagger when he visited the baby Jesus in the manger."

Jemmie emitted a soft, resonant sigh and touched the dagger's point.

"When you draw pictures, you bring things to life. That's a precious gift. Do you know how precious?"

"No, Miss Laura." So her name was Laura. Like Petrarch's Laura. Perfect.

"It's a gift from God. Only God gives the power of life, and He has given it to you. You should feel very, very proud." He gave a little hop. "What are you planning to do with this special gift?"

"I dunno. Draw stuff, I s'pose."

"God doesn't like it when you waste his special gifts."

"I better keep drawin' stuff then."

"You must do more than that. You have a gift. You must make it your calling."

"Callin' what?"

"A calling is something you must do more than anything. St. Paul's calling was to preach the Gospel."

"What's yours?"

"I suppose mine is to help boys like you." She hugged him. His pliant body conformed to her curves.

"I got me a callin'."

"Yes, you do." The boy beamed with pleasure and bounced upon his toes with a new sense of purpose. "And if you follow that calling, you can also make an excellent living."

"I can?"

"Certainly."

"They pays you fer fightin' injuns?"

"Why are you talking about fighting Indians?"

"That's me callin'."

"Your calling is making beautiful pictures. Like Mr. Henry."

"He don't make no more money'n me and he's all growed up."

"How can you be so sure of that?"

" 'Cause I seed him in the park makin' drawin's."

"Mr. Henry earns his living drawing in the park?"

"Sometimes he lays on the grass and sleeps."

"Mr. Henry's calling is his own concern."

"Yes, Miss Laura."

"Remember to use your God-given gifts in His service."

"Yes, Miss Laura."

She gave him another hug. "Now run along." Hickok squeezed her tight before he scampered off.

I busied myself aimlessly, hoping Laura had not detected my eavesdropping. She brought me Jemmie's drawings.

"Here. I doubt I made much of an impression."

"You made an indelible impression, I'm sure, but Hickok is most insistent about his lack of interest in his own talent."

"Perhaps he'll one day see the light."

"Like Saul of Tarsus on the road to Damascus."

"Perhaps."

"Would you like to keep his portrait of Marco? He'd want you to have it, I'm sure."

"It will be more use to him in your hands, but I'd be curious to see some of your work."

"It's nothing, really. I have a certain facility. Not enough for a career as an artist."

"I should like to see your work."

I had fallen into the practice of storing my materials at the Lodging-house as it was in such proximity to City Hall Park. I located my portfolio and brought out my view of the Park and my portrait of Alger, acutely conscious of every blurred shadow and misplaced line. She held my drawings in her hands. I could feel the soft pads of her fingertips against the paper.

"You do yourself a disservice. These are lovely. This landscape has a delicious play of light among the trees."

"You're too generous."

"And you've captured Mr. Alger's particular energy and dynamism. You've done him justice."

I fear I flushed red. "If I have any strength as an artist, I suppose it's in my ability to capture character in a few strokes."

"I'd like to sit for you."

"That would be my great pleasure."

"I will of course pay the usual salon fees."

"I'd be honored to have you as my subject, but I cannot accept payment. We're colleagues."

"But I must pay. Otherwise I deprive you of your livelihood."

"No work of mine could possibly be worth the time you'd spend posing. To have you as my subject is more than payment enough."

Laura laughed. "Then I see we're at an impasse. Should you ever come to regard your own work as sufficiently worthy to be commissioned, I hope you'll remember my request."

"Should you ever allow me the great pleasure of drawing your portrait *gratis,* I would consider it a signal honor."

She laughed again and extended her hand. For someone with such *gravitas* she laughed easily. "Let us then agree to disagree, Mr. Henry."

I shook her smooth, white, weightless hand. "Please, call me William. Or better, Willie." The word tickled my tongue. I never called myself Willie. Only my oldest intimates used the name.

"Willie it is."

She spoke it with casual insouciance. I flushed. "And may I call you Laura?"

"You may, but it isn't my name."

"Oh. Oh. So terribly sorry."

"Think nothing of it. A pet name Jemmie uses with me. I don't know why."

"Like Petrarch's Laura."

"I doubt that's his inspiration."

"No, no, of course not."

"Good-day, Mr. Henry. Willie." She turned away. I watched her don her cloak to leave, adjusting the shoulders with a single sure gesture, and I felt that I had been shaken into place with equal calm precision. Yet I did not feel used or humiliated. On the contrary, I felt the tingling exhilaration which normally manifests itself only in the shadow of great accomplishment.

———

⌒CHAPTER ELEVEN⌒

JEMMIE USED HIS CRUMPLED BILL WELL. WHEN HE AND THOMAS Lackey picked up the *Star*, Thomas made to pay as usual, but Jemmie held out the tired paper and said in a strong voice that he was buying his own.

"Where'd that come from?" Thomas asked in a querying tone.

"None a yer business," said Jemmie.

" 'Tis if it belongs to me."

"If you was missing a penny, you'd a turned me inside out."

"Stole it."

"Did not."

The newsman resolved their dispute by taking Jemmie's bill and making change. Jemmie lugged off his pile of sheets without another word to Thomas Lackey, thanks to Dannie's largesse a free man.

However, Jemmie did not return to Harry Hill's or the Bowery Theatre. He called the places to his mind with considerable pleasure, but when he contemplated revisiting them the pleasure turned, like bad milk, into a sour taste in the back of his mouth.

Many of the boys who came to the Lodging-house stayed

only a night or two, but Jemmie settled in as a regular. Unless rousted by a larger boy he slept each night in the same location, an upper bunk near the windows on the square side. The uppers were hotter, but the older boys claimed the lowers, and here he could lie upon his stomach and look down on Printing House Square, not a square, speaking strictly, and devoid of any central defining feature, more a widening of the streets where three came together, a trapezoidal funnel, but an open space nonetheless, and often the moon was visible to him in the broad wedge of sky. Seeing the moon reminded him of the man with the rough voice, and the gold piece which had propelled him to this place. The gold piece made him think of his sister and his tiny brother, and bury his head under his arm to make them go away.

Not long after his ensconcement Jemmie and the other boys were summoned to be addressed by a sad-eyed man with a gentle voice. The man spoke knowledgeably of the difficulties which beset the boys. He told them that the Supreme Being was everywhere by their side, even at the worst of times, and that His hand reached constantly for theirs, if only they would take hold and allow His touch to lift them from their mire of troubles.

Much as Jemmie would have welcomed such a benefactor, the appeal left him unmoved. He had never felt such a touch, and he did not know where he might put his hand to feel it. The thought of a loving touch, however, put him in mind of his mother. He made it a rule never to think of her, because her image caused a sickening torpor to invade his limbs and a heavy blanket of woe to smother him, but the man's words

145

brought forth the memory of her firm hands about his chest, and a dizzying sensation of soaring hawk-like through the air clasped in their grip, and the thump of a landing upon her scratchy woolen breast. He wept hot tears, which he pushed off his cheeks with his thumbs that the other boys would not see them, though the other boys took no notice, lost as they were in their own recollections.

Even as sadness enveloped him, Jemmie heard words which shone with hope. This man was sending boys West, to be matched with families who needed them. No boy would be settled against his will. So many needed boys that families would vie for the right to take them in. They would be fed well and treated fairly, and when they came of age they would be given one hundred dollars and a horse.

Jemmie saw his future astride a white stallion, dashing across the plains with a family of Indian fighters, clad in buckskin fringe that shimmered in the wind. He sensed the insistent pressure of the mysterious hand the man had spoke of impelling him toward the Lodging-house, toward this moment. The plains wind blew him forward to register his name.

The line moved slowly. O'Connor spoke to every boy with deliberate care. When Jemmie's turn came, O'Connor took his name and handed him a piece of paper.

"Here. See your father signs this."

"Me father?"

"Mr. Brace can't up and ship you out without your father's say-so, can he?"

"But I's here. You said I'd stay here anyways."

"He can't be shipping you halfway across the continent. Your father might say you were stolen. Mr. Brace can't have that."

The cool prairie wind had dropped to naught. Jemmie took the stiff paper. He found a pencil on Alger's desk and drew a horse upon the back. Then he crumpled it into a ball and kicked it around with some other boys until Mrs. O'Connor gathered it up and sent them all to bed.

———

Jemmie's momentary exultation had a lasting effect. What had been an airy fantasy hardened into bedrock resolve. As his own boss Jemmie every day brought home almost thirty cents, which he was careful now to entrust to O'Connor's slotted table so that he would not be enticed to spend it in ways he would regret. He spoke to no one of his intentions. He was going West, and he could not expect a helping hand from any quarter to get him there.

Evenings he drew pictures with Mr. Henry and a small group of other boys, and often Mr. Alger. He drew because Mr. Henry and Mr. Alger wished him to. Unused to the friendly attention of adults, he had feared at first he would be beaten or expelled from the Lodging-house if he did not attend the sessions, but by the end of the first week tentative forays into inattention and disobedience had convinced him that Mr. Alger and Mr. Henry were incapable of harsh treatment. Indeed, they seemed oddly concerned that he think well of them. To his surprise he found their interest to be as compelling as threats or blows in keeping him in the group of would-be artists, though their compassionate concern made

147

him no more dedicated to his art than had they exercised violence upon his person.

Alger and Henry's esteem for Jemmie did not go unnoticed among his peers. In the showers they set upon him with their towels. One boy they called Hammer was particularly adept at snapping his wet cloth so that it raised bee sting welts upon Jemmie's tender flesh. Jemmie withstood their attacks without complaint and made it his business never to show vainglorious pride in his work. Eventually the true weight of Mr. Henry's respect for Jemmie outbalanced the boys' resentment at the special attentions, and they abandoned their game.

On Tuesdays and Thursdays Jemmie cheerfully deserted Mr. Henry, and instead of drawing people or things in the world he copied the curves and angles of Miss Laura's letters, objects he viewed as pleasingly graceful but of no particular significance, like the intricate latticework grates which adorned the nearby *Tribune* building. Entranced like the other boys by her beauty, her kindness, and her mystery, he laboured hard to please her.

The boys debated Miss Laura's origins and the reason for her presence among them. All agreed she was fabulously wealthy. Some said she was an orphan who had been lifted from poverty by a love-struck tycoon, and in return dedicated herself to helping fellow orphans. Some said she was raised in wealth and comfort but that one day, when her attention was elsewhere, her son had been kidnapped from his perambulator by an evil Italian, and had perished under the Padrone's blows while sawing on a violin for a beggar's pittance. According to this theory, she taught to atone for her momentary lapse. The most popular theory, however, held that her boy child had been abandoned by a drunken nanny and had wandered into the urban wilderness to be raised by poor folk as their own. Its adherents believed that she taught among them so that she might discover her long-lost son, who might be any one of them.

Jemmie was certain that she was Laura Courtland. He knew that plays were only a copy of life. He understood that the actress he had seen in the Bowery Theatre was only pretending to be the brave and heart-strong lass of the scenario. Yet he also knew that this woman possessed all the qualities that the actress had laboured to portray, and when he called her Laura she answered to the name.

Finally, at the end of a very long month, O'Connor sprung the padlock and opened the slotted table, and Jemmie decided it was time to collect his earnings. Finding himself the possessor of nine dollars and twenty cents, he thought it best to consult with his fellows about his future plans. Hammer wrapped his meaty fist about Jemmie's pipe-stem arm and threatened to scalp him. Boys his own age gave better counsel. Lemon Lip, who sold post cards at the Grand Central Railway Depot uptown, told him he would need twenty-five dollars for a rail ticket, and Scratcher said he would need to buy at least two guns and plenty of bullets, which expense would be considerable. Tammy the Red had heard a cart man yelling at his fallen horse that the nag was twenty dollars thrown in the gutter. Jemmie and his advisors calculated that in order to fight Indians he needed minimum capital of one hundred and thirty dollars. Even with nine dollars and

149

twenty cents in his bank it seemed a distant dream. Iron despair banded his heart like Hammer's hand about his arm.

The bank was opened upon a Thursday, Laura's day, and when she appeared Jemmie sat in the front, as being closer to Miss Laura helped him not to think about one hundred and thirty dollars. After letters Laura beckoned him and held him close while they looked at drawings he had made for Mr. Henry. She stroked his hair and praised them, and fastening her warm eyes upon him, she told him that God wanted him to go West, and that God wouldn't let anything stop him, and she enfolded him in her gentle arms and squeezed him until the despair relinquished its grip upon his heart. He clung to her until she patted him on his bottom and told him to run along. No matter how much money it took, or how the big boys sneered, he was going to fight Indians.

Laura's inspiring words had a further effect upon Jemmie Hickok. When he clung to her, his frail body stiffening with strength and resolve, what had once been mere suspicion firmed into certainty: Jemmie knew as surely as he knew his own hand that they shared a common past. He did not believe he was her lost son, for he did not believe she had a son, but he believed that everyone knew his own family, and trusting his own heart knew she was his. "Switched at birth." Was he switched at birth?

While Laura conversed with Mr. Henry, Jemmie skipped downstairs to the square. He singled out her carriage stationed at its usual spot, where the boys had often studied it to fuel their speculations. It was a modest but finely finished brougham, sober black but shining with the mirror luster of many coats of lacquer. Even Jemmie's unschooled eye could discern that the horses were exceptional, a rich chocolate colour, perfectly matched and exquisitely formed. They were tended by a lone well-tailored coachman. More than once Jemmie had seen passers-by attempt to converse with him about his steeds only to be told that he was forbidden from discussing his employers or their horseflesh.

Jemmie waited out of sight until Laura appeared and entered the conveyance. As the coach accelerated he ran behind and leapt upon the boot, which the uneven pavement swung like the stern of a ship in weather, banging Jemmie against the spokes, but he held fast, and the roughness of the terrain covered the sound of his landing. Clinging to the leather straps, Jemmie tried to make himself invisible between the splash board and the trunk.

The coach jounced up Broadway, keeping to the center of that capacious avenue, further shielding the boy. At Union Square the street narrowed, and he caught the eye of a push-cart peddler, but the man was too deeply engaged in maneuvering his clumsy barrow to betray him with a sign. A tow-haired boy threw a stone his way.

At Madison Square they turned onto Fifth Avenue. He had never been this far north. From his hiding place Jemmie could make out only a sliver of street rushing away from the carriage, yet he experienced a profound change in his surroundings, a fresh ambience of generous, meticulous attention. Lurching smoothed to a gentle jiggle as tilted Belgian blocks yielded to smooth Fisk concrete. Smells of manure and horse piss evaporated, and with them the cries of vendors,

151

the curses of teamsters, and the clatter of street-cars, leaving such bucolic silence that he could hear the chirrup of sparrows in the trees which sprang from the pavement. Broad sidewalks that would have been welcomed in the crowded lower reaches of the city stood swept and empty, awaiting the well-shod foot. The ample avenue flowed away from him as if he were cruising up the vast East River, the occasional carriage sailing past heading downtown. Jemmie basked in the luxury of space.

The vehicle slowed to a halt, forcing Jemmie to shrink back to avoid detection. Blind now, his ears served as eyes. He heard the creak of the coachman's glove upon the door handle and the tap of Miss Laura's shoes descending. He heard her velvet voice release the coachman for the evening and her feather step mount stone stairs. The carriage jolted into movement, bringing him a glimpse of Laura at the door of a brick and brown-stone building. He wiggled out from his secure position, and as the carriage slowed to turn the corner for the coach house he leapt off.

Miss Laura was gone when he approached the house. He thought it big as a bank but not equally imposing, for it was sparsely adorned and lacking the sheen of marble. In aspect if not in scale it appeared no different from the rows of houses where he had hawked his matches, save that its stoop was broader and flanked by a fat stone balustrade. A low locked gate guarded stairs down.

Had Laura entered A. T. Stewart's imposing mishmash of gleaming columns and entablatures a few blocks north Jemmie might have been satisfied with the intelligence he had uncovered, but this plain exterior challenged him to learn more. He vaulted the gate. Below, an ironwork grille blocked a niche hollowed from the stoop. Jemmie pressed against the grille until his thin chest squeezed past. He faced a locked iron door beneath a small transom cocked open to admit air.

Jemmie clambered atop the door handle and hoisted himself to the transom. It was wider than the grate. He thrust his head inside and saw a dark corridor lined with casks and bins.

A dozen feet down the corridor a door opened and a young woman in starched kitchen whites appeared. Jemmie's breath froze in his lungs. She walked toward Jemmie but did not see him, intent as she was upon the bins, from which she gathered some apples into her skirt. She straightened, her face a few feet from Jemmie's, but eyeing her load returned whence she came, leaving the door ajar.

Jemmie's lungs exploded with a whoosh. When his heaving chest subsided he pushed first his arm, then his shoulder through the transom, and dropped with a thump to the floor.

The stone was cold and smooth, refreshing underfoot, the air starchy sweet. He crept past the door the servant girl had used, past laughter and the odour of poultry and potatoes, as it swung open again, and he ducked between a tin bin and a large sack of something hard and fine. A different servant girl hurried past him, supporting a tray artfully arranged with foods he did not recognize. She opened a door at the far end of the corridor and tripped up a flight of stairs.

The tray could only have been meant for Laura. Jemmie followed its trajectory. At the head of the narrow stair a door

153

admitted a lemon slice of light as it awaited the immediate return of the servant girl. If Laura was his family, this was his
home. Jemmie climbed the stair and slipped past the door.

Carpet soft as sand rubbed his feet, but everything around
him was cold and hard and elaborately incised. He had entered a dense world of metal and stone, a forest of fluted
columns and brass chandeliers crowded with polished, scant-
ily clad figures. A boy danced on goat feet, a naked woman
concealed her intimate parts behind a large goose, men
wrapped in bed sheets raised their arms to speak, all throb-
bing with the pulse of life, frozen for the moment in stone as
Jemmie had been frozen at the transom by the servant girl.

The boy with goat hooves leered at Jemmie and beckoned
with a pudgy hand. Jemmie backed away. He knew about statues, having seen them supporting pigeons in Union Square
and on the Park Bank building and many other places, but no
chisel could have shaped these creatures. He could see the
veins in their hands and the puckers in their skin and the
crescent moons of their fingernails. God had made these people. He wondered who might have turned them to stone. He
had heard a story once about a man who had turned his
daughter into gold.

Jemmie stood in the center of the room as far as could be
from the stone people, upon his comforting red and blue path
through the column forest. Silver clouds hovered in a blue
sky above, whence winged babies waved at him and pink people smiled down, clad only in bed sheets that often left the
women's breasts bare.

He heard thumping. Through the columns he made out the

sweep of a marble stairway and a skirt descending. He did not wish to discover if the intruder could turn him into stone. He dashed away from her toward a beckoning open door.

He reached the room, panting hard, and peered back in time to see the servant girl with her empty tray disappear down to the cellar. He caught his breath in frightened, disappointed little gasps. This was not the home he had imagined for himself and Laura but an alien and forbidding place, a stone residence for stone people.

The new room was also filled with them, but here they congregated in a double row in the center, each an island of dynamic immobility raised upon its own pedestal stand. Against each pedestal a gold frame leaned. The walls of the room were broken into gold squares as well, some no larger than a folded newspaper and some as big as the slotted Lodging-house table, all cunningly fitted to cover every inch of wall. Each square was carved with twisty leaves or geometric designs, and each was a golden window into a tiny world, a world of happy people eating and drinking, or misty hills and rivers, or dead rabbits and fruit, or people bedecked in complicated clothing. The largest depicted a perfect horse, almost of a size to ride.

Jemmie did not understand why someone who owned a house would hand it over to this crowd of strangers and animals. As surely as he knew that Laura was family he knew that this was not his past. Perhaps she was not of this place. Yet her carriage lived here. Perhaps she was a bewitched princess held by a magician who turned people to stone. Perhaps his spell allowed her flesh and blood existence for the hours she visited the Lodging-house, each night at the stroke of nine returning her to stone.

A picture caught his eye. It was long and thin, wedged between a naked girl on a crimson bed and a heap of pheasant carcasses. The picture showed many bison, so many they carpeted the rolling hills like fields of corn. The bison were charging furiously. The closest, the largest and angriest, was being chased by an Indian upon a spotted pony. The Indian wore a hat of feathers and carried a bow and arrow and a spear, and showed no fear. He rode without a saddle but had risen up by clasping his mount between his knees, arm cocked to hurl his spear into the side of his enormous prey.

Jemmie was captivated by the precisely captured details of the hunter: the red and yellow daubs streaking his cheeks, the jagged scars disfiguring his bare chest, the blue and white beading adorning his footwear, the flint tip lashed by rawhide to his spear. Jemmie knew now that he had been brought into this house to see this image and remember it. One day he would kill this man.

When he had absorbed the man into his mind Jemmie carefully left the room, creeping through the columns. He paused at the hidden door from which he had emerged. He dared not return that way. Looking up the carpet path toward the great stair and the front entrance, he prayed for speed and dashed forward. At the moment his feet left carpet for the cold marble of the entrance rotunda he saw the servant girl who had carried Laura's tray mounting the stairs. The slap of his feet upon the stone caught her attention and she turned. The sight of him froze her in amazement. Jemmie hoped she had been turned into stone and he ran for the door. She sprang to life. He lunged at the great handle as she lunged for him. The door was heavy and slow-moving. Her nails cut his arm. He twisted from her grasp and dashed down the steps along Thirty-second Street and didn't look back until he reached Broadway, where he hopped upon a downtown stage and headed for the Bowery, tingling with the thrill of his narrow escape and fervor for his calling.

CHAPTER TWELVE

My weeks at the Lodging-house had taught me much about the newsboy's behaviour but little about his essential nature. Motive was too deeply buried in the deed. It had become evident that my observations would give me no more moral insight than observing the orangutan in the forests of Sumatra until I should witness an incident which, like an experiment in physical chemistry, would impose such extreme conditions upon my subject that he would decompose into his constituent parts. The newsboy's life was sufficiently harsh that I knew such an event to be inevitable. When it occurred, however, I was not observer but participant.

In my own struggle on the streets I was offered a reprieve of sorts by an earnest young fellow with an eager smile. I had seen him pass by upon earlier occasions, head craned forward as if leaning into a strong wind, with barely a glance at my work, obviously a man without the time or the inclination, or to judge from his clothing the surplus capital, to indulge in even the swiftest of portraits. This day, however, he wished to talk. He declared himself Noah Wapner, journalist for the *Christian Union,* penning an article about a new voice for reform in the city, a certain Anthony Comstock. This gentleman had yet to attain the power and notoriety which the name now brings to mind. Although Comstock then was little more than a lone man on a personal crusade, he was already exhibiting his genius for attracting both praise and condemnation by bringing a remarkably lurid obscenity suit before the Criminal Courts. Noah had decided that an illustration would make his piece more appealing. Would I be interested in earning five dollars?

Of course I would. When, from exigency, I asked for half in advance I learned that he was not in fact in the employ of the *Union* but was working on its strong expression of interest in such a piece. The five dollars would be mine when it accepted our work for publication, the merest of formalities as he described it.

My labors had taught me a new skepticism in matters of the purse. I dickered like a costermonger. "And if they accept the piece but not the illustration?"

"Why would they do that? Your drawing will be our prime attraction!"

"What if the editor doesn't share that opinion?"

"You're investing in your future. Once you're in print, you're an illustrator! You'll be making ten times what you're making now."

His insistent optimism made me wish to believe in his plan. Whatever the reality of the *Christian Union*'s interest in Mr. Wapner, his energy and good cheer lifted my spirits. Success would move me off the streets before winter.

"Come," said Wapner, closing the bargain, "I'll stake you to lunch."

Selecting the necessary drawing materials, I paid a lad five cents to return my other equipment to the *Sun* building and accompanied Noah the few blocks up Centre Street to the Halls of Justice while he amused me with tales of Comstock's derring-do. With a physique as powerful as his will to purify, and the secret financial support of the Young Men's Christian Association, Comstock had declared war upon obscenity in New York, and the press was feasting upon the spectacle. "It has all the salacious allure of the most degrading pornography and all the moral appeal of a temperance crusade," said Wapner. "Last week Comstock went after a purveyor of the most astounding filth, and the constable he brought along to make the arrest slipped round back and warned the fellow off. Comstock ran the man down and hauled him personally to jail, then had the constable dismissed from the force."

As we neared the Halls of Justice, Noah pointed out a nondescript building bearing a banner forty feet long emblazoned with bold letters proclaiming "HOWE & HUMMEL." The columns on either side of the entrance bore the same inscription, as did the shop windows, which revealed a motley assortment of men and women arrayed upon wooden benches, from fashionable souls to threadbare petty thieves, all united in the evident desire to be elsewhere. Hummel and Howe were then as unknown as Anthony Comstock, as yet unsung in vaudeville and the press, and I innocently inquired of Noah if we might be looking into a pawnshop. No, he replied, that was the law offices of the attorney who would challenge Mr. Comstock that day in court.

The Halls of Justice, aptly dubbed the Tombs in general parlance, was a somber Egyptianate building chill with the damp rising from its swampy foundation, a granite imitation of a pharaonic temple fronted by a portico of thickly bunched lotus-sheaf columns which crowded out the sun. The case was a minor offense and would be adjudicated without a jury, but it had been moved to the Court of Special Sessions, the larger of the courtrooms, because of growing interest in Mr. Comstock's work.

Though the trial was already under way spectators milled about in the dank hallway, chatting in gay anticipation. When Mr. Comstock was summoned as witness all hastened into the cadaverous gloom of the courtroom. Wapner found us a place which afforded me a clear view of the principals, and I prepared to sketch.

Comstock swore his oath in a firm baritone, hand pressed hard upon the Bible, peering out through truculent blue eyes from beneath a steep, balding forehead. He would tell the whole truth, so help him God, and woe to the man who impeded him. Comstock dressed the reformer, in plain rumpled black wool and stiff white shirt, but beneath bulged the bull neck, thick thighs, and heavily muscled torso of the shoulder-hitter. His aura of massive determination was enhanced by bristling ginger whiskers which swooped from his sideburns to join above his upper lip, as if it were a bridle and God held the reins. Under the gentle urging of the prosecutor he clearly and succinctly described his visit to a concert saloon named Maude and Mabel's, at which he witnessed the defendants in a state of practical nudity gyrating their stomachs in a revoltingly suggestive manner, such as to breed lust in the minds of the beholders. When his words provoked titters among the spectators Comstock glared them down.

"Lust," he said, in precise tones, drawing down his upper lip as he searched for the exact words, "defiles the body, debauches the imagination, corrupts the mind, deadens the will, destroys the memory, sears the conscience, hardens the heart, and damns the soul. It unnerves the arm, and steals away the elastic step. It robs the soul of manly virtues, and imprints on the mind of the youth visions that curse him throughout life. Like a panorama, the imagination seems to keep this hated thing before the mind, and it wears its way deeper and deeper, plunging the victim into practices that he loathes. The family is polluted, home desecrated, and each generation born into the world is more and more cursed by the inherited weakness, the harvest of this seed-sowing of the Evil One."

The spectators rumbled with admiration for his oratory. Wapner grinned. "Spoken like a man on intimate terms with the emotion."

The prosecutor asked Comstock to identify the women who had thus debauched their audience. This proved impossible. Three souls, ostensibly female, were seated at the defense table, but they were swathed head to floor, faces covered with heavy veils in the Moslem tradition. When the judge instructed them to remove the veils their attorney shot to his feet and objected in dry, quick words. This was young Mr. Hummel.

The artist in me rejoiced at the contrast between Comstock and his antagonist. If Comstock was a stallion for the Lord, Hummel was a sleek deadly mink, barely five feet tall, slender of frame but immaculately tailored in black, his tapered legs ending in pointy 'toothpick' shoes. He had a huge pear-shaped head and he moved quickly, peering at the world through the mink's beady black eyes, probing for a weakness but revealing none himself, speaking forcefully with never a ripple in his noncommittal expression.

"Your Honour, to ask a Moslem woman to bare her face to public view is to dishonour her. We are prepared to stipulate that these are the women in question."

The spectators stirred while the judge pounded for order. Comstock could not keep silent. "Spare us hypocrisy's foul stench!"

"Mr. Comstock," said the judge, "this is my courtroom, not yours. Mr. Hummel, instruct your clients to remove their veils."

The women stirred anxiously. "In that case, Your Honour," Hummel replied, "I move we clear the room of all males save officers of the court."

"Ladies," said the judge over more hubbub, "kindly remove your veils."

The women hesitated. Hummel leaned over them and whispered. They briefly lowered their veils sufficiently to reveal three moderately attractive women who could have been Semite, Teuton, or Celt. One, henna-haired, had the freckled pug nose of an Irish colleen. Comstock identified them as the women he had witnessed.

Mr. Hummel, consulting a paper, now cross-examined the accuser. "This complaint specifies the obscene act as, and I quote, 'lewd and lascivious contortion of the stomach.' Is that correct?"

"I have already testified to that effect."

"Thank you. You may step down." Comstock removed himself from the witness box. "Your Honour, I move for summary dismissal of this outrageous accusation."

"On what grounds?"

Hummel hefted a tome. "I have here a current edition of *Gray's Anatomy.* It is the acknowledged authority on the human body. I wish to offer the following quotation into evidence: 'The stomach is the principal organ of digestion. It is the most dilated part of the alimentary canal, serving for the solution and reduction of the food. Its form is irregularly conical, curved upon itself and presenting a rounded base, turned to the left side.' " He held up a diagram of the human viscera. " 'It is placed immediately behind the anterior wall of the abdomen, above the transverse colon, below the liver and diaphragm.' Your Honour, those of us who have overindulged on heavy foods know that gyrations of this organ may cause intense discomfort, but they do not attract lascivious attention. In truth the movements of this organ are completely invisible. Therefore this complaint should be summarily dismissed."

The judge said he would take the motion under advisement. Comstock drew down his upper lip to speak, but chewed on it instead.

When it came Hummel's turn to present the defense he called as his witness one of the veiled dancers, and when the bailiff raised his Bible to administer her oath Hummel pushed it aside and produced a Koran. Over the prosecutor's objections she swore to Allah to tell the truth. At the mention of Allah, the other two raised their hands reverently toward the east.

The woman identified herself in a quiet voice as Zelika. The judge instructed her to speak out. Louder she betrayed a distinct Philadelphia accent. This did not prevent Hummel from presenting a fervent argument on their behalf based upon ancient texts. According to Hummel this so-called dance was a ritual act of ecstatic devotion which it was their Islamic duty as practicing Sufi mystics to perform. He expounded at length, maintaining the neutral demeanor of a man explaining the physics of the bicycle, and limited Zelika's testimony to yesses and noes. Whenever he mentioned Allah, a frequent occurrence, the three women would supplicate to the east while Comstock fumed in silence. When the judge recessed for lunch Hummel cleared a space in the hallway for the women to spread prayer mats, on which they knelt facing east and with considerable mumbling performed their ritual obeisance oblivious of the amusement of passers-by.

As promised Noah hosted me for lunch, at a dirty restaurant barren of décor but serving a savory beef stew for twelve cents a portion. When I complimented the food he told me it was the uneaten remnants off the plates at Delmonico's. I thought he spoke in jest. Proud of his bargain, he assured me he did not. Noah was ebullient, pleased with the food, pleased with my rough sketches, and pleased with the course of events. When I remarked there was little evidence of justice on either side, he said he'd give it justice in the telling.

After lunch, before Hummel could swear in the self-styled Fatima, the judge dismissed the case. "Mr. Comstock," he said, "you should stay out of other people's business. In the future do not put your nose where it is not welcome. It is not welcome in this courtroom." Comstock rose upon thick legs and opened his mouth to speak, then thought better of it. He clamped his jaws closed with a contemptuous snap heard across the courtroom and marched out.

Some spectators applauded; others voiced angry words. The three Moslem ascetics emitted suspiciously sybaritic squeals of pleasure. Noah thought the outcome perfect. "Now I can strike a tone of moral indignation. Shocking miscarriage of justice *et cetera*. The *Union* will buy that."

"And if Comstock had prevailed?"

"Morality triumphant. Not half so marketable. The *Union* is Henry Ward Beecher's rag. It's laden to the scuppers in morality triumphant."

"So you don't believe these women are Moslem mystics?"

"Were they Mohammed's own wives and raised the dead with their gyrations, the *Union* would call this a miscarriage of justice."

"Will you label them impostors? Evidently the judge believed them."

Noah laughed. "Hummel likes to say there are two kinds of lawyers, those that know the law and those that know the judge. Over lunch, I wager, Hummel made the judge's acquaintance."

Noah's enthusiasm made him impatient for my illustration. I promised I would have a drawing by dinner and repaired to my room imbued with his confidence in the project. The scene seemed ripe for caricature. As I walked the dozen blocks to Washington Square, I framed my drawing in my mind: the shrouded Philadelphian Zelika upon the witness stand, accepting the Koran from huge-headed Hummel while her two mummified mates gesticulated toward the east and Comstock bristled at the lot of them, sucking on his upper lip: a dynamic and amusing little *mise-en-scène*. I entered Mrs. Frye's pregnant with anticipation, hoping for hope.

I was surprised to find Alger sitting in the parlor. I could not imagine what would bring him home in the middle of the day. I waved in passing. Alger followed me up the stair. He spoke furtively.

"I apologize for the intrusion. I went to the park . . . the *Sun* building. . . ."

"Not at all, not at all. Come, sit." Alger was blessed and cursed with a transparent visage. When in good spirits his joy radiated forth. I had often warmed myself at that fire, but now the fire was banked. His eye was dim, his mouth drawn. He rubbed his moustache with a nervous forefinger.

Alger dropped into my armchair, his back to the glare from the window, as if he knew how clearly his distress could be read and wished to obscure his face in shadow. I pulled out my desk chair and left a goodly space between us. He needed distance as much as solace. He searched for his words.

"I've had a terrible . . . I'm sorry . . . I shouldn't . . ."

"Horatio, please. I'll do everything in my power to be as good a friend to you as you've been to me."

"Thank you, that's very kind, very large-spirited."

"Not at all. Now how can I be of help?"

"I left here this morning, as usual, to write at my desk at the

167

Lodging-house. The mornings are a good time for me because the boys are all at work and I find it very productive to sit in that empty room and write. I can imagine the boys . . ." He lapsed into silence. I believe he was embarrassed. I waited. I could not discern whether he was speaking for my benefit or his own.

"I was in the square there, enjoying a glass of fresh water from the portly man who dispenses it *gratis*," he mused, "when I was accosted by that boy with the notched ear, Dannie O'Connor. He calls himself O'Connor, at any rate. I believe he chose the name to foment confusion. I was friendly enough. I apologized for his treatment at his namesake's hand." Alger spoke tartly, pursing his lips as if the words were leaving a bitter aftertaste.

"Would you like something to drink? I'm afraid I don't have anything but Mrs. Frye's pitcher."

Alger waved away my suggestion, intent upon his tale. "I asked Dannie how he was faring. He replied that he was quite fine. He thanked me for asking. He hoped I was feeling well also. He had business with me which required I be in tip-top condition. I could not imagine what he meant. He claimed that he had seen Jemmie Hickok last night. Wasn't Jemmie at the Lodging-house last night?"

"I talked to him there."

"He claimed to have spoken with Jemmie. He claimed Hickok had deputized him to be his agent."

"Agent for what?"

"He claims that Hickok said I . . ." Alger filled his chest with air. When he continued, he kept all emotion from his voice.

THE NEWSBOYS' LODGING-HOUSE

"He said that I performed unnatural acts with the boy. He said I gave the boy a suggestive picture of nude men, and I . . ."

Alger again fell silent. His eyes darted into mine and away again, gauging my response without confronting it. I thought it more therapeutic to express sympathy than outrage. "And how did you respond?"

"I was struck mute."

"I can well imagine."

"He told me that if I did not meet him at noon tomorrow with five thousand dollars he would bring Jemmie to the station house and have me charged with pederasty and unnatural acts."

"Good Lord."

"Yes. And then he ran off."

"And what do you make of this?"

"I've no idea. You saw Jemmie at the Lodging-house. I don't imagine he even saw Dannie last night."

"What do you propose to do?"

"Why, talk to Jemmie, I suppose." Alger's voice squeaked in anguish.

I thought it best to put the kindest interpretation on events. "Dannie's a self-styled comic. This could be his demented idea of a prank. He sends you charging after little Hickok, and the boy won't have the first idea why you're so worked up. He imagines a cruelly amusing dialogue at cross-purposes."

"That had occurred to me. He might wish to create trouble for Jemmie. Though I can't imagine why."

"Let me talk to Hickok. I see no reason why you should give Dannie the satisfaction of playing out his vicious scenario." **169**

He leaned out of the shadows toward me, hope illuminating his features. Evidently this had been his plan from the beginning. "Would you?"

"I'll talk to him tonight."

"If he shows his face."

"Of course he will, and his presence will be proof of his innocence. Now I suggest you take a walk. Write. Put this from your mind. We'll have it resolved by dinnertime."

"Thank you."

He held out his hand. I clasped it firmly between my own. "Dannie's plan was to upset you, and he's succeeded. Don't give him any additional satisfaction." I spoke with all the assurance I could muster, and was rewarded with a rueful smile. We both preferred to believe in the power of Dannie's twisted wit, but neither of us believed as fully as we wished.

CHAPTER THIRTEEN

I drew all afternoon, and by evening I had completed my illustration for Noah. When he came to collect my work he praised it mightily, but I took scant pleasure in his words, thinking only of poor Alger's dilemma. His tale had a gnarled and ugly shape. Tumorous. As the gas was being lighted I accompanied my anxious friend to Printing House Square, where he took refuge in a saloon and I mounted to the Lodging-house.

I arrived before dinner. Pushing past the line of boys signing in, I searched for Jemmie and located him at last hunkered down in a far corner, watching an arm-wrestling contest. When I called him aside he willingly followed.

"Where we going?"

"We must have a private talk."

"We can use the broom closet."

"Let's talk outside." I hoped Jemmie was as ill used as Alger in this matter, but I had no desire to test my faith in his innocence by being sequestered with him.

Jemmie skipped down the stairs, to all appearances his usual dreamy self. I walked us away from the *Sun,* toward the center of the square where the clatter of carriages afforded us privacy enough, searching for a way to broach my foul topic to this child placidly watching horses pass.

"Jemmie, tell me, have you been well treated at the Lodging-house?"

"Yessir."

"You haven't been bullied or abused by the older boys?"

"No sir."

"Nor by anyone else?"

"No sir."

"Are you satisfied with the way I've treated you?"

"Yessir."

"And Mr. Alger?"

"Yessir."

"Mr. Alger has treated you well?"

"Yessir."

A wave of relief passed through me. Jemmie seemed calm and friendly enough, if lost in his own world. "You haven't been in contact with the O'Connor boy, then?"

"Why?"

"He says he saw you yesterday night, but you were here yesterday night."

"I went out after." Jemmie twisted away from me.

I put my hand upon his shoulder and turned him back. He stiffened at my touch. "Did you talk to Dannie about Mr. Alger?"

"I's going inside now."

Jemmie pulled at me, eyes averted, but I gently maintained my grasp. "Dannie says you told him Mr. Alger abused you. Did you say that?"

"I's going inside."

I could not understand how Jemmie could maintain his presence at the Lodging-house, speak well of Mr. Alger, and perpe-

172

trate such a vicious lie. I spoke more harshly. "Did Mr. Alger abuse you?"

His only response was sullen silence. I squared him to me and leaned close, so he could not avoid my eyes. He stared through me to a point across the square, his features hardening into a cruel perfection, less Donatello than Caravaggio. I did not detect guilt in his look, rather the determination not to be dissuaded from his aims.

"If Mr. Alger abused you then you are duty bound to report him to the police, to protect the other boys. Did he hurt you in any way?" Jemmie remained stubbornly silent. "If Mr. Alger did not take liberties with you, when you say such things you commit a terrible injustice. You bring pain and dishonour to a good, kind man. You might even ruin him."

"Dannie says it won't hurt Alger 'cause nobody'll know."

"It has hurt him already, but it will hurt you and Dannie more. What you're doing is called blackmail. It is a serious crime and we shall summon the police and you and Dannie will be sent to Blackwell's Island."

"Dannie says you'd say that. He says that's bunkum. He says Alger'd cut off his own head afore he went to the law."

Jemmie squirmed, but I would not let him free. "Why are you risking your freedom for money? What will you do with five thousand dollars?"

He kicked at a paving block with his naked toe. "Hunnerd. Five hunnerd dollars."

"Dannie's squeezing Mr. Alger for five thousand. So he's cheating the both of you."

"All I need's five hunnerd." 173

"Why?"

"Callin'."

"What?"

"Me callin'."

Again he tried to free himself. I thought of his abortive talk
with Laura. "You mean your plan to go west and fight Indians?"

Jemmie nodded.

"Dannie's way leads only to Blackwell's Island."

Jemmie contorted his bony shoulders, and I let him slip from
my grasp and scamper across the square. We had nothing more
to say to each other. I stopped a boy and gave him a note telling
Mr. O'Connor I would not be teaching that evening, and I
walked as quickly as I could to the saloon where Alger waited.

The place was noisy and drenched in a tobacco fog, its
denizens disporting with the rambunctious insouciance of the
press. Alger played with an empty whiskey glass at an obscure
table in the rear, darting looks at the door. He could tell from
my manner that I did not bear good news. "They're in it together," he declared.

"I wish I could say otherwise."

"I'd never have thought it of the Hickok boy."

"Nor I. I tried to dissuade him. He was well fortified by
Dannie."

"That Dannie must be the devil incarnate."

"I'm not the person to advise you on this any further. You
must consult a lawyer."

"No lawyers."

"A good intimidating lawyer will scare Dannie out of this."

"Dannie won't be scared off."

"Surely you don't propose to pay him off?"

"This can't reach the police."

"It's arrant extortion. A proper lawyer will have it summarily squashed. I believe I can even recommend one." I thought of what Hummel could make of the notch in Dannie's ear.

"Word would leak. The penny sheets will feast upon it. Even the *Sun.* They'll craft some amusing headline about my Ragged Dick." He smiled thinly. "The Seligmans won't see the humor in it."

"You overestimate your importance."

"I'm of no importance, but the press will find the irony amusing. No boy will touch a book with my name on it. No parent or library would let him." He leaned into me. "Do you think he'll take a thousand?"

"A thousand or ten thousand, what difference does it make?"

"I can raise a thousand."

"If you pay, you prove their allegations."

"They're lying!"

His vehemence startled me. "I'm talking only of appearances."

"I'll collect a thousand dollars. Will you deliver it to Dannie?"

"You must go to the police." He glared at me. "I understand your reluctance. It's natural and human."

"You've no idea!" Spittle flew.

"My dear Alger, if I can be of any help as a friend it's to see your dilemma from a more objective perspective."

"If you're my true friend you'll do as I ask."

"It is my friendship, the profound debt I owe you, which prevents me from abetting the criminals who will ruin you." **175**

"This is not the time for moral niceties!"

"If you pay Dannie he'll bleed you dry."

"Jemmie won't."

"Dannie will find another pretty little boy."

"I could always kill him." Alger giggled mirthlessly. If Alger had thought murder would have extricated him from his dilemma, at that moment he would have seized upon it.

The barmaid appeared. I ordered soft cider, to preserve my faculties. Alger ordered another whiskey. He waited for her departure before he spoke.

"You must believe me when I tell you I am utterly blameless in this matter. I've never even been alone with the boy."

"Then you have the perfect defense."

"Perfect." Alger spoke with no conviction. "As perfect as Jemmie." He saw in my eyes that I thought the remark an odd one. "Come, come, William, he's a beautiful boy. You've told me that often enough. Doesn't his beauty cause you the least discomfort?"

"No."

"I find that difficult to believe."

"Well, I find it unsettling, I suppose. As Kant says, when I see such beauty, I cease to stand at the center of my own world."

Alger viewed me skeptically. "All that perfection, all that purity doesn't rouse the least desire to possess it?"

"No." The waitress returned. Alger downed his whiskey in a single gulp with the grimace of a man unaccustomed to hard liquor, and handed her the glass for another. "Have a drink."

"One of us should have a clear head."

176   "Ah, yes. Clear."

I had never seen Alger in such a sour and sullen state. I thought it my duty to cheer him. "Buck up, Horatio. The truth will out."

"Ah yes. The truth."

"Come, come, you of all people must give some credence to the sanity and common sense in the world."

"Why me?"

"Your books—"

"My books." The waitress returned. He downed another whiskey and handed over his glass for more.

"A bottle's three dollars."

"Alger, let's return to Mrs. Frye's. In the morning you'll see this with a keener eye."

"Bring on the bottle! And a glass for my friend!"

"Alger, I pray you—"

"You're a simple man, William, but you can't believe the world is like my books." He gave a drunken scowl. "What brought you here?"

"How do you mean?"

"Why did you magically appear at the Lodging-house in a well-cut suit without a penny to your name? Oh, of course, the thirty-four dollars, but that's hardly a birthright, is it?" He glared at me, daring me to answer.

"I don't wish to discuss it with you in your present state."

"But I do. The writer in me senses a story here. The prodigal son . . . Joseph in Egypt . . . What do you want with my boys?"

"You're drunk."

"And you are hiding something." The woman brought his bottle, and he poured us both a whiskey. He drank his own, **177** and when I did not touch mine he eyed it covetously and I pulled it beyond his reach. "As you'll not tell me your story, let me tell you a story of my own," he said, his speech slurring, "about a minister's son, stuck off in a dreary parish town, having tea with would-be dowagers."

"Really, Alger, I don't need to hear this."

Alger waved away my objection. "One of his duties, one of his less odious duties, was tutoring a boy in Bible, a boy quite like Jemmie in form, with the most delightful way of hopping onto a chair. His pious parents wouldn't have him play with the other boys, for fear they'd corrupt him." Alger laughed at that. "Of course the other boys despised him, and terrorized him." He poured himself another glass. "Imagine Jemmie in form, but Dannie in spirit. A boy never blessed with innocence. Though his tutor treated him with exaggerated propriety the boy sensed what he roused in the man, and took demonic pleasure in tormenting him, sitting upon his lap, touching his chin or his cheek. The tutor longed for and dreaded their daily hour. One day in late fall, after a nasty cold rain, the boy appeared at his tutor's door soaked in mud. He had been shoved in a puddle by some boys. He should have forgotten the lesson and returned home, only a few streets away, but no, he feared his parents' punishment." Alger barked a harsh laugh. "The fire in the room consumed much wood but emitted little heat, and when the boy intruded, the tutor had been huddled in its shallow aura with a blanket over his lap. He stripped off the boy's sodden clothes and wrapped him in the blanket, and they sat by the fire together. Chilled to the core, or playing for attention, the boy shivered beneath the heavy wool. The tutor rubbed his hands up and down the boy's body to warm him, conscious of the crisp bones and tender flesh beneath the fabric. The boy curled into the tutor, and smiling like a cat, he kissed the man. The touch of those lips dissolved the tutor's good intentions. . . ." Alger gazed at me, his eyes pathetic with drunken concern. "Is the tutor a monster, then?"

I said nothing. Though Alger's tale provoked a wave of nausea I could not attach my revulsion to this anxious creature. Alger, more intent upon confession than absolution, continued.

"The boy told his parents immediately. The tutor left town the same day, hiding in his father's house while his future was decided. The boy's father wished to prosecute, but the church council feared scandal, and satisfied itself with banishing him from the ministry. The boy's father, unhappy with the outcome, warned that should the tutor ever touch another boy, he would send him to hell *via* the penitentiary."

"So Dannie has found the perfect victim," I said.

Alger smiled his helpless smile. "New York is a sinkhole of depravity. Had I wished to become a predator of young boys I could have done so, and no one the wiser. I chose to inure myself to their baser attractions by elevating their virtues into literature." He drained his glass. "I reject those feelings, and by rejecting them, I become the person I wish to be."

I raised my whiskey in silent toast to Alger, a gesture which purged the last of his truculence. He was such a mediocre writer that I assumed his life came easy to him, but Alger's life was the greater work of art. He daily faced down demons as pernicious as my own, and shaped for himself an honourable existence. "If I may ask an impertinent question."

179

"You may."

"Do you pray?"

Alger made a sour face. "No God that I'd pray to would put these feelings in my chest."

"Then how do you find the will to live as you do?"

My evident sincerity embarrassed Alger. He supposed correctly that I was paying him a significant compliment. "I won't be living this way much longer unless I clean up this mess. I find it difficult to believe that Jemmie's a part of it."

"He's only asking for five hundred dollars, you know. The rest is Dannie's idea. Jemmie's obsessed with going west to fight Indians, and believes five hundred dollars will get him there."

Alger perked up. "He wants to go west?"

"To fight Indians."

"Let's ship him out with the Children's Aid Society! I can think of no one I'd rather be separated from by the Mississippi." Alger straightened his jacket with renewed sense of purpose, resurrecting his remarkable ability to spontaneously generate optimism. "I shall arrange it, but first I must speak with the darling little boy." He rose abruptly, staggered, and with a hiccough sank back into his seat.

"Return to Mrs. Frye's," I said. "I'll speak with him."

CHAPTER FOURTEEN

I framed my argument as I made my way back to the Lodging-house. I had appealed to Jemmie's moral instincts without success, yet I was convinced that the boy did have some sense of right and wrong. Apparently he believed he was serving a higher good by maligning Alger, sinning, but in the cause of fulfilling his destiny. If I could point him on a straighter road to the same end he would follow it. Dannie was a formidable opponent, however, and I had scant means of convincing Jemmie we could serve him as well. My best weapons, I decided, were truth and trust.

When I reached the *Sun* building the boys had returned from dinner. I searched for Jemmie, fearing that our previous encounter might have driven him off, and discovered him squirreled among the others. His presence, however, was not reassuring as to his state of mind, for it implied that he had such confidence in Dannie's pronouncements that he had no fear of my exposing him to O'Connor.

I kept a wary eye upon that gentleman while I closed on my quarry. Jemmie saw my approach and tried to keep his distance. I followed. With O'Connor watching I could not cut him from the flock, but he could not shake me either. We talked while we moved among the boys, guarding our words. **181**

"Jemmie, do you trust me?"

"Yeh."

"Do you trust Mr. Alger?"

"Yeh."

"Do you trust us more than you trust Dannie O'Connor?"

"I dunno."

"I think you do. Am I wrong?" Rather than reply Jemmie veered away toward a group of laughing boys. I intercepted him.

"We know that you are only trying to do what is best, and we wish to help you. You want to go west; we shall help you." Jemmie was mute. "If you take Dannie's five hundred dollars, how are you going to go west?"

"Locomotive."

"Have you ever taken a train?"

Jemmie nodded vigorously.

"Then you know that a small boy alone on a train is prey to all sorts of calamities. You can miss your train, or lose your ticket, or have it stolen from you. If a bigger boy learns you're carrying hundreds of dollars, how long will you hold on to your money? You need protection. You need guidance. If you let us help you, we'll make certain that you're safely transported. You will be sent with a group of boys and delivered to a good family who will love and look after you until you're old enough to fight Indians."

"Dannie says I kin fight Indians now."

"He says what he knows you wish to hear. Once you're west you may decide for yourself if you're prepared to fight Indians. You can't know from this distance what faculties it requires."

"I knows what I needs to fight Indians."

"Look at me, Jemmie." In trying to avoid me, Jemmie had backed himself into a corner and was casting his eyes about searching for an avenue of escape. I knelt to his level and waited patiently until his gaze met mine. I could not discern in his eyes if I had convinced him. I had nothing more to argue but the right on our side.

"You are at the crossroads of your life," I said. "Our way offers you the means to realize your dream, with hard work and determination. Dannie's way offers only money, and at a terrible price, for if you choose Dannie's way you'll look back on this day as the last that you breathed honest air. You'll live your life in degradation, cut off from all the good in the world. You'll wish for the power to return to this day, but it won't be granted to you. You'll live in hell, a hell you'll have made yourself, today."

Jemmie listened with opaque eyes, but the growing tension in his body revealed that my words had their effect. When I sentenced him to hell his face contorted in a mask of misery. "Are you afraid of Dannie?" I waited for tears that did not come. I knew then what he most needed to hear, because I knew what I most wished to hear. "Jemmie," I said, "you're a good boy, a brave boy, and you are not alone." I encircled him with my arms and held him close. Jemmie crumpled against my chest choking out great gasping sobs. O'Connor watched from across the room, but when my eye caught his he looked away.

———

Jemmie agreed to meet me in the square late the next morning, when Alger would have made the necessary arrangements and he could learn the details of his journey. I thought it important to provide him a specific chain of events to fasten upon. I even

183

told him Alger would buy him a new suit that day in anticipation of the trip. Jemmie appeared at the appointed time, arms laden with the late-morning edition of the *Sun*. Alger did not.

Anticipation rendered us both mute. I bought him an ear of hot corn. Jemmie sold a few papers. I could not discern if his faith was faltering. Mine was. I produced my Breguet repeater, and amused Jemmie by playing him the time.

When my watch struck noon, Alger's appointed hour to *rendezvous* with Dannie, he had yet to appear. Presenting Jemmie my timepiece to divert himself, I sequestered him in the stairwell of the *Sun* building and went forward in Alger's stead.

My memory of Dannie from our Lodging-house encounter was pleasant enough. He had charmed me with his wit and easy manner, and I had admired the strength with which he withstood O'Connor's intimidation. My own warm feelings frightened me, for now I saw his charm as seductive camouflage for an utter lack of compunction. With his winning ways the boy had blackmailed Alger and no doubt lifted my wallet. I thought it more than chance that he had stolen money from the one person most reluctant to pursue the matter and had blackmailed the one person most poorly equipped to resist his baldfaced lie. He had a genius for divining the weaknesses in others, and he found special pleasure in taking from us what we could least afford to lose. I wished to protect Alger, but I feared exposing my own frailties to a young man who could exploit them so ably and with such relish.

I met Dannie in the square, on the steps of the *Staats Zeitung* building, beneath the bronze gazes of Gutenberg and Ben Franklin. He greeted me with a friendly "Hullo," betraying no surprise at seeing me in Alger's stead. I kept a stern countenance, intent on revealing no more than was absolutely necessary to convince him that his plan had failed.

"Figgers Alger sends you to wash his linen for him."

"You know that Mr. Alger is blameless in this matter."

"There's blameless and there's blameless, ain't there?"

"I don't know what you're talking about."

"The man snogs boys. It's as plain as that weed of a moustache on his pretty little mouth."

"I'm not here to discuss Mr. Alger."

"Right, then, give us the money."

"I'm not here to pay you off, either."

Dannie darkened. For a moment an altogether different character emerged, hard and shrewd, as he scanned the square for trouble, and I realized he had chosen the steps of this building because they afforded him an unimpeded view. When he saw no evidence of a trap his grin returned. "A stall's no good. We got no patience. Jemmie's hot for justice."

"Jemmie's backed out."

"I'll have to hear that from him."

"He's leaving town."

"So it's kidnapping now, is it? First buggery, then kidnappin'."

"Think what you like. Jemmie doesn't want to see you again. If you go to the police he'll tell only the truth, that you tried to coerce him into betraying Mr. Alger."

"Now that's a lie. The story's Jemmie's. I was helpin' out a friend."

"I don't believe you. I can't imagine who will. Without Jemmie you've got less than nothing."

185

"Jemmie searched me out. He told me a story, I believed him. Now he's tellin' you another one. No sayin' what he's savin' for the police."

"How can you possibly think that I'd believe such swill?"

"You think you've got a baby saint there by his shiny little balls. It's t'other way round. He's leadin' you by the shorts, jes' like he led me, and when the time's ripe he'll give 'em a yank."

"Stay away from him. If O'Connor catches you skulking about he's likely to notch your other ear."

"You wasn't so happy 'bout that first time."

"This time I shall be."

"No sir. You're a soft-hearted fella. You'd feel sorry for Satan hisself."

"I'll do whatever is necessary to protect that boy from you."

"That I believe you would." Dannie grinned. "You tell Jemmie to take care now." He ambled off, as casual as if we had been discussing the weather. I watched him depart with a peculiar sense of dread. Dannie's words did not convince me that Jemmie had initiated this scheme, but they forced me to confront the obvious truth that he had been a willing, perhaps even active participant in perfecting it, and that thought caused the hairs on my neck to stand, as my old dread of Evil's place in the world took on Jemmie's perfect face.

I fought off my dark musings by concentrating upon more immediate concerns. Dannie had not behaved as if he had seen the last of Jemmie.

Jemmie awaited me at the door of the *Sun* building, peering at Dannie's departing figure.

186 "What'd he say?"

"What could he?"

"He's plenty sore."

"He won't hurt you. He's not the sort to use his fists."

Alger hallooed us from across the square, fast approaching with a bounce in his step. He patted Jemmie on the shoulder and told him to pack his bags because he was traveling to Kansas in two weeks. Kansas had recently been Indian territory, he explained, and the boys would travel by train, and when they arrived in Kansas the locals would hold a meeting in a church where everybody who wished to take in a boy would come and meet them. There would be many such families, Alger explained, because food grew in such abundance that children were counted a blessing, and the mere feeding of a young boy was not considered even the smallest of burdens. Jemmie replied that he would choose the Indian fighter who gave him a white horse, which he would name White Cloud. I saw no reason to deny Jemmie the pleasure of his hope. I congratulated Alger.

"It required some persistence. I donated fifty dollars to the Society and paid a boy twenty to put off his trip." Alger started up the Lodging-house stairs. "As he's been a Lodging-house resident, O'Connor must attest to his good character. I imagine he'll be happy to oblige." Alger produced a piece of paper which, oddly, made Jemmie flinch. He sat down on the bottom stair.

Alger drew me up the stairs with him. "How was your interview with Dannie?"

"I'd feel more secure if Jemmie stayed off the streets until he leaves for Kansas. Perhaps we can rent him a room."

187

Alger scowled. "That might be misconstrued."

"No doubt O'Connor will take charge of the boy." I could not fight Alger over this. My fears were purely speculative, likely the result of too great a regard for young Dannie's powers of mischief. In fact, Dannie's twisted attempt to exploit little Jemmie had resulted in his redemption.

The door to the common room was locked. Mrs. O'Connor opened to our knock. Alger kissed her upon the cheek in his enthusiasm and sought out her husband to trumpet Jemmie's good fortune. O'Connor agreed that this was a rare opportunity for a sensitive child and saw no difficulty in writing a sterling letter of recommendation. However, when we asked him to shelter Jemmie he was less amenable. He bade us summon Jemmie from below.

Jemmie would not come at first. I descended and took him by the hand. He returned me my pocket watch with the glum demeanour of a man on his way to the gallows. I did not realize that O'Connor inspired such dread.

Facing O'Connor, Jemmie covered it well. O'Connor spoke in his usual mild tones. "Tell me, Jemmie, and tell me true, are you afraid to go out on the street?"

"No sir."

"These gentlemen say you are. They say you fear the boy Dannie, whose ear I nicked. Is that true?"

"Yessir." Jemmie stole a glance at Alger and myself.

"Are you afraid he will hurt you?"

"No sir."

"What are you afraid of?"

"His eyes."

"His eyes?"

"Scary."

"He scares you with his eyes?"

"And words."

"He threatens you?"

"His words dig in. Like lice."

O'Connor was nonplussed. "I think what he means," I inter-jected, "is that Dannie is capable of persuading him to do bad things."

"Is that true, Jemmie?" asked O'Connor. "Does Dannie tempt you to sin?"

"Yessir."

"You know what I think of Dannie."

"Yessir."

"In this life you'll find many paths to damnation, and most will appear as rose-covered bowers. You must learn to shun them. Dannie is evil. You know that, don't you?"

"Yessir."

"When he speaks, don't listen. Tell yourself that he is evil and what he says, he says to hurt you. Shut your ears to his seduc-tions." Jemmie appeared to be paying scant attention. "I can't shield you from evil. Evil is all around us. You must teach your-self to recognize evil for what it is and shut it from your life. No one can do that for you. Do you understand what I'm saying?"

"Yessir." Jemmie pulled away, and O'Connor let him go. He ran to the window and gazed longingly down at the square. Minnie O'Connor, who had hovered just within earshot, drifted in our direction.

"He's no match for Dannie," I said.

189

"Whatever danger that boy's in is of his own making."

"He's nine years old."

"Then it's time he stood on his own feet. He's welcome to sleep here, but he'll be sent off with the rest of them."

Mrs. O'Connor touched his arm. "Dear," she said, "I can look after him."

"You are not his mother!" O'Connor shot back with uncharacteristic vehemence, before continuing with his usual intimidating calm. "Whatever his age, like it or not, the world has made a man of him."

O'Connor's tartness of tongue provoked me to retort with rather too much emphasis, "You're endangering the boy's whole future for the sake of principle."

O'Connor favored me with a rare smile. "If you're so concerned, place him in his father's care for the next two weeks."

"He's an orphan!"

"He's no orphan."

"Yes, he is."

Alger, who had kept silent in an endeavour to disguise his great stake in the outcome, could not refrain from speaking out. "Of course he's an orphan."

"Jemmie!" barked O'Connor. "Come here, please!" Jemmie ambled over. Dannie's dark prediction echoed in my head. "Tell me, Jemmie, and tell me true," said O'Connor. "Are you an orphan?"

"No."

"But you told everyone you're an orphan."

"So's I could stay here."

I looked at Jemmie's slack face and recalled his grotesque

disfigurement. What horrors he must have experienced to deny his parents. "Do your mother and father know you're here?" I said.

"Me mum is dead."

"Does your daddy know?"

"No." The blank expression had set in place.

"Why not?"

"He'd take me home."

"He beats you?"

"Only when he's drunk."

"He's drunk often."

"Mostly always."

Alger's cheek twitched. I surreptitiously waved him away so that his anxiety would not pollute Jemmie. I knelt close to the frightened lad and spoke in a low voice to emphasize that I was speaking man to man, the two of us. "Your father can't hurt you any more." Jemmie looked unconvinced. "Do you trust us, Jemmie? O'Connor and Alger and myself?"

"Yessir." The reply was mechanical.

"We're all committed to sending you west, but first we must consult your father. Your name isn't Hickok, is it?"

"No."

"What's your name?"

Jemmie's lips formed a tight line. Behind him, O'Connor smiled again. Apparently he found our predicament amusing. "We must know your father's name and where he lives so we may get his permission."

"He don't want me to go west. He don't want me to go nowheres."

"We'll convince him." Alger hovered too near, then backed off. "Jemmie is your real name?"

"Yes."

"And what is your surname?" Jemmie's face could have been a death mask. "We are very determined and very persuasive men. We'll convince your father to send you west."

"Won't do no good."

"Have I ever lied to you?" The lip bent, a tiny fissure in his façade. I persisted. "You're right to be afraid. If we fail, your father could reclaim you. But saying nothing is also a choice. Saying nothing is choosing no to Kansas and no to White Cloud." I was nose to nose with Jemmie, but he made no move to pull away. I waited. He whispered a word I did not catch. "What?"

"Swear."

"I swear to you we'll get you west."

"Swear on Laura's head."

I raised my hand. "I so swear."

"Larkin."

"Larkin," I repeated.

"Jonas Larkin. Thirty-eight Baxter Street."

I hugged his slender body to my chest. "You are as brave as any Indian fighter who ever lived." Jemmie tolerated my grip but did not reciprocate. Alger and I set off in search of Jonas Larkin, and with a kiss upon the top of his head Mrs. O'Connor turned Jemmie out into the world.

———

CHAPTER FIFTEEN

In my fragile condition, I had responded to the mass and density and tumultuous velocity of this city as do many of the more vulnerable New Yorkers, by carving a particular path as an animal might cut a path through dense jungle and hewing faithfully to that route in my comings and goings from my lodgings to Printing House Square and City Hall Park. I now accompanied Alger in a new direction, northeast on Chatham Street, walking in the shadow of an elevated metal road, absorbing the grit and clangour of that raw iron artery as it pumped streams of workers to and fro from upper Manhattan. In our brief stroll the character of the street changed with astonishing rapidity, the great buildings of politics, press, and commerce yielding to a crowded street of crumbling structures: cheap lodging-houses and cellar concert saloons interspersed with shops crammed with all manner of clothing from rags to faded finery, and pawnbrokers offering their random collections of hostage goods, no doubt much of it stolen. We were accosted several times by shabby Jews pulling at our sleeves, steering us toward their troves of 'sheap' clothing, eager to offer us a bargain and expropriate our funds. Alger remarked that he was never accosted when he walked the street alone. They never bothered city men; apparently I still had the aura of *Ausländer* about me.

In a scant three blocks we reached Baxter and turned north, abandoning the street bazaar for blank brick interlarded with crazily leaning board barns, blind façades hiding hives of activity. Garbage lay in drifts, like summer snow. The odors of the stable succumbed to the offal odors of slaughterhouse and bone-boiler.

Amid this desolation crowds of local inhabitants went about the business of their lives, to the din of peddlers hawking rotting produce. A woman and her daughter scuttled by bent in half like crabs, carrying mounds of half-sewn garments like huge soft shells upon their backs. In three more blocks Park and Worth converged on Baxter forming a jagged star of streets marked by a tiny park, two forlorn trees protected from neighborhood children and goats by a fence pocked with gray rag shreds hung by scavengers to dry. This, said Alger, was the notorious Five Points, and the park was Horace Greeley's accomplishment. It seemed a small victory. We continued up Baxter. The street narrowed further. Wooden structures were crowded out entirely by brick. Men loitered upon crudely built stoops eyeing us through hooded eyes, as if wondering what grief we had come to inflict and who would be our victims.

Alger and I avoided their stares by discussing the best strategy for dealing with Jonas Larkin. Alger had recovered from his earlier dismay and was now confident of success. "I'll present it, of course, as a great service he's performing for his son. Surely even Jonas will see that it's best for the boy. I'll threaten prosecution for abusing the child if he refuses."

"And if he says no?"

"Impossible."

"If he does?"

"Buying off the father is worse in ethical terms than buying off Dannie, I suppose, as Jonas is selling his own flesh, and he'll squander the money on drink, but it's definitive. Once Jemmie's gone Jonas can't extort more." Alger lowered his voice. "I have in my pocket five hundred dollars' cash I collected for my visit to the Children's Aid Society. The sight of greenbacks will be irresistible. For cash, that sort of man would sell his son to Gypsies."

I was not heartened by Alger's disclosure. We were bringing a small fortune into the toughest section of the city, to negotiate with a man of whom we knew nothing except the awful dread which he inspired in his son. A father who evoked such a response must be an extraordinarily malevolent presence. Even if Alger could convince Jonas that his interests were served by accepting the bribe, Jonas might yet refuse if more satisfying mischief could be caused another way. I imagined an adult with Dannie's wile and lack of compunction, vicious and goaded by drink. I imagined how he might react when a stranger waved money in his face, offering to send his son away from him forever. The fact that the son feared him and had been hiding from him for weeks would only make such a man more likely to strike out. Myopic Alger at five foot two and myself hobbled by ailments would hardly present formidable opponents. If he was bully enough to beat a nine-year-old, our weakness would only goad him on. "Perhaps we should engage a constable to escort us."

"Prudence," replied Alger, "lies in keeping this matter far from the authorities."

Thirty-eight Baxter Street was a narrow brick box punctured by four rows of featureless windows. To call it a bleak warehouse for humanity would be to slander the elegantly constructed buildings west of Broadway which housed more valuable merchandise. We descended to the basement grog-shop, a cave barren of furniture save for a few stools and a keg of sour beer, where in the dark shapeless forms huddled over tin cups and a toothless hag argued with a man who had drawn too much beer. When we entered, she ceased. All eyes examined us. Before we could frame a question she asked her own, in heavy Cockney brogue.

"So yer lookin' for Larkin then?"

Alger concealed his surprise beneath an air of official dignity. "Jonas Larkin."

"You've taken yer bloody time about it." The proprietress rapped the keg sharply, eliciting a dull throb, and spoke to her clientele. "I 'ears what's there and I's back in a flash."

We followed her outside and into a meanly proportioned entry. I had never before visited this class of dwelling. I had anticipated the utter absence of ornament, the cramped proportions, the lack of air and light as the logical if inhumane result of cheap construction, but I had imagined it in a sort of ideal state of arid deprivation, and instead I found a rank world crawling with the filth of decades, alive with the fetid odors of grime and soot and cheap candle grease, of rotting food and rotten timber and effluvia of human, pig, and goat. The old woman trod upon a baby at play in the muck.

She led us through the house and out the back, to a cramped shadowed yard of mud and broken bricks overhung with a web of clotheslines. Eight rickety privies occupied the space like drunken sentinels. She pointed to the building behind. "Basement."

We picked our way forward until the old woman halted just before it, where a four-foot manhole revealed a sluggish cataract of human excrement dripping into a cesspool a few feet beneath. She pointed to some steps. We descended.

A narrow pane of glass, its bottom level with the manhole, admitted a view of oozing effluvia but no air. The room was filled with the honeyed odors of the cesspool wafting from beneath the floorboards, infused with the more immediate smell of stale vomit. A heap of rags lay upon a dun pallet, once straw, now matted with human excretory fluids. I went to it. The rags concealed a withered man with sunken face and blue skin, frozen by *rigor mortis* in a pose of twisted agony, drained as if by a giant suction pump of all his bodily fluids. I stepped back. "Cholera."

"Dead?" asked Alger, hanging by the door. He made no effort to keep hope from his voice.

"Yes." I felt a peculiar mix of emotions. This man had met with a terrible fate, yet if he was the monster I had imagined, his death might have lessened the *quanta* of misery in this world. At any rate, Jemmie was free.

I heard a whimper, perhaps a dog's whine. I followed the sound to a pile of crusted rags in the darkest corner. When I turned it toward me I saw a ghastly blue face distended in the agonies of cramping. It appeared to be a young woman.

"Please . . ." With her last strength she held out a bundle, as besmirched as herself. I accepted it. The bundle weighed nothing at all.

I parted the cloth to reveal an infant's perfect form, but so desiccated I might have been viewing mummified remains dead a thousand years. The eyeballs were shriveled, and the skin had contracted about the skull, drawing back the lips from the tiny toothless mouth in a grimace of ghastly delight. From its stiffness I judged the child dead at least four hours.

I prised open the young woman's half-closed eye, and the eyeball showed only white. Drained of life by vomiting and diarrhea, she was only with great effort maintaining consciousness. If she lapsed into a stupor I was quite certain she would die. "Can you hear me?"

She reached out to touch the baby. "Sam." She stroked him in my arms as if he still had life. Apparently the work of saving him was all that kept her from her coma.

"Don't worry about the baby. Worry about yourself. I'm a doctor."

"A doctor." She spoke the words with a lilt of hope.

Though the exact span of the disease may vary from two days to a week, cholera follows a predictable course. After the initial purging diarrhea and subsequent vomiting, the blood pressure falls and the pulse is faint. Muscular cramps may be severe, and thirst intense; as dehydration occurs, the patient becomes stuporous and comatose, and lapses into shock. If a patient reaches this final phase he will not recover. This young woman was in the cramping phase.

Traditional treatment was blood-letting, though its benefit was not established. Calomel or tincture of opium had proven useful upon occasion. In truth, medical science had no more than a descriptive knowledge of the disease. The patient lost fluids, the patient died.

I used my handkerchief to clean her caked lips. She looked at me with eyes soft with illness and trust. My duty was to bolster her reserves of strength. My only tool was her faith in me. Though I was utterly convinced of the impotence of medicine, I had to act with the sure competence of the surgeon. To do otherwise would be to murder my patient by killing her hope.

"Water!" She gestured at a filthy pail. I procured it. British army doctors withheld all liquid from cholera victims, administering purgatives instead. Their patients died as quickly as any. I took the tin cup from the pail and poured the murky liquid down her throat. She swallowed weakly.

I strove to move with authority and speak with assurance. "Alger! Find me clean water. And salt. Immediately." He disappeared. "Do not be afraid," I crooned, "there is nothing to fear. Your body is purging itself of fluids. We must simply feed it fluids in sufficient quantity to replace them."

"How long?"

"Until your body tires of purging. I shall feed them to you. We must add salt because the fluids rob your body of salt."

"Not me. Sam." Weakly she pushed me to care for the infant.

I feared the baby's death would drain her of purpose, but I could not have her spirit divided and sacrificing itself. "Sam is dead."

"No!" With surprising force she wrenched the stiff bundle from my grasp and rocked it at her bosom.

"Sam is dead," I said. "I cannot bring him back."

"No!"

"Jonas is dead, and Sam is dead. Only you're alive." She rocked and cooed to Sam. Though she acted as though Sam still lived, I suspected she had long known he was gone. I spoke what I thought she wished to believe. "If you die, Sam's memory is erased from this earth. If you live, Sam lives in you. Live. Live for Sam." She gave a cry of pain. "You will live. I shall save you." She sank into my arms.

I brought more water to her lips. This time she drank with animal thirst. Her stomach convulsed, forcing liquid from her mouth and her nether portions, spreading a fresh wet stain across her smock, subsuming her thirst in intestinal agony. "Drink," I said. She shook her head. "Drink," I repeated. Her eyes brimmed with pain. I smiled my most Hippocratic smile. She forced herself to swallow another sip.

Alger appeared with a pail of water and a handful of salt. He mixed the two, and I fed it to the girl, chatting to keep her conscious and alert.

"What's your name, my dear?"

"Emma. Emma Larkin."

"Are you Jemmie's sister?"

"Yes."

"Jemmie is alive and well and sends you his love." She smiled. "You must get well for Jemmie."

"We'll take you to the hospital," said Alger.

200   "No," I said, "No hospital. She's under my care." If they didn't bleed or purge her to death they would kill her with neglect. I touched her brow. "I will see you well."

"The grog-shop woman thought we were public health officials. They must be on their way. When they arrive, she'll have no choice."

"Then we must move her now."

Alger walked to the door. "Let me see what I can find."

I do not know how long Alger stayed away. I did not think of him, or the imminent health officials. I devoted my attention to Emma, coaxing her from one sip to the next. She fought me, knowing I would force her to drink. Her resistance seemed to give her strength.

Alger returned bearing a clean smock. With gentle speed we stripped Emma's dry, cold limbs of her stinking rags. Her breasts showed no swelling in the *aureolae,* her belly no *Linea Negri,* the darkened line of hairs and pigment which marks the recent mother. Sam was her brother, then.

"What?"

"We're moving you to a better place."

"Sam."

"We can't take him."

"Sam!" She twisted away from us as we lifted her, but her frail efforts barely added to her weight. A stain spread across her midriff. She continued to struggle as we carried her out the courtyard and through the tenement to the street, and I spoke to soothe her. "Sam is beyond all pain. Beyond our reach. We can't take him with us. I promise you I'll see he's properly laid to rest." She ceased her agitations, soothed by my words or depleted of her last stores of strength. I meant to honour my

201

promise. If the public health men did their job they would transport Jonas and Sam to the new morgue, where I might claim the bodies and arrange proper burial.

A white-smocked cart man awaited in the street with his flat-bottomed two-wheeled vehicle. "This is the best I could manage," said Alger. We laid Emma flat upon the platform. Alger jumped up beside the driver.

"Where does he take us?"

"The grog-shop woman named a place."

We had no time to discuss the matter further. While I attended to Emma, placing my coat beneath her and resting her head upon my lap, a large black wagon with the markings of the Public Health Service appeared and two men in bowler hats alit, making toward our patient in the cart, shouting, "You there! Stay!"

Alger must have paid the cart man well, for when he punched the man's shoulder the cart jerked into motion, leaving the bowler hats in our wake, its single axle jouncing violently over the cobblestones. I tried to cushion Emma from the worst of the shocks and prayed she would live until we reached our destination.

We bounced up Baxter to Canal Street and thence to Broadway, faster than this primitive conveyance was meant to travel, Alger trying to keep his seat beside the driver and I clinging to Emma upon a bed more commonly used for transporting bed posts or turnips than human beings. Bad as the pounding was, I felt constant fear that we might be brought to a halt by the traffic and the nature of my patient's disease be revealed, leaving us to the mercy of a populace furious at its dissemination. Emma would certainly be taken from us.

We reached Broadway without incident and lost ourselves among the mass of traffic until Broome, when we turned west and soon stopped at a brown-stone residence. Alger mounted the steps. I watched him converse with a large, once-handsome woman in a plum-colored gown and follow her into the house. Emma begged for water. "Soon," I said. "Soon you'll have clean sheets and a soft bed."

Alger returned. "It's settled."

"Does she know we have a cholera patient?"

"I didn't say and she didn't ask. She's very discreet."

We carried our patient carefully up the steps and into a well-appointed entry. The woman, whom I came to know as Mrs. Rutledge, greeted us with a silent nod, and led us without comment upstairs to a bed-sitting room at the back of the house. She indicated a wash stand with a tap, a rarity then. "Water. I understand you wish salt."

"Please, and additional sheets and towels."

She left us to settle our patient into bed. We stripped off Emma's smock, and I made a crude effort to wash her limbs before we laid her down. The water made her twitch, but the clean sheets acted like a balm upon her skin. Mrs. Rutledge appeared with the salt, and I prepared the saline solution and administered it to Emma. She drank with great gasping gulps, oblivious of the sour taste, and her weary eyes closed. I feared she was comatose, but no, she slept.

"Alger," I said, weak with relief myself, "I can't imagine how that crone could have directed us to such a discreet and generous woman. We're in the hands of a true Samaritan."

"I can't speak to Mrs. Rutledge's virtue, but I know she makes a good living by not asking questions. You're in a house of assignation."

"Aha." I washed my hands at the basin with a fine lavender soap. "This room must be costing a fortune. We'll move her tomorrow."

"I've paid for a month. That was required. She'll be fed as well."

"You're the true Samaritan."

"I'd already said good-bye to the money. I was certain it would end up poured down Jonas's throat. This is a far better use for it." He stammered slightly, embarrassed by his own largesse. "I should be off. Jemmie will be at the Lodging-house by now."

"Bring him this evening. He'll lend Emma strength."

"He'll be eager to see her."

"Perhaps you can provide me with a change of clothing from Mrs. Frye's. I shall be here for a few days."

"You're the Samaritan, William."

Alger departed. I sat beside Emma and watched her sleep. I was not feeling virtuous. I had not chosen to act well. I had not chosen at all. Perhaps I was committing the greater evil by spreading the cholera. Emma would in all probability die despite our efforts. A weariness overcame me, but also a certain peace. Oddly, in spite of the jostling of the dray cart and the burden of conveying Emma to her present abode, I experienced no dorsal spasms. I slept.

Emma's moans awoke me. Outside, the gas was lit. I poured a tumbler of saline and held it to her lips. She drank, and I poured another, and another, and when she refused I persisted, encouraging her with the promise of Jemmie's impending visit. The good woman of the house brought a tray of barley soup and beef stew. I poured some of the soup down Emma and ate the stew myself. As I was mopping the last of it with a crust of fresh-baked bread, Alger announced himself below. I heard his solitary step heavy upon the stair. Emma looked to the door, hoping for her brother. Alger entered. His eyes bore an indecipherable expression of loss.

"Jemmie is gone."

CHAPTER SIXTEEN

Alger spoke heartily, exuding a forced confidence that Jemmie would materialize at any moment, saying that he had, with O'Connor's permission, sent the newsies abroad to spread the word that Jemmie had nothing more to fear from Jonas, with the promise of a ten-dollar bill for the boy who brought him home. Nonetheless Jemmie's absence weakened Emma, and I tended to her crisis while Alger watched, torturing his moustache with such violent twists that I finally asked him to leave, lest his fears cause unintended harm. I walked him out the door with reassuring words.

Alger was not appeased. "Jemmie betrayed Dannie, and Dannie has a perverse sense of justice."

"Dannie won't injure him. Assault lacks wit."

"Then he may be planning worse." Alger gave his moustache another yank. "To speak the truth, I'm afraid for myself."

"Engage a private detective."

"Private detectives are a suspicious lot, and assume the worst of all parties, most especially their employers."

I clasped his shoulder to reassure him. "By this time tomorrow you'll be bringing Jemmie here to see his sister."

"Of course, of course," he said, without conviction, and hurried down the stairs. I returned to my patient.

I attended Emma without assistance, not only to conceal the presence of the cholera but also because she needed my personal attention. Saturating her digestive system with salt water would most probably do no harm, but I had no assurance it would do much good. The efficacy of the treatment lay in her faith in me and my powers as physician. I played the role to the best of my ability, solemn and precise at times, cheerful and encouraging at others, always serenely confident in my result. She retched and spasmed, in agony ejecting from the anus what I forced in the mouth, but still she drank, eyes slitted by pain and exhaustion, suckling like a hungry lamb on the rim of the glass. Her faith swallowed my doubt. I could not allow myself to question my role as saviour lest my misgivings break the spell which kept her grasping for life. Holding the glass to her lips, I became the person she required of me. For those moments I knew who I was and what I believed the world to be.

When, drained of sustenance and exhausted by her continual purging, she lapsed into a comatose sleep perhaps never to awaken, my doubts rushed back redoubled. Then I would lave her person and change the bedclothes certain that I would never be required to repeat the task, berating myself as an arrant charlatan, a liar, and a hypocrite, denying this woman her sole possession on this earth, the right to a dignified death. I would lapse into an agitated sleep, vowing that when I awoke I would upend the damnable pitcher and tell her firmly that she might spare herself considerable pain by accepting her fate, only to be roused by her cries for water, and her beseeching

207

look would once again bury my doubts and summon the strong doctor to her side.

We struggled on in this fashion for some days, I know not how many. Alger did not reappear, and I had no one else in my life who would remark upon my absence, save perhaps Mrs. Frye and Noah Wapner, and no responsibilities save earning my keep, which necessity seemed distant and abstract compared with my current occupation. We lived, the two of us, in a cocoon of timeless isolation. Finally, one evening as I changed her linen Emma turned away from me with feminine modesty, and I knew that she would live. Her skin lost its bluish hue and took on a more supple texture. She gained control of her bowels and the strength to take herself to the lavatory.

If I had not saved her, I had provided her with means to save herself. For the first time in my thirty years of life, I could honestly claim to have landed more than a glancing blow upon the life of a fellow human being. Yet what had I actually done? I had only provided Emma Larkin with the opportunity to believe in her own future. Such is the gap, I thought, which separates us one from the other.

Emma did not victimize herself with such hairsplitting. As her organism ceased dying and began to heal itself her energy of spirit returned, fueled with the optimism of her growing strength. Though frail, she reasserted the mystery of her body, as if I had never washed and tended to her most intimate parts. I of course respected her pretense, and as her form and color returned it was pretense no longer, for the blue shriveled corpse I had watched over was an altogether different creature from the one that now occupied that same bed. A delicate perfection of feature, so similar to Jemmie's, emerged. She was a wounded faun, a denizen not of Baxter Street but of the Forest of Arden, a slender woodland nymph with skin of ethereal translucence and amber eyes still liquid from her illness.

Her wraith-like aspect was enhanced by her silence. She shared her brother's quality of pensive introspection and seemed content to lie quietly, rapt in thought. At first I deemed this a phase of her illness, but I discovered with time that such tranquillity was essential to her nature. Emma was not stupid, but she did not parade her wit. She would answer my questions simply and directly, without elaboration, and she did not inquire much of me. It sufficed that I was a friend of Jemmie's. In consequence I spoke little as well. In silence I maintained my appearance as the confident healer, a manner I could not have sustained beyond the privacy of that chamber but one I wore well in her presence, and a role which in the playing imparted a gratifying sense of self-assurance. We spent hours together virtually mute, yet I was not bored. She radiated peace. My time with her left me cleansed and refreshed.

Her first concerns were for her brother Sam. True to my word, I visited the new Dead House in the basement of Bellevue Hospital by the East River, a dungeon with a tiled floor where corpses lay exposed upon stone slabs beneath a constant spray of water. I saw a young woman, to judge by her bloated form reclaimed from the river, a pale man badly slashed about the neck, an infant, not Sam, and, mercifully, no Jemmie. Cholera victims, I was told, were buried immediately in the potter's field.

Upon my return to Emma's lodgings Alger awaited, mightily

relieved to see Emma risen from the dead, but bearing no word of Jemmie. I reported to Emma that Sam was gone to the potter's field. As was her habit Emma took the double blow quietly. Alger bantered gamely, without raising her spirits, that the news his sister was well would bring Jemmie at a run. I saw him to the door.

There his heartiness faded. He reached into his pocket and pressed some bills into my hand. "She'll need fresh clothing, and you must pay your rent."

"This is beyond generous." I tried to return the money, but he would not take it.

"I've moved in with the Seligmans."

"So it's Fifth Avenue for you now."

"No more of Mrs. Frye's indecipherable stews."

"Are you done with Printing House Square, then?"

Alger nodded. "The five boys are all I can handle. I'm more of a guardian, really. Mrs. Seligman is quite ill."

"The newsies will miss you."

"I shall miss them." He smoothed his moustache with a bashful smile.

"You will continue to write."

"Certainly. I'll discourse with the boys through my pen."

"And we shall talk."

"Yes."

We shook hands for what we both understood to be the final time. Just as Alger could not afford to remain among the boys, he could not maintain our friendship. He knew too little of me and I too much of him. "You're a good man, Alger," I said.

"William," he said, "whoever in hell you are, I hope to God

you find a worthy place." And he skipped down the steps and from my life. I had followed Alger to New York. Now I was on my own.

———

Emma held out no hope of seeing Jemmie again. I did not explain the tangled causes of his disappearance, and she seemed to take it for granted that the city had consumed him. She focused her energies instead upon seeing that Sam had a decent resting place. I made enquiries with the Health Department, which directed me to the office of the Charity Commissioner, and it offered small solace, but said that a family member might take its packet boat to Hart Island and attempt to claim the body. Emma wished to leave immediately, but I insisted she first regain her strength and then purchase some presentable clothing. She professed satisfaction with her stained smock, which was indeed far superior to the rags we had found her in, but knowing the effect of clothes upon women, I hoped that a fair ensemble might allow her to view herself with sufficient *amour-propre* that she might lay aside her tragedies and plan a better future.

Emma gained strength with such rapidity that she seemed to will herself healthy that she might attend to Sam's requirements. First, however, I attended to hers. Ignorant as I was of the subtleties of female attire, I escorted her to A. T. Stewart's, which vast emporium I was told would fulfill all her needs. It was housed in a gigantic iron cage, clad entirely in window panes, and the ground floor was a cornucopia of dry goods of every description, from the most elaborate silk brocades to the simplest muslin for the poorest clientele. I was charmed

211

by Emma's remarkable ease among the crowd, unintimidated even by the most richly appointed ladies, as if conscious she belonged to the natural aristocracy of beauty but evincing none of the vanity usually attendant upon this realization. When at her insistence, and to her delight, we rode in the 'elevator' to the second story, where ready-mades were located, I understood that her comfort lay in a girlish excitement of curiosity, and that I was the one who thought her beautiful.

When Emma was confronted with the panoply of finished garments delight turned to awe. I selected a sensible young saleswoman and entrusted Emma to her care, with the understanding that she would outfit the girl with all the necessaries but not exceed fifty dollars in total cost, as Alger had given me eighty-five. I toured the displays of silks and laces and calicoes, shawls, gloves, and Yankee notions, conspicuous in the crowds by virtue of my sex, mutually avoiding the glances of my few fellow males, and took refuge for a time in the basement carpet-making department, reportedly the largest room in the world, but upon my return Emma sent me away again, and I was reduced to sitting in a corner, watching the traffic fight its way onto Broadway from Ninth Street, until I felt a hand upon my arm and I turned to see my willowy sylph transformed by corset and bustle into a shapely young lady of fashion. I rose and bowed with mock solemnity. Emma curtsied with an uncharacteristic gaiety. She wiggled her hips, remarking with a giggle that she had never worn a bustle before and it made her feel like a horse in harness, and drew back her skirt to show off the kid boots encasing her delicate feet. The saleswoman, seeing my pleasure, remarked that as a result of Emma's natural

good taste in matters of fashion, with even the most parsimo-
nious care we had spent seventy-five dollars, but that of course
we might find inferior goods at the lower price if I insisted.
Emma sagged in disappointment and stripped off her glove. I
told her that would not be necessary. She threw her light arms
around my neck, hugging herself to my chest. The laughter on
her lips was well worth the added sum.

––––

Though I tried to dissuade Emma from what I knew would be
a frustrating and painful excursion, she was determined to
make her peace with Sam. Her insistence was all the stronger
because Jonas was never mentioned. When I saw I could not
stop her, I arranged for us together to ride the Charity Commissioner's packet boat to Hart Island. It was a day of unseason-
able heat, a final spasm of summer before the inevitable cold.
We sat at the bow to catch the breeze and to spare ourselves the
sight and smell of tiny caskets piled upon the deck. Emma had
brought a bouquet of pansies to lay on the grave. She said Sam
would not recognize lilies.

Hart Island was a low windswept desert, a barren corpse of
land. Potable water was shipped in with the pine coffins. Con-
victs dug the pits. I consulted a baton-wielding guard, who
pointed vaguely at a field behind him. We traipsed in the heat
among acres of trenches proportioned as coffins but wide as a
coffin was long, shrunk in the presence of these massive graves
to the relative size of maggots, until we came upon a freshly
covered trench marked by a pine board which enumerated the
likely date for Sam's interment. The occupants were itemized
by their approximate ages. There were many. The coffins were

213

laid three stories deep, shoulder to shoulder. Even here, space had value.

Emma scrutinized the list. It contained Jonas Larkin's name, and half a dozen male babies, most listed as John Doe. "Is Sam in here then?"

"Almost certainly."

"How may I claim him?"

"We don't know which he is."

"I would know."

"After weeks in the ground, I think not."

"I would know."

"I've enquired already. They won't allow you to disturb the others. It's not possible."

She contemplated the secrets beneath the turned earth. "When we had a bureau, Sam slept in the drawer. He liked feeling shut in. Can he go to heaven from here?"

"So far as I know, the believers of the world are unanimous that the soul of a baby, wherever he may lie, rises straight to heaven."

"If his soul's in heaven, it don't matter where his bones lie."

"No."

She held the pansies to her chest, kissed them, and placed them beside the marker. Then she handed me her hat, placed a blue kerchief upon the ground, and kneeling with care so as not to soil her clothes she placed both hands on the rough earth and pressed her cheek against it. With eyes shut tight, witness to some inner vision, she spoke in a clear declarative tone. "Good-bye, Sam." Then she rose, cleaned her face with the kerchief, retrieved her hat, and made for the dock without a backward glance.

We caught the packet's return run. Emma gazed into the waters and spoke little during the trip. I too refrained from conversation. The raw, inescapable fact of the potter's field made soothing words worse than meaningless and mocked idle chitchat. I feared that the ferocity of our excursion might crush my patient's rising spirits, as indeed those of any sensible human being, and I felt the peculiar conviction that were I not so concerned for my patient, I should myself be plunged into the depths of despair. When we landed at the Battery in the early afternoon, I therefore put on a cheerful countenance and told Emma that having made her excursion, there was time yet in the day for an excursion I had always wished to take. Maintaining an air of mystery, I bade her board the Broadway stage. By keeping her guessing about our final destination I hoped to lead her mind away from sorrowful contemplation.

While the bustle of the trip up Broadway succeeded in distracting Emma, the heat and noise drained her energy. I worried that I might be taxing her strength to take such a protracted journey, but when we reached Madison Square and I wished us to transfer to a Fifth Avenue omnibus, Emma insisted we continue. Atop the vehicle in the open air we surveyed the stately march of sumptuous dwellings and the spidery scaffolds erecting St. Patrick's Cathedral and alit at Fifty-ninth Street. There I hoped to find my antidote to the horrors of Hart Island in the sylvan reaches of Central Park.

We passed through a simple iron gate in a low stone wall,

and descended to the shores of a pond girt by the craggy granite spine of Manhattan Island. Though the effect was romantic wilderness the hand of man was no less present than at Hart Island, and that knowledge made the vista all the more soothing. Emma picked up a flat pebble and expertly skipped it across the water. I tried to match her skill and plunked one to the bottom. She rooted among the stones until she found a fistful of likely candidates, and instructed me in the art of angling the stone and snapping my wrist. I was a poor student, and that amused her. I observed that she must have practiced a great deal to attain such proficiency, and she admitted she had, when she had lived on a farm and tended cows. She spoke of the cows by name and described their foibles with precision and grace, as those of close friends, and even now, as I think back upon her words, I believe they revealed a ready wit and a clear eye for the beauty in simple things. Her greatest pleasure, she said, had been once when her father had procured a quantity of ice at Easter, and after services he had mixed it with salt and miraculously transmuted milk into ice cream.

We ambled through twisting paths, kicking fragile gold and russet leaves, and climbed a grassy hill to a rusticated Gothic barn crowded with children, where pure milk and other childish refreshments were served. Here I purchased us ice cream, the first for Emma since that Easter transubstantiation. We sat among the youngsters rolling in the grass while Emma lapped her dollop with a dainty tongue, sculpting it in small careful licks to prolong her enjoyment.

Emma was growing fatigued. The Dairy, as the structure was called, was situated above a sunken road which led from the park. Extravagantly I engaged a waiting hack to return us to Broome Street. After such a tiring day the stopping and starting, the swaying and bouncing exercised on her a soporific effect. She leaned upon my chest. I encircled her slight shoulders with my arm and attempted to shield her from the roughest jolts while she slept. Although I could not imagine sleeping through such jostling, my back, usually a sensitive barometer of agitation, recorded no discomfort.

At Broome Street I gently disengaged from Emma, intending to bid farewell for the evening. She awakened much refreshed. Another carriage was pulling up, and a belle swathed in emerald satin entered Emma's building.

"How long I's at Broome Street?" she said.

"Until next Tuesday."

"I must find me a place." She spoke with matter-of-fact resolve. "Find work."

This inevitability had been in both our minds from the moment we knew she would not die, but I had thought it better for us not to discuss her future until she had the strength to voice her own concern. "What do you do?"

"Whatever. Piece work. Sew. Feather fans. Glue paper to cigar tins."

"Hard work."

"Easier without Daddy drinkin' all the money. Gluin' tins was best. I made more'n fifty cents a day, the days Sam let me. Glue gived me headaches though."

I thought of the girl working every hour there was light while tending to the baby. "What would you prefer to do?"

"I'd like a clean place. A place to wear these fine clothes. **217**

A. T. Stewart's maybe, but they don't need me. I asked. The woman what sold the clothes said they's full up, and anyways they needs experience in the trade."

"Perhaps we could find you a place in a store which is not quite so prominent."

"Or domestic service. A good house would be grand. I asked Mrs. Rutledge, but she's full up. Good house'll ask for good word on me from another good house. I'll be gluin' tin."

"I'll see you find your place."

"How you gonna do that? You need a maid?"

"No. I'm a lodger."

"You got work?"

"Not exactly."

"So help yourself. Don't worry about me." She spoke with evident sincerity and a touch of pride.

"I saved your life. In the South Seas, when a man saves another's life he's responsible for that person forever."

She laughed. "They got that backwards, don't they?"

"It makes perfect sense. They believe that in saving a man's life one cheats the gods, causing them to abandon the man in anger, so the saviour now must act as that man's personal god."

"Here we got but one God and he's not around much anyways."

"The principle remains. If I intervene on your behalf, that creates a responsibility on my part to see you safe."

"You save someone, they's the one owes you!"

"They didn't choose to be saved. It's the act of one's own free will that creates obligation."

218

"You got a way a thinkin' so hard you turn things inside out. Let's eat."

She descended from the hack. I remained, thinking to take the vehicle back to my lodgings. She gestured impatiently. "Food's paid for."

In my defense, let me explain that lodgings at Mrs. Rutledge's included the cost of meals, to justify a greater fee, as most days the rooms stood empty, but also because her clientele preferred not to be seen dining together in public. On the day or two each week when they frequented her establishment they wished to exploit the privacy of their chambers and they appreciated good food. Mrs. Frye's table had consistently deteriorated since she had filled her lodging-house and a captive clientele had allowed her to tighten her purse strings. Plain if undistinguished fare had devolved into starch and suspect beef. I sent the hack on its way.

Once in her room, Emma disappeared behind a screen. After considerable manipulation of hooks, buttons, and laces she emerged in a loose cotton nightgown to busy herself beating the dust from her dress. Freed from the female paraphernalia, her sylph-like form pressed intermittently against the flowing folds. The nightgown draped demurely about her person except when her movements swirled the hem from her bare calves, or later when we dined and she leaned over her food, causing the loose collar to fall away from her rising breasts. She ate with relish, conscious no doubt that in a few days she would find herself dining on bread and potatoes, dexterously dismembering the glazed squab, afterward licking her fingers clean of the sweet fatty residue with exceptional care. The determined intensity of her indulgence convinced me I had been naïve to think Central Park would allay the terrors of Hart Island.

I was forcibly affected by the sight of this slim, exquisitely featured woman voraciously indulging her appetites. Her sensual delight made me acutely conscious of the contrast between the amorphous cotton cloth and the lithe limbs beneath, of the supple arcs formed by her pink tongue caressing her tiny fingers. Her complete lack of pretense, her easy trust in me as her protector only made her more appealing.

I ate little. My body had concluded that my stomach was an irrelevant organ. I watched her dine, and when I showed her with my fingers how best to parse the squab, her tongue licked glaze from them with a playful puppy gesture. I let her lick them clean. She must have seen them shake.

She ate everything there was to eat. When the bones were picked white she mopped her rosebud lips with linen, threw her arms about me, and drew me to the bed.

One afternoon in Manáos, after a mind-numbing week packing specimens, I had visited my friend Hunnewell, hoping to convince him to accompany me on my impending return to the Solimões to find more fish. I was surprised to see him answer his door dressed in the easy but revealing attire of the Brazilian native, a short white shirt and white linen drawers. He had converted his front room into a photographic studio, where in his unlikely costume he was recording the charms of a pair of delightful *moas,* dressed in European fashion in white muslin and jewelry and flowers in their hair and exuding an excellent smell of pripioca. He invited me to assist him, and I happily did. The ladies, while not at all sluttish, were remarkably free of prudish inhibitions, and without much trouble Hunnewell induced them to strip and pose naked. They moved gracefully, with casual disregard for their state. Hunnewell adjusted their poses, and soon to general merriment they were adjusting his. I was invited to join in. Though my blood was stirred, I was not prepared to yield myself to these mysteriously free creatures. I feared the implications of surrender. I left Brazil as virginal as I arrived, but when I think of that country the image which predominates is not the majestic river of my researches but these two laughing young women clad only in pearl earrings. I had often wondered how my life might have been altered had I spent my months in Brazil collecting fewer ichthyofaunal specimens and more personal sensations. I long suspected that the changes I had most feared would have been in actuality the most salutary.

As Emma drew me to her, thoughts of Manáos pulled me closer. She placed her half-parted lips delicately against mine, as if fusing furnace-warmed Venetian glass. Her arms were remarkably strong. This was for her the natural and inevitable outcome of the evening. She was squeezing the most from her hard existence; she was paying her life debt by giving life; she was laying Sam to rest. I had not the meanness to deny her.

Do not think that I was simply serving Emma. I was wild with desire. Yet I might have restrained myself as I had in Manáos and avoided my later troubles. I knew that against all Emma's good reasons stood the unassailable truth that this was wrong, a despicable sin, a base abuse of intimacies granted me as her physician and self-appointed guardian, as bad as Alger's

221

abuse of his young tutee. Summoning the will to resist, I re-strained my urge to return the touch of her lips, the crush of her arms. I conquered my lust.

I could not conquer my loneliness. Saving Emma's life, I had glimpsed the depths of the abyss which divided us one from the other; holding her now, I saw that this chasm was the ultimate cause of my solitary agonies. Simply put, I saw that Evil was the moral term for isolation. When our lips brushed and her breasts compressed against me, I knew that if ever I were to bridge that gap it would be here and now, with this gentle fer-vent creature whose life was mine. Whimpering with delight I leapt for the far side of the gorge.

⌒CHAPTER SEVENTEEN⌒

JEMMIE LEFT THE LODGING-HOUSE DETERMINED TO EARN money for his trip West. Mr. Alger and Mr. Henry had spoken brave words as they parted company but Jemmie had not attended, because if he had listened he would have had to ponder where they were going when they left him, and he preferred to think about earning money for a pair of riding boots with spurs. His morning papers were worthless at this hour, so he headed for the *Herald* building, intent upon securing the commission of an early edition of its evening paper, the *Telegram.* He was halfway across the square when Dannie joined him stride for stride.

"Hello, partner."

Jemmie hastened his pace and kept his eyes fixed upon the looming *Herald* building.

"I hear you're going West. Congratulations."

Head down, Jemmie mounted the *Herald*'s steps. Dannie stopped him with an outstretched arm. "What have I ever done to harm you? It's thanks to me they're sending you West, ain't it? Think about it."

"Thanks." The word was spoken with a dull patina.

Dannie acted hurt. "Alls I ever wanted was the best for

you. Who took you to the theatre? Who gave you four dollars? You ever eat half so well as you et with me?"

"No."

"So gimme your hand. Lemme congratulate the man what's goin' West to slay injuns." Jemmie did not see how he could refuse. Dannie pumped energetically. "They sendin' you Children's Aid Society?"

Jemmie nodded. "I's getting me a white horse. White Cloud."

"I'll buy you a present." Dannie grinned as if they shared a secret. "Maybe a Remington rifle. How 'bout a Remington rifle?"

"That'd be swell."

"Your dad must be pleased as punch to be rid of ya."

"I told you I's a orphan."

"I always figgered you was colourin' the truth a bit there." Jemmie was silent. "C'mon, you's no more'n orphan than me."

"You ain't no orphan?"

"Hell no. Me dad got liquored up alla time and whomped on me and the rest of us, and I jus' got sick of it and tore out. Know what finally ripped it?"

"No."

"We never had no food in the house, but one day Dad comes home with a jug of brandy and a fair-sized ham, drinks hisself flat. Sister takes his razor and cuts us some ham. Nothing else in the house could cut through spit. Dad wakes up, decides he's gonna shave, sees his razor all slimy with ham fat, and goes berserk. He takes the razor strop to my sister till I says I done it, and he busts off a chair leg to use on

224

me. I's smaller then, but plenty quick, and I smacks him with a iron skillet and he drops, blood oozing out like warm honey, and I's out the door. Boom."

Jemmie listened to this tale with complete attention. "What about your sister?"

"She had any sense, she took off too."

"Did she?"

"How's I suppose to know? I tol' you I took off." Dannie's peevish tone betrayed the pain of the memory, but when he saw that Jemmie understood his smile crept back. "We's free now, boyo. Eh?"

Jemmie gave a tentative nod.

"But I still ain't no orphan. Damn skillet didn't do the job. Priest says I gotta go back, kiss me dad's feet, beg forgiveness and whatnot. This priest, he's a good enough fella as priests go, but he got his church idea what me father's like. I knows me father. One time a pig bumped me father, I seed him crush its skull with his shoe. Father sees me, he bashes me head flat with the first thing to hand. Won't mean it a course. Feel right terrible 'bout it after. Scab his knees with a million novenas fer that damn priest. I's still dead."

Jemmie stared up at him with saucer eyes. Dannie tweaked his nose. "Why's I tellin' you this bunk? Yer off to kill injuns and yer daddy'll be a million miles away. When the Aid Society knows where you's settled I'll send on that Remington." He turned and walked slowly away.

"Wait! Wait!" Jemmie pursued his diminishing form.

"What now?" Dannie kept walking, and Jemmie had to hasten his step to keep pace.

"I lied."

" 'Bout what?"

"I ain't goin' West."

"Why not?"

"I jes' ain't."

"Where you goin' then?"

"I dunno."

"You stayin' here then?"

"Cain't."

"Why not?"

"Cain't."

"Why not then?"

"I gets me head bashed in."

Dannie stopped with a show of concern. "Your daddy." Jemmie nodded. Dannie whistled a long tailing note. "Yer daddy, is he like my daddy?" Jemmie nodded. "That is troubling news." They walked for a while. Dannie stroked his chin. Jemmie could see he was deep in thought. Of a sudden Dannie snapped his fingers with a crack that ignited his playful grin. "Got it." Jemmie stared at him, agape. "You can come with me." He extended five thick fingers. Jemmie offered his tiny paw. They walked hand in hand.

Reaching the Chatham Street side of the square, they walked in the latticework shadows of the overhead railroad. A tremendous clattering and a shivering of the iron trellis blotted out the diamonds of sunlight at their feet. Showered with burning ash, Jemmie looked up in fearful expectation of imminent entombment. Dannie laughed.

226   "Never rid the elevated then? Don't you worry, it's not go-

ing nowheres, 'cept back and forth uptown." The locomotive overhead spit steam and its pistons creaked. "Want to go for a ride?" Jemmie nodded emphatically.

Dannie pulled him up the iron stairway. At the top a diminutive, domesticated version of the behemoth from the Bowery Theatre awaited, panting and coughing like a saddled bison. Jemmie rode beside Dannie along Chatham and up Bowery, flying upon his personal steed above the bustle of the street, gazing like a god into hard lives of sweatshop labor that crowded the upper floors of the passing structures. At Thirtieth Street the railway terminated and the boys descended and crossed to Fifth Avenue, where Dannie put them on the uptown bus. Jemmie tried to recapture the elevated sensation by mounting to the roof, but he was perched too close to the noise and dust and moved too slowly to feel the same gratifying separation from his surroundings. As they progressed northward and the structures thinned he was soon beyond the range of his roving, and at the barren blocks above Ninety-fifth Street he had the satisfaction of being in an altogether new part of the world, and the relief of knowing he was surely beyond the reach of his father.

At the top of Central Park, where the coach turned back south, Dannie alighted and led Jemmie toward Sixth Avenue. They marched the margin between Olmsted's manicured wilderness of lake and leafy hillock and the flat fields of genuine open country, until they reached a rambling building situated where the winding paths of Central Park debouched onto a wide dirt road that ran off at an angle through the empty land. Carriages of all descriptions crowded into the forecourt, two-wheeled and four, covered and open, united only in their elegance of line, the refinement of their horses, and the celebratory attitude of their finely clad inhabitants. Dannie ran ahead, searching among them until he found a two-wheeled vehicle so slender of form it appeared to be drawn in ink rather than constructed, pulled by a large gray stallion champing at his harness. The reins belonged to a massive man thick with muscle, clad in a suit which perfectly matched his steed. Jemmie saw only the man's back, a bulging gray mountain perched upon the tiny seat, and marveled that his weight did not crush the conveyance. The man leaned down to speak with Dannie, and when Dannie gestured in Jemmie's direction the man turned his heavy head, and Jemmie recognized him. The man gestured with his whip. Jemmie advanced cautiously.

"Dannie says you're a stand-up fella."

"Yer Harry Hill."

"That's my name. What's yours?"

"Jemmie."

"Hello, Jemmie." Harry's huge hand rubbed the top of Jemmie's head. Jemmie was surprised at the lightness of his touch.

"You talk poetry."

"Not on Harlem Lane, my lad. Here the horses do the talking."

"What's his name?"

"Runnymede."

"Funny name."

"I bought him from an English lord. English lords aren't governed by the rules of reason."

"I'll have me own horse when I go West."

"Would you like to try this one?"

Jemmie's eyes shone. He nodded energetically.

"Come aboard then."

Jemmie eyed the carriage. Harry filled its single seat to excess. "How?"

Harry plucked the boy like a dandelion and deposited him in his gargantuan lap. Jemmie was engulfed in gray wool too fine to make him itch, encased in Harry's thick arms converging before his nose upon the supple reins. With a snap of Harry's wrists Runnymede started off at a lazy trot, leaving Dannie behind in the courtyard. Harry sat upright and held his arms stiff, and greeted other drivers in his deep voice. Nestled between the solid thighs and massive chest, watching the power of the prancing stallion quivering in the strips of leather clasped in those mighty fists, Jemmie thought himself in the safest, strongest place on earth.

Harry turned away from the park. Harlem Lane stretched before them dusty and straight. Harry snapped the reins and the horse stepped up his pace, inducing vibration in the fragile carriage. Jemmie jounced in his little nest, content. "Put out your arms." The bouncing gave an oddly resonant quality to Harry's voice.

"What?"

"Hold out your hands, like you're serving a platter." Jemmie complied. "When I hand you the reins, grasp them tight.

If you drop them, we'll be in a right pickle." Harry closed the boy's hands around the reins. In Jemmie's tiny grasp they appeared thick and unwieldy. When Jemmie squeezed down on them, Harry dropped his own. "He likes a firm hand."

Sensing anything but a firm hand Runnymede stepped up his pace. Jemmie sat upright as he had seen Harry do. Without Harry's arms around him he felt himself precariously exposed, levitated by the bouncing and pulled toward the horses by the weight of the reins, which hung much heavier than they had appeared in Harry's grasp. He pulled them tentatively. The horse shook off the mild pressure and broke pace. He was galloping wildly now. Jemmie, fearful, looked to Harry. Harry was unperturbed. "Firmly!"

Jemmie stiffened his legs against the bouncing to no avail. He longed to drop the reins and clutch the wool beneath him, but he would not. He would never relinquish the reins. He yanked with all his strength. Runnymede shook off the annoyance with a turn of his head. Instead of pulling in the horse Jemmie pulled himself off his seat. He slid down, still jerking ineffectually, into the thundering hooves. He closed his eyes and prayed to God.

An angel's grip girded his waist and hauled him into the carriage. Clamping Jemmie under one arm, Harry put his giant fist over Jemmie's two and drew Runnymede back to a trot.

Jemmie opened his eyes, his voice aquiver with relief. "I's sorry, sir."

"Nothing to be sorry about. You're a right bulldog pup." The words made Jemmie sit tall. He'd proved himself to

Harry Hill. They rode for a distance, both holding the reins, past a few more inns and stables, and when they reached the final building on the road, a gentleman's bar, Harry slowed his horses. "You'll be wanting a drink. Chalk it up to Harry Hill." He dropped the boy to the ground. "When Dannie shows, you tell him I said you're a proper British bulldog." Jemmie watched him trot on up the lane.

The fine clothes worn by the saloon clientele made Jemmie conscious of his bare feet and hatless pate and the gaping rents in his coat and pants, so he decided to wait for Dannie outside. He sat upon the steps, watching the fleets of furiously high-stepping trotters urged on by their riders. The saloon crowd pressed against the porch railing, identifying well-known titans of finance who raced with the same reckless abandon they showed on Wall Street, dashing hither and yon without order or pattern. The actor Lester Wallack received encouragement, and all cheered lustily for the Reverend Henry Ward Beecher. Jemmie enjoyed the prancing horses, the fine equipage, and the spirited competition, thinking himself a privileged member of the racing fraternity.

Dannie soon appeared. Though his attire was scarcely better than Jemmie's he marched them boldly into the saloon, answering the stares of the bartender by ordering beers on Harry Hill's account and compiling a thick sandwich from the heaps of meats and cheeses upon the counter. Ravenous and fearful of expulsion, Jemmie gulped his beer and crammed his mouth with bread and ham.

"Hey, go slow there, you're among gentlemen." Jemmie made unintelligible sounds. "How's that?"

"How come they don't think you's gassin' 'bout Harry Hill paying?"

"Nobody what wants their arms and legs in working order would make that up."

Jemmie munched and thought. "Harry says to tell you I's a British bulldog."

Dannie grinned and slapped Jemmie on the forehead. "I knowed it! I said you was aces! You'll be glad you met Mr. Harry Hill!"

"How's that?"

"You'll see." A commotion from the yard interrupted the boys and caused a general exodus toward the locus of excitement. Dannie jumped up. "C'mon."

All eyes were fastened upon a cloud of dust far up the lane, blooming into a golden halo from the lowering sun. Jemmie leapt upon the railing for a better view, and discerned three light vehicles careering toward them in the semblance of orderly competition, two running side by side, filling the road, the third pressing from behind. Even from this distance the skill and reckless determination of the drivers were evident. Porch sitters speculated upon the stakes.

A four-wheeled carriage pulled ahead powered by a sorrel and a bay. Onlookers murmured admiration, and one claimed to recognize the beasts as Myron Perry and Daisy Burns, champions of the Lane and pride of Commodore Vanderbilt, and the steed close behind as Robert Bonner's Dexter, for which the owner of the *Ledger* had paid thirty-three thousand dollars.

The trailing carriage made a daring play to pass Robert Bonner. As he swept to match him wheel to wheel Jemmie recognized the hulking form of Harry Hill.

"Five cents says Harry takes him!" said Dannie. Jemmie was silent. He would not bet against Harry, even if the opposing horse cost a million. The two raced side by side step for step. An irregularity in the road or the contact of Harry's wheel caused Bonner's vehicle to take a sudden hop and wobble drunkenly, and Harry sped past as Bonner fought to keep himself on the road. The boys cheered. Harry cracked his whip and Runnymede found more speed. He closed on Vanderbilt.

As the racers fast approached the inn, which Jemmie guessed to be the finish line, Runnymede's nose pulled even with Daisy's tail. Vanderbilt, a stern, snowily bewhiskered gentleman with a lap robe warming his legs, glanced severely at Harry from the side of his eye. Harry grinned and snapped his whip, inching forward. Vanderbilt gave his reins a brief, decisive flick in reply, and his pair shot ahead with a jolt that unseated his silk hat, revealing a pate so bald that Jemmie thought his scalp must have migrated to his cheeks. Runnymede fought to match them, but Harry's mass was too great a burden. To applause from the porch crowd Vanderbilt flew past the inn a carriage length ahead.

Harry slowed Runnymede to a trot and the boys scampered in his dust. Bonner drew alongside, red-faced with effort and anger. "Harry, you son of a bitch!"

Harry saluted him with his whip. "If you can't take the

strain, shun Harlem Lane." Bonner drove on in disgust. Harry and Runnymede disappeared into a nearby stables with a wave to the boys.

"C'mon then," said Dannie, striding toward the smithy's yard. "It's late."

"Late fer what?"

"Have I let you down yet?" Dannie flashed his wickedest smile.

Jemmie ran to catch up. Though he had abandoned the trail leading West he felt closer to his goal. He had driven his first horse and proved his mettle to Harry Hill, a gentleman whose spirit contained more of the Indian fighter than those of all his would-be guardians at the Lodging-house combined.

‿CHAPTER EIGHTEEN‿

DANNIE GREETED THE BLACKSMITH, A BRAWNY LAD NOT MUCH older than himself, with a curt "Give us the tongs, then." The boy went to a wall of implements and took down a yard-long pair of slender levers with iron squares forged to one end. He handed them to Dannie as if he'd been anticipating his arrival. "That'll be a penny."

"G'wan," Dannie said to Jemmie. "Pay up."

Jemmie fished out a penny and handed it over to the young man, who deposited it in the pocket of his sooty leather apron. "Just a penny?"

"Fer luck," said the smith. Dannie selected a few good-sized burlap sacks from a pile in the corner. He strode out the door deaf to Jemmie's questions, only voicing concern that they reach their mysterious destination before sunset. At the entrance to the park he found a waiting hansom cab, and for thirty-five cents engaged it to convey them southward through the picturesque lanes, beneath the reds and golds of autumn. Jemmie, however, was oblivious of the brilliant leaves shimmering in the diminishing light, hearing not the evening birds but only the creak of the axle, thinking that each turn brought him closer to his father's haunts. He was relieved when they halted at the Seventy-second Street entrance, although the hansom driver refused to risk his carriage on the rough tracks. They picked their way on foot in the lengthening shadows among squatter shanties which dotted the craggy hillocks of the West Side.

"So where we goin'?"

"Huntin'. You ever been huntin?"

"No."

"It'll juice you up. Pays good money to boot. You'll want the practice, fer going West."

"Huntin' what?"

"A cunning, vicious foe. Worse'n injuns."

As they neared the river the stench of rot announced the dumping-barge wharf. An orderly cluster of shacks gathered nearby. Though composed of nothing more than bits of old boxes and discarded wood, roofed with scraps of tin, and vented with a length or two of stovepipe, they had a neat, homey air which Jemmie found appealing. Small children played with dogs and chickens. Goats and geese wandered freely. Bundled rags lay by the door of each shanty.

When the children saw our boys they let out a shout, drawing older boys from the dwellings. A large fair-haired lad called to Dannie, "What you wantin' then?"

"Moon's full."

"So?"

Dannie raised his tongs. "We're going rat huntin'."

The younger boys cheered. Their spokesman was more circumspect. He disappeared into the shanty and returned with an adult version of himself, wiping his hands upon a rag, whose presence silenced the children. He spoke with a guttural German accent.

"Who hunts?"

"Harry Hill."

"Vat you pay?"

"The usual."

"Vat usual?"

"Two cents per for what they catch. Up to four hunnerd. Live a course. Plus your boy and the cart to haul 'em to Harry's."

"Dat's extra."

"What?"

"Fifty cents to haul."

"Okay."

"Unt fifty cents to hunt."

"What?"

"You hunt my estate."

"You the Duke a Garbage now?"

"You hunt, you pay."

"Okay, okay. Done." They spit in their hands and shook on the deal, and the children disappeared noisily into their dwellings. The blond boy led Dannie and Jemmie behind, where rose small mountains of scraps and bones, guarded by an old man who sat upon a bundle of rags chucking the occasional stone at dark scurrying forms. He barked German at the boys.

The blond boy translated. "He says pay him fifty cents."

"Why?"

"He's paid to keep 'em off. You're costing him a night's work."

"I'm bein' squeezed like a lemon, I am."

"You don't pay, he chases 'em."

"Not no fifty cents. That's robbery. Twenty-five cents tops."

Another discussion in German ensued. "He says thirty."

"That's the lot now? No surcharges or special levies or nothin'?"

"No."

"Your mom kicks in dinner."

"Okay."

Dannie handed over the thirty cents. The old man left his post, muttering harsh syllables.

The boys reappeared bearing an assortment of nooses, traps, and self-made tongs. Dannie and the blond lad, Otto, organized the hunt, dividing the half-dozen older boys into equal groups and assigning each to a bone mountain. Otto caused much anguish among the younger ones by firmly refusing them permission to join in. They pointed at Jemmie. "He's no bigger'n us! He's huntin'!" Jemmie felt a surge of pride.

"You seed what happened to Rusty. Think about it." They quieted somewhat. "It ain't gonna happen to none a you."

"But he's goin!"

"That's not yer affair."

"What happened to Rusty?" Jemmie asked, not a little
curious.

"He got et. He was chasing 'em and he slipped and his foot stuck and they jumped on his eyes and tore at his belly till his guts come out," Otto said, pleased at the sobering effect of his words upon Jemmie. "Chomped on his eyeballs like they was onions. Wasn't but last week."

"How old was Rusty?"

"Dunno. Why?"

"Well, how big was he?"

" 'Bout so." Jemmie tried to calculate how much bigger he was than the span of Otto's hands.

"Course Rusty fought back. Ripped up a couple right proper."

"How'd a little boy like that rip 'em up?"

His informant guffawed. "Who said nothin' about a boy? Rusty's Gunther's terrier." Jemmie felt scant relief, but he recognized that in the danger lay the honour of the act.

Jemmie and Dannie had a bone mountain to themselves. Dannie handed the tongs to Jemmie. "Don't worry none 'bout squeezin' too hard. They don't squish." Jemmie climbed upon the slippery pile, holding the iron levers like a club should a beast attack his bare toes.

The flies had subsided with the cool of evening, but the stench of putrid meat lay heavy in the air. In the monotonous gray light the bones glowed with a greasy sheen. Shadows flitted among them like wounded spirits searching for their resting place. Whatever drove these wraiths, Jemmie's presence inspired no fear. Stumbling and clattering he crested the pile to arrive nose to nose with a sleek pink-tailed creature the size of a small cat, oblivious of his presence, placidly munching on gobbets of meat that clung to a sheep skull. Reassured by its arrogance Jemmie readied the tongs and swooped, catching the animal squarely between the iron plates. Its soft sides quivered in his grip. Bracing himself against a large bone, he lifted it proudly in the air. The beast twisted free and scurried off.

"Squeeze!" Dannie called with amusement. "Squeeze that sucker in two!" Stung by the cheers and gibes which wafted from the other piles signaling greater success among the other boys, Jemmie scrambled with renewed determination, his greased feet sliding out from under him, and clasped another rat, and another, and another only to have them squirm free, but each attempt taught him more of the dexterous arts required. Finally he snared one of less impressive proportions, squeezed with vigor, and dropped it into Dannie's waiting sack with a satisfying plop.

"Bravo, boyo. Want me to have a go?"

"I's just gettin' the hang."

"Have it your way. Jes' squeeze 'em like you love 'em."

Jemmie prowled the pile like an Indian. His prey were plentiful and fearless. He learned to snap his tongs shut and sweep the animal into the air with a single firm motion, shocking it into passivity, then swing it to Dannie's waiting burlap before it regained its rebellious nature. As he found his rhythm he became a mighty giant striding through a pallid wasteland, plucking his unsuspecting prey from their routine existence and dashing them into the closeness and turmoil of the sack. Danger was forgotten. He who had never wielded power over another living creature, with the exception of his futile attempt to control the runaway Runnymede, was now god of this ossuary, deciding the destiny of his subjects with a single snick of his mighty iron tool.

He chose his antagonists carefully, searching for a stance or a manner which marked them as particularly deserving of their fate. Some ate too greedily, some too brazenly pushed aside their fellows, some were too oblivious of his prodigious presence. He meted justice with a firm and impartial hand.

But Jemmie was human, and small, and the weight of the tongs and the exertion of scrambling and sliding over the hill wore him down. When he grew too weak to clutch the rats securely Dannie ordered him to trade places. Jemmie held the sack with heavy arms, giving it a poke with his toe now and then to discourage the inhabitants from gnawing to freedom, while Dannie hunted with strength and persistence. Hours passed. Jemmie fought the urge to sleep. When he dozed, Dannie would cuff him with the tongs and tell him to mind the pulsing sack.

By moonset the resident boys had gleaned their quota, and Dannie and Jemmie joined them for a meal of stiff bread and cold sausage while they calculated the value of the catch. Dannie paid Otto eight dollars and Otto helped them load the sacks onto a cart pulled by a pair of eager spaniels. A young boy was detailed to accompany the cart, and Jemmie and Dannie set off beside it, poking the bags regularly to prevent the rats from chewing their escape.

Jemmie trudged with leaden legs down Eleventh Avenue

and the Hudson shore. The sky lightened as blocks stretched into miles. Each step brought him closer to his father's haunts, but he was too tired to feel much fear. Dannie walked easily, apparently impervious to exhaustion, and finally he took pity upon Jemmie and bade the sagging boy jump upon his back. Clinging like a monkey, Jemmie fell into grateful slumber.

Jemmie had spent a long and eventful day. In the span of a single sun he had abandoned his plan to migrate West, and with it his friends at the Lodging-house and their mode of existence; he had embraced the very man they had warned him against, and the way of life they said would ruin him; he had ridden his first elevated railroad, driven his first horse, conducted his first hunt. Such upheavals did not go unremarked in his sleeping brain. As he rocked along upon Dannie's broad back he dreamt he was an Indian in fiery paint flying upon a stallion over western hills carpeted with rats the size of bison. Exhilarated by his effortless speed he singled out the chief of the thundering monsters. He stretched back his arm to launch his spear. The rat bison bared its teeth. He could not thrust. The spear hung heavy in his hand. Horse hooves flashed. The velocity which had thrilled him moments before was now a terrifying menace. Something he knew so intimately that he could not give it a name was closing on him, and he was frozen in place. The thing engulfed him and still he could not move, though the hard thing crushed the life from his malleable chest. As the last dregs of spirit were squeezed from his tissues he forced his eyes open, gasping for breath. With his cheek pressed gratefully against Dannie's warm neck he watched the world sway by in the rising light until his eyes again refused to see.

———

Jemmie awoke upon a hard bench in the dark, smelling apples and ham. Raucous sounds slipped under the door with a band of light. He was in a store room on the margin of riotous activity.

He emerged into a hot, smoky, gas-golden hall filled with tiered benches packed with well-dressed sports. The commotion was occasioned by the appearance of a wooden cage being carried by half a dozen men to a cube in the center of the room no larger than a dray cart. Jemmie climbed up the bench supports to peer inside its walls and saw only an empty space sheathed in metal.

A stern gentleman called for silence and the room responded as a single person. He continued over the hush in measured judicial tones. "Are the enumerators ready?" Two gentlemen seated upon the lip of the cube responded in the affirmative. "Let them in!"

The cage was thrust over the walls and a man in a suit the color of persimmons opened its door. A crowd of rats nosed to the edge and leapt under watchful eyes.

"How many, gentlemen?"

"One hundred," both enumerators replied.

"The count is correct. One hundred rats in the pit."

The beasts searched for an exit from their prison, their claws skittering frantically upon the tin, as the enumerators examined them and used tongs to replace weak or injured animals with healthier specimens. The audience loudly critiqued the animals. Money changed hands. Jemmie recognized some of his quarry; one, whom he dubbed Giganta, found the strength and speed to climb the slippery wall. Jemmie hoped he would clamber to freedom, but he fell back when he reached the inward-curving lip. Soon the rats came to accept the dimensions of their world and raced about more comfortably, concerned less with escape than with mutual harassment. "The rats have their ease!" proclaimed the referee. "Ready Jack Underhill!"

Talk ceased. A ginger-headed man cradling a scarred fox terrier approached the pit, whispering soothing words in his animal's shredded ear. The dog, though eager and alert, was no larger than the bone-collector's disemboweled Rusty. Jemmie could not understand what satisfaction would spring from sacrificing him to the rodents.

The referee began a deliberate count. "One! Two! Three!" The dog set his jaw and spread his limbs, and his owner searched for an open space in the swirling mass below. "Drop!" Ginger gently tossed the terrier toward a likely spot. A bell sounded.

The terrier alit in a frenzy of motion, clamping his jaws on the closest rat and shaking him with ferocious efficiency. As the crowd roared approval, Jemmie thought he heard the faint crack of snapping spine. The terrier hurled the body in the air and with a warlike growl assaulted another.

The terrier swam in a sea of enemies. They fastened themselves upon his face, his back, his legs. They hung from the remnants of his ears. He sank beneath their brown bodies, hushing the crowd until he surfaced, shaking his head for fighting room but otherwise oblivious of their onslaught, his attention ever centered upon the victim in his jaws until its spine gave, when he would toss it aside and methodically seize the next. Jemmie was awed by the terrier's demonic intensity of purpose, but the unrelenting mayhem made him uneasy. This was not a contest but a slaughter. His rats were sacrificial sport. He had no desire to witness their destruction, yet he could not remove his eyes from the butchery, and he could not but respect its agent.

The bell rang to general shouts of approval. The referee intoned, "Gentlemen will now have the usual half-hour refreshment." Jemmie pushed forward while men unclamped one side of the pit to admit the terrier's master. The bloodied animal licked his hand and yelped triumphantly. Jemmie liked the careful manner in which the man examined Jack Underhill's wounds, and the soothing words he spoke, like an Indian chief to his wounded warrior. He wished to pet the animal, but his way was blocked by piles of broken rats. He would not walk upon their bodies. Though he was drawn to the dog, his loyalties lay with the hunted.

He was suddenly very hungry. He joined the crowd at the food table and concentrated upon worming his way to the forefront. As he was piling ham and turkey and cheese upon a slab of bread a hand gripped his arm.

"I been lookin' for you, boyo." It was the toff in the

245

persimmon suit. Up close the suit had pink piping. A floppy bow tie graced a celluloid collar. The dandy waved a ten-dollar note in Jemmie's face. "Here. Yer share."

Jemmie eyed it cautiously. The toff had a familiar chin. "Me share a what?"

"The rats a course. Harry pays eight cents a rat. Five hundred rats. I's givin' you one-third. Less expenses. That's more'n fair."

Jemmie spied the clipped ear beneath the derby hat. "Dannie!"

"You've got someone else shovin' ten dollars up your nose?"

Jemmie grasped the note and examined it. "You look like a regular swell!"

" 'Tis me average me. T'other is me labourin' costume. You should take yer new wealth and buy some togs yerself. You stink of lard and rotten meat."

Dannie's presence returned Jemmie to the world of his concerns. He looked at the crowd of men with apprehensive eyes. "Where is we?"

"Abe Conkling's rat pit. Abe runs it for Harry."

"That near the Five Points?"

"Near enough. Why?" He saw the fear on Jemmie's face and rubbed his fingers as if thumbing cash. "There's more'n distance between 'em. Yer dad got four dollars for a rat fight?"

"Four dollars fer this?"

"Yer gettin' the bargain of a lifetime, boyo. You might wanta stretch that tenner with a sagacious wager." He called to a large man standing nearby. "J.G.! What's the odds on

Jack Underhill?" The man turned, and Jemmie recognized J.G. as the man he had seen at Harry Hill's, who might be his benefactor from the shadowy ferry. His boxer's body was clad in the same sober finery, and his nose was similarly mashed. Jemmie was concerned that J.G. would not approve of the choices he had made to arrive at a rat pit, but the man smiled at him, and Jemmie smiled shyly back.

"Well now, I couldn't recommend laying down good money at this juncture. Only a fool'd bet on Henry Hubbard topping Underhill's time." J.G. spoke in a sweet tenor, nothing like his benefactor's abraded tones, and Jemmie realized he had mistaken J.G.'s identity. The thought made him more at ease with J.G., but less comfortable with his surroundings.

"Colin, he raised Jack Underhill to be a champion," said J.G., savoring the melodious sounds of his own voice. "Rears him from a pup in his own private rat pit. Feeds him naught but raw meat on the bone, to toughen his teeth. When he's a whelp his only playmate is a rat big as him, only his teeth is pulled, and they only play at meal time, and he's gotta kill his pal afore he gets fed. One month in, Jack Underhill's barking for his rat 'cause it means food, and Colin starts slipping him rats with just their top teeth, just enough bite so he'll respect their jaws, until he's knocking off five afore dinner. By the time he sees a rat with all its teeth he's a regular Angel of Death. So what I'm saying is, keep your money in your pocket. Henry Hubbard never bettered twenty-five minutes."

"Pity no one took that kinda care raisin' you," said Dannie to Jemmie. "You'd be out there this minute killing injuns." They all laughed. J.G. was called away.

247

"Right regular fella," said Dannie. "I was wantin' you two to get together."

"Why's that?"

"You'll see."

Jemmie watched J.G. shoulder his way through the throng, shaking hands and patting backs. He seemed a very amiable man for one so large. He passed a lanky, ragged, beak-nosed boy. Jemmie's heart stopped. "Ain't that Mickety?"

"Who?"

"Yer hangman at the Lodging-house."

Dannie scrutinized him from afar. "Could be."

This time Jemmie knew he was making no mistake. He shrank under the protection of the table. "Go see."

From his hiding place Jemmie observed Dannie amble over to the boy, speak with him briefly, then grab him roughly by the arm and drag him to the door. Jemmie waited anxiously until Dannie reappeared with his usual saunter. "Nothin' to worry about. He snuck in anyways. He's gone."

"Did he say about my father?"

"He says your daddy showed hisself at the *Sun* building, raving drunk, saying he wasn't sending you West if Alger pays him a thousand dollars, and now he's got the boys on the lookout with a five-dollar reward."

"How'd he get five dollars?"

"Don't rightly know. Maybe he's lying about that, but Mickety believes him. Lucky thing you laid low."

"Did he say anything about my sister?"

"Why you askin'?"

"I ain't seen her since I took off."

"You miss her, don't ya?"

"I do. I's scared now I's gone he's maybe hurtin' on her."

"I have bad news for you there. Seems she took sick and died."

"Died?"

"Dead and buried."

"And the baby?"

"And the baby." Jemmie staggered. Dannie steadied him. "Yer all yer daddy's got, and he wants you somethin' fierce."

"I never shoulda left 'em."

"The cholera killed them. 'Tain't your fault."

" 'Tis."

" 'Tis God's will."

"I wished him dead. God took Emma instead."

Dannie put an arm around Jemmie. "God's done His deed. Now you gotta do what's best for you." The little boy looked up at him in anguish.

"What's that?"

"Later." The boy clung to Dannie's orange legs. Dannie stroked his hair. "You got me, boyo." Jemmie had known moments when he resisted Dannie's blandishments, and moments when he chose to yield to them. This was neither. For young Jemmie, choice ended here.

～

CHAPTER NINETEEN

The following morning I left Emma with only a touch and a kiss. I trembled with pleasure for life. Where I had once sensed evil all about me, I now found only goodliness and grace.

I had much to say to Emma but could not decipher what it should be. I could not articulate the profound unspoken intimacies which had passed between us, and while I felt immensely grateful in the fullest sense of the term, both thankful and indebted, expressing that emotion upon leaving Emma's bed would only have demeaned the both of us. Though I felt something which might honestly be described as love, any profession of sentiment on my part felt equally inappropriate, as it would have appeared as a bald attempt to elicit from Emma a similar avowal.

Honesty and tact dictated that before we spoke at any length I consider carefully the consequences of my impetuous act, and for that I required the perspective of time and distance. For her part, Emma had no words for me. She seemed content to speak through the kiss, a frank, straightforward affectionate pressing of the lips which promised nothing and precluded nothing. Confused as I was when we parted, one truth I knew with absolute clarity: As her quondam saviour I had previously recognized my moral obligation to safeguard Emma; now I felt a visceral compulsion to fulfill that role.

But I had also to attend to my own survival. I returned to Mrs. Frye's to find a pressing note from Noah Wapner. It included three dollar bills and a page from the *Christian Union* which featured a coarsely etched rendition of my portrayal of what Wapner had labeled 'The trial of the pulchritudinous Moslem mystics.' He coupled apologies for the diminished payment with the prospect of further employment were I to join him at the Tombs that very day. I gathered my supplies and hastened thither, though my mind still churned with thoughts of Emma.

Any event as much anticipated as the loss of one's virginity is sure to amount to less in the actual realization. The very ignorance which breeds anticipation creates its own obstacles. The clumsiness, the messy incompatibilities of life intrude. I had thought I would bridge the gap which sundered me from others. I was naïve. The act itself was primordially selfish. Even at my most melancholic I had never been so utterly concerned with my own inner state, and judged from appearances Emma was equally self-absorbed. Yet her pleasure afforded me deep gratification. Her pleasure, which I could not feel, could not as a man even adequately imagine, completed my own in a fashion I could never have foreseen. The gap remained, but a spark had leapt between us. For those ecstatic moments I did in fact feel less alone.

She was an extraordinary woman, I had no doubt of that, and my duty to her and to my own spark of life commanded that I make her my wife. I longed for a steady flow of current between us; I longed to learn what she would teach me about my selfishness and hers; I longed for the right to lie chest to chest in the shadows of the night, to feel the flutter of her heart against mine, to synchronize my breath with her whispery exhalations.

Since the onset of my ailments I had banished all thoughts of matrimony. Not only did I fail the standard of wholesomeness required by society, but I considered myself ill adapted temperamentally to the condition. Though I believed marriage to be essential to a full and fruitful existence, I recognized it as an elevated state requiring a perfect partner, and I was convinced that were I to marry an imperfect woman, a manifest inevitability, whatever small flaws she possessed would over time grow in my mind to unbearable proportions.

These reservations lost their force when I considered Emma's case. My duty to the young woman outweighed any constraint society imposed upon me as a result of my dorsal condition, and my perception of Emma was, I believed, sufficiently clear-eyed that the magnitude of her faults was already obvious to me. She was unschooled and ignorant of the basic amenities of existence. Yet I wished her for my wife.

These faults, I felt, were superficial signs of deeper strength. Emma did not share the fanciful illusions born of luxury and ease indulged by women of my class such as my pampered sister. Emma had a direct, unmediated experience of the world. She knew hard work. Her moral strength was purchased with sweat and adversity; moreover, her difficult life had taught her to value the guidance and sustenance which a man could provide. For however much a man might shrink from saying the naked words, the wife his heart more or less subtly craves is at bottom a dependent being.

Under the circumstances, I could not ask Emma to accompany me to Boston as my fiancée. I must marry her in New York. I would resurrect Alger to stand as my best man. I could not think what I would write my parents to prepare them, so I concluded it was best to say nothing at all. We would appear together in Cambridge and I would introduce her to them as my wife. Father and Mother would be shocked by the sight of her youth, but they would greet her with enormous good will. Alice would eagerly interrogate her on womanly issues. Aunt Fannie would maintain an appalled but discreet silence. After five minutes of talk all of them would be even more perplexed by my choice. They would wonder what power Emma held over me. They would fear that our wedding was proof of my continuing weakness of mind.

Ultimately, they would have nothing to say to her. I could not summon to mind a single friend or relative who would. She was as sharp-witted as any of them, and had opinions as strong, but she had not been equipped with the tools of rational thought. I did not even know if she could read.

She could learn, Lord knows she was young enough, but that would require an enormous commitment of time and energy on her part, and great resolve. The more she learned, the more she would realize the gulf which separated her from the well educated. I saw no evidence that she would wish to recreate herself in such a fundamental fashion. I could not expect her to become a different person to satisfy my family's concept of a proper mate.

253

The alternative was clear. Here, away from Cambridge expectations, I could nurture her at her own pace. We could grow together. I could earn my living as an artist sketching caricatures for the papers. Wapner's note promised a steady stream of work. This was my unequivocal course.

When I saw that this was to be my lot I was overcome with nostalgia for my life in Boston. Until this moment I had been curiously bereft of any sentimental longing for my former existence. The price exacted for such an intense and unremitting life of the mind had seemed unbearable. Now its burdens and uncertainties appeared as ripe potentialities. For the first time since I had arrived in New York I longed for the lectures, the nights of ardent disputation, the family dinners where we resolved the crises of the nation. I wished to hear Peirce speak passionately for hours on things beyond my understanding.

Filled with such vexing thoughts I arrived at court in the midst of the final summations, and found a seat which gave me a reasonable vantage point though at a distance from Noah. He gestured that I should focus my attention on the defending attorney and his client. I did not require Noah to note that these were the most intriguing men in the room. The lawyer was addressed as Mr. Howe and I concluded he was partner to the somber and ferret-like Mr. Hummel, though in appearance his colleague's absolute antithesis. Whereas Hummel moved and spoke like a shadow, trying to deny his very presence in the room, Howe strove to occupy the maximum amount of space. He was a man of enormous girth, which he bore with the grace and buoyancy of an actor confident that his great mass added

substance to his performance. He draped himself in imperial

purple, accented with diamond studs; in place of a necktie, a cloverleaf of white, pink, and black pearls held a diamond dewdrop at his collar. Diamonds twinkled from his fingers and his immense golden watch fob.

The defendant, by contrast, was an absolute Caliban of dishevelment. His hair was matted and stiff as old stable straw, his shirt tattered and black with filth, his coat and vest greasy and encrusted with dribblings of food. He sat silent, staring gloomily at nothing through mournful black eyes. The prosecutor, an earnest and indignant young man, was reminding the jury that before the defendant had shot and killed his father's attorney in a dispute over his inheritance, he had been a richly dressed and well-spoken man about town. He forged on to assiduously prove the absurdity of the defense attorney's allegation that a fall from a horse five years before suddenly had rendered his client mad, strongly implying that only upon meeting Mr. Howe had the defendant lapsed into his incapacitation. Unfortunately he spoke with such didactic precision that the jury abandoned the effort of following his argument long before he concluded it.

Not so Howe. Howe possessed the weapons of a champion orator—undulating mane of hair, large expressive features, orotund tenor—and wielded them with relish. He cajoled, flattered, wheedled, sermonized, and shouted, running the gamut of emotion as a pianist might run the scales, tripping from indignant, sarcastic, injured, and irate to imploring, sentimental, and pathetic without regard to logic or consistency, but with a careful eye on the enthralled inhabitants of the jury box. I had no doubt of the outcome.

255

As I sketched the putative madman, I could not help but compare his mental state with my own. Searching his filthy, pallid features, peering into his dead eyes, I saw nothing which separated us, save the hypocrisy of my self-delusion. Hiding in Manhattan from my responsibilities to those who had borne and loved me, those who had sacrificed to give me a place in the world, was no more honest than this young fop hiding behind the crusted bits of food upon his lapel. We both sought absolution we had not earned.

Marrying Emma and remaining in New York was a scheme as blind and foolhardy as shooting one's father's attorney. Neither addressed the true issues of patrimony. Was I expecting to remain incognito forever? What would my family make of my new situation? I would escape nothing. I would resolve nothing.

I could not leave. I could not stay. I must marry Emma. I could not marry her. Whatever I did was an act of betrayal. My future was a logical impossibility. As I contemplated the conundrum my lumbar muscles commenced to spasm, making sitting too painful to sustain. I signaled to Noah that I had made sufficient sketches and I hobbled from the court, cursing my cowardly constitution. I lay upon the bench in the corridor until I could gather the strength to return to my lodgings.

What should have been an afternoon's work became a two-day battle with dorsal paralysis. I lay transfixed with pain, striving for the strength to complete my task, my mind circling back upon itself in an endless sequence of identical unanswerable questions. Observing the pattern of my dorsal attacks I was quite conscious of their connection with my emotional state, but that knowledge did not diminish the pain or reduce their frequency.

I battled on with patience and will. When I sensed a dorsal lull I would force myself to my sketch pad, standing against the hearth since sitting was impossible, and work until my eyes refused to function, when I would crawl back to my bed and lie victim to my thoughts until again I found the strength to defy them.

I completed the sketch. It was wooden but sufficiently precise to please Noah. I dispatched it, and I slept, or more accurately lay in bed for the hours of darkness, and in the morning I forced myself upright and went to visit Emma.

I was not blind to the irony of my situation. I had come to New York, I had told myself, to investigate the question of evil by observing the children of the streets, and to learn from their behaviour if there was hope for humanity—for me—in a Darwinian universe. Now the objective stance had vanished, yet I searched nevertheless for my future in the wisdom of an illiterate sixteen-year-old. I had been appropriately humbled. The absurdity of my quest and its outcome would be comical were it not for the toll it would take upon the innocent.

I could see by now that my true motives for descending on Manhattan were more complex than I had allowed myself to imagine. My quest was genuine, my admiration for Alger sincere, but what I had portrayed to myself as a research expedition was more a flight from personal oppression. I was cursed with a constitution too frail to support the edifice of expectations which had been raised upon it. My back and my eyes were inadequate to the task, yet I could not ignore the deep conviction that they were the least of my deficiencies. My moral foundation was built of sand. I had neither the certainty of purpose nor the purity of intent to fulfill my nobler destiny. I was fated to live a lesser life.

My experiences in New York had taught me an unexpected truth. Living in Cambridge, traveling through Europe with my family, studying in Germany and at Harvard, searching for my future in the world of reason and higher morality in which my father raised me, I had sought a thread of purpose which would sew my disparate experiences into a unified garment, a coat of many colors which I would don as my destined calling, tailored to conform to the lineaments of my deepest soul, wherein lay dormant the future William James. I believed that I had only to transform the potential into the actual. Was I *in esse* a painter? A biologist? A doctor? I need only open myself wide enough, I thought, and he would emerge. I prised myself open, and when that failed, I prised myself wider, and wider, and wider, until I lay like a corpse upon an autopsy table.

I now realized that my search had been misguided. My deterministic fatalism was less a philosophy than an excuse for abdicating the tyranny of choice. Whatever the hidden truths about the ultimate forces directing our destiny, those forces were not what paralyzed me. I had let myself be frozen in my hapless state by a childish desire for that very inevitability which I pretended to loathe. I wished for destiny to determine my outcome so that I might avoid the trauma of creating it myself. It was becoming clear to me that whatever its essential stuff, my practical identity consisted entirely of those choices which I had made in the course of my life. I did not exist apart from those decisions, or if I did exist upon some higher Platonic plane, that essence of William James was invisible and unknowable, functionally non-existent. I had chosen to flee to New York. I had chosen to lie with Emma Larkin. I had chosen to earn my living as a caricaturist. My future would not search me out. I was creating William James with every choice I made.

I existed as a continuous entity because while each choice was discrete, each was dependent upon the choices past. That sum of actions which equaled William James had begun with my first consciousness, and veered when I departed McLean. No inner essence would make me live with Emma Larkin as a caricaturist in New York. No inner essence would prevent it. The choice was mine. The prospect was terrifying but also liberating. My dorsal spasms eased.

I recognized that my navel-gazing ignored Emma's half of the equation. I was her protector, and I would do the best for Emma or I would become a William James I had no wish to be. I would explain my position frankly and lay out the choices which confronted us. Voicing my thoughts and hearing hers would, I hoped, make the decision self-evident.

I approached her brown-stone unsure of my welcome. I had sent her a note explaining my absence but had received no reply, and I feared it had not been delivered or she had not believed my words and thought me to be avoiding her. Upon entering the building, I was told that she was absent. I elected to await her return in the velveted parlour. She arrived as they were lighting the street lamps. The cool air had burnished her cheeks to a coppery glow. She greeted me cheerfully, without mention of my truantry, and led me upstairs. It was impossible to imagine that this fresh and vital creature had once been the shriveled skeleton I had first encountered.

She opened the door to her room and waved me inside. I entered taking care not to brush against her, which provoked a smile. "I don't bite." She took my hat and hung it by the wash stand. "How you been?" She straightened her hairbrush and comb with proprietary pleasure. How long had she been without a comb before we met? I wished to ask, but the question would insult.

"So you been workin'. I been lookin' myself. Askin' drapers and such if they need a shop lady."

"Any luck?" She had read my note, then, unless it had been read to her. I despised the condescension in the thought.

"The clothes get me a look, but I ain't got no experience nor the know-how nor the lingo. Mainly I ain't got no employer to put me a good word. There's dozens of us fer every openin'."

As I watched her arrange her brush and comb so proudly, my mind, inflamed with my urgency of purpose, leapt unexpectedly to the narrow stair at the Lodging-house, tangy with printer's ink, to a moment when I had been impelled by a similar sense of mission, and I saw again Charles Loring Brace's heavy gaze of careworn greeting. The peace, the certainty in those eyes revealed at once the hypocrisy of my current undertaking. I had not come here that we might jointly decide our course of action. I was here to explain to both of us why I could not marry her, and the more elaborate my explanation, the greater would be the insult to Emma. She would think I had used her callously or, worse, think I was implying that she had maneuvered to ensnare me. Either way her sense of injury would deprive her of what pleasure and comfort my ministrations had hitherto provided.

Why did I wish to explain myself to her? Not to learn from her, nor to instruct her, nor to reach a common understanding.

My true motive, I now realized, was in keeping with my usual infantile pattern. I wished to win her absolution, so that abandoning her would not constitute betrayal. I wished her to carry my burden. Just as I had relied upon my father's and my aunt's support to indulge my intellectual pursuits, and then relied upon Alger to subsidize my New York experiment, now I wished Emma to subsidize her own abandonment by assuring me that I was correct in not making her my wife.

It was time I changed my pattern. If I was to wrong this woman I would shoulder the burden myself. I would not explain; I would not ask self-exculpatory questions; I would act as a grown man should and accept the consequences.

"Have you pursued the possibility of domestic service?" I asked.

"Can't see how, beyond Mrs. Rutledge," she replied with a puckish grin. "Mrs. Rutledge says she don't know no one needs a servant, but she knows a lady with a beautiful house what needs a pretty girl like me. I's skinny, she says, but there's those what like that. Says she'd pay me well and see I's decked out beautiful. All lace and satin. Eat well too."

"What did you tell her?"

"I says I's thinkin' on it." She laughed.

"Are you?"

"I dunno." The laughter dried up. She looked at me with tired eyes. "I cain't go back to gluin' tins. It ain't in me no more."

"You know where her path leads. You'll have a few years of luxury, and then the woman will need fresher faces, and you'll descend to a lower sort of house, and lower still, and if you don't succumb to drink or consign yourself to the river you'll

261

end up an old woman at forty, robbing sailors in a wharf-side panel house or peddling needled beer in a stinking basement on Baxter Street."

"Ain't you the one for sermonizin'. Where you gonna be ten years from now?" Her black eyes bored into me, searching out my secret.

"If I can secure you a good position as a domestic, will you take it?"

"Course I will."

"Then I shall."

"We don't got but two more days."

"I hope to have it by tonight."

"You best be off then." Emma dismissed me. I left with the disquieting sense that in spite of my reticence Emma had heard what I had originally intended to say to her. Our exchange had been my unspoken bid for absolution, and she had refused either to grant or to deny my petition. I respected her the more for that, and respected myself the less.

―――――

Autumn had arrived at last, with a sudden blast of arctic air. I had brought no overcoat from Boston. As I waited outside the *Sun* building the cold crept through my summer suit and crawled into my veins. I was stiff as a trout in a frozen pond when promptly at seven the sleek carriage arrived, its chocolate horses snorting plumes of vapour. As I approached, she opened the carriage door.

"Pardon me, Madam—"

"Mr. Henry, come out of the cold." She was swathed in a cashmere cloak of red so deep it was almost black, and her words emerged from the shadowy depths of the hood like those of an apostolic abbess. When I joined her in the carriage she threw it back, the blood-black fabric framing her pale features to perfection. "How have you been, Mr. Henry?" Her lips voiced genuine concern.

"I've been as well as could be expected, thank you."

"The boys have missed you."

"I miss them. I've had pressing matters which couldn't be delayed."

"I was so sorry to hear about Jemmie."

"That was a blow."

"Have you any word of him at all?"

"No."

She gazed at me with such compassion that I could not bring myself to impose upon her. I sat mute, framing my argument.

"Are you certain that you're well?"

"Quite well. If I look otherwise it's due to the cold and the awkwardness of my task."

"And what is that?"

"I must request a signal act of charity."

"And what is that?" She favoured me with a welcoming smile.

"As you may have heard, Jemmie has a sister I discovered at the brink of death from the cholera."

"Mr. Alger was rapturous about your gifts as a physician."

"It was a close thing. She saved herself, in fact."

"Alger said your fierce dedication pulled her through. He said you wouldn't let her die. He called you a born healer."

"Alger has a weakness for the melodramatic."

263

"He's left us also."

"So I gather."

"Are you returning to us?"

"I'm not certain." Was I? Likely not.

"You were speaking of an act of charity."

"Oh. Excuse me. She's bright. She's a hard worker. She tended her baby brother under the most horrific conditions."

"Her poor baby brother."

"She was willing to give her life for his. She insisted we travel to the potter's field to visit his grave in spite of my efforts to dissuade her." I spoke with particular fervour. My companion smiled with understanding. This woman had many smiles.

"She's healthy now and requires employment."

I nodded, relieved that she had spoken for me. "She's a good young woman."

"You vouch for her?"

"Yes. I've seen her fierce loyalty toward her brother. I've seen her fight off death's grip. I've seen her determination to better herself."

"You talk as if she were your charge."

"She is."

"Then she shall be mine as well. Bring her here at nine o'clock."

I thanked her, and left. I had solved my problem and I had solved Emma's. I was face to face with William James. I liked him not.

⌒CHAPTER TWENTY⌒

NOW THAT IT WAS COLDER, THE TRANSOM WAS SHUT. JEMMIE swaddled his fist in cloth and rapped sharply. The pane shattered with the blow. He removed the broken shards with thumb and forefinger as he had been taught. The putty was dry and stiff, and the glass pulled out in big jagged slivers, like knife blades. Striving for silence, he folded the shards in the cloth and dropped them outside. They landed with a muffled tinkle.

He poked his head through the hole. The hallway was cold and black. Good. He wished to be cold and black himself, a shadow in the shadows. He dropped to the stone and crouched like an Indian. When he was certain that the sound of his fall was met by silence he tripped forward as quickly as he could through the darkness, but his stiff shoes clumped upon the stones. He stopped to remove them, tied the laces in a knot, and threw them around his neck. Now he could feel the smooth hard path, and he made only the faint rubbing sound a snake would make.

He felt like a snake sliding up the stairs, a slippery animal sneaking through the dark. He had no more fear than a snake, no more desire than a snake. He was doing his snake job simply because that is what snakes do. He could remember when he did not know he was a snake. He once thought he would be an Indian fighter, but the harder he had tried to fight Indians, the more snake-like he had become.

He nudged open the door at the top of the stairs and peered through the crack into blackness, straining to make out the stone people who guarded the stone forest. Did they come to life in the dark? Even snakes feared stone people. He crept forward, feeling the safety of soft carpet between his toes. If his foot touched stone he hopped back. If the smallest part of him strayed from the path, the hunters and the goat-footed boy would make him stone like them.

When he reached the middle of the room he could discern the entrance hall in a tepid pool of light from the street, and slipped toward it. He wondered if the gods above in their sheets and towels could see him. He could only make out a rare gilded glimmer up there, like the wink of a celestial eye.

The locks were forged for larger hands than his but he muscled them loose. He had to pull with all his weight against the door to start it moving. Then its mass carried it rapidly inward on buttery hinges, and he struggled to slow it before it compressed him into the wall. When he emerged, Dannie and J.G. were topping the steps. Dannie rubbed Jemmie's head and whispered in his ear, "That's my boyo."

J.G. lit a bull's eye lantern, and Jemmie followed them back down the carpet in the safety of its flickering rays. They moved quickly and said nothing. J.G. swung the lantern back and forth, searching. The stone people were frozen by the light but their shadows danced across the walls, taunting

Jemmie. "You're a shadow too," they seemed to say, "one of us."

When J.G. discovered the dining hall he led them past gnarled chairs and through the door into the butler's pantry, where he waved his lamp across glittering cases, dappling the room with its reflections and revealing the three of them in the glass fronts, ghosts of shadows hovering over a sparkling silver treasure.

J.G. let out a low whistle. "Well, shit me bricks."

Dannie pushed Jemmie out the way they had come. "You're our eyes. Give us a hiss if there's trouble."

Jemmie felt his way back through the dining room and lurked in its doorway, where he could watch the faint yellow stain of the entry. Behind him cabinets squeaked open and heavy silver thumped and rang. The sounds carried too well in the silence. Removing his eyes from the entry, he lost his vision in granular blackness. He peered into its depths, fearful he would miss a telltale movement, and discerned the faded flutter of a white robe. A statue was coming his direction.

Jemmie fumbled back toward the pantry and hissed at its door. When the clunking continued he hissed again louder. The sounds stopped. The thread of light beneath the pantry door turned black. Jemmie shrank into the refuge of the massive marble hearth and strained his blood-clogged ears for sounds of the statue's approach. Did statues make sounds? Footsteps. A white-robed body entered and froze itself into a listening posture at the pantry door. Jemmie listened with it.

They remained, statues both, for long moments of silence as blank as the blackness until a faint but indisputable metallic clink floated from the pantry. The white figure broke into motion and shoved open the door, emitting a shrill and very human "What the hell!" as he was yanked inside. The door slammed shut and Jemmie heard the clattering of silver upon silver and the softer sound of silver crushing flesh and bone. He waited through muffled oaths and more silver colliding with itself and then the pantry door sprang open and Dannie and J.G. swept out hauling fat hemp sacks. J.G. hurried past but Dannie peered about for Jemmie, calling his name in a loud whisper until Jemmie stepped from his place of conceal-ment. Dannie waved him onward and rushed ahead but Jem-mie could not follow, rendered immobile by the sight of the pantry door and the thought of what it concealed.

When he tore himself away, Jemmie saw Dannie limned in the pale entry, gilded by street glow washing through the door that J.G. had left ajar in his flight. Dannie gestured to Jemmie to quicken his pace, then vanished onto the street.

To attain the light Jemmie had to run the gauntlet of the statues. He could make them out, edged with luminescence from the entry, as still as any hunters who ever stalked a deer. If he did not see them perhaps they would not see him. Squeezing his eyes tight shut he trusted to his bare toes to find their way along the carpet, watching the purple of his eyelids brighten toward red, expecting at any moment to feel a cold stone hand upon his shoulder or a bronze arrow through his chest.

Footsteps forced open his eyes. Before him stairs flowed

toward the dim pink gods overhead. A young woman was descending, wrapped in a rippling cloud of white. When her features caught the light he turned to stone.

His knees caved and he dropped, mumbling a prayer, eyes tight shut, but when he opened them Emma was before him still.

"Jemmie?" The voice sounded human.

"Is you a ghost?"

"Jemmie!" She ran forward and clasped him in her arms. Her bosom felt as warm as ever. The room darkened.

"Boyo!" Dannie loomed in the doorway.

Emma cried in fright and backed up the stairs, dragging Jemmie with her. Dannie bounded after them and grabbed Jemmie's arm. Jemmie dug his fingers into the folds of Emma's robe. She screamed again. Dannie ignored her, speaking to Jemmie with deadly urgent calm. "Boyo, you cannot stay here. You'll hang."

"You said she was dead."

"We git or we's all dead." Dannie pulled Jemmie hard.

Jemmie locked his fists on Emma's robe. "You said she was dead!"

Dannie gave a great wrenching yank and jerked Emma and Jemmie off their feet. Their tumbling weight pulled Dannie off balance as well. Buried in the spicy scent of Emma's robe, Jemmie heard again the soft crack of bone.

CHAPTER TWENTY-ONE

I arrived at the mansion in the Pale Lady's sleek black brougham. I had been rousted in the small hours by an irate Mrs. Frye, who had presented me with a brief note on fine paper stating simply that if I wished the best for Jemmie Larkin I should come at once. I expected I was being called to identify his body. I could not imagine how the boy alive could stimulate such urgency. I was saddened at the prospect but had long ago reconciled myself to this outcome. I did not see how it was in Dannie's interest to let the boy survive.

I suspected that Dannie took such an unnatural interest in Jemmie for intensely personal reasons. He viewed our efforts—mine, Alger's, and even O'Connor's—to provide Jemmie with life choices as an unjust allocation of opportunity. He wished to prove to the boy that in spite of never having had such concern lavished upon himself his life path was the superior one, and he wished to punish us for our profligate attentions toward the pretty little lad. I feared that Dannie had devised for Jemmie some particularly grisly and humiliating demise. I almost felt relief that our suspense was at an end.

I viewed the resolution of the mystery of Jemmie's disappearance as an appropriate, if tragic, capstone to my New York adventure. I had grown to welcome the prospect of returning to

Cambridge. As I had predicted, Emma had proved herself conscientious and amenable to instruction and soon her position, and her future, would be secure, a comforting prospect but one which did nothing to ease the escalating tensions in my lower back. I vowed when certain she was fairly established to return to the ministrations of McLean. I would have nothing to hold me in New York.

As I indulged such elegiac thoughts the carriage sped up the most exclusive stretch of Fifth Avenue, empty at this hour of all activity save a sweeping wagon which scrubbed the gutters of the already immaculate street, and alit at a brown cube of a mansion where clustered several carriages and a police wagon. I entered under the suspicious eyes of a uniformed policeman.

Another stopped me in the entry. The simple exterior concealed a foyer of staggering luxury, the antithesis of the restrained elegance I had come to associate with the Pale Lady. *Putti* peered down from the domed entry ceiling and the hall was crammed with bronze and marble wrought in every configuration from satyr to girandole, the whole creating an imposing but claustrophobic effect, as if to impress upon the visitor that the owner possessed not only the resources to purchase every object on earth but also the will to do so.

I showed the policeman my note and was immediately escorted into the salon. Approaching, I heard a dry, cracked voice speak in the didactic tones a peevish cook might use with a scullery maid who had scalded the stew. "This is a domestic issue. I leave it entirely in my wife's hands. Mrs. Vanderbilt runs the domestic corporation!"

The speaker, a lean, stern-faced gentleman, was seated in a   **271**

worn, overstuffed horsehide chair orphaned by the ornate décor. A robe covered his lap. Luxuriant side whiskers compensat-
ing for an utter lack of hair upon his head rendered him readily
recognizable from numerous illustrations, though he was leaner
and more sinewy than they depicted, as if he were the famous
Cornelius Vanderbilt, richest man in America, sculpted in beef
jerky. He spoke to a man firmly planted on strong shoes clasping
a bowler deferentially to his chest. My Pale Lady, wrapped in a
gown the subtlest shade of violet, sat upright in a stiff-backed
chair, composed and attentive. Vanderbilt interrupted himself at
our approach, surveying me with an annoyance milady rose to
dispel. She introduced us and identified the bowlered gentleman
as Mr. Isaac Stanley of the municipal constabulary.

"Mr. Henry," she continued, "Jemmie needs your help."

"I'll help that boy," said Mr. Vanderbilt. "I'll help him to an
early grave." So he was alive, then.

"Please, Cornelius, you were saying I had your permission to
handle this."

"A man is murdered, ma'am," said the detective. "This is
hardly a domestic affair. The law must take its course."

In response to my shocked look, Mrs. Vanderbilt explained.
"Jemmie was caught breaking into this house. My butler has
been slain."

"I can't imagine Jemmie as party to burglary and murder."

Vanderbilt glared at my presumption. "The boy won't talk to
us," said Mrs. Vanderbilt. "I'm hoping he'll talk to you."

"Surely he wishes to exonerate himself."

"He only asks for Emma," said Mr. Stanley.

"His sister." Stanley nodded. Their relationship was already known to the police, then. "What has he told her?"

"We're keeping them apart," said the detective. "We've reason to believe that she's involved as well."

"That's absurd."

"I would say it's obvious," said Vanderbilt. "We employ the sister, and in a matter of days the brother robs us. Why did we employ that girl, Frankie?" He looked sharply at Mrs. Vanderbilt.

"You're describing an unfortunate coincidence," I said.

"Coincidence is a lawyer's word for collusion," said Mr. Stanley.

"I'm certain Jemmie can provide another explanation."

Vanderbilt snorted and rose stiffly. "I'm going to bed. Tell him about the other burglar."

"So you've captured another man?" I dreaded what I knew would follow.

"Yes," said Stanley. "It seems a third escaped. Our other prisoner claims the job was Jemmie's idea. He says Jemmie planned it with his sister."

"Does this prisoner have a notched ear?"

"Yes."

"How do you know about that?" said Vanderbilt, pausing by the door.

"I know him from the Lodging-house," I said. "He calls himself Dannie O'Connor. A notorious liar and thief."

"He is a cheeky little beggar," said Stanley.

"Dannie's very clever, and he has a particular knack for creating confusion and hurting others. Let me talk to Jemmie.

When he understands how he's being betrayed he should reveal the truth."

"If he planned this caper, nine or ninety he'll swing for it."

"He's an innocent, Mr. Stanley, misled by his elders."

"Then he can tell us the name of the third burglar. Your Dannie is tight as a drum on that."

———

A constable led me to the root cellar, a rough stone room lit only by a grate high in the wall which admitted a dim patch of brightening sky. Save for its sacks of potatoes and onions and turnips, the chill place created the perfect impression of a dungeon cell. If Stanley had placed the boy here by design to create in him a terror for his deed, he had succeeded. Jemmie sat in a corner like the madman of my dreams, knees drawn up to his chin, arms wrapping them tight. In the oubliette light I could see little more than the matted hairs upon his head. He made no move to acknowledge my presence. I feared he was catatonic.

I ordered his guard to bring us a lamp to enliven the room. "How are you, Jemmie?" He did not stir. "Have they treated you well? Do you want for anything?" He did not reply. "It's good to see you." He buried his head deeper. A response of sorts. "Perhaps you think I'm angry with you for running away. I was disappointed, that's true, but I'm not angry with you. I know Dannie's power. I know you did what you thought you must." I waited for some reaction. He rocked slightly. "Well, it is good to see you. I feared you were dead." I rose as if to leave and turned my back on him, moving slowly for the door. His voice stopped me.

"Sam is dead." When I faced him, he was again as still as if he'd never spoken.

"He was too small and weak to survive the cholera. Your father died from the cholera also."

Jemmie showed no reaction. "Are you sad for your father?" His dark huddled form shivered lightly. "I remember how you feared him."

"I want Emma." Jemmie spoke with the merest bobbing of his head upon his knees.

"They won't allow you to speak with her at present."

Silence. All movement stopped. The policeman returned with the lamp. Jemmie shied from the light, so I shortened the wick to a glimmer while casting about for a proper avenue of approach. "Are you angry with me?" The silence took on a different quality. "You're angry that I didn't protect you from Dannie."

"I chose." The words dribbled out.

"And you can choose again."

"I's dead."

"No. You're not dead."

"I's hung."

"No."

"Dannie says I's hung. They all say I's hung."

"Dannie says this was your idea. He says you put him up to this. Is that true?"

"Yes."

My chest tightened. "Tell me how."

"I been here. I seen it."

"You came here before?"

"To visit Laura."

"Mrs. Vanderbilt?" He nodded. "Her first name is Frankie. That's an odd name for her, don't you think?"

He nodded. "She's a Laura."

"Did she invite you?"

He shook his head.

"Then why did you come?"

"I had to."

"Did you talk with her?"

He shook no. "I come through the little window. Then I run away."

"And you told Dannie about this?"

"Dannie says I's a right jimmy, says I goes anywheres. He says I's his now, and I goes anywheres fer him. I tol' him 'bout here."

"So Dannie heard you'd been here, and he decided you should both return to rob the building."

Jemmie nodded. I breathed more lightly.

"That first time, did you take anything?"

Jemmie froze again. I sat as still as Jemmie.

"Did you take anything that first time?"

Jemmie nodded. My breath left me.

"What did you take?"

"Indian."

"You took an Indian?"

"And bisons."

"Did you take a painting perhaps?" He nodded. I could not conjure an image of Jemmie sneaking out a window with a painting beneath his arm. "You didn't steal a painting."

He nodded. "In me head."

"So you looked at the painting."

He nodded.

I smiled. "You're not a thief; you're a connoisseur." He looked at me, fearful. "That's a fine thing. That's a person who loves pictures and understands them."

His voice rose in anger. "I chose Dannie like you said not and I chose hell like O'Connor said not and I's gonna hang."

I put my hands upon his narrow shoulders. He dug his chin deeper into his knees. "I know you. You're no thief."

"I chose. I's dead. You said."

"You can choose again."

He looked at me suspiciously. "You said not!"

"I was wrong."

"Then why listen to you!" He spit out the words with all the fury bottled inside his tight little frame.

"You needn't. Look inside. Where is the Indian fighter?"

"Gone!"

"I don't believe that." I caught his eye, and saw beneath his angry denial a glint of possibility. "When you're free of Dannie you'll be straight and strong. You'll fight Indians and hunt bison." He sank his head into his knees in despair. "You can be free, but you must fight back. You must tell the name of the man who ran away."

"Dannie don't die." The words sifted through gritted teeth.

"Dannie will hang for murder. Tell me the name of the man who ran away."

Jemmie's rigid features betrayed hints of a deep inward struggle. I waited him out, convinced that more words would

277

only weaken his nascent resolve, instead peering into his eyes in hopes of imparting my strength of purpose.

"J.G." He spoke softly, in a voice tight with despair.

"J.G.," I repeated, eliciting a small nod. "Do you know his full name?" A small shake. "How is he formed? Is he big? Small?"

"Big. With a sweet voice."

"Where is he found?"

"Harry Hill's."

"You're a brave strong lad."

He squirmed away from the compliment. "Hangin' don't kill Dannie. I seed it."

———

Upon leaving Jemmie I noticed that the glass was missing from the transom window at the end of the hall. I rolled a barrel beneath it, and upon climbing up I saw shards wrapped in a cloth strip lying outside. I had discovered Jemmie's little window.

Returning to the stairs I passed the kitchen, where I spied Dannie chatting with a policeman and a scullery maid while munching on an apple, as cheerful and relaxed as if he were the woman's suitor instead of a suspected murderer. Seeing him inspired me with the usual combination of fascination and dread. Against my better judgement I intruded, addressing him gruffly from the door.

"Mr. O'Connor!"

He welcomed me with his habitual grin. "You're meanin' me, I suppose."

"And what name are you going by these days?"

"Henry. Dannie Henry." My annoyance pleased him. I resolved not to be drawn into argument, harbouring no illusions that I could inculcate a conscience in the man, but for Jemmie's sake I thought his remarkable serenity worth probing. "You seem to find this tragedy amusing."

"I don't sees how bein' grim and gloomy's gonna bring back the dead."

"Contrition on your part might make the law show some compassion."

"I's sorry I's caught. I's sorry t'other fella killed that butler. I's sorry I ever met little Jemmie Larkin and ever let him seduce me into a life of crime with his sweet talk of Vanderbilt riches."

The smooth conviction with which he uttered these words chilled my heart. "You'll have to concoct a less ridiculous lie than that."

"Weren't my sister set up the job. Weren't me cased it out."

"One look at Jemmie will prove you wrong."

"The devil comes in all shapes and sizes. 'Twas his air of innocence seduced me. I imagine my lawyer'll call you and Mr. Alger to testify about the corruptin' influence of the little snot, him lyin' 'bout Mr. Alger and almost ruining Mr. Alger's reputation and all."

I should have anticipated this tactic but did not. I stifled my revulsion and spoke harshly, to disabuse him of the ploy. "Your neck will stretch before a lawyer can stretch that fable to fit the facts."

"Ever heared of Abe Hummel? Howe and Hummel?"

"You can't afford him."

"Cain't I though?" He took a large bite from his apple.

Dannie's bravado, then, was inspired by faith in his representation. Yet that did not explain his positive good cheer. **279**

"You're lying to save your hide," I said, "that's understandable, but what's the pleasure you find in this?"

Dannie munched apple and smiled. "Now if I told you that, I'd lose the half of it."

———

I returned to the detective and Mrs. Vanderbilt, agitated at the thought of Mr. Hummel twisting a judge and jury into Dannie's knots at the expense of Jemmie and poor Alger. Frankie, impressed that I had managed to penetrate Jemmie's silence, offered me tea. "Tell us, Mr. Henry, how you reached the boy."

"I appealed to his faith in justice," I said, with an eye on Mr. Stanley. "He's an innocent who's been ill used by the older boy, who, by the way, now claims my own name as his, purely for the pleasure of vexing me." I sipped the excellent beverage in that overdecorated parlour, thinking of Jemmie squatting among the turnips. "Apparently Jemmie came here one day to visit Mrs. Vanderbilt. Mrs. Vanderbilt has an extraordinary influence over the boys at the Lodging-house," I said, elaborating for Mr. Stanley's benefit. "Jemmie apparently felt he had to see where she lived."

"He presented his *carte de visite*, no doubt," said Mr. Stanley.

"He squeezed in through the cellar transom."

"Of course!" said Frankie. "We had an intruder, a boy, a few weeks ago."

"Did he ask for you?" inquired Mr. Stanley.

"No. He fled when we discovered him."

"Nothing was taken," I pointed out.

"No."

280   "That was Jemmie, no doubt overawed by your establish-

ment. Recently, Jemmie has been seduced by the older boy into abandoning his usual haunts, and he has fallen under Dannie's sway. He told Dannie about his adventure, perhaps to impress him with his daring, and Dannie saw an opportunity to steal the Vanderbilt silver. Dannie was, I believe, grooming Jemmie to be a cat burglar in any case. He called Jemmie his jimmy."

Stanley listened, noncommittal. "That doesn't explain his sister's role."

"His sister is in this house as an act of charity on Mrs. Vanderbilt's part instigated by my intervention upon her behalf."

"A coincidence," said Mr. Stanley derisively.

"Not precisely. Their presence is connected, but in a subtler fashion than Dannie's lies would have it. If Jemmie hadn't been at the Newsboys' Lodging-house I'd never have met Emma, and if Mrs. Vanderbilt weren't such a charming and magnetic woman she wouldn't have attracted Jemmie's attention, or mine, nor would she have had the grace to accept Emma into her employ."

"Whatever you say." Mr. Stanley had little patience for the finer points of my argument. "I'm taking them all to the Tombs."

"Surely not Emma," I said. "Look at the transom window. Jemmie entered with no help from the inside. If his sister had been involved, he would have entered by the door."

"Unless he wished to conceal her involvement."

"If he entered by the transom he didn't require an accomplice. In the sciences, we look for the simplest explanation that fits all the facts. I believe I've supplied that."

"You're a scientist, then?"

"Of a sort."

"And what sort is that?"

Trapped, I could think of nothing else but "I concern myself with the contradictions of the human *psyche*."

"Not a branch of science with which I'm acquainted," said Mr. Stanley, rising from his seat. "I assume your scientific methods didn't uncover the third burglar."

"As a matter of fact they did."

The good detective regarded me with surprise and a hint of respect. "For an innocent, he's quick to rat out his pals."

"They're not his pals. The man's name is J.G. He's a big man with a sweet voice who frequents Harry Hill's Saloon."

"We'll take the boy's cooperation into account. If you'll excuse me, Mrs. Vanderbilt, I'll be off."

"Mr. Stanley," she said, holding him with her steady open gaze, "surely Jemmie's assistance convinces you that he wasn't conspiring with his sister."

"That's a matter for the courts."

"In the meantime, let her remain in my household. I shall be responsible for her."

Stanley placed his bowler upon his head and squared it carefully. "I admire your generosity of spirit, ma'am, but if I were you I wouldn't count on finding its match in the likes of Emma Larkin."

"I'll take my chances with her."

"As you wish. But I'd watch her closely if I were you."

"We're all closely watched, Mr. Stanley, by someone far more powerful than I."

When Mr. Stanley left I asked to see Emma, but was told the

girl was sleeping. I apologized to Mrs. Vanderbilt for putting her in this position. She waved that away. "What perturbs me," she said, "is that my presence among those boys brought this about."

"I don't see what you could have done differently."

"Why do you think Jemmie followed me home?"

"I don't know."

"As a specialist in the human *psyche,* give me your hypothesis."

I flushed. "I only claimed expertise to lend my interpretation a presumptive legitimacy."

"You've assumed the mantle. Speculate, please."

"I'd say the boy's in love with you."

"Mr. Henry!"

"They're all in love with you. The child in Jemmie sees the mother he wishes for, and the man in him sees the woman of his dreams." She laughed, blushing. "Jemmie said he had to come here," I continued. "I can't think what else that would mean."

"Does Dannie truly believe that a court would declare that little boy to be a criminal mastermind?"

"It's the sort of lie that has the charm of fable about it. He says Abe Hummel is representing him. I can imagine the circus he'd make of Dannie's devil child. I shall try to dissuade Hummel from accepting the case, but I fear it's a fool's errand."

Frankie lifted the inlaid lid on an *escritoire* and penned a brief message. "Present this to Mr. Hummel with my compliments."

"Do you know the man?"

"No, and it's better I don't." She handed me the note as if it were a bridge between us. "I trust to your discretion. We shall

283

save Jemmie and his sister, Mr. Henry, you and I together." I pocketed Frankie's note, determined to do everything in my power to insulate her from this nasty business.

———

I entered the barren offices of Howe & Hummel at the earliest decent hour, but the splintered benches were already replete with supplicants. I gave my name to a sharp-faced young clerk and requested to see Mr. Hummel. When I undertook to state the purpose for my visit he cut me short. "Don't want to know. Don't need to know. Don't mean to know." He pointed me at a bench where an overrouged young woman ceded space for me beside a man in an apron that smelled of fish. We made it our mutual business to ignore one another, and stare at the passers-by who paraded between the giant letters of the firm name painted upon the store-front windows.

The dull sky had trapped the night cold, and the chill radiated from the glass and spread among us like an icy bath. The doll-faced woman implored the clerk for heat. At her third request he squatted at a large safe in the center of the room, spun its dials, and opened the ponderous doors, revealing nothing more valuable than a bucket of coal with which he fed the stove.

The office was a rambunctious place. Message boys came and went. Junior attorneys joked and toiled and consulted with suspicious-looking men, perhaps detectives. A moment of general hilarity erupted when one young fellow was called into Mr. Howe's office but could not attend him because his shoes were glued to the floor. At last the diminutive black figure of Mr. Hummel appeared in the windows, in conversation with a bull of a man in immaculate gray. When they parted at the door they shook hands and the bull said, "Save my boys and I'll buy you toys." Hummel reminded the man that he had expensive hobbies.

Hummel surveyed our bench, and we looked at him expectantly. As his eye lingered on mine I grasped the opportunity to introduce myself, excusing my rudeness by telling him that a nine-year-old boy was enduring the traumas of prison at this very moment, unjustly accused of murder. To the annoyance of the other suitors he waved me in.

Hummel's office was as simply furnished as his waiting room, save that the walls were covered with portraits of stage beauties, affectionately inscribed. His desk was a schoolteacher's table. A molasses barrel sat incongruously in one corner. Hummel himself created an oddly contradictory impression. Viewed from close quarters, and freed from the solemnity of the courtroom, his extreme youth emerged. He could not have been more than twenty-two. His boyish gestures and enthusiasms reminded me of Alger, but whereas in Alger they expressed simplicity and naïveté, in Hummel they were tempered by a contrary solemnity and calculation. He would jest; then he would subside into a carefully adopted neutrality of expression. I could not determine if his shifting was a natural expression of a dual nature or a well-crafted façade designed to draw the most from our encounter.

"You saved me the trouble of searching you out." He spoke in a high breathy voice as he rummaged through a pile of documents upon his desk. With a satisfied "aha" he extracted a copy of the *Christian Union* open to my sketch of the trial of the nubile Sufis. "We made my head a tad balloonish, didn't we?" I was dumbstruck. "Come, come, Mr. Henry, you can't expect your work to go unnoticed."

"Well, sir, it's a cartoon. It was my job to exaggerate, so as to capture a larger truth."

"Sometimes I think that's my job as well. But I don't see the truth advanced by giving me a watermelon head."

"I tried to be equally unflattering to everyone concerned."

"You've revealed the Brahma bull in Comstock, I'll grant you that. Here, inscribe something witty and I'll have it framed." He proffered me the drawing and a pen.

"I thought you found it unflattering."

"It makes me into a Mongoloid idiot. But it draws attention to the firm."

I wrote, "For Mr. Hummel, who creates the truth."

"I'll take that as a compliment," he said, upon examination, "though I suspect you're a man who believes there's only one truth, and not made by the likes of me." Pointing to a chair, he hopped onto the molasses barrel and from his high perch struck an attentive pose. "So. You're here about a murderous nine-year-old."

I sat myself and described in detail Jemmie's dilemma. As I talked, he absently twirled his death's-head watch fob and asked incisive questions about Jemmie's life in the Lodging-house and his previous relations with Dannie. I described Dannie in the most unflattering terms, but I saw no need to mention his blackmailing of Alger. Hummel chewed on the ramifications.

286   "If Jemmie swung, he'd be the youngest ever in this state, by

a good two years." The thought seemed to intrigue him. "But what do you wish of me?"

"Dannie said you'd represent him. I assumed he was lying, but were you planning to defend him I wish to warn you off."

"What that you've told me constitutes a warning?" he said combatively.

"Nothing, not precisely," I stammered, taken aback by his inquisitorial tone. "I suppose this is more a petition than a warning."

"Do you wish me to defend Jemmie? My fee for capital cases is three thousand dollars cash in advance. That includes the cost of an appeal." He watched me through slitted eyes.

"I hadn't thought of that. I'd assumed if Jemmie had a fair trial he would be fairly treated, whoever defended him."

"You've seen enough of Dame Justice to know better than that. You mean you've no wish for me to defend the boy because you think I'm a shady character who twists the truth, and your Jemmie doesn't need truth-twisting to be exonerated."

"Sir, I'm here to appeal to your higher instincts."

"Nonsense on both counts. Jemmie is a little thief, and the others would never have been in the Vanderbilt mansion were it not for him. He's guilty, and as the murder was a direct result of his criminal actions, he's guilty of murder." He watched me until he was certain that I had absorbed the truth of his analysis. "I've been somewhat disingenuous myself," he continued. "As it happens, I am taking Dannie's case." He hopped off the barrel, ending our interview. "I would like to thank you for this frank exchange of views."

I flushed hot. "You have taken advantage, sir."

"That I have. But you came here with the purpose of taking advantage of me. Good-day." He extended his hand.

The result of my interview had been only to fortify Dannie's case. Fearing disaster for Jemmie, I could see nothing to do but produce the envelope from Mrs. Vanderbilt. The name engraved thereon stifled his flippancy. He tore it open and focused upon the note with intimidating intensity. When he looked at me again, his face had taken on a mask of neutrality. "Do you know what is in this letter?"

"It was not addressed to me."

"Well, Mr. Henry, it appears you've been playing a stronger hand than I." He summoned a clerk, then returned to his desk to pen a hurried note which he handed over for immediate delivery.

"I've withdrawn from Dannie's case."

"Thank you."

"Thank Mrs. Vanderbilt. I'll be representing Jemmie."

"Did she hire you?"

"The wife of the richest man in America, and arguably the most powerful, expressed deep concern for Jemmie's welfare and asked me to do whatever I could for the boy. You may tell her that I shall represent Jemmie *gratis,* as an act of charity on her behalf."

"Is that what she intended?"

"Do you wish to save the boy or not?"

"Of course."

"Can you think of anyone who is more likely to free him?"

"No."

"Of course not." He twirled his fob impatiently. "She also

said I should respect your wishes in this matter. Mr. Henry, the choice is yours. What shall it be?"

I saw myself shake his hand. I heard myself say, "I place Jemmie in your care."

"I'll have him out by dinner time."

———

That afternoon I was summoned from my lodgings to the Tombs. Hummel had persuaded a judge, by what means I know not, that Jemmie was the victim of an unfortunate coincidence. According to Hummel, young Jemmie had been sneaking into the mansion to visit his sister when the burglars chanced to break in. In fact, according to Hummel, had young Jemmie not roused his sister, Dannie would never have been caught. The myriad contradictions between this account and the facts of the case were no obstacle to the bench. Jemmie was freed upon my recognizance, with the proviso that he be available to testify at the murder trial. Hummel had saved the boy, and skewered my hypocrisy by forcing me to choose between the True and the Good.

Jemmie stood with a blue-suited constable while I signed the day book. We walked together past the crowded columns. "You signed fer me," he said.

"Yes."

"Does that make me yours?"

"After a fashion."

"How?"

"It means I've promised to look after you until they need you."

"When's that?"

"I don't know. Weeks or months."

"What happens then?"

Jemmie had cut to the quick. I had no ready answer. I took the Hippocratic approach. "I'm your protector. No harm will come to you, I promise."

We descended the steps. Jemmie pondered my words, and spoke with decisive finality. "Yer my protector fer good and all."

I nodded. For the first time he put his hand in mine, allowing himself to be a child with me. "I want Emma."

I returned him to my lodgings to wash the stink of prison from his person, using my experience with Hummel to navigate the turbulent waters of Mrs. Frye. I announced decisively that Jemmie was joining me in my chambers for an indeterminate period, and before she could roil too mightily I showed her the letter by which I had been summoned the previous evening and informed her that I was caring for the boy at the request of a lady who wished to remain nameless. Mrs. Frye recognized the letterhead, and was most accommodating. She herself saw to his bath. "Tell me, Mr. Henry," she said as the servant girl poured in the steaming water, "you're on intimate terms with this woman, then."

"We share an interest in helping homeless children."

"She could buy them each a mansion if she chose, but she'll never grace the drawing room of Mrs. Astor." She tested the water with a gesture of superior gentility. "I can well understand her desire to help the poor, herself a refugee from the ashes of Atlanta, plucked from destitution. She is truly among the fortunate of the earth." She poured from a ewer of cold water with a dismissive flick of her wrist.

"Please, Mrs. Frye," I interjected, "I don't wish to hear such things."

She gave me a coy smile. "Mr. Vanderbilt won't live forever, of course, but don't count on her getting much out of it."

"Really, Mrs. Frye."

"They say she signed a contract with the man. She's even forbidden to have children, they say, to protect the others' inheritance. I have clothes a boarder left when he couldn't pay the rent that look to fit your boy."

She departed, and I eased Jemmie into the bath, trying unsuccessfully to banish her gossip from my mind. I was certain it was the baseless talk of envious tongues, yet it cast Frankie's involvement with the newsies in a suitably tragic mould, which made me lend it credence. If Frankie could not be a mother, she would mother a hundred. Mrs. Frye's attempts to disparage Mrs. Vanderbilt had the opposite effect, making Frankie appear even nobler than I had already conceived her, if that were possible. Jemmie interrupted my musings by complaining that I was scrubbing him too vigorously.

Shadows were lengthening when we reached the mansion. Jemmie, polished and presentable, remained in the carriage while I summoned Mrs. Vanderbilt to her door. Under the circumstances it did not seem appropriate for Jemmie to enter the house, so I asked that Emma be allowed to join him in the carriage. Frankie sent for her, and we stood in the obscurity of the entrance, watching their reunion in the hack. They hugged briefly, they spoke little, yet we could see in their gestures and their posture that simply being in each other's presence strengthened their spirits.

291

I related to Mrs. Vanderbilt my adventures with Hummel, stressing that her intervention had determined this happy outcome. She replied that my role had been equally essential. I daresay we each felt greater satisfaction in the other's achievement than in our own. Watching the brother and sister, I daresay we felt like brother and sister in spirit. At length a maid appeared and requested Emma's presence, and I went to the carriage to summon her. As she stepped to the pavement I took the opportunity for a brief private word.

"How are you bearing up, Emma?"

"Jemmie's free for good and all?"

"There are formalities, but I'd say the danger has passed."

"That's a blessing."

"Mrs. Vanderbilt has been an angel of mercy for the two of you."

"That she has."

"And you? Are you being treated well by the other servants?"

"Well enough. Katie Rourke, she was sweet on Edgar what died, and she's hard on me."

The thought appeared to burden her. "Do they believe you're involved?" She would not answer, but hung back from the door where Mrs. Vanderbilt awaited us. "Emma, speak. I'm here for you."

"I's pregnant."

CHAPTER TWENTY-TWO

With Mrs. Vanderbilt standing in the doorway, conversation was impossible. Having told me her news Emma was content to regain her post without further comment, but she seemed relieved when I would not allow it until she consented to a *rendezvous* later that night.

I returned with Jemmie to my lodgings dazzled by contradictory emotions. My satisfaction in extricating him was stifled beneath anger at the Fates, fear for Emma, self-pity, self-castigation for succumbing to self-pity, and, against all reason, a rush of paternal pride. Struggling to sort my way through it all, I could not but discern a pattern in the chaos of recent events. Since I had lain with Emma, I had followed a course which could only be described as choosing the Good above the True.

Searching myself, I detected no guilt for consorting with Emma. Whatever the ultimate consequences the decision at that moment had been correct, for her and for me, and I would not unmake that experience nor exchange it for any other in my life. The problem, as I came to define it, was that I had not sufficiently honoured the meaning of that moment. Having accepted its goodness, I must also accept its truth, and instead I had chosen to act as if it had not transpired.

Once I had chosen to deny my interlude with Emma my

dealings with Hummel were predetermined: I had perforce to engage him to save Jemmie by any means possible. Having chosen to preserve my own future at Emma's expense, how could I then sacrifice Jemmie's future to some abstract concept of justice?

However, I harboured no guilt on that score either. What was one more mockery of justice in this city where injustice was more the norm than the exception, compared with Jemmie's life? Yet I knew that if the whole world acted as I had, social order would collapse. Who but criminals would wish to live in a world where justice was dispensed by Howe & Hummel? I recognized that I had chosen the evanescent, temporary good over the higher good. I was confident of my choice, although knowingly choosing the lesser over the greater good should be a philosophical impossibility, since the very act of choosing might be described as the act of deciding which possibility affords a greater good.

I could not deny my own emotions. Perhaps I sensed that the great benefit served to the concrete reality of Jemmie's life outweighed the minuscule erosion to the abstract concept of rule by law. Perhaps. I suspected that beneath my emotions lay the irrational certainty that the preservation of a single human soul was a worthier goal than the protection of any abstract good, no matter what logic might assert to the contrary.

This perception put a different colour to the notion of absolute evil, and the dread that had prompted the emotional collapse which relegated me to McLean. The horrors I had encountered pondering evil in the abstract receded before the simple need to resist all efforts to destroy a single human spirit.

This was not an arcane perception. Emma would acknowledge its obvious truth. However, this truth could not be learned through logic and study. My studies served only to obscure it, based as it was upon irrational insight grasped in the lived moment, through honest interpretation of one's own inner spirit.

My problems, then, derived from denying the truth of my actions with Emma. In acting as if our carnal encounter had never existed I had stifled our fumbling efforts toward the Good; I had become, in effect, Evil. Fortunately, I had now been offered an opportunity to undo what I had done. This time I would accept the implications of my choice. I would marry Emma and raise our child, and Jemmie, here in New York.

Time passed on turtle feet until I could meet Emma. Jemmie saw my drawing from the *Christian Union*, which I had in my vanity placed upon my mantel. When he learned I had been paid three dollars for it, he sought out my drawing supplies and declared that he would become an artist. I reminded him of his passion for fighting Indians, but he dismissed that with a shrug and asked me what to draw. Thinking to unburden the boy, and to learn something of his inner life, I said he should draw the images which he saw in his mind. He set to work assiduously on a large black vehicle with enormous wheels, which he told me was the locomotive at the Bowery Theatre. My interest provoked him to describe his impression of the play and his own experiences of locomotives, a remarkable reversal from his previous taciturnity in my presence. Apparently as Jemmie's protector I shared with his Laura of the Lodging-house access to his thoughts.

At supper he ate with such gusto that he had to be restrained **295** from bolting his food. Mrs. Frye made much of his Vanderbilt association, provoking a pomaded young clerk, a *Star* reader, to quote its breathless account of murder and mayhem at the Fifth Avenue mansion. Though the article made no mention of Jemmie, Mrs. Frye's imagination was piqued. I avoided her barbed inquiries, except to remark that Mrs. Vanderbilt had complete confidence in Jemmie, as did I. Mrs. Frye kept her eye on the boy until I led him upstairs.

At last, long after Jemmie was asleep upon a cot in my room, when theatres were closed and the evening crowd thin, I engaged a hack and ascended Fifth Avenue. Emma was waiting at the corner of Thirty-fourth Street, shivering in the chill air. She jumped in beside me and pulled the blanket about her slight body, clasping the hem with two hands at her chin like the child she was. I instructed the cabbie to drive slowly toward Central Park. From his perch above and behind he clicked to the horses and we set off at a leisurely pace. We talked in low tones, conscious of his thickly clad body hovering over the thin roof of the cab.

I thanked Emma for telling me of her condition. She gave a dry laugh. "Yer welcome."

"No, Emma, I'm sincere. I behaved badly before. You've given me the chance to make up for that."

"You set me up plenty fine. I got no complaints."

"I had no business palming you off on Mrs. Vanderbilt."

Emma pouted. "I ain't some playin' card."

"No. Certainly. That's exactly what I'm trying to say. I didn't treat you—treat us—with the respect the situation demanded."

"So now yer talkin' like I sold you a railroad."

296

"No. No. I'm not. I am not trying to diminish our relation."

"Did I say you were?"

"No." Whatever I said, Emma chose to understand as an insult. "Let me start again."

"Good."

"Emma, please marry me."

She laughed again.

"Please, this is a serious matter."

"Course it is." She sat up straight and brought the blanket tight about her, assuming the majesty of a Cleopatra meeting her Mark Antony. "If yer askin' my hand in marriage why ain't you on your knees?"

Though I suspected she was playing with me, I had no alternative but to comply. I knelt in the cramped, bouncing carriage, struggling to maintain my balance. She held out her hand. I took it lightly, and aimed my wobbly gaze as well as I could manage into her dark impassive eyes. "Will you marry me?"

"Why?"

"Excuse me?"

"Yer askin' like you already know the answer. Why should I marry you?"

"Emma, you're mocking me."

"You the one doin' the mockin'. You say 'marry me' and you can't find a single reason fer it."

"Our lives are bound together."

"Do you love me?"

"I love you."

A dryness in my tone caused her to pull her hand from mine. "You don't."

"Emma, we're from different worlds. We know little of each other. I admire your courage and your strength of will and your clean common sense."

"How romantic is that? A girl gets proposed to, she don't want it 'cause she's full a common sense."

"You're very beautiful. That goes without saying. You've a purity of features and a lithe and graceful form."

"Sounds like yer describin' a prize horse."

I struggled back to the seat. "This is not a game."

"It sure ain't. No fun in it at all."

"You may not love me, Emma. I'd be surprised if you did. You probably find me a rather comical figure. However, you'll discover that I'm a kind, fair, and affectionate man."

She grew more serious. "I knows you're those things."

"Then marry me."

" 'Cause I's pregnant."

"Love will come if we treat each other well. This isn't a romance-tale fantasy. Look at the choices before you. When your pregnancy can't be concealed, Mrs. Vanderbilt will dismiss you. You'll sink into the slums, or worse. Or we can build a life together."

"You think I told you I was pregnant so's you'd marry me?"

"Certainly not."

"Then why'd I tell you?"

"You were duty bound to tell me."

"Yer a right strange man. I told you so's you'd help me to get rid of it."

"That we cannot do."

298   "Yer not gonna get religious of a sudden?"

"We haven't the right."

Emma leaned out and called to the driver to turn the cab. She fell back into her seat with a thump as the cab altered its course. "I's gettin' rid of this thing in me, with you or no."

"Emma, this child is mine as well as yours. I have a share in this decision."

"No."

"Let's make the most of what's befallen us."

"It ain't yers."

"What?"

"The child ain't yers."

Suddenly the carriage felt exceedingly warm. "I trust you're not saying that simply to shut me up."

"I was late already when we did it."

I pondered the cruel miracle of that tiny homunculus surviving Emma's vicious bout of cholera. "It makes no difference. It could as easily have been mine. It's mere chance that it isn't."

She laughed, a harsh animal bark. "Yer a right piece a work."

"It doesn't matter who the father is. Really."

"It matters to me!"

I'd been blind and egoistic. "Forgive me. I didn't mean to take you from the man you love. You've never mentioned him or even hinted he existed."

"He don't!"

"The father died, then?"

"Yes!"

"Then marry me."

"You idiot!" Her face wrenched itself into horrific contortions, every muscle fighting to pull its own direction as if each had no wish to share in this poor woman's physiognomy. She gave an inhuman groan, a feral cry of helplessness and pain, and pounded on my chest.

The driver halted the cab. His voice penetrated the roof. "Everything all right in there?"

"Yes, please," I said. "Walk on."

"We're God-fearin' folk, we are, and we won't have nothin' befall that girl in our cab."

"Continue, please."

"You all right, miss?"

"Yes, go!" she called through her sobs.

"Say the word, miss, and we're driving straight to the station house."

"No! Take me home!"

The cab started up. I realized what a fool I'd been. "You poor girl."

"You don't know!"

"I can imagine."

"No!"

"No, I suppose I can't." I gathered her to my chest. Her sobs ebbed. We rode for a period in silence. I risked her displeasure by speaking. "It's not the infant's fault. Let's raise him together."

"Never."

"Then I'll see he's well adopted."

"No."

"You'll live comfortably while you carry the child to term." She buried her head in my chest and shook a vigorous no.

"Give me a single reason why we shouldn't." She mumbled something into my coat. "Excuse me?"

She turned her face to mine, and with a resigned, defiant look, she spoke. "This baby's my brother."

I touched her bare head. She jerked away. My hand hung suspended, a hairy male appendage. I snatched it back. She sat upright and apart from me, as if we repelled each other with an electrostatic charge. Bile rose bitter in my throat. I forced myself to reach for her again, though I knew she would find my touch repulsive. Her fingers stiffened beneath mine, but she did not draw them back. The soft skin belied her awful secret. When the cab slowed at Thirty-fourth Street, I broke the silence. "Do you have Sunday afternoon off?"

"Yes."

"Meet me here at two."

She darted from the carriage.

———

The following day I visited the library at the pathological museum of New York Hospital and familiarized myself with abortion procedures. All the alternatives were brutal and dangerous, and fell into two categories, crude abrasive surgery or the ingestion of highly toxic poisons. She could not have been more than eight or ten weeks gone or her condition would have been evident to me. If she was less than two months with child the chance of safe success was greater. I considered performing the procedure myself, but my reading quickly dissuaded me. Experience was the single most valuable attribute in the surgeon. The preferred method required a practiced, sensitive touch and a small wire. The more elaborate the equipment, the more invasive the procedure, and the more ways it could cause harm.

Since abortion was a crime I could not ask for referral to the most prominent practitioner. That was not necessary, however, as she was a favorite topic at Mrs. Frye's dinner table. She called herself Madame Restell, and the newspapers dubbed her the Wickedest Woman in New York. She was also said to be among the wealthiest, and had constructed what the papers referred to as her 'palace' on Fifth Avenue and Fifty-second Street. She scandalized Mrs. Frye and the rest by behaving like any other wealthy matron, riding afternoons behind an excellent pair in a sober black victoria in Central Park, where the women stared and the men refused to lift their hats to her.

Restell held the fascination of overt iniquity. Though she had spent a comfortable year at the penitentiary on Blackwell's Island two decades ago, the papers were fond of trumpeting her invulnerability. She spent lavishly, advertising her pills in coyly worded placements in their pages and purchasing influential support, but her principal defense was said to lie in a small black book reputed to contain the name of every customer. She did not earn her mansion on Fifth Avenue by tending to the poor and powerless. Through all this speculation she maintained a politic silence. Not only did her profession demand the discretion of a priest in the confessional, but the overheated workings of the public imagination promoted her interests more than any statement she might concoct. I meant to determine if her skills were the equal of her reputation before I entrusted her with Emma.

Madame's mansion was sufficiently far north that the promise of Fifth Avenue had been as yet only partially fulfilled. The fine Fisk paving ended a block below, leaving the Avenue a dirt road, and a farmer grew vegetables across the street. The building itself was impressively tall, a *sous-sol* and four stories above, removed from the street by an exaggerated moat. It did not, however, present a fortress aspect, for the moat allowed light to the basement, and the walls were as much glass as brown-stone, as if to proclaim to the passers-by that the house held no secrets. This transparency was mitigated, however, by heavy curtains of satin and lace, which concealed while proclaiming a sumptuous world within. The impression overall was of a calculated use of private luxury to public effect, a contradictory assertion that the dwelling had nothing to hide, indeed welcomed the visitor, while nonetheless concealing unutterable mysteries.

I mounted its elaborately balustraded stoop and pulled the bell beneath its Rococo canopy. A man servant opened the door onto a grand hall of marble and mirrors. I presented him with a note for Madame and was ushered through a maze of bronze, silver, and gilded knickknacks that rivaled the Vanderbilt collection into a green satin parlour to await her response. Such rooms, crowded with chairs, sofas, and settees awaiting occupation, usually have an expectant air when empty; this chamber, however, felt oddly devoid of such anticipation, as though the space belonged exclusively to its carved, stuffed inhabitants, among whom a human being was a rare alien intruder.

Soon enough Madame appeared, a petite, chalky, elderly woman with black hair, clad in black silk, her shoulders draped in a black velvet mantilla trimmed in silver thread. A thickness

303

in her person suggested a fondness for eating well. She held out her hand to me sheathed in creamy black kid. I had expected the fine tapered fingers of a surgeon, but hers were thick and stubby, though her wrist was small and finely boned.

"In the future, if this is not a social call, please use the basement entrance on Fifty-second Street." Her elegance was betrayed by a Cockney accent.

"Certainly. Would you rather I repair there now?"

"No thank you." She smiled thinly. She had the weary, penetrating gaze of a sea captain who has spent his life scanning an empty horizon. "It pleases me that my neighbours see a gentleman paying a social call. How can I help you?"

"I'm here on behalf of a young woman who finds herself in tragic circumstances."

"So you've written."

"I'm sure you hear many such stories." She inclined her head slightly in assent. "I must admit that I'm not a proponent of your form of treatment. I believe that most cases do not justify such draconian methods."

"I've yet to meet a gentleman who believes in the morality of what I do, or one who'll pass up the opportunity to use my services."

"This is truly an exceptional case."

"They all are."

"Even among the exceptional, this cries out for attention."

"Why is that?"

"That, I'm not at liberty to disclose."

"How old is the young lady?"

"Approximately sixteen."

"Healthy?"

"Yes, though recently recovered from the cholera."

"How advanced is her problem?"

"I don't know precisely. Not further than the third month."

"I will not treat beyond the third month. You're certain she wants this?"

"Yes."

"You're not only speaking your wish, but hers?"

"I'm not the father of the child. I'm her physician."

"They're never the father."

The woman's sarcasm was more resigned than bitter. She was speaking an objective truth, more for her own benefit than mine. I felt obliged to explain that I was not like the others, not merely to justify myself but to reassure her that all men were not the beasts she imagined. "She's lonely and afraid," I said. "I nursed her through her cholera. She needs the support I can give her. I'll be at her side during this trial as well."

"That's impossible. There can be no witnesses. For her protection and mine."

"But she needs me."

"No doubt that thought gives you comfort. More comfort, I wager, than it gives her."

"You seem convinced that I do not have this woman's best interests at heart."

"Your motives are no concern of mine. I'm treating the girl."

"Then your interests and mine are identical. If you'd be so kind, could you describe your method of treatment?"

"Again, that would be proposing a crime and you would be the witness."

"Assure me that you won't use oil of savine or pennyroyal."

To my surprise she rose and presented her hand. "Mr. Henry, let's prove my neighbours right and call this a social visit. We'll shake hands and part friends and pretend we never had this conversation. Thank you for braving my front door."

I remained seated. I had to decide whether to trust this woman upon no more evidence than rumour, gossip, and her confident bearing. I imagined my alternative, holding Emma's hand in the dirty back parlour of some seedy former doctor who eagerly accommodated me while clumsily pawing Emma. "Please, Madame, I apologize if I've insulted you. That wasn't my intention. I'm here because all the world knows you're the queen of your profession. I assure you, if you knew the story of this poor girl you'd consider it your duty to assist her."

"I have a bad feeling about this, Mr. Henry. You haven't told me enough lies. Lie to me a little."

"Please. Help this girl."

"She's an orphan, I suppose."

"Yes."

"That's better."

"I'm telling you the truth. If you're any judge of character, and I know you are, to have thrived in your profession, look into my eyes, and believe me when I say that this poor girl needs you as much as any girl ever has."

My earnest gaze provoked a look of mild amusement. "As a student of character," she said, "I've learned that the most convincingly sincere are those who most practice faking it."

"I don't know what else to say."

306   "Tell me why I should help this girl."

I searched her hooded eyes. She gave me nothing back. The words formed: Emma's father was her child's father. They could not pass my lips. I had not the right to violate Emma's confidence, even to save her. In despair I stood and bowed. "Thank you for your time."

"I'll take your girl."

"Thank you."

My relief and confusion pleased her. "You should learn to lie, Mr. Henry. You'll be chewed up if you don't. My fee is five hundred dollars."

"I don't have fifty."

She held up her stubby gloved hand to cut me off. "Mr. Henry, I'm a rich old woman. I'll die before I spend my last dollar. But my fee is five hundred dollars."

I nodded. "May I bring her on Sunday at two o'clock?"

"If all is as you describe we'll attend to business that evening. You may call for her Tuesday morning. She'll be very weak."

I left Madame Restell's perplexed by our encounter. Apparently she had no more liking for her profession than did I, and was searching for reasons not to practice it. Yet she was not ashamed of what she did. Quite the opposite. She was proud of the succour she offered young women in need. It was, however, a tired pride. She appeared to be exhausted by the effort of sustaining belief in her work in the face of universal reprobation.

She no longer needed the income. She worked from conviction. She would gladly have abandoned her conviction, but she could not. Therefore she set up barriers for herself, to make it harder to undertake her labours. It was as if she were a Jewess in Spain during the Inquisition, exhausted by the isolation and

307

the subterfuge required in maintaining her faith, wishing with all her might that the Christian God were her God, but unable to embrace Him.

However, when the time came she would perform to the limits of her ability. My duty was clear. I must raise five hundred dollars. Had I still been close with Alger I might have appealed to him even for such a sum, but that was no longer possible. Mrs. Vanderbilt was not likely to perform this particular act of charity. It was time to sell my grandfather's minute repeater.

A Breguet minute repeater is a unique work of watchmaking art. Any reputable jeweler would quickly trace the provenance of mine and contact my father to determine its rightful owner. I resigned myself therefore to receiving a fraction of its value from the pawnbrokers on Chatham Street. I selected the shop which displayed the most expensive goods, determined to receive a thousand dollars for a watch worth four or five times that amount.

The proprietor was a portly Jew dressed in a well-fitting coat of fine wool, with the nervous habit of pulling on his long side locks. I waited while a pinched woman pleaded with him for more money for a gold brooch. He did not seem to hear her. Finally she succumbed to his deafness, took what he had given her, and fled. Her face glimpsed behind her shawl showed the pain of abandoning the final vestige of a life once lived in hope.

Thinking that the Jew's deafness might be ignorance of the language, I presented my watch in German. Though I indicated the Breguet mark and described its value, he offered me fifty dollars. I demonstrated the minute repeater. I doubt he had ever heard one before. His interest piqued, he raised his offer to two hundred. I asked a thousand. He turned his back on me in disgust. I walked out.

After showing my goods to the neighbouring businessmen I settled with my first bidder for five hundred dollars. When he paid me my money, he deducted fifty dollars as a "safe deposit" fee, and I snatched back the watch until he gave ground. Necessity made me a hard bargainer. Had I truly needed a thousand, I wager I would have found a buyer at that sum.

As I left with the thick roll of bills fattening my pocket, I thought of the face of the woman who had sold her brooch. I had feared that parting with the watch would spiral my spirits into a whirlpool of despair. Not only was it my sole treasure, my entire patrimony, but its sale must be described as a betrayal of my father. He had not given me his precious heirloom that I might sell it for a fraction of its worth to finance the abortion of a destitute sixteen-year-old. He had not given it to me to be sold at all, but as a symbol of his faith in me and of the continuity of achievement in our family.

I suspect that he had many moments when the price of the watch, honestly sold, would have been of enormous value to him, and I am certain that he had many bitter thoughts about his father. Yet he never succumbed to the temptations of necessity or anger to liquidate the watch. He kept it as a symbol of a connection he could not deny. He had given it to me in the same spirit. Now it was gone.

I waited for my sight to cloud and my lumbar muscles to clench my spine. Instead I felt a bewildering lightness in my body, as if I had cut a raft loose from its moorings and was drifting out to sea, giddy with the prospect of unknown adventure and the impending terrors of the open ocean.

———

I had to prepare Mrs. Vanderbilt for Emma's absence. I briefly considered telling her the truth but quickly abandoned the notion. When I contemplated informing her that Emma was pregnant but refusing to specify the father, I could imagine many scenarios in which Frankie would find offense and one only when she would not, and that single scenario required her to be a woman of superhuman understanding and boundless trust. Frankie was an extraordinary woman, but I had not the strength of heart to put her to that test. I resolved to heed Madame Restell, and lie well. I had become more practiced in that shadowy art since my arrival in New York, but I was still a novice, and had succeeded in my ruses only because those I misled had no great stake in seeing through them. This was a more delicate situation. Mrs. Vanderbilt had committed herself to believing in my probity. I valued her good opinion of me. I had not yet lied to her, although of course I had not told her the entire truth. That had been difficult enough. Now I must actively mislead her and risk the consequences.

I sent her a note requesting an interview. She replied with her habitual grace, inviting me to tea. We discussed the funeral of her unfortunate butler, and the mourning of his fiancée, and the news, which I had not yet received, that Detective Stanley had that day apprehended the J.G. of Jemmie's description. We speculated as to the effect upon Jemmie of his inevitable visit to the Tombs to identify the man. Conversation turned to the subject of Emma.

"I'm afraid I must ask you for yet another charitable act," I said.

"What is that?"

"Emma hasn't had a chance to spend any time with her brother. Jemmie is hungry to be with her, and I'm sure she feels the same." I spoke quickly, not wishing to engage her in an exchange for fear I would falter and reveal my subterfuge. "When we saw them together it was clear they benefited from each other's company, more by contact than by actual conversation. Such encounters take time. Emma's still weak from her bout of cholera, and a day or two with her brother would strengthen her considerably. If you would excuse Emma, I was thinking I might take them up the Hudson for a few days."

"How solicitous of you. Please, let one of my husband's men make the arrangements."

"That's not necessary." I smiled, but let an edge of stiffness enter my voice. "I'm requesting charity for Emma, not myself."

"As you wish." I had embarrassed her. Good. That would deflect her suspicions. When Emma reappeared in her weakened condition I could ascribe her troubles to the cholera. Lying, I discovered, was not difficult, if one's purpose was clear and one's motive sufficiently strong.

CHAPTER TWENTY-THREE

I escorted Jemmie to the Tombs to identify J.G. Detective Stanley led us into a darkened closet and stood Jemmie upon a chair that he might spy through a peephole into the next room. Jemmie peered gravely, and nodded assent. The detective asked for a positive statement and Jemmie said in a quiet voice that the man was J.G., and could he leave now? As we departed, Stanley warned me that the boy would surely be called to testify at the trial and suggested in a voice tinged with contempt that Hummel prepare him for the inevitable cross-examination. Apparently Jemmie's betrayal of his associate was a graver sin in Stanley's eyes than J.G.'s thuggery.

The image of tiny Jemmie perched upon a stool in the witness box being hammered by J.G.'s lawyer disturbed me. In our few days together Jemmie had been an easy roommate, obedient and clean. He had devoted himself to his drawing, creating a collection of pictures which reflected his adventures since he ran away from Jonas Larkin, and had faithfully explained them for my benefit. In spite of my urgings, however, he would not draw anything about Indians or the west, and he refused outright to draw the painting which had so captivated him at Mrs. Vanderbilt's. The pain of abandoning his true calling still burned in him. I wondered if he would ever value an artist's work as much, and I worried he was rather too bent on pleasing me.

As we left the Tombs hand in hand I tested his resolve. "You will have to go up before a judge and jury," I said, "and tell what happened."

"What do I tell?"

"Well, do you know what the lawyer said to free you from the Tombs?"

"I was visiting my sister."

"I suppose you'll have to say something like that. Mr. Hummel will make it very clear to you."

"Do I swear a oath?"

"You'll put your hand upon a Bible and swear to tell the truth."

"Oh."

"Can you do that?"

"Do you want me to?"

I nodded. He nodded in reply.

"What if someone calls you a liar?" I said.

"Once I swears, it's the truth."

————

Sunday, I collected Emma at the Vanderbilt mansion and drove her the twenty blocks to Madame Restell's. She was wrapped in a warm shawl and carried a well-crafted traveling case, both gifts of Mrs. Vanderbilt. We said little. When I explained that I was entrusting her to New York's most respected practitioner, she listened with an air of acceptance and gazed out the window for a view of her famous abode. The sight of the building seemed to give her confidence. I realized that its peculiar

313

combination of the welcoming and the impregnable was designed precisely for this moment.

We entered from Fifty-second Street, descending to a door on the *sous-sol* patio. A maid escorted us to a comfortable basement parlour, where we were soon joined by Madame Restell, again dressed in black. Her husband had died the year before; perhaps, like Mrs. Frye, she was in a perpetual state of mourning. Madame asked for a history of the pregnancy. Emma said only that she had missed her menstrual cycle and had reason to think herself pregnant. Madame bade me wait while she took Emma into an adjoining room for a physical examination. When they returned, Madame pronounced herself satisfied that Emma was carrying, and in her second or third month.

Madame's wariness in greeting me was replaced in her dealings with Emma by a sure nurse's manner. She sat the girl close and took her hand, and with unaffected understanding asked Emma if she was quite certain she wished to lose this child. Emma nodded diffidently, head bowed, looking as tender and vulnerable as the most innocent sixteen-year-old.

"If making the baby was awful," said Madame, "losing it will be worse. Don't think that killing the foetus will make the memory go away."

"I don't." The words were almost whispered.

"The memory I'll make won't go away either. Like it or not, this creature is part of your body. When I tear it out you'll feel you're losing a piece of yourself. And once done you cannot change your mind. Done is done. If you believe in souls, you're snuffing one out."

"No I ain't. I's sending it to heaven." She spoke with a vehemence which revealed that Madame's questions were not new to her.

"You're upset," said Madame. "Good. If you wish to have the baby I can find a home for it."

Emma shook her head vigorously. Madame rose with a rustle of stiff silk. "Very well." She turned to me. "Payment, please." I handed her the wad of bills. She counted it carefully and placed it in a purse which hung from a strap upon her shoulder. She opened a phial, handed Emma a large round pill, and poured her a glass of water. "This is to soothe and relax you." She looked at me. "Not pennyroyal." We watched while Emma swallowed it. Emma was unused to medication and repressed her gag reflex only with difficulty. Madame rewarded her with a nurse's smile. "Excellent. Now you will have to sit for an hour or so while the pill takes effect." She turned to me. "Mr. Henry, you may keep her company. Then you'll have to leave us."

I reassured Emma that I would stay with her as long as permitted and return as soon as possible, and the maid led us down a corridor fronted with doors, depositing us in another, smaller parlour. For all we knew, behind each door sat a poor unfortunate like Emma. Our room was papered in blue silk but simply furnished with a *chaise longue,* a pair of ladder-backed chairs, a wash basin and accessories. Emma reclined upon the chaise, awaiting the effects of the medication. "What'd she give me?"

"I don't know. Perhaps an opiate. Laudanum, perhaps."

Emma smiled. "I'd like that."

I took her hand. "Tell me what you feel."

We sat there, silent, Emma scrutinizing her inner state, myself scrutinizing Emma. Her inward concentration isolated her from the faintly medicinal surroundings as if she were sheathed in an impermeable membrane. We sat there for perhaps half an hour. Emma's eyelids drooped as she succumbed to medication.

Of a sudden the hallway resounded with the tread of heavy boots and the crack and crash of doors opening and closing with great force. The noise stirred Emma, who forced open her pendant lids and struggled onto one elbow as the door burst open, revealing a bull of a man with flaming ginger whiskers and ice blue eyes.

"Aha!"

We stared in astonishment at Anthony Comstock. He stared back. Disposing of me with a glare he spoke gently to Emma, his whiskers crinkling about a paternal smile. "There, my dear, you're safe now. Nothing to worry about." He reached into his pocket and presented her with a hard candy wrapped in waxed paper. "Cherry." He searched roughly around the sink.

"What are you doing here?" I asked his burly back.

"I should ask the same of you," he replied without turning around.

"That is none of your affair."

He turned and bristled at me. "There, sir, you are mistaken. You will protect this poor girl's good name by remaining in this room until my business is concluded. If you do not, I shall crush you." He spoke with such ferocity that I could not deter-

316

mine if he meant to crush my reputation or my skull. Before I could frame a reply he departed.

Emma sat up. "Who was that?"

"A dangerous man." I went to the door and listened to the continuing commotion. I was consumed with curiosity, but I did not doubt the sincerity of Comstock's threat or the risk to Emma, and I could not see what good would come of intruding upon the scene beyond.

I stood listening to muffled talk and the clomp of boots for perhaps half an hour. Then all was silence. I ventured into the hallway. The reception room was empty. I found the stairway and mounted to the lavish marble hall. Servants stood at parlour windows staring disconsolately down Fifth Avenue. The maid who had greeted us approached me, distraught, and reporting that Madame had just departed with Mr. Comstock for the station house, she presented me my roll of bills.

I returned for Emma, who greeted me with a wobbly smile. The drug had attained its full effect. I explained that Madame had been taken by the police and we must leave at once. She insisted upon walking, swaying gently, the few blocks to Central Park in the chill afternoon air. We sat in the pallid light by the craggy pond we had visited before, among trees now denuded of their leaves, the crags and skeletal branches a suitable setting for my bleak mood. Emma, however, showed no distress. She produced Comstock's cherry candy, carefully unwrapped it, and placed it between her cherry lips.

"Don't lose heart," I said. "There are dozens like Madame Restell in New York. I'll find another just as good."

She shook her head, sucking on the candy. "No."

"Not as famous, but certainly as able."

"No need. I'm having this here baby." She stated this surprising fact with simple certitude.

"That's the pill talking," I said, "and the thrill of fear."

" 'Tain't. That man was sent by God, and I knows why." She looked at me with a dreamy smile. "I's carrying Sam."

"You told me Sam was in heaven."

"You says that. You says all babies go straight to heaven, but you's wrong about Sam. Sam's growin' inside me. That man knowed it. He come to save me from killin' Sam."

We sat together watching the sky in the water. My gentle questions could not shake her resolve. Her cavernous pupils told me that this was not the time to disabuse her of her epiphany, but hearing the strength of her conviction, I doubted if I ever could. Seeing the purpose behind those opiate eyes, I wondered if I should.

In Emma's mind the burden in her belly had gone from curse to blessing. While the forbidden consanguinity of the parents might cause the baby to be born a monster, the chances were not great. That the child existed at all was certainly monstrous, but if Emma's belief was as enduring as it was intense the child's life might well add to the sum of joy in the world. I did not relish the thought of depriving this girl, who had known such hardship, of a source of love and hope. I had to adapt to the fact that Emma would bear this child.

Before I had learned her terrible secret I had decided that my proper course was to marry Emma and raise Jemmie and her child. I did not see how knowing her secret changed my responsibility. I did not know if Emma would accept me, and certainly this was no time to broach the subject, but I resolved to raise it at the first opportune moment. In the meantime, the best course of action was for Emma to remain at her place of employment. Emma wished to return there, and I hoped I would have some weeks to think things through and plan the next steps in our lives before facing the difficult task of informing Mrs. Vanderbilt of Emma's condition.

We rode the omnibus back to Thirty-fourth Street. I escorted Emma to the door, and having no desire to explain myself to Mrs. Vanderbilt I conveyed my apologies through the butler, saying that Emma had been too ill to take aboard ship, and asking that she be allowed to rest for the day before resuming her duties. The good man bade me settle her in. We carried Emma, sagging from her opiate, to the room she shared with three other servant girls beneath the eaves. I worked with unseemly efficiency, wishing to be done and out before encountering Mrs. Vanderbilt, but Frankie met us on the stair, her smooth forehead creased with concern. She insisted on helping Emma to change into night-clothes and tucking the girl into bed while I waited in the hall. When summoned, I made a show of taking Emma's pulse and examining the whites of her eyeballs while Frankie hovered nearby. I took my leave, but she escorted me to the door. I apologized for this most recent disturbance.

"Nonsense. We're partners in this. How can I help Emma?"

"She needs rest. She should be excused from heavy labour for a few days. She'll be stronger soon enough."

"Is it the cholera?"

"After a fashion."

"Is there chance of contagion?"

"No. It's weakness from the after-effects of the disease."

"She didn't appear feverish. Should she have a warm bath?"

"No. Really, you needn't concern yourself. She will recover."

Every word of concern was a lancet in my flesh, bleeding more lies from me, sapping my soul. I ceased to be William James and I became a person I did not know or like, a mealy-mouthed double-talker preying upon the best intentions of a good woman, my every lie adding to the cruelty of the inevitable reckoning.

Descending through the house as we talked, I achieved the entry at last. The butler held open the iron-bound door. I had only to shake her hand and disappear. Frankie's fingers lingered in my own.

"Emma's in greater danger than you're telling me."

The lying, I decided, had to stop. "No, and yes." Instead of making my escape I led her down the stoop that we might speak in the privacy of the open street. "Forgive me, I've been misleading you. I've been afraid to trust your forbearance and compassion when you've given me not the slightest cause for doubt."

"Our interests in this matter are identical."

"Emma isn't feeling the after-effects of cholera. Emma is pregnant."

"Pregnant." Mrs. Vanderbilt spoke the word carefully, considering its manifold implications.

"A coupling not of her choice."

"Poor child." Her Southern lilt stretched the words with sympathy.

"I know you're not one to blame the victim, but in justice to Emma I thought it best to hold my tongue."

"That isn't a lie one can sustain for long, unless one plans to lose the baby."

"Precisely."

"The trip up the Hudson was a lie as well, then."

"I was honouring her wishes. I didn't know your feelings on such matters, and I didn't wish to compromise your beliefs."

"But you say she is presently pregnant."

"She had a change of heart."

She stared long at the high window shielding Emma. When she spoke, her lush Southern vowels had taken on a drier tone, as if a switch had been thrown inside her and her thoughts had been shunted onto a different track. "You've not been fair with me, Mr. Henry."

"I'm well aware of that, and I profoundly regret my decision. Whatever mistakes I've made, I've made only in the interests of preserving Emma's honour."

"Your labours on her behalf are positively Herculean." Acid eroded her words.

"Having saved her life, I bear a responsibility to help her live it well."

"An admirable if unorthodox sentiment."

"Emma shares your opinion in that regard."

"May I ask when you learned of her pregnancy?"

"Only last week. I assure you, when I asked you to take her in I had no idea she was carrying a child."

"You can imagine the complications this causes with the other girls."

"I intended to tell you before her condition became apparent, and arrange other accommodations."

"And what would those be?"

"I hadn't made that determination. She only this afternoon decided to keep the child."

"Speculate with me." I hesitated. She remarked upon my indecision. "I believe you've misled me quite enough, Mr. Henry."

I might have lied to her, told her anything or nothing. I told the truth. "I have not broached this with Emma, but I'm planning to marry her."

"Yes. Perfect. The honourable thing." Mrs. Vanderbilt's symmetrical features distorted into an unbecoming smirk. "I'm grateful for your candour. Now please remove your bride-to-be from my house immediately."

"It's not what you think."

"Please, say no more. I can't sort the truth from the lies. Just take your child bride and go." She stepped brusquely toward the mansion, then turned back sharply. "No. Stay here. I'll send her out."

CHAPTER TWENTY-FOUR

Emma appeared, groggy still, carrying the traveling case Mrs. Vanderbilt had given her. "I've been let go. They don't say why. They say you'll say." I took her bag and led her down the stairs. "You told her I's pregnant."

"It's no reflection on you. She's punishing me. She thinks I'm the father."

She clung to my arm. "Where's I goin'?"

"I'm taking you to the Grand Hotel for the night. Tomorrow we'll try to find a lodging-house that will have the three of us."

"The four of us." She patted her belly. "You still want to marry me?"

"Yes."

"I accept." She put her arm around my neck and drew me to her for a kiss. I hoped Mrs. Vanderbilt was not watching.

———

We rode the omnibus downtown and I enrolled Emma in the hotel, for one night only. The clerk noted her small valise and requested I pay in advance, reminding me pointedly that only paying guests were allowed on the upper floors. I deposited Emma in the 'elevator,' relieved that I could not accompany her. Excited at again traveling in such a conveyance, she threw me a proprietary little wave as the doors closed upon her.

Walking back to Mrs. Frye's, I diverted myself from the contemplation of my own precarious condition by trying to make sense of the two remarkable reversals of character that I had just witnessed. Emma's transformation, while the more mystical, was the less problematical. She had undergone what could best be called a conversion of faith. Confronted with Sam's grisly death, it had suited her to believe that the souls of dead babies rose to heaven. Now it suited her better to believe that the souls of dead babies were reincarnated. Her grief at losing her baby brother, her impotence watching him die, her anger at her own degradation, her shame at carrying her foetus, and her guilt at aborting it were distilled by the shock of seeing a kindly Comstock into a liquor which happily assuaged all her tumultuous emotions. Logic was not at issue. Neither belief could be proved or disproved, although the fact that Sam had died after Emma was impregnated mitigated against the transmigration theory, unless the soul was not formed at conception.

Emma did not select her belief by choice. Such a selection would not have been true belief, indeed would have felt like a pale simulacrum of her passionate new-found faith. Yet whatever Emma needed most to believe she believed. Now that her foetus was Sam and her purpose in life was to raise him, for instance, Emma no longer viewed my marriage proposal as a pathetic joke but as the best way to realize her ends. I do not mean to imply that she was using me. Quite the opposite. She was grateful for my attentions and was, I believe, in the process of falling in love with me. Her love, however, did not spring from a romantic notion of the merging of two spirits, but from a deeper inner need.

Before her own change of heart Mrs. Vanderbilt could also have been said to be in love with me. Not that she desired any inappropriate liaison. She was, I believe, in love with the idea of me as the gentle, knowledgeable, child-man, like Alger good with the newsboys because he was himself still a boy at heart, but more diffident than Alger, more sensitive, and above all more artistic. Alger was, in truth, an execrable writer. His childlike enthusiasm hurt his ability to judge his own work harshly enough to raise it to a worthy level. I had a child's naïveté, perhaps, but I did not suffer from an exaggerated estimation of my creations, being if anything too acutely aware of my own shortcomings, and my self-inflicted wounds appealed to Mrs. Vanderbilt. In contrast with her husband's overbearing certainty, she found my tentative manner endearing.

I am not claiming to be the man she thought I was. In summing up the qualities she observed, she compiled a man purer than I. Childish naïveté became childlike innocence. A desire to learn from the newsboys became a selfless act of sacrifice. Self-doubt became humility. An act of medical common sense became the saviour's touch. Consequently, when she saw that I was no perfect person but an arrant sinner her disillusionment was stronger than it might otherwise have been. She was angry not only with me but with herself for believing in me. I had humiliated her, and the way to explain away her own self-deception was to conclude that I was a master of duplicity, as monstrous as she once had thought me saintly.

But I overstep my story. Up to this point, Mrs. Vanderbilt had behaved as any proper, pious woman would. The fault lay in me. As she had overestimated my virtue, I had overestimated hers. Instead of seeing a gifted woman bound in a marriage of convenience no different from Emma's engagement to me, save in the scale of its magnificence, I beheld an angel of mercy bestowing blessings upon the poor. I believed in her purity as much as she believed in mine, and ultimately I could not imagine that she would be anything other than utterly empathetic and forgiving. I could not summon the lack of trust to see my lies through to their conclusion. In truth, no woman would have been capable of hearing what I had told her without passing judgement, and I deserved her poor opinion for grievously overstepping my Hippocratic boundaries with Emma.

Until this moment I had thought true belief to be absolute and beyond one's control, the inevitable expression of one's most fundamental knowledge of the workings of the world. Now I saw that we created our beliefs even as we cherished their eternal permanence. All of us are bound up in beliefs which express not our deepest truths but our deepest needs.

Why, then, could I not believe in the Divine Spirit as my father did? I wished so desperately to believe that I had almost annihilated myself in my struggle. My happiness, perhaps my life, depended upon my believing that a higher good existed. Why did I not believe? Though I tortured myself for my disbelief, was I even certain that I did not?

Consumed with these thoughts, and with more mundane financial concerns now that my five hundred dollars had to provision four souls, I arrived at Mrs. Frye's. When I told Jemmie that he and I and Emma would soon be a family together, he betrayed no surprise. However, he cleaved to me until the dinner bell and made certain to sit beside me at table.

As the plate of gray beef was being handed about, a gruff bowler-hatted man appeared at the door requesting Mr. Henry, and urging me to accompany him post-haste upon an important matter which he refused to specify, except to say it would require no more than an hour of my time. I thought it best to acquiesce. He looked vaguely familiar, and by the time he delivered me to Pontin's Restaurant on Franklin Street I had recalled that I had seen him in heavy conversation with a clerk at the offices of Howe & Hummel. He pointed me toward the rear of the establishment and told me that the hack would be waiting in front when I was done.

Noah had mentioned Pontin's, darkly paneled and crowded with sober-suited men, as the restaurant of choice for those in the criminal bar and judiciary. I passed through the room, searching fruitlessly for Howe's bulk or Hummel's diminutive form, and was about to abandon my quest when a door opened revealing an inner sanctum holding but two tables. One was filled with distinguished men of judicial mien. At the other sat Howe with a pile of cash before him and Hummel scribbling numbers on the tablecloth. At my approach Hummel looked up from his labours, affecting surprise. "Mr. Henry, you've come during banking hours."

"I was summoned."

"Not by me."

"I'll be gone, then."

"No, no, while you're here, have a seat." I sat. He returned to his count, as if to demonstrate the triviality of our meeting. "Your ears were burning this afternoon?"

"Only from the cold."

327

"I was referring to certain conversations of which you might be unaware in which you were the subject of a great deal of nasty attention."

"I can't imagine why."

"That strains my credulity, but no matter. Not why but what, that's the point." Here he looked up briefly before resuming his calculations. "I've been talking to a certain party who recently has been of great help to you. This party now regrets her efforts on your behalf. This party now believes that a certain young man she once thought a blameless boy is in fact a dangerous felon, and she has instructed me to see that he is arrested for murder."

"Jemmie? You've already had him cleared."

"When the Municipal Courts open tomorrow morning I shall inform the judge that his previous ruling was based upon erroneous evidence. I shall petition the court to issue a bench warrant for the boy's arrest on murder charges and for his sister's arrest as an accomplice, and I shall be very persuasive."

"She knows that's a lie!"

"My party is fully persuaded that I'll be serving the truth."

"Why are you telling me this?"

"It's not the why, it's the what."

"You can't expect me to talk you out of it."

Hummel looked up impatiently from his jottings, articulating his words with the precision one uses in speaking to a simpleton. "If a warrant is issued for their arrest, the police will come and take them to the Tombs. If the police arrive and cannot find them, they do not go to the Tombs."

"You're telling me to hide them?"

"He's telling you nothing of the sort," said Mr. Howe, nibbling on crackers and caviar while thumbing his cash. "If he did I'd shut him up."

"A few days ago you'd do anything for that party of yours," I said, "even fire an old client. Now you're frustrating her purposes. Why?"

"Good-bye, Mr. Henry."

"Kindly stop eating and piling up your money, and talk to me!" I felt a flush of righteous anger, not at Mrs. Vanderbilt's sincere if cruel betrayal, but at the lawyers' disgusting *nonchalance*. Hummel was exploiting us both for some advantage I could not fathom. "Whatever game you're playing, I won't be your shuttlecock."

"Wrong metaphor," said Hummel without breaking count. "This is a gift horse. Nothing gained looking in its mouth."

"Don't pretend you're acting from altruistic motives."

"Not the why, Mr. Henry, the what."

"You find this very amusing, but you're playing with the lives of innocent children!"

"Please, spare us the homilies," said Howe. "Have some caviar."

"What is your game?"

"I've made enquiries about you," said Hummel. "You're a man with a very shallow past."

"Nothing to be ashamed of," said Howe. "I was a doctor in an earlier life."

I gaped at him in amazement. "If you left this city and

started afresh somewhere else," said Hummel, "you wouldn't leave much behind."

The frustrations and absurdities of the preceding weeks welled up inside me. I struggled to maintain control over my emotions. "The 'why's' are important to me, Mr. Hummel. I won't do your bidding blind."

"If you care as much for this boy and girl as you pretend, you'll do what's best for them."

"I need to understand!" I pounded the table in frustration, upsetting a stack of bills.

Hummel collected them. "Really, Mr. Henry."

I stood, tense with rage, staring my fury at the complacent pair. Of a sudden my anger dissolved in understanding. I contemplated them with an emotion bordering on delight. "Of course! J.G.! If Jemmie's gone, they've no case against J.G.!" I pointed my finger at Howe. "Hummel's working for Mrs. Vanderbilt, but you're serving whoever's behind J.G.!"

Hummel awarded me with an ambiguous smile. "You should consider following Mr. Howe's example and becoming a lawyer in your next life."

"I wouldn't go north," said Howe, "certainly not to Boston." He handed me a much-folded rotogravure. When I flattened it out, I was staring at a self-portrait I had drawn a few years before. "This chap has been the subject of discreet inquiries by the Pinkerton Agency. Without your beard, you could be his brother."

———

I entered the waiting hack composed and purposeful. My course of action was clear. We three must leave the city with the first train in the morning. Jemmie was free on my recognizance, and when he disappeared I, or Mr. Henry, would be criminally responsible. I must become William Larkin and lead the Larkin family west.

I had the driver drop me at the Grand and arranged for him to pick me up at Mrs. Frye's at dawn. Emma, on the American plan like all the tenants, dined beneath the cavernous dome. I was forbidden to enter the hall, lest I cadge a free dinner, but Emma was summoned. She left table reluctantly and, eager to return to her food, listened without comment to my instructions.

I informed Mrs. Frye of my departure and presented her with a spurious new address. Jemmie helped me pack, pleased to be leaving New York City but showing no anticipation about traveling west. We slept with our bags guarding the door.

I slept like the dead. How many nights had I lain upon that mattress forcing my eyes to close, hearing every creak and clock tick as a hammer blow? This night was blank. No doubts crushed me; no despairing abyss opened beneath. Whether Evil and Good were logically distinguishable was a remote and abstract question without bearing upon the course of my life. Events had conspired to lift the burden of choice, and I slept as I had not since I was eight.

We dressed in the dark. The street lamps were still lit and the first snow of the year was falling when the cabbie appeared. We drove through feathery flakes shimmering in the gaslight to the Grand. Emma awaited us in the lobby, shawl about her shoulders and valise at her feet.

We continued uptown through a thickening storm to the

massive, lumpy form of the Grand Central Railway Depot, where I deposited my family in the stifling warmth of the waiting room of the New York and New Haven. I trudged from railroad to railroad, traipsing through mounting snow, until I located a New York Central train leaving in an hour which would take us to St. Louis. I purchased our tickets savouring the irony that Mr. Vanderbilt's machine would be carrying us to safety, though this was no great coincidence as the depot and all its railroads belonged to him.

I collected Emma and Jemmie, and we passed from oppressive heat into the frigid air of the train shed. To call this a shed was to call St. Peter's a parish church. Its galvanized trusses arched in one unbroken span over the largest roofed space on the continent. We searched the platforms, tiny inconsiderable creatures in this vast interior universe, hemmed in by Vanderbilt's trains but liberated by his soaring iron beams and their lofty promise of the ultimate triumph of mechanical man.

We located our car and settled in our seats. The train was filling rapidly with travelers of all sorts, some making a journey of only a few hours, others families like ourselves with belongings gathered about them, boring deep into the continent. Emma and Jemmie sat facing me, holding hands, watching the bustle on the platform. I summoned the image of myself as a doctor in St. Louis, treating the likes of my traveling companions from a consulting room in a household run by Emma. I could not envisage the architecture of the place, but my St. Louis Emma was content.

My thoughts were interrupted by the harsh gutturals of lowland German. A man with farmer's hands was asking me if the snow was going to prevent the train from leaving. I answered in German that I did not know. He didn't seem satisfied with my response, and was asking again when his *Frau* shut him up.

My German would prove useful in my medical practice. I felt a hunger to read German again, Schopenhauer, Goethe, Fechner, and Fichte. Once established, I would locate a good bookseller and resume my reading.

There would be a time not distant when I would reconcile with my family. Once my course was set I could write them and explain my new direction. Only now that I was seated in the St. Louis train did I feel how much I missed them all, and the pain I was causing them. Foraging in New York City had freed me from the constraints of their expectations, but it had also cut me off from their energizing wit and their sustaining love. Mr. Henry had a life which did not allow for their presence. Mr. Larkin longed for their company.

Moving to St. Louis was my only course of action. I was responsible for these two souls who sat across from me watching latecomers hurry toward our train. I again summoned the image of our house to be. I saw nothing. Outside, the conductor called, "All aboard!" The words sank into the mighty void.

I put one hand upon Emma's knee and one on Jemmie's. They turned away from the window. "You looks like you see'd a ghost," said Emma.

"I cannot go with you."

"What?"

"I can't go."

"Why not?"

"I can't will it."

"What?"

I took my billfold from my pocket and handed it to her. "Here's all my money." I kissed her on the cheek. "You saved my life."

She shied away. "You're crazy."

"You're staying here then?" Jemmie wore his distant look.

"I've another life. I'm returning there." I stood. "Jemmie, I leave you the artist's supplies." I jotted my name on a scrap of paper. "Emma, my true name is William James. I live in Cambridge, Massachusetts. If ever you're in need, you can find me there."

Emma turned away in anger. "You won't be hearing from us again."

"I'll be thinking of you, every day." I walked down the aisle and descended the steps as the conductor sealed the doors.

————

I sold my St. Louis ticket and hired a hack to carry me downtown to the pier where the *Bristol* docked. My desertion was at once the basest act of my life and the bravest. I should have been consumed with shame and thrilled with despicable pleasure. I was neither. I felt fully responsible for what I had done, yet I could not have done otherwise. I felt only the regret and relief of an actor relinquishing an important but ill-fitting role.

At the pier I purchased a Boston ticket and a copy of the *Sun*. Comstock's arrest of Madame Restell was prominently featured on the first page. According to the account, Comstock had entered her mansion posing as a desperate husband with too many children and a pregnant wife. When Madame supplied him with medicine to bring about "the desired results" he immediately produced a warrant. Summoning policemen concealed outside he searched her house, discovering pills, powders, suspect obstetrical instruments, and, it was rumored, even a young client.

Apparently, Comstock's moral outrage was so great that he could not be dissuaded by Madame Restell's notorious black book or her powerful allies. According to the *Sun*, he escorted Madame to the station house in Madame's black victoria. During the ride, said the *Sun*, she offered him forty thousand dollars if he would step down from the carriage and forget all about her. Even as the *Sun* mocked Comstock's pomposity and puritanism it marveled at his incorruptible temperament.

The story did not address the true mystery of the tale. Though Comstock was early in his career, his bristling side whiskers and taurine gaze were already anathema to those in her profession. Madame was a practiced survivor. How had she allowed herself to be cozened by Comstock?

The *Bristol* did not sail until five. I purchased a late paper in search of further insights and was rewarded with another first-page story. Madame Restell, released on bail, was to have appeared in court that morning. Her maid found her dead in her bath. She had slit her own throat, a relatively painless death, according to the *Sun*, but one only accomplished by a practiced surgeon. The paper talked of her guilty conscience and her horror of prison life. Comstock boasted that she was the fifteenth miscreant he had hounded to suicide.

I thought of the tired, lonely woman who had interviewed me, and imagined her using Comstock for her own dark purpose. The Madame Restell of my acquaintance had lost the

335

strength to practice her beliefs but could not summon the will to reject them. Perhaps she had channeled the force of Comstock's zeal to push herself to action. I thought of Alger trapped in his ministry without a calling. Perhaps he had succumbed to the boy's seductive nature for a similar reason.

By late afternoon the snowfall had become a swirling blizzard cloaking the city in a paralyzing layer of pure white, and the *Bristol* sailed from a Manhattan momentarily purged of its magnificence and filth. For a few hours the struggles there would cease. Rich and poor were equally idled. When the storm abated their children would play side by side in the streets.

I stood by the rail and watched until the island disappeared into the furious mists. Then I went below and had the *Bristol*'s barber remove my beard. For the destitute the snow was heaven sent. They would be hired to scrape it away, that the struggles might resume.

EPILOGUE

Rather than return to Cambridge I traveled to McLean Asylum, and there sent word for my father to collect me, thinking that he had most likely maintained the fiction, even with my mother, that I was still convalescing there. Dr. Tyler was relieved to see me intact. I offered him no explanation, other than to report that our course of treatment proved beneficial.

My father arrived more relieved, no doubt, than Dr. Tyler, but determined to ask me nothing about my disappearance. Though I had behaved with complete disregard for my duties as a son, causing him great anxiety and I suspect no little expense, he expressed nothing but his joy at finding me healthy and in good spirits. In all his remaining years he never mentioned those missing months, or the absence of the Breguet minute repeater. Perhaps he saw himself as partially to blame in some unfathomable way for my absconding.

True to her word, Emma never contacted me. I knew nothing of her or Jemmie until William James MacReady paid me his visit. I don't know why she didn't name him Sam. Fortified with a fresh sense of purpose, I secured a position lecturing at Harvard, met my wife Alice soon thereafter, and built a life upon those twin foundations. Though Alice has been the core of my existence, not a day passes when I do not think of little Emma's fingers on my lips, or Jemmie's look of veiled inward musing. Choice ends nothing. We all carry within us the people we have chosen not to be, stunted by lack of light and nourishment but perpetually requesting their day in the sun.

Of all the participants in this tale, Jemmie's future remained the most intriguing, and the most opaque. Perhaps his anger at me for abandoning him made him abjure drawing. I like to think not. If I could not give him a vocation, at least I started him upon a fitting path. He had a sensibility which a wealthy man might have mined for a lifetime of aesthetic appreciation, a temperament which an artist might have nurtured into a lifetime of creation. Perhaps he became one of these. More likely he painted tobacco tins on the sides of barns.

Alger and I never spoke again. When he removed himself from the Lodging-house his writing lost the freshness of observed experience, and his books became copies of his earlier models. Never more than modest successes while he lived, when Alger died a decade ago they seemed destined for oblivion. This year they sold one million copies.

The New York papers that reached Boston were not the sort that followed Dannie's trial. I suspect J.G. was freed for lack of evidence, and Dannie convicted and hanged. Had Hummel capitalized upon our flight to cast Jemmie as the mastermind he might have saved Dannie, but he would have flouted Mr. Vanderbilt's yen for retribution. I suspect Dannie wasn't worth that price.

Dannie was as close to a perfectly evil creature as I have ever met, yet I cannot honestly say I feel pleasure at the thought that he was hanged. Dannie did not think himself evil. He wielded what weapons he had at his disposal in his battle for survival. That he was born incapable of empathy or remorse, or nurtured by those incapable of better arming him, was not his doing. A dog that kills a baby is not evil. Dannie made us laugh. Jonas Larkin, whom I never met, exceeded even Dannie in his crimes, yet I suspect that had I known him, his life would have presented exculpatory circumstances. He might have been a charming man when he was sober.

I came to New York to determine from the Darwinian struggle of the newsboys whether we live in a moral universe. I failed. When I read this account I am amazed that a man of thirty could have been so naïve. Up to that time I had endeavoured to be virtuous by freezing myself in a state of perpetual innocence. In New York I confronted not evil in the abstract but evil as palpable living thing. I learned through my gut what I could never have absorbed through the intellect: that to be truly good one must sin and know the consequence. If evil has a purpose, perhaps that is it.

In retrospect, it is clear that I came to New York searching for my faith. I did not find it. Faith, I discovered, was a sly predatory cat who could not be captured in pursuit but came in her own time, for her own reasons, and struck without mercy; yet her elusive and peremptory nature only intensified the urgency of the hunt.

Until I fled to New York I had lived as if morality were solely a matter of inner concern and transcendent significance. In my morbid self-absorption I had blinded myself to the obvious truth that my life was a cog wheel in the intricate machinery composed of all the lives around me, and that my moral worth, my essential nature, was determined by my place in the mechanism. After New York I saw that I had been holding myself pure not from love of the good but from childish fear. I was guarding myself from making hard choices. The hard choices, the choices which teach us and define us, are those which exact their cost on others. I was a man of thirty before New York forced upon me those choices. Jemmie was only a boy of nine when the city forced those choices upon him. His and mine were indivisible. We were two cogs grinding our teeth one against the other. If, in writing Jemmie's tale, I have been illuminated by the spirit of my friend and mentor Horatio Alger, it is because we were both, in our own ways, fit subjects for his tales.

FINIS

AUTHOR'S NOTE

While a novel is its own explanation, a novel in the voice of William James requires a word or two. By his own admission, James suffered a mental collapse soon after graduating from medical school, which he described in a disguised version in *Varieties of Religious Experience.* I have incorporated his tale, in which he reports his image of a black-haired youth with greenish skin and talks of suicide, as my point of departure for my own description of his illness. Though the exact events of this period are a mystery, twenty-one pages (as much as forty-two pages of writing) having been cut with a sharp blade from James's diary, it is likely that he spent time at McLean, where he met Alger's cousin and might have encountered Alger as I described. While he fought depression all his life, James emerged from this crisis with a surer sense of his own future. He had found the strength to commit himself to creating the William James who shaped so much of American thought in the late nineteenth century.

I have sown through the book occasional phrases and sentences belonging to James. Otherwise, I have created my own James, striving to be consistent with his later beliefs and the facts of his life. His description of the newsboys' demeanor on page fifty-nine is from a contemporary account, and the relaxed wooden palings of the empty lot on Broadway in Chapter Three are his brother Henry's recollection. Comstock's courtroom testimony on lust in Chapter Twelve and William Morris Hunt's exhortations in Chapter Nine are in their own words. Dannie's doggerel in Harry Hill's saloon is a poem from the period. The play I describe in Chapter Eight is *Under the Gaslight* by Augustin Daly, who later sued those who appropriated his idea of tying someone to a railroad track. The single most useful item in my research was the four-foot-by-six-foot perspective rendering of *The City of New York,* published by Galt & Hoy in 1879 and available from the Library of Congress, which purported to show every building on Manhattan and afforded me the pleasure of walking the streets of New York with William James.